HOLLYWOOD LEGENDS
BOOK THREE

Dreaming
Of Your Love

MARY J. WILLIAMS

About the Author

Writing isn't easy. But I love every second. A blank screen isn't the enemy. It is the opportunity to create new friends and take them on amazing adventures and life-changing journeys. I feel blessed to spend my days weaving tales that are unique—because I made them.

Billionaires. Songwriters. Artists. Actors. Directors. Stuntmen. Football players. They fill the pages and become dear friends I hope you will want to revisit again and again.

Thank you for jumping into my books and coming along for the journey.

How to Get in Touch

Please visit me at these sites, sign up for my newsletter or leave a message.

http://www.maryjwilliams.net/home.html
https://www.facebook.com/pages/Mary-J-Williams/1561851657385417
https://twitter.com/maryjwilliams05
https://www.pinterest.com/maryj0675/
https://instagram.com/2015romance/
https://www.goodreads.com/author/show/5648619.Mary_J_Williams

More Books by Mary J. Williams

Harper Falls Series
If I Loved You
If Tomorrow Never Comes
If You Only Knew
If I Had You (Christmas in Harper Falls)

Hollywood Legends Series
Dreaming with a Broken Heart
Dreaming with My Eyes Wide Open
Dreaming Again (Coming in July)

One Pass Away Series
After the Rain
After All These Years
After the Fire (Coming in June)

Contents

Prologue

LIGHTS FLASHED FROM every direction. It blinded and dazzled all at once.

Screams drowned out every other sound. This was Los Angeles. Busy streets in every direction. Jet patterns overhead. The excited—in some cases rabid—fans that surrounded the roped-off red carpet made it seem like nothing existed but them and the bright lights.

It shouldn't have been a pleasant experience. Alighting from the over-the-top luxury of a Rolls Royce into chaos and mayhem? No normal human being would willingly seek out such an experience.

However, Colton Landis was not a normal human being. He was an actor.

Colt turned his world-famous megawatt smile on the crowd, eliciting another deafening burst of heartfelt screams.

"We need to get inside, Colt. The movie starts in ten minutes."

"Relax, Deb."

Colt's publicist had been with him for five years. Deb Kline knew how to spin a press release like nobody else. They saw eye to eye on most things. Except how much he should expose himself to his fans. If she had her way, he would zip from point A to point B as quickly as humanly possible.

1

In this case, point A was the limo, and point B was Grauman's Chinese Theater.

"I'll relax when you are safely inside. Have you forgotten Dallas already?"

"Dallas was an anomaly."

Colt continued to wave and smile. Deb wanted him to curb his accessibility. She had always been cautious, but after a fan somehow breached security during a press conference to announce his next movie, she was particularly leery of events like this one.

"Colt."

"Don't go over there, Colt."

Deb knew the second Colt observed the waving autograph books, her words fell on deaf ears. He believed in giving his fans what they wanted. It was one of the things that made Colton Landis a huge movie star. He genuinely loved his fans. He loved meeting them, speaking with them, having his picture taken with them. Most of her clients searched for any reason to avoid these moments. Not Colt. He didn't have a public persona and a private one. What you saw was what you got— twenty-four hours a day, seven days a week.

Colt made her job as a publicist a dream. Keeping him safe was a nightmare.

He refused to have a bodyguard. Part of it was ego—and he had plenty of that. Many of his parts portrayed him as a big, macho, tough guy. How would it look if he had a bigger, more macho, tough guy constantly shadowing him? Not great for his reputation. He would look weak. And in Hollywood, perception was everything.

It was a valid argument. Not so valid? Colt believed that, for the most part, his fans were harmless. Not that he was a naïve Pollyanna. There was no need for Deb to point out the entertainment world's tragic examples of the heinous acts obsessive fans could commit.

Colt lived the life. He grew up watching his superstar mother traverse that fine line between making herself accessible to fans and maintaining some much-needed privacy.

However, he didn't have a family to consider. No wife. No children.

His life was his own. A bodyguard would mean he was giving in. Turning his life over to fear instead of embracing every single moment of his fairytale existence.

"Ten minutes."

Deb didn't know if Colt heard her over the screams. Nor did she care. She was getting him into that theater if it meant grabbing his ear and dragging him along like an errant five-year-old. And wouldn't that make a great picture in *People* magazine? Okay. No ears. *Ugh. This man was going to make her old before her time.*

Colt held a woman's phone at arm's length, including himself in a selfie of her and her three friends.

"I love you, Colton."

Colt couldn't single out the speaker. The cry came from every direction. He waved and called out, "I love you, too."

He signed a few more autographs, moving along the line. Deb was right. He needed to get inside. It wasn't fair to keep everyone waiting. Ten more, he promised himself. It killed him to see the expressions on the faces of the fans who were left out.

"Thanks. See you soon," Colt called out to the crowd.

Handing her signed book to a dreamy-eyed woman, Colt gave the crowd a final wave.

"Ready?" Deb tried to maintain the *stern teacher* expression she had spent twenty years cultivating.

Colt had a way of making her professional mask slip. Thank goodness she was old enough to be his youngish grandmother. While his charm was undeniable, her age and experience allowed her to put the sexual pull that radiated around him into perspective.

Until he turned his smile on her. Full blast.

"Am I that big of a pain in the ass?"

There it was. That naughty twinkle in his deep blue eyes that made the world swoon. On screen, it was irresistible. Paired with dark hair and a tall, muscular frame, was it any wonder the camera loved him?

Reluctantly, Deb returned his smile.

Colt was her client. He was also her friend. She knew he wasn't trying to be difficult. He was being himself. For a man who was adored by millions, catered to on a daily basis, and could buy and sell two or three third-world nations without raising a sweat, Colton Landis was surprisingly down to Earth. And hard-headed. And opinionated.

On top of that? On occasions such as this one, a major pain in the ass.

Still, if she were honest, there wasn't a single thing about him that she would change. As movie stars went—hell, as human beings went—Colton Landis was a joy to be around. Not that she would ever tell him that. The last thing he needed was another person extolling his endless virtues. Colt hated that kind of treatment. One of the reasons they worked so well together was because Deb didn't kowtow.

Deb was about to hit him with one of the nifty sarcastic one-liners he loved, when a scream came from the crowd. Not a *we love you* cry, but one of terror. Before she could react, Deb saw a man jump over the velvet rope. He carried a knife.

Colt pushed her to the side, effectively putting himself between her and the attacker. *He isn't after me*, Deb wanted to protest. But everything happened so fast, she didn't have time.

In the blink of an eye, the man raised the knife and stabbed Colt.

Chapter One

THE GLAMOUR OF Hollywood was a tissue-thin façade rolled out for red carpet movie premieres and award ceremonies. Anyone hoping to find Oscar night glitz would have their dreams dashed by a fast dose of reality.

Hollywood was built on sweat, backbiting, betrayal, and ruthlessness. The founders didn't care about talent or dreams. Getting ahead took more than a pretty face. It took ambition and a hell of a lot of luck.

Staying ahead was another game altogether. This town loved a winner. Until that winner had two or three box office duds. It was amazing how quickly people lost your phone number and forgot your name.

It was brutal and not for the faint of heart.

Colton Landis stood on the street outside Landis Productions, taking in the noise and the smog. He took a deep breath. This was Hollywood. The *real* Hollywood. Nothing got done—not a frame of film rolled through the camera—without money. The more, the better.

And no one was better at extracting large sums from reluctant investors than his brother Wyatt—not even their father. He took everything Caleb Landis taught him and added his spin. The result? The toughest deal makers in Hollywood sported the same last name.

"Excuse me. Aren't you Colton Landis?"

So much for traveling incognito. Colt left his home this morning wanting a bit of rare anonymity. Sunglasses. An old cap sporting the logo of an obscure Midwest Minor League baseball team pulled low to shadow his famous face. Rarely was he recognized in this part of town. Still, some minor camouflage never hurt.

As it turned out, he shouldn't have bothered.

With an inward sigh, Colt smiled at the fifty-something woman and her friend. Graciously, he signed their tourist brochures and posed for a few pictures.

He didn't mind. Not really. He loved his fans. So what if this was one of those blue moon days when he wanted to be Joe Smith—everyman. The ladies didn't know that. They were sweet and a little giddy. By the time he was finished making their day, they had made his.

"Good morning, Colt."

"How are you?"

"Good."

Colt was never certain what to make of Wyatt's assistant. Derrick ran his brother's office with the brutal efficiency of a staff sergeant—wearing Italian leather loafers and tailored suits. He didn't know what kind of salary the man pulled down—that was between him and Wyatt, but it had to be impressive if he could afford to dress like a Gordon Gekko wannabe.

"Wyatt is on a call to Tokyo, but he said to send you right in." Derrick led Colt to the office. "May I bring you something? Water? Espresso?"

"No. Thank you."

"Hmm." Derrick closed the door with a snap.

Strange. There was no other way to describe the man. Colt wasn't thirsty. Why did Derrick care? Did he get a bonus from the vendors for pushing their products? A little kickback if the office went through a certain amount of coffee every month?

"Hey," Wyatt grinned. Moving around his desk, he pulled Colt in for a hug. "Right on time."

Colt slapped his big brother on the back. The Landis boys were a tight-knit group. However, perhaps because Garrett and Nate were twins, Colt felt closest to Wyatt. If he had a problem, Wyatt tended to be his first call. When Wyatt's marriage made its final gasp, he spent a lot of nights crashing at Colt's place.

From the outside, Wyatt seemed like the buttoned-down, serious Landis. In many ways, that was true. Colt knew there was a wild side. He'd seen it. And would just as soon never see it again.

"I know the difference between an invitation and an order. The message you left was from my producer, not my brother."

Wyatt didn't correct him. They were brothers first and forever. However, their careers meant a lot. Colt spent his time in front of the camera. It was Wyatt's job to make sure the production side of the shoot ran smoothly.

"I wanted to share this information in person. As of this morning, *Playing with Fire* is a go."

"That's fantastic, Wyatt."

Colt's name was enough to get most movies made. For some reason, the romantic comedy found more obstacles than anyone anticipated. The money people didn't like that the script had been written by an unknown who insisted on directing. What they didn't say, except in whispers, was that they didn't want a woman behind the camera when she didn't have a proven track record.

How could she get experience if no one would give her a job? The money people didn't care about that—Colt did. He liked Rene Longtree. She was smart and no matter what anyone said, he was certain she knew how to direct a movie. She should. She learned from one of the best. Colt's brother. Garrett Landis.

"Who finally pulled his head out of his ass. Marks or Blankenship?"

"Blankenship. You and I know it was only a matter of time before one of them decided there was too much money to lose if they didn't agree to your terms."

"*Our* terms," Colt reminded Wyatt.

"I fought for Rene because it was important to you." When Colt stared him down, Wyatt caved a little. "I'm for giving a deserving person a chance, Colt."

"Who heads the DIF?"

Diversity in Film was an organization that their father had founded last year. The main purpose was to push for the use of minorities and women in Hollywood. Last spring, Caleb Landis delivered a rousing speech, encouraging his peers to think outside the box when casting films and hiring talent.

While publicly the industry met the ideas with enthusiasm and praise, getting them implemented was another matter. True, hiring someone because it promoted diversity was a bad idea. Hiring the best person, no matter their gender or the color of their skin made complete sense.

Colt refused to budge. It was Rene or no one.

"It's settled?"

Wyatt nodded.

"When do we start shooting?"

Colt wanted to get back to work. A vacation was great, but it had been too long between jobs. He had turned down half a dozen projects in anticipation of this one getting the green light. It was time to get off his ass and back in front of the camera.

"I spoke to Candice last week. She's as anxious as I am."

Candice DeMarcco would be his co-star—much to Colt's trepidation. The actress had a reputation for being a bit of a diva. But he refused to take gossip at face value. He knew how to deal with difficult co-stars and Candice was perfect for the part. He was willing to take a chance it it meant making the best movie possible.

"The casting is set. Locations booked. Rene wanted a woman assistant director."

"And?"

"Kiki Donahue."

Another of Garrett's disciples. Better and better

"Full speed ahead."

Colt loved this script. He had made a few comedies. And a few romantic dramas.

Wishes, the movie that made Hollywood sit up and recognize him as more than a pretty face, had been called the most romantic movie in decades.

After reading *Playing with Fire*, he knew he'd found the perfect blend of humor and romance. Not an easy balance to get right. Many tried, few succeeded. Wince-worthy attempts at the genre littered the Hollywood landscape. Colt believed this would be one of the rare exceptions.

"Colt."

"I don't like the way you said my name."

Wyatt's tone told Colt his brother was about to knock the sweet cherry off his hot fudge sundae.

"There is a caveat attached to the money."

"Go on."

"You need a bodyguard."

Great. Wyatt hadn't knocked the cherry off. He had decimated the entire dessert.

"No."

"I'm not giving you a choice, Colton."

Shit. Wyatt rarely called him Colton. When he did, he meant business.

"If this is about that minor incident at my last premiere."

"Minor?" Wyatt pounded his fist on his desk. It was a rare show of temper. "A man stabbed you."

"Stabbed is an exaggeration. Nicked. Once the nurse wiped away the blood, it didn't even require stitches."

"It was luck."

"It was fast reflexes." Colt wasn't bragging. His quick moves prevented his attacker from causing major damage. *And*, he disarmed the man before security could arrive.

"Colt... "

"A bodyguard would have gotten in the way. I know. I've worked with them."

Colt's dismissive tone made his opinion clear.

"The backers don't agree."

"Talk them out of it." Wyatt had the gift of persuasion. Smooth words. His brother never left a meeting without a signed contract. Getting the money men to drop the bodyguard stipulation would be a piece of cake.

"No."

"What?"

"I agree, Colt."

"Come on."

"You weren't on the other side of a phone call informing you that your brother was attacked on the red carpet. The media reported everything from a massive injury to your death."

"Deb phoned Mom and Dad first. She was shaken up. It took her awhile to get to you."

"I understand that, Colt. The point is, I love you. I would feel better if you let someone watch your back."

"Don't play the brother card, Wyatt."

As plays went, it was damn powerful. Though not as much as Wyatt's next.

"Mom agrees."

"Low blow," Colt muttered. "We aren't kids, Wyatt. I can't believe you would go running to Mommy."

"I didn't do that when we were kids. We settled things brother to brother."

"Then—"

"Unlike when we were kids, you're acting like a selfish brat. Calling in Callie seems appropriate."

"You're bluffing."

This time, Wyatt stared *him* down. And won. His brother didn't bluff. Resorting to dragging their mother into a dispute wasn't his usual style, but he did what was necessary to close a deal.

"The only reason I'm caving is because I don't want to worry Mom. Her boys are a bit accident prone lately."

Not long ago, their brother Nate broke his arm—then was almost blown to pieces. As crazy as it sounded, Nate's job as a stuntman turned out to be less life threatening than his recent stay in Montana.

"I have an idea."

"Don't you always." Wyatt spent his childhood trying to curb Colt's wild ideas. And having a damn good time in the process. He grinned. They'd had a great childhood.

"Yes." Colt crossed his arms. "You'll like this one."

"Okay."

"Get me a female bodyguard."

"That's something *you'll* like. Me? I say hell no."

"Hear me out. We present her as my girlfriend. The world loves a love story. No one will suspect the truth."

"It's not the worst idea you've ever had."

"It's right at the top."

"Two conditions."

"I should have known." Colt scrubbed his face. "Fine. Shoot."

"We tell the family the truth."

"Naturally. I don't want Mom, or Dad, getting any ideas. She's already planning two weddings. That's plenty. What else?"

"Keep your hands to yourself."

"Wyatt!" Dramatically, Colt clutched at his chest. "I'm hurt. I do not harass women."

"No," Wyatt agreed. "You charm and seduce."

"You make it sound like that's a bad thing. I haven't heard any complaints. Have you?

"This woman will not be a giggly supermodel or one of your co-stars. You have hired her to do a job—to work for you. That is a line you cannot cross."

"What if she crosses it first?"

"Jesus, Colt. Are you so hard up for new blood? I repeat. Promise to leave the bodyguard alone or you'll spend the next five months bunking with the hairiest, smelliest man H&W Security has on staff."

"H&W." Colt sat up straight. "Is that who you're using?"

"We always do." Wyatt picked up his phone. Now that Colt had agreed, he wasn't wasting any time. "At the rate we're going, they should start offering us a bulk discount. I hope they have somebody who fits the bill."

On the outside, Colt nodded, his expression sober as a judge. On the inside, he grinned ear-to-ear. He knew damn well H&W had the someone. The perfect someone.

"DON'T BE AN idiot. Stay down."

The man on the ground shook his head, clearing the ringing in his ears. And letting everyone watching know that he wasn't listening.

"I can't believe it. He's getting up." The men exchanged looks. Idiot didn't begin to describe this guy. Obviously, he had a death wish.

"Do what they say." His opponent danced from foot to foot. The bounce of a boxer. Or a warrior. Both fit. "I don't want to hurt you."

"You think I'm worried?" He spat a mouthful of blood. "You got in a lucky punch. You won't take me down again."

Thirty seconds later, he was flat on his back, gasping for air.

"Had enough?" Someone called out.

"Come on. Let's call it a day."

He batted away the hand that reached to help him up.

"Fuck that. And fuck you."

With a shrug, his opponent turned. He took the opportunity to shoot his foot out, aiming for the vulnerable knee that was only a few feet away. His eyes widened with surprise when instead of connecting with bone, his foot twisted painfully, the hands that securely held him one move away from breaking his ankle.

"You have two choices. Walk away, or crawl. Which will it be?"

"Like I said, *fuck you*."

"Have it your way."

The pain was excruciating. Before it became much worse, he cried uncle.

"What the hell is wrong with you?" One of the men helped him up. "You lost. Fair and square."

"I was holding back," he insisted, trying unsuccessfully to save face. "Fighting a woman is bogus. Goddamn cunt."

"Arlington." The shout came from the back of the room. "Pack your gear and clear out."

"But—"

"You're fired. Get your gear and clear out. If you're still here in thirty minutes, I'll throw your sorry ass through the gate."

"Alex."

"Not now, Sable. Get cleaned up and meet me in my office."

Sable Ford followed her boss into the hall.

"I've been called worse. I don't want to be the reason a man loses his job."

"I didn't fire him because of that. Though, it isn't a word I like my crew to use. He's out on his ass because he tried to blindside you."

"I handled it."

Alex paused at the base of the steps. The nearby elevator didn't get a lot of use, especially by management. Men who spent so much time behind a desk needed to stretch their legs every chance they got.

"You could have broken Arlington's foot, and nobody would have blamed you. The fact that you didn't is why you're still working for me, and he isn't." Alex's blue eyes met hers. He was ex-Army. So was she. They no longer wore the uniform, but some things went deeper. When your commanding officer gave an order, you didn't argue. "Anything else?"

"No, sir."

"Shower." Alex pushed her toward the locker room. "No hurry."

Sable was the only female bodyguard working for H&W Security. It meant she was in high demand. It also meant dealing with men like Rod Arlington. During training drills, and on the job. It wasn't very different from what she experienced in the Army.

A band of brothers sounded good, but even in the twenty-first century, some things never changed. Brothers meant men. They tolerated women. Barely. From the lowest grunt to the brassiest of the brass. Sable, and women like her, had to put up with a lot to forge a career.

Words were nothing. Abuse against women, physical and sexual, was the military's dirty little secret. Now and then it popped to the surface, only to be washed away with promises of reform. Promises that, for the most part, were not kept.

Sable joined the Army straight out of high school filled with ideals and ambitions. Six years later, stuck in a bad situation for which she could see no solution, she turned in her dog tags.

Quitter.

Sable tried to shake the thought from her head. She'd been trying for almost two years. Sometimes, when one walks away from the family business, the backlash was harsh. Her father hadn't wanted reasons. He wanted a daughter who fulfilled her commitment to her country and her fellow soldiers.

The papers she kept in a safe deposit box were stamped honorably discharged. In her father's opinion, they should have read AWOL.

The water that poured over her short, dark hair didn't wash away her somber thoughts. It never did. Most of the time, she kept her nasty little demons at bay. When they slipped under her guard, she rode out the melancholy and moved on. She couldn't change her father's attitude. All she could do was live her life.

Shutting off the shower, Sable grabbed a towel and headed for her locker. It was a damn big room for one person. H&W needed to hire more women. She knew plenty who could do the job. Old friends. And new ones she had met since leaving the service.

Alex wanted a meeting. She would add her thoughts to his agenda.

Pam Stoddard sat behind her desk. She served as executive assistant to three men. Now and then she made noise that she needed help, but the truth was, Pam didn't want anyone else invading her territory.

"Are Jack and Drew out of the office?"

The founders of H&W Security kept strange hours. However, self-made billionaires could do pretty much anything they wanted.

"They were in earlier. It's double-date night. They are taking their wives out for dinner and dancing."

"Sounds nice."

"My husband is going to hear about it." Pam winked. "My not so subtle hint about our anniversary next month. Go on in. Alex is free."

Sable liked that her bosses were married. She knew their wives and considered them friends. Family. It made her strained relationship with her father a little easier. She took the seat opposite her boss/friend/family and jumped right in.

"You need to hire more women."

There she said it.

"I agree." Alex sat back, his steeped fingers tapping his chin. "Any suggestions?"

Sable had a list of ten names tucked in her pocket. Just for fun, she threw in a ringer.

"Dani."

Alex frowned, his complexion turning slightly white.

"My wife? Really?" Suddenly, his tan disappeared altogether. "Have you mentioned this to her?"

"No." Sable hid her smile. "On second thought, never mind."

"She would be damn good." Alex might not like the idea, but his first instinct was to defend the woman he loved. "Are you suggesting she couldn't handle it?"

"Dani would be perfect. Kickass to the extreme. You'd be the problem."

"Me?"

"Be honest," Sable shook her head. "Can you see yourself sending her out on a job? South America? Japan? Those were my last locations."

"Fine. I'll admit I want my wife close to home. And out of danger."

"Which is why she is not on my list." Sable handed Alex the paper. "Besides, you guys are thinking about starting a family. That would be difficult with her in another country."

"She told you that?" Alex didn't wait for an answer he already knew. "Why do women need to share every bit of information?"

"You haven't told Jack and Drew?"

Sable grinned when Alex shrugged.

"Not that long ago, nobody knew my business. Now, everybody does."

"And?"

"It's strange. Disconcerting and more than a little unsettling." Alex grinned. "And I wouldn't go back for anything."

Sable looked around the luxurious office with a spectacular view of Harper Falls. She hadn't known Alex when they were in the Army. However, experience told her this was eons away from his life in the field.

"No restless feet?"

"No." Alex's expression was the one of a man truly content with his life. "If I do feel a pull? If I get to wondering what is over the horizon? I tell Dani. She understands better than anyone."

"What happens then?"

"She takes my hand, and we go exploring together. A week. Two at the most, and we're happy to come home."

"Must be nice," she said wistfully.

Sable's gaze traveled out the window, over the town and the river, to the horizon. The unknown. She liked Harper Falls. Loved her friends and her job. However, when Alex spoke of the connection he and Dani shared, she knew it wasn't likely she would find that here. Or playing bodyguard for the rich and famous.

"Is there a problem?"

Alex prided himself on reading people. On a good day, it was hard to get a bead on Sable. She seemed laid back. Happy. Lighthearted. And he supposed she was. However, as with many ex-soldiers, there was more than she showed on the surface. Sable had watched people die— strangers and friends. No one came back from that unchanged.

Alex had no doubt that Sable had her shit together. Still, even she had her demons—ones she hadn't shared with him, or her friends.

"I've been feeling restless lately," Sable answered, using Alex's words. It described her feelings as well as any.

"If you ever need to talk."

"Your door is always open." Sable had heard it a hundred times. She doubted she would ever take him up on the offer, but it was good to know she had the option.

"I have a job for you." Alex picked up a file and handed it to her.

"I figured."

"Wyatt Landis called this morning."

"Is there a problem? Jade?"

Sable's stint as Jade Marlow's bodyguard hadn't been long. But a bond developed. They kept in touch, speaking at least once a week. Two days ago everything had been fine. But the world was a crazy, unpredictable place. Change, when it happened, could be sudden—and dangerous.

"Relax. Jade is fine. It's another member of the family that needs your services."

"Really?" Sable ran the Landis family through her head, eliminating each as she went. Caleb and Callie. Unlikely. Wyatt? Probably not. If Jade was all right, so was Garrett. Nate went through his drama and came out the other side happy, healthy, and in love.

That left— Uh, oh.

"Colton needs a bodyguard for the duration of his next movie shoot."

"Why me?"

Under her breath, Sable added, *God, why the hell does it have to me?* Of all the Landis family, why did she get stuck with the egocentric pretty boy. The one whose kiss she still thought about from time to time. Nope. Not a good idea.

"Colt isn't thrilled with having a bodyguard. The backers insist, so he's insisting the girlfriend angle."

"Of course he is."

Sable had played that part before. No one looked hard at the eye candy hanging off a man's arm. The goal wasn't for her to blend into the woodwork so much as decorate it. No one would suspect a tall brunette with perfectly manicured fingernails of carrying a concealed weapon. Or that she could take out men twice her size without breaking a sweat.

She liked those jobs. For all her tough ass ways, deep down, Sable was a girly girl. High heels and designer labels suited her just fine. No one needed to know that she had acquired her Louis Vuitton luggage on eBay, or the few good pieces of clothing in her closet she supplemented with bargain basement finds.

Sable wore the items as if she were born to money. Except with a greater appreciation.

"This is why you need more women around here. I've worked for the Landis family. Won't my return generate questions? The wrong kind of questions."

"I checked. No one gleaned on to who you were. There were hundreds of stories about Jade, her father, and the Landis family, but not a single mention of you."

"I don't know whether to be relieved or insulted."

Alex smiled. "For now, go with relieved. If someone remembers you, the family knows what to say, You and Jade—old friends. Romance bloomed between you and Colt, etc."

"Mmm."

"You've met?"

"Oh, yes."

"Ah."

"Ah? What does that mean?"

"Colton Landis has a reputation. Did he hit on you?"

Sable nodded.

"You turned him down?"

"Naturally." *After she kissed him.*

"Will it be a problem if the inevitable happens and he hits on you again? Repeatedly?"

"I've dealt with the situation before."

Alex waited for her to finish the thought.

"Fine. He's a bit more attractive than the average client." *That was putting it mildly.* "I'm a professional, Alex."

"You're also human."

"Meaning?"

"Don't beat yourself up if you slip."

"Alex!"

Sable was shocked. Rule number one. The thing he drilled into the head of every person who worked for H&W Security. Stay detached, and don't cross any lines.

"Are you encouraging me to sleep with Colton Landis?"

"No. Of course not."

"Good."

She planned on keeping her feet planted firmly on the ground. No kisses. No nothing. Having her boss's okay to *slip*, as he put it, was the last thing she wanted.

Like setting a kid loose in a candy store with no supervision. Things were bound to end badly.

"You can turn down the job, Sable." Alex handed her the file. "Look it over. If you decide to go, you leave in a week. If not, no problem. They can find someone else."

Sable lay in her bed, going over the particulars of Colton Landis and his recent problems.

A delusional man convinced the movie star was having an affair with his wife, attacked Colton. The man breached security, easily getting past the pitiful red rope that blocked the public from the celebrities.

According to the report, Colton's quick reflexes prevented anything more than a flesh wound to his upper arm. He tackled the attacker; the EMTs patched Colton up, and amazingly, the premiere continued. With the movie's star in his seat.

Not surprisingly, the backers of Colton's next movie insisted on better security. A bodyguard wasn't foolproof, but it was an extra layer of protection. No one wanted their star out of commission and unable to finish the film.

Sable set the open file aside. She had known before she read a word that she was taking the job. Professional pride. She had never turned down an assignment; she wouldn't start now.

So what if she felt a jolt of anticipation—an excitement missing from her life lately. It had nothing to do with Colt. Well, maybe a little. She was only human.

Sable picked up his picture. Dark hair and killer blue eyes. A face that the camera, and millions of women, loved. Too good looking. And too aware of it. She could personally attest to his charm and sex appeal. The combination overwhelmed a person, making her forget herself and her job.

Last time, she had the luxury of walking away. It wouldn't be as easy this time. Colton Landis's girlfriend? What was she getting herself into?

Chapter Two

BEVERLY HILLS, CALIFORNIA. Rodeo Drive. Movie stars. Swimming pools.

Hillbillies.

Sable smiled. Never underestimate the influence of television and reruns. They were her friends during her early childhood. Was it any wonder her brain referenced the Clampetts rather than something more recent?

Sable relaxed against the soft, leather seats, lulled by the smooth-riding limousine and watched mansion after mansion pass by the tinted window. Quite an upgrade from her life in the military. Luxurious cars. Fancy homes. Bone china and sterling silver place settings.

As with her former life, all of this was temporary. Tonight she would sleep underneath bedding that cost more than she used to make in a month. However, as with the government-issue sheets she used in a tent in Afghanistan, they didn't belong to her.

Sable couldn't complain about the upgrade. She wouldn't wake up with sand in her eyes and her mouth. Still, it would be a nice change to be an owner instead of a renter.

Roots. The older she became, the more she longed for them.

Moving from Army base to Army base hadn't been easy. She and her mother followed her father. North Carolina. Japan. Germany. One year she attended three different schools.

That was unusual. However, the life of an Army brat was unpredictable. She learned early not to become attached. Friends, when she made them, didn't last.

Television had been her entertainment, her companion, and more often than not, her babysitter. The life had been difficult for Sable. It had been brutal for her mother.

Iris Freed married Mathias Ford expecting non-stop excitement. Living in a foreign country sounded exotic to a girl from Treetop, Tennessee. She pictured parties and shopping and—well, she didn't know. But it had to be better than the crushingly boring life she had lived during her first nineteen years.

Reality crashed in on her fast. There were no parties. Shopping meant the PX. Mat claimed the base was in Italy, but for all she knew, they were still in Tennessee. Military housing looked awfully like the shack in which she grew up. The men and women sounded the same. Acted the same.

Iris spent her days cleaning, cooking, and waiting for her husband. To her horror, she was stuck in the same routine, the same life from which she had run. She wasn't a glamorous jet-setter. She was the one thing she swore she would never become. She was her mother.

Iris didn't have the tools to leave. No work experience. No education. She found herself ruled by fear of the unknown. She couldn't go back to Tennessee. After bragging up her new life, she would never live down ending up where she started.

The most logical move was to find another man to take care of her. One not in uniform. Iris was pretty. Soft blue eyes and a young, curvy body. How hard could it be? She caught Mat when every girl in eastern Tennessee wanted him. If she put her mind it, she could attract someone better. Richer.

Two things worked against Iris. Mat received orders, sending them to Guam. And she discovered she was pregnant. It was a bad combination for a woman planning to start a new life. Iris was stuck.

Ten more years. A child to lug from base to base. A few affairs that her husband chose to ignore.

The day she turned thirty, Iris looked in the mirror. She wasn't young. Nor was she old. The pretty on her face had worn off long ago. The prematurely deep lines around her mouth told the tale. Years of discontent. She was tired. Too tired to keep fighting a losing battle. Nothing would ever change. She was stuck.

Iris stopped thinking about leaving. Instead, settled in, resigned to live the rest of her life with a man she tolerated and a daughter she never wanted. Television had been Sable's early companion. It became her mother's last refuge.

Sable sometimes wondered how different her choices might have been if her mother had taken the slightest interest in her. Instead, she grew up guided by a stern, yet undeniably loving, military man.

Never, no matter their disagreements, did Sable doubt that her father loved her. It made their current estrangement all the more difficult. She tried, every day for a year, to make him listen. To explain why she walked away from his world. Every day, her efforts were met with silence.

Sable continued to reach out. Not every day. Sometimes once a week. Or once a month. All she could do was hope that one day, he would answer.

Closing her eyes, Sable adjusted her earphones, letting the music on her playlist wash away her troubled thoughts.

At the same time her mother embraced television as her method of virtual escapism, Sable turned to music. It filled her soul like nothing else. When she ran. Or lifted weights. Or sought a few minutes of peace in a crazy, war-torn country. Sable found solace in the melodies and words.

Moving to Harper Falls came with a huge bonus. She met, then became friends with Rose O'Brian. When she stopped to think about it, it never failed to amaze Sable. Long before they met, Rose's songs filled Sable's iPod. They helped her through some bleak moments when she found consolation in nothing else.

Life had a way of handing her unexpected pleasures. Calling Rose friend was one of them.

The car slowed, taking a right, stopping at the tall, wrought-iron gate. Sable didn't remove her earphones. The driver knew the routine. Through the intercom, he spoke to a faceless voice, dutifully presenting his face for the camera. Less than thirty seconds later, the gate opened.

The surface of the driveway was smooth, not a bump or pothole in sight. Lined with trees and flowers of every color, it reflected the lady of the house. Bright and welcoming.

Exactly how Sable would describe Callie Flynn.

It wasn't Sable's first visit. Last year, while protecting Jade Marlowe, she had the pleasure of meeting the superstar and her equally famous husband, Caleb Landis.

At this point, after working for H&W for over a year, Sable didn't experience the nerves she felt the first few times she met someone rich and famous. She had quickly found out that the old saying was true—they put their pants on one leg at a time—just like everyone else. True, their pants were more expensive, but that didn't make the person special. They were average people living above-average lives.

Callie Flynn *was* different. No matter the setting or the clothes, the legendary beauty could never be called average. Sable expected movie star. She found the most down to Earth person she had ever met. Callie had a light soul. A fact reflected in every thing, and person, who surrounded her. She didn't have a pretentious bone in her body.

The first time they met, Callie ignored Sable's outstretched hand, drawing her into a warm hug. Lemons and an elusive fragrance. Sable later found out it was a perfume made especially for Callie. It suited her perfectly.

They hadn't spent a lot of time together, but Sable knew, without a doubt, that Callie was exactly the person she appeared to be.

This job was filled with all kinds of potential pitfalls, beginning and ending with Colton Landis. However, knowing she would get to spend time with his mother almost made up for the trouble she knew was ahead.

Before the car came to a full stop, the front door opened. Callie Flynn, her famous screen goddess face free of makeup and beaming, rushed out. Dressed in jeans and a t-shirt the exact color of her famous gray eyes, the dark-haired woman with bare feet was not how the world would picture Callie at home.

To her family and friends, this was the real Callie Flynn. The woman they knew and loved.

"Welcome back."

Sable breathed deeply. Lemons and Callie. The other woman's embrace was warm, lasting longer than the normal greeting between acquaintances. Returning the hug, Sable reveled in it, wondering if this was what it felt like to know a mother's love.

A prickling of tears made Sable blink. Whoa. Put on the breaks. There was no way she would use Callie as a balm for her mother issues. It was foolish. Not to mention dangerous.

Callie welcomed her into her home. As an employee and, perhaps, as a friend. Expecting more would be looking for trouble.

"I had hoped the next time we saw you, it would be strictly social." Callie linked her arm with Sable's, guiding her into the house. "Oh, well. The reason you've come is unpleasant. That doesn't mean we can't enjoy having you with us."

Before Sable could comment, a booming voice filled the room.

"There she is."

Caleb Landis lifted Sable off the floor, his strong arms holding her close. He set her down, a grin lighting his handsome face. Tall and fit, no one would guess he was in his sixties. He looked and acted twenty years younger.

"Ever think about changing careers?"

"Caleb," Callie warned with an indulgent laugh.

"What?" Caleb slipped his arm around his wife's shoulders. When Callie was around, he had to touch her. It was as natural as breathing and just as necessary. "Sable has a face the camera would love."

"Really?"

The last thing she wanted was to be an actor. However, Sable was only human. The idea that a man of Caleb Landis' stature and experience thought she could be a star gave her ego a nice boost.

"Don't encourage him." Callie's gray eyes darkened with speculation. "Unless you're interested. You have a very expressive face, Sable."

"I do?"

That was news. Sable worked hard on her poker face. In her Army days, she bluffed her way through quite a few card games, winning more often than not. Expressive? Really. Her Army buddies would find that as surprising as she did.

"Absolutely. *Are* you interested?"

"God no." Not wanting to sound ungrateful, Sable added, "I'm flattered. However, it isn't for me."

"I didn't think so," Callie smiled. "Think of it as an option. It's nice to have them."

Sable thought of her mother. Stuck for most of her life with no idea how to get out. Callie was right. Life was better with options.

"Come along. Everyone is out on the terrace."

"Everyone?"

"This is one of those rare, wonderful times when all my boys are in town. When it occurs, I like to have them near as often as possible."

Sable trailed behind the couple. Light poured into the room from more windows than she could count. Bright, cheery colors added to the feeling of perpetual spring. Flower arrangements. The scent of roses.

Unlike the places where Sable grew up, it wasn't merely a place to sleep and eat. It was a home.

"Sable."

Laughing, Sable watched as a beautiful redhead rushed across the lawn. Unlike the first time they met, Jade Marlowe radiated happiness. It looked good on her.

"How are you?"

"Great." Once more, Sable found herself returning an enthusiastic hug. "I don't have to ask. You're glowing." Sable lowered her voice. "A great sex life does wonders for the complexion."

"You won't make me blush," Jade insisted though a telltale trace of color bloomed on her cheeks.

"And love," Sable added.

Jade's gaze shifted over Sable's shoulder, the emerald color deepening. "Yes. Love makes all the difference."

Garrett Landis, sensing his lady's interest, winked. He and his brother Nate stood on the lawn with a tall, slender blonde. From the look on Nate's face, Sable deduced she had to be Paige Thornton. Love was definitely in the air.

"Wyatt. Pour Sable something to drink."

Callie patted her oldest son's arm before taking a seat next to Caleb.

"Tea or lemonade." Wyatt gestured toward the table. Two blue pitchers with matching glasses and plates of cookies and sandwiches covered the surface.

"Lemonade, please. I remember it from the last time I was here. I've craved it ever since."

Colt exited the house, a glass of lemonade in one hand. Well-worn jeans emphasized his long legs and a t-shirt proclaiming his love for Pat Benatar. His dark hair mussed. Natural or artful? Sable decided to give him the benefit of the doubt. He too was barefoot. To her chagrin, Sable decided even his toes were sexy.

"Taste and beauty. You're a woman after my own heart."

"Oh, brother," Sable groaned at Colton's corny line. She thought she had mumbled them under her breath, but Wyatt's laugh told her he heard her comment.

"Finally, a woman not instantly swayed by the famous Colton Landis. Forget his heart, you can have mine."

"I don't know about your sons, Callie. They seem awfully free and easy with their vital organs."

"Watch it, boys. Sable can give as good as she gets. Sit. Tell us what you've been up to."

"There isn't much to tell." Avoiding the seat next to Colt, Sable walked to the nearest empty chair—all the way across the patio.

"Come on," Jade urged. "You don't have to name names. Tell us about your last job. Where did you go?"

"The Ukraine. Come on," Sable looked around. "Wouldn't you rather talk about something else?"

"Was there a handsome man involved?" Callie asked.

"Yes."

"Then spill."

Sable spent the next hour recounting her last adventure. She hadn't lied. The job was as routine as they came. She played babysitter to the three-year-old son of a high-powered businessman. His business took him to the Ukraine to conduct some sensitive negotiations, involving what, Sable didn't know.

Rather than miss his son's birthday, he brought his family along. It was up to Sable to make sure no one kidnapped the boy. It wasn't as ridiculous as it sounded. Things like that happened all the time. However, the closest Sable came to anything dangerous was some suspicious-looking borscht. She skipped the oddly colored soup and returned to the United States.

"Sounds boring."

"In the best possible way," she assured Nate. "I never hope for trouble. Especially when there is a child involved."

"As a mother, I agree. As a woman?" Callie's eyes sparkled. "What about the handsome man?"

"Richard Cullen IV." Sable waited for a beat. "Three years old and already a heartbreaker. It was love at first sight."

The rest of the afternoon flowed in a similar vein. Casual and relaxed. It would have been easy for her to forget that she was there to do a job. Feeling Colton's gaze reminded her.

Sable met his laser-blue eyes, causing a funny jump in her pulse. It wasn't fair. Colt was the first man in a long time to interest her libido. He was the job. Hands off. It didn't matter that Alex had given her the green light. She knew the rules. Bend them once and there could be a whole slippery slide effect.

Discipline. In both body and mind. How many times had her father said that? It was the code she lived by. She sure as hell wasn't going to break it for a casual fling.

"This has been fun, but we need to get down to business."

"Can't it wait until tomorrow?" Jade asked.

"Sorry," Sable shook her head. "I'm on your brother's dime. It isn't right for me to take advantage."

"Take advantage all you like." Colt's smile slowly widened, his eyes never leaving hers. "I'm easy."

"He's your son," Wyatt said to his father. "Tell him what's what."

Before Sable's eyes, Caleb morphed from genial to serious.

"Colton. My office. Now."

"Oh, boy." Nate rubbed his hands together with glee. "Colt is in for it now."

"You get too much pleasure out of this." Paige looked around. Wyatt and Garrett's expressions mirrored Nate's. "Look at you. He's your brother."

"Our pampered little brother." Wyatt took a sip of tea. "Now and then he needs to be put in his place."

"Should I go with them?" Sable started to rise.

"Stay." Callie patted the seat Caleb had recently vacated. When Sable joined her, she took her hand. "Caleb is going to set a few ground rules, nothing more. I'll admit that too often, Colt gets his way."

"He won't with me." Sable's firm tone was for her benefit as much as for the Landis clan.

"Naturally. Colt would never force himself on you. Never," Callie said emphatically.

"I never thought he would."

Satisfied, Callie nodded. "He will make comments. It's in his nature to tease and flirt. I'm afraid he gets that from me."

"On you it's adorable." Wyatt winked at his mother. "Colt can come off as obnoxious."

"You're making too much of this." Sable refused to let them treat her as if she couldn't take care of herself, or handle any innuendo Colt might shoot her way. "Nothing Caleb says will stop Colt from being who he is. He flirts. Sometimes I'll ignore him. Sometimes I'll tell him to go to hell."

"We know you can handle Colt," Callie said with an easy smile.

"Then what is this about?"

"Caleb believes in treating people with respect. Men, women, and children. That is how we raised our boys. Sometimes, one," Callie looked from son to son, "or more of them needs reminding. In private."

COLT FOLLOWED HIS father. Caleb always used his office when having a talk with one of his sons When he was nine and broke his mother's favorite vase, Colt shook in his shoes. Now, at the ripe old age of twenty-seven, he couldn't help it. He felt a little quake. It didn't matter what he'd done or hadn't done. His father meant the world to him. If he in any way disappointed the best man he had ever known, Colt became slightly sick to his stomach.

"Shut the door and sit down."

"Yes, sir."

Caleb sat in his large, leather chair, silently contemplating his youngest child.

"I trust you, Colton."

Colt knew he wasn't expected to answer. Not yet.

"Sable can kick your ass. Any day of the week and twice on Sunday."

"I know that."

"That does not give you the right to disrespect her."

"You think I would?" The implication hurt—and pissed him off.

"Not intentionally. Sable isn't like the women you're used to."

"I agree. She's special."

Caleb raised his eyebrows but didn't ask what Colt meant by *special*.

"All I'm asking is that you refrain from your usual banter. You and Sable will live together. No dropping her at her door. She's your shadow, Colton. Around the clock."

"I'll tone it down."

"That's all I ask," Caleb nodded.

"Dad."

Colt frowned, his eyes pensive. God, Caleb thought with affection, *he looks like his mother*. Colt had his father's eyes; the rest was pure Callie.

"Yes?"

"That thing I said about Sable being special. I didn't mean special, special. Like Jade is to Garrett. Or Paige to Nate." It was clear that Colt regretted bringing it up. He jumped to his feet. "You know what, never mind. Forget I mentioned it."

After Colt had left, Caleb sat alone in the room where he did his best thinking and let his mind wander.

Colton? And Sable? Caleb closed him eyes and smiled. Too soon. But interesting.

Chapter Three

"I THOUGHT YOU lived in Beverly Hills."

"I did." Colt shifted gears, his Maserati purring like a well-oiled machine—which it was. He treated his cars with the greatest of care. "When Garrett and Jade moved to his house in Laurel Canyon, I decided to buy his downtown loft. It's a great place."

"I agree." Sable had stayed there when she guarded Jade. "It's more practical. From a security standpoint."

"Right."

The awkward silence drove him crazy. Colt never had a problem finding something to talk about. He was naturally outgoing. Part of what made him a good actor was his interest in people. He listened and observed. Every conversation was another opportunity to pluck information he could later use for a role.

Talking to a woman was especially easy. Next to getting one naked, it was his favorite activity. He liked the way they sounded. The way they smelled. Just looking at a woman, any woman, was a pleasure.

It was his father's fault. Until he pulled him into the office of shame, he and Sable had been doing fine. A little lighthearted banter. Give and take. Colt was certain he hadn't read her wrong. She enjoyed it as much as he did.

Not that Dad was wrong. The situation was a new one for him. He dated. He carried on a few long-term relationships. However, the last woman he had lived with was his mother. Now, he had Sable. Twenty-four hours a day. Seven days a week. Strictly hands off.

Colt sighed. He should have done a better job of thinking this through. A single glance at the woman sitting next to him and his sigh became a groan. A male bodyguard would have been a much better idea.

"Are you all right?"

"Right as rain."

Colt rolled his eyes. *Right as rain? Really?*

"That groan sounded…"

Sexy? Titillating? Intriguing? Colt's thoughts didn't fall in line with his father's edict, so he kept them to himself.

"How did it sound?"

"Constipated. Do you have enough bran in your diet?"

So it's come to this. Never had a woman commented on his bowel movements. Either he was getting old, or Sable was different. Crap. There it was again. *Special. Different.* Colt didn't know why those words kept popping up.

Sable Ford was a beautiful woman. Gorgeous. But not in a cookie cutter, *I've seen that face on a million magazines,* kind of way. Sable didn't look like anyone else. Hence, special. Different.

Colt felt his shoulders relax. That was it. Everything about Sable was unique. From the top of her glossy dark hair to the tips of her brightly painted red toenails. And everything in between.

Long and lean, with just the right amount of curves, Sable made his mouth water. She had from their first meeting. She knocked him on his ass, literally and figuratively. That kiss. Unexpected and memorable. He'd thought of it more than once.

Had she? At the time, Sable seemed unaffected. And uninterested. It would be best if that didn't change. His ego could take the hit. Colt shifted in his seat. His libido was another matter. Damn. It served him right. His thought to ask for Sable was a way of getting around the bodyguard issue. Wasn't he clever? Hell, no. He was not. He was going to suffer for his smartass ways.

God, if Wyatt found out, he would laugh himself sick.

Colt pulled into the underground parking garage. It was another perk to living in this building. Direct access to the loft using an elevator that bypassed his floor unless he had the proper code.

"A retinal scan? Nice."

Sable worked for a cutting edge security firm. She appreciated the best of the best. Especially when it made her job easier.

"I'll get your scan added tomorrow."

"That isn't necessary," Sable assured him.

"Sure it is. While you're in Los Angeles, my home is your home."

"Theoretically."

"Positively."

Sable smiled. She liked to get to know her clients. It made her work easier if she understood what made them tick. She already knew the basics about Colt. Add to them, he was stubborn. Borderline argumentative—in a casual way.

"When you leave the loft, I leave the loft. When you come home, I come home. If I do my job properly, we will never enter the building separately."

"Stubborn."

"I agree—you are."

Colt leaned against the elevator wall, arms crossed. The lighting wasn't great. However, Sable could swear his eyes glowed. Bright blue. It disconcerted her. And damn, it turned her on.

"If this keeps up, it's going to be a long two months."

"Amen." She heard Colt sigh. "And yes. I like to have the last word."

"Me too." Colt let her exit the elevator ahead of him. "And here it is. Retinal scan. Tomorrow."

"But—"

"In a fair fight, you can kick my ass." Colt leaned close. "I don't fight fair."

Asshole.

"Did you say something?"

"Are you a mind reader?"

"Nope."

"Then I didn't say anything."

Sable walked into the living room. It felt familiar and different all at once.

"You redecorated," Sable said when Colt returned from putting her luggage in the guest room.

"I made a few tweaks. Fresh paint. New furniture. I did a complete overhaul on both bathrooms."

"Why? The guest bath was a dream."

"Compared to what?"

Any place I've ever lived. In her head, it sounded pathetic. A real, *poor me* moment. Her apartment had a sweet little setup, including a large bathtub and a balcony overlooking the Columbia River. It didn't compare to what Colton was used to, but it suited her.

"Are you a bathroom snob, Colton?"

"Damn straight. And proud of it." Colt opened the refrigerator. "Beer? Water?"

"Nothing, thanks."

"I live well, Sable." He twisted the cap off a bottle of something imported. Sable didn't recognize the brand. "I won't apologize."

"Good. There is nothing worse than a self-hating millionaire. I know. I've worked for people who spend so much time downplaying what they have, they get no pleasure out of life."

"Perhaps that *is* their pleasure."

"Well said." Sable started to kick off her shoes, then paused. "Do we need to set some ground rules?"

"Dad already did."

Sable laughed. "We'll get to that in a second. I meant how do you want to do this? Should I stay in my room?"

Colt did a perfect spit take. Luckily most of it hit the sink.

"Why would I want you to do that?"

"I'm not your girlfriend. Or your friend."

"Bull —" Colt caught himself. "Pucky."

Damn, he was cute. "I'm your employee."

"I didn't hire you."

"Many of my clients prefer not to socialize. I'm fine with that."

"I'm not." Colt toed off his boots. His socks followed right behind. "Take off your shoes, Sable. Stay awhile."

Colt took her hand, led her to the big, comfortable sofa, and gently gave her a push.

Like landing on a pillow. Sable closed her eyes. Heaven wrapped in the softest fabric imaginable.

"I want one. Unfortunately, it wouldn't fit in my apartment."

"It comes in smaller sizes." Colt knelt to remove her shoes.

"That isn't necessary." But it made her insides jump—in a good way.

"I'm a good boy. I'm a good boy. I'm a good boy."

Sable lifted an eyelid. Colt seemed transfixed—staring at her foot. "Problem?"

"You have no idea. Rule number one. No teasing or flirting. Rule number two. Do not make a pass."

"Good rules." *If you were dealing with underage virgins.* "Caleb laid down the law."

"Umm." Reluctantly, Colt set down her foot and joined her on the sofa. On the far end of the sofa. "He's right. Your job does not include indulging my baser instincts."

"Did Caleb use that term? Baser instincts?"

"It amounted to the same thing."

"That's why you played Zombie in the car? You were editing your words?"

For a man like Colt, it had to be brutal. Flirting came as easily as breathing. How did he suddenly stop without blowing a gasket?

"I don't want you to feel uncomfortable. And if you say it's part of the job, I swear I'll ..."

"You'll?"

"How do you threaten a woman who could twist your balls off without breaking a sweat?"

Sable's eyes narrowed. "How do you threaten any woman?"

"Fair question." Colt gave it some genuine thought. "This is a first. I've never met a woman who annoyed me the way you do. May I be honest?"

"There's a reason it's called the best policy."

"And silence is golden. Best I keep certain things to myself."

"We could spend our time together speaking in clichés. Or I can break the ice. I have a good idea what you were going to say."

"I doubt it."

"You don't argue with women; you sleep with them. If things start getting sticky, you end it. How many non-arguments have you had?"

When Colt groaned, Sable didn't try to hide her grin. "Come on, Mr. Movie Stud. You can't be embarrassed."

"Embarrassed? No. I prefer to call it discreet."

"You never kiss and tell?

"No. Never."

Colt said it with simple conviction. He wasn't selling her on the idea. It was up to her to believe him or not. Sable believed him. Colt wasn't as easy to figure out as she once believed. The superstar gloss wasn't an act. Neither was the down to Earth man she saw in front of her.

As with most people, Colton Landis had multiple facets to his personality. He wasn't a shallow pretty boy. His complexities made him human. And, to her chagrin, more irresistible than ever.

Sable needed a diversion—something to take her mind off her increasingly inappropriate thoughts.

"So you like feet? Is it a fetish?"

"Pardon me?"

"Before? When you removed my shoes? I got the impression you wanted to kiss my feet."

Not the best segue. Kissing feet? Colt kissing *her* feet? *So* inappropriate. And oddly appealing. Perhaps she was the one with the fetish.

"Not a fetish." Colt looked uncomfortable. "Is this a test? I'm trying to be good, Sable, but you aren't making it easy."

Neither are you. She desperately wanted to push that stray piece of hair off Colt's forehead. Was it as soft as she imagined? If she ran her fingers through the dark locks, would he purr or growl?

"Your eyes are all dreamy. What are you thinking about?"

Sable wondered if Colt was aware that he had moved closer. His head bent. His deep blue eyes locked with hers.

"You don't want to know. It would be better if we dropped this, Colt."

"That's the first time you've said my name."

"Is it?"

"Mmm. It's always, pretty boy. Or movie stud. Colt sounds good."

Colt's voice lowered, the timbre sending shivers down Sable's spine. One night. Not even that. And she was ready to forget her moral stand against sleeping with a client.

"What would your father say?"

Sable thought that would pull Colt up short. She was wrong. Instead, he smiled. A smile that did nothing to cool her overheated blood.

"His message was clear. And that was the plan. *Is* the plan."

"Good." Sable wanted to sound firm and in control. Instead, she sounded like a breathy fangirl. Ugh. It had to stop. Now.

"You like me."

"You're a Landis. What's not to like?"

Smart. Make it about his family. There was nothing sexy about that.

"You like *me*. Colt. My last name has nothing to do with it."

"Your last name is the reason I'm here. Your family has a connection to H&W."

"You. Like. Me."

With each word, Colt moved closer. Sable could have stopped him. A simple *no*. Hand to his chest, checking his progress. That's all it would have taken to make him retreat to his side of the sofa.

Colt wasn't pushing. He gave her ample time to object. The problem was, she wanted him right where he was.

"Colton."

"Mmm. Colton. Even better. I know what you taste like, Sable. Sweet and spicy. How can I resist those lips?"

"Because you know it would be a mistake?"

"Would it?"

Colt's mouth hovered over hers, close enough for her to feel the warmth of his breath.

Yes or no? Sable didn't know what her answer would have been. Caught by his eyes, she hesitated. Then pulled back.

"My phone." The ding indicating a new text was a lifeline. Gratefully, Sable twisted away. Glancing at the screen did more to kill the moment than a dozen buckets filled with icy water.

Two words—*call me*—and Sable crashed back to reality.

"I need to answer this."

"Is everything okay?" Colton frowned. Gone was the warm, pliant woman whose voice dripped with honey. In her place, an unfamiliar Sable. Cool. Stilted. He had never seen anyone switch gears so quickly.

"Do you have any plans for the evening or are you staying in?"

"No plans."

"Let me know if you change your mind. Remember, if you go out, I go with you."

Sable headed toward her bedroom.

"Damn it, Sable. Talk to me. What's wrong?"

She paused, not turning. "It's personal. No reason for you to worry."

Puzzled, Colt watched her close the door with a strangely controlled click. It wasn't a slam. However, he knew by the set of Sable's shoulders that she was upset.

Colt walked to the window. The view was his favorite. He couldn't get this in Beverly Hills. Los Angeles at night. The lights, the energy. It spoke to him. He loved to stand and observe. It looked like a huge, constantly changing mural—painted for his pleasure.

Tonight, he didn't see any of it. His mind was on Sable.

No reason for you to worry.

How could he not? One moment he saw laughter in her eyes. Her words teased, inviting him in. The next, the life went out of her. Something flipped a switch inside her, and Colt wanted to know what it was.

Did Sable need help? And if so, how could he get her to ask?

Chapter Four

"SABLE! THANK GOD you called."

"How are you, Mom?"

"Desperate."

What else was new?

Sable sat on the edge of the bed and did the only thing expected of her—she listened. The litany of problems never changed. Not in tone or length.

How could a woman who confined her life to eating, sleeping, and watching television, have so many complaints? Sable could count on one hand the times their conversation varied.

Number one, Sable's first date. Iris objected. Vociferously.

The moment Sable announced that she had accepted Tanner Pearson's invitation to the movies, her mother never let up. Men, no matter their age, wanted one thing. Women were weak and always gave in. The only way to avoid temptation was to stop the madness before it began.

Her mother's solution? No dates. Ever. A woman was better off alone than tied to an ungrateful, selfish man.

Sable listened, as she always did. On Saturday night, she showered, put on her nicest dress, and a touch of makeup. Precisely at seven o'clock, she left the house. She half-expected her mother to follow her to Tanner's car. It would have been better than the warnings Iris shouted for the entire Army base to hear.

Sable wasn't discouraged. She dated—often. She never told her mother ahead of time.

The next, and biggest, blowup came when Sable joined the Army. No amount of screaming or brow beating would change her mind. By the time her mother found out, it was a done deal.

Iris reminded her on a regular basis that she had thrown her life away. Sable listened, as always, in silence. Her mother did not greet the news that Sable had decided to leave the service with the approval she expected. Why? Because a good daughter would get a job near her mother, not across the country. A good daughter would want to visit. A good daughter.

What did that mean? Sable had no idea. She tried. She asked the questions she knew her mother wanted to hear. How is your back? What did the doctor say about your heart palpitations? Are you taking your medication? Pills Sable doubted she needed.

It hurt her heart. She loved her mother, but speaking with her was a chore of gargantuan proportions. Most of the time she tuned out the words, her mind drifting to mundane subjects like grocery lists and dentist appointments.

This evening she thought about Colt. Something almost happened. He made her forget herself—something she never did. Her mother's phone calls were painful, but, for once, her timing had been flawless. It stopped her from making a big mistake.

An hour later, her mother finally ran down. The brief lull allowed Sable to ask the question she most wanted answered.

"Is Dad there?"

"Is he ever?" Iris reserved that shade of bitterness for her husband. "I had hoped when we settled here in Florida that I would see more of him. What a pipe dream that was. He's taken up golf. Can you imagine?"

Sable knew it wouldn't do any good, but she had to try.

"That sounds like something you could do together." As far as Sable knew, the last thing her parents did as a couple involved her conception. "A little fresh air and sunshine? It might do you good."

"Me? In the sun? Hello, skin cancer. Honestly, Sable. You have no consideration for me."

"You're right. I wasn't thinking."

"No, you were not." Iris sighed. "I have to go. Wheel of Fortune is starting."

"Mom. Tell Dad to call me." Sable always asked. Almost two years and still no luck.

"If I ever see him. Take care, baby."

"You too."

Sable headed for the bathroom for a much-needed shower. Speaking with her mother wore her out. She had completed twenty-mile hikes in full gear that left her with more energy. Right now, nothing sounded better than hot water and blessed silence.

She stepped into the newly remodeled room and briefly wondered if a bathroom could bring on a religious experience. Because Sable swore she heard angels singing.

"Hello, gorgeous."

Reverently, Sable ran her hand over the rim of the beautiful jetted tub. Grinning, and feeling her spirits rise, she turned on the taps. *Oh, blessed water pressure.* In the blink of an eye, she was chin deep and halfway to nirvana.

Thirty minutes of alone time, plus bubbling water that relaxed every muscle in her body, and Sable felt like herself again.

She quickly dried her body with what had to be the softest towel ever created. Gray? Who owned gray towels? Colton Landis. Sable didn't know if he chose the dark slate color, or it was someone else's influence, but it worked. Smiling, she briefly considered slipping one in her suitcase before she headed home. It wasn't going to happen. Still, the silly thought banished the last bit of lingering sadness.

Sable opened her suitcases and removed a jar of body cream. It was a necessity, not a luxury. No matter where she went, Afghanistan or Miami Beach, she always carried lotion.

She wasn't a snob. High end or drugstore brand, Sable didn't care. She learned early on that the desert played havoc with your skin. She slathered it on her body after every shower. The result? Soft and smooth. Not like a baby's butt. Like a woman.

It didn't take her long to transfer her things into the outrageous walk-in closet. She didn't know where the extra space had come from, but she swore it was twice as large as before.

Great for an extensive wardrobe. Something that, by no stretch of the imagination, described Sable's clothing. Perfectly adequate. She wouldn't embarrass herself, no matter the situation.

Besides, every piece was hers. Paid for by the sweat of her brow, so to speak.

Sable stood back and surveyed the closet. Her clothes barely filled a quarter of the area. Her underwear and various sundry items occupied the top two drawers of the polished mahogany bureau. Plenty of room for the shopping she wasn't going to do.

Sable grinned. There would be no *Pretty Woman* moment for her—thank God.

She glanced at her phone. Eleven-thirty? It was later than she thought, but her stomach didn't care what time it was. It told her the little sandwiches and delicious cookies Callie had served with her famous lemonade were not going to get Sable to breakfast.

The living room was dark. However, the light that shined through the windows was sufficient. Sable walked to the kitchen, enjoying the feel of the cool hardwood floor under her bare feet.

The refrigerator was new. Again, Sable wondered why Colt felt the need to swap out something that hadn't been more than a few years old.

To make the place his own.

Sable understood the impulse. She did the same thing. Always had. Army base to Army base. Whether she was a child trying to find a foothold in her ever-changing universe, or an adult, looking for something she couldn't put a name to, Sable found little ways to personalize her space.

Sub-Zero refrigerators and crazy-ass closets were not in her budget.

However, the principle was the same. She recognized Colt's need to transform the loft into his, not his brother's, vision of home.

"Holy crap."

Sable's eyes widened. Now she knew why he needed such a big refrigerator.

Who the hell did Colton plan on feeding?

"It's embarrassing."

Sable didn't jump out of her skin. However, it was a near thing. Calmly, she set the jar of fancy stuffed olives onto the shelf. Instinct had her grabbing the first handy weapon. Good reflexes kept her from smashing it into Colt's pretty face.

"Do not sneak up on me." She grabbed an apple before closing the door.

"I didn't sneak. See that chair?" Colt pointed to the one in the corner. "That is where I was when you came out of your bedroom. All you had to do was look."

"In the shadows of a darkened room. I'm not a raccoon."

"Point being, I was here first."

"The excuse of a man who grew up with siblings."

"It isn't an excuse. It's a fact."

"Oh, shut up." Sable raised the apple to her mouth and took a bite. Was there anything better? Crisp and juicy, the sweet/tart flavor filled her mouth. "Yum. I'll give you this. You know how to pick your produce."

"You're feeling better." Colt handed her a paper napkin.

"A hot bath and a little perspective." Sable wiped the juice from her lips. "They do wonders."

"You liked the tub? You're the first to try it out."

Sable appreciated that Colt didn't ask about the phone call.

"On a scale of one to ten, I rate it a twenty. And the towels? Heaven."

"Mom will be happy to hear that."

"Callie? I figured you hired a professional decorator."

"When I have Mom? Not a chance." Colt turned on the electric kettle. "She has impeccable taste."

"Is she the one who stocks your refrigerator?"

"No." Colt rubbed his neck, his expression sheepish. "The thing is."

"Yes?"

"People like to do things for me."

Sable hid her smile. He *was* embarrassed. Interesting.

"*People?*" She prodded.

"Fine." Colt pulled two mugs from the cupboard, slamming them onto the poured-concrete counter. Why they didn't shatter, Sable couldn't say. He put a tea bag in each one, then filled them with boiling water. "Women. They stock my refrigerator. They do my laundry. They clean my house."

"How does that work? Please. Tell me you haven't given a bevy of beauties access to your home?" If that were the case, she needed to change his security immediately. Sable made a mental note. Why take any chances? Either way, the system needed to be updated.

"Of course not." Colt frowned. "My assistant, Nancy, handles letting them in and out. She stays the entire time and never leaves anyone alone."

Nancy Flicker. Sable remembered the name from the list of people on whom H&E had done extensive checks. She passed. Before Sable left Harper Falls, Alex had cleared everyone Colt dealt with on a regular basis

"Okay."

"Okay? That's it?" Colt picked up the mugs and followed her into the living room.

"What else is there to say? It isn't any of my business. Or it wasn't. I'm afraid that from now on, you'll have to get things done the old-fashioned way. Do it yourself. Or hire somebody I can have checked out."

"Fine," Colt huffed.

"It is the way most of the world works."

Seeing his expression, Sable almost felt sorry for Colt. Up until now, he lived a life where tedious chores were miraculously done for him. She forced him to leave a little of his Peter Pan ways behind.

"It made my life easier."

"You don't need to apologize."

"I wasn't." *Exactly*. "I wanted you to understand why I have enough food to feed an army."

"An army? Speaking from experience, it's close. But not quite." Sable hid her grin behind another bite of the apple. "What happens to all that food? Wild parties? Please tell me you throw food orgies."

"Sure." Relaxing into the banter, Colt sipped his tea. "Explain the difference between a food orgy and a regular one?"

"You gorge yourself on food and sex."

"At the same time."

Sable gave him a *well, duh* look.

"Ah. Sorry. I have to revise my answer. No food orgies. I donate it to a homeless shelter."

Of course, he does. Another piece to the Colton Landis puzzle. Gorgeous. Charming. Funny. She could add good guy. His one annoying quality? He had a few, but to her consternation, she couldn't find anything that turned her off.

His few flaws made him human. Sexy imperfections. She needed something, anything, to make him less attractive.

"When was the last time you kicked a puppy?"

"Never. Next question."

Sable's eyes narrowed. He knew what she was doing. The smile on his mouth bordered on self-satisfied. *Okay, she might be grasping at straws, but she could work with that.*

Smug didn't look good on anybody. Though Colt almost pulled it off. Damn him.

"Regular orgies?"

"By your definition, how many people make up an orgy?"

"Five."

"Not even a hesitation?" Colt sounded impressed. "Why five?"

"Three people? There's a name for that. Four? Not enough. What if two couples are having dinner. They imbibe in too much wine. Somebody pulls out a little weed. One or two joints later, things get funky. Not an orgy. Add the plumber who stopped by to unclog the sink? Wham, bam. That, my friend, is an orgy."

"Impressive."

"I read. A lot."

"So you've never…?"

"Orgied?"

"Is that a word?"

"If it isn't, it should be. And no, I never have. One on one only."

A few seconds ticked off the clock. Then a minute. Then two.

"Aren't you going to ask me?"

"I did."

Colt thought about that, then nodded. "Right. I became distracted. Five? You're certain?"

"Five," Sable said emphatically. "Or more."

"Then no."

"Four?"

"Nope?"

"Three?"

Sable saw it in his eyes. A twinkle in a sea of blue. Intrigued, she waited.

"You want me to kiss and tell?"

"Hell, yes. Change the names to protect the not so innocent."

Sable prepared herself to coax the story from him, but Colt surprised her.

"It was a dark and stormy night."

"Oh, come on."

"Seriously. There isn't a lot to do in Northern Alberta in the middle of January. My co-stars made the suggestion." Colt laughed. "Boredom and chivalry got the better of me."

"Chivalry? Come on."

"I consider it rude to turn down not one, but two beautiful women."

Two women. Sable should have known.

"What if it had been a woman and a man?"

"Probably not." Colt rubbed his chin—considering. "If no one objected, I would have watched."

Sable laughed. Somehow, their conversation about sex wasn't the least bit sexy. She found herself relaxing and enjoying Colt's company.

"Is that the time?"

"Two-thirty? I'll be damned."

"Shouldn't you get some sleep?"

Colt started filming his movie tomorrow. No, today. She felt guilty keeping him up.

"I don't go in until one o'clock."

"Good."

"I want to apologize, Sable."

"Why?" Puzzled, she frowned.

"I left my parents' house filled with good intentions. We barely walked through the door, and I began flirting. Hard."

"And I flirted back." Sable planned on doing this in the morning, but since Colt brought it up, now was as good a time as any. "That was on me, Colt. I crossed the line."

"We crossed it together."

"Fair enough." Deliberately, Sable wrapped the apple core in her napkin and set it aside. It gave her a moment to collect her thoughts. "We can flirt, Colt, as long as it is without intent."

"Interesting choice of words." Colt gathered their cups and her napkin and headed for the kitchen. It seemed she wasn't the only one who needed to think things through. "I can't make a pass unless I know you want to catch the ball."

"I don't." *Liar.*

The look Colt gave her echoed her thoughts. Thankfully, he didn't call her out.

"How do you want to play this, Sable?"

"Friends?"

"Of course."

"Nothing more."

It wasn't a question. Sable could tell Colt didn't like her answer, but again, he kept his opinion to himself.

"About sex."

That perked him up.

"Yes?"

"My role as your faux girlfriend doesn't follow us behind closed doors. It isn't necessary to remain celibate simply because I'm staying here."

"Meaning what?"

"Bring a woman home." Sable almost choked on her words, but she managed to spit out a few more. "Going to her place isn't practical. Though if you'd rather, we can work that out. I prefer you don't meet in a public place. Hotels are harder to secure."

"I see. And you do what? Sit outside the door in case my partner's motives are more nefarious than simply getting me off?"

"That won't be necessary." Sable could hear the anger in his voice. In her opinion, it was unwarranted. "I can hear you from my room. Yell if you're in trouble."

"What about you?"

"Me?"

"Yes, Sable. You." Colt moved until he stood inches away. His eyes didn't twinkle. They glowed. "You're a young, healthy woman. What about your needs?"

"I can take care of myself."

Colt's bark of laughter held no humor.

"I want to work out and have breakfast at my parents' place. We'll leave at eight."

"Fine."

"And Sable?" Colt paused at his bedroom door.

"Yes?"

"When you're taking care of yourself? Remember, I can do the same. Who knows? We might be *taking care* at the same time."

It took some effort, but Sable held in her groan until she was certain his door had closed.

Bastard. Planting that image in her head was cruel. Inhuman. How was she expected to sleep?

There was no help for it. Sable entered her room, tossed off her robe, and crawled into bed. Without hesitation, her hand slipped between her legs. It wasn't a slow build.

Fast. Intense.

Sable closed her eyes as her orgasm hit. She couldn't help herself. She wondered if across the loft, in his room, Colt did the same.

Chapter Five

COLT NEEDED TO work off a lingering case of frustration—tinged with a touch of anger. Nate seemed like the perfect outlet. His brother was always up for some sparring. This morning it was their version of cage fighting. Without the cage. Or the anything goes rules.

A few blows in, Nate figured out that Colt's demeanor wasn't as casual as his.

"Watch the low blow. I need my balls in working order."

"I didn't touch your precious balls."

They circled each other; the easy grin wiped from Nate's face. If Colt wanted to play hard, so be it.

"I wanted to put the warning out there. I would hate to beat up that movie star face. Wyatt wouldn't be happy if his star shows up bloodied on the first day. However, touch the cojones, and you're asking for it."

Colt glared at Nate. The look could intimidate most men. Nate, all six five, two hundred and twenty pounds of him, wasn't impressed. Damn, he loved his brother. But being the youngest could be a pain in the ass. He would always be the *baby*. That was difficult to overcome.

"Suck it up, Colt. It was one night. You've gone longer without sex." Nate raised an eyebrow. "I hope."

"This isn't about—" Colt growled. "Forget it. I need to get cleaned up. And pancakes. Many, many pancakes."

"Forget the carbs," Nate called out, chuckling. "Remember. The camera adds ten pounds."

"Fuck you."

Nate's laughter did nothing to help Colt's mood. He hadn't slept and the fact that Sable looked fresh as a daisy added to his frustration. She encouraged him to bring a woman home. Damn her. It was tempting to see how she would react if he did just that.

Unfortunately, the only woman he wanted was out of his reach. For now. Colt wouldn't give up that easily. He would be patient. When she caved, the reward would be all the sweeter.

Colt hurried through his shower, throwing on jeans and a button-down shirt. He didn't notice that the color matched his eyes. His mother gave it to him on his last birthday. She knew what he liked. Easy, yet stylish.

A glance in the mirror told him he looked presentable. At the last second, he ran a hand through his damp hair. It tended to curl when wet, and a quick fluff gave him the perfectly tousled, *I don't give a shit*, look that women loved and men tried to emulate.

This time, Colt laughed at himself. Yes, it was ridiculous. However, after so many years, looking good was second nature. He liked who he was and every time he stepped outside, he represented the Colton Landis brand. Actor first. Movie star second. It was fun as well as frustrating. And he wouldn't change a damn thing.

"That's all it takes? One move?"

"With practice."

"Show me again."

Colt paused at the top of the stairs. Sable smiled at Jade. And what a smile it was. He longed to find out if that smile felt as good as it looked. One day soon, he would kiss her just as her lips began to curve upward.

"Here."

Wyatt waved a napkin in front of his face.

"What's the big idea?"

"I thought you might want to wipe that drool off your chin before Sable sees it."

"Hilarious. You and Nate should take your act on the road." Colt shoved past Wyatt. "Far, far away."

"Garrett." Jade pulled him from his seat. "Be a love and let Sable demonstrate on you."

"No thanks." Garrett wrapped his arms around Jade's waist and whispered something in her ear.

"Later." She made a not so convincing attempt to break his hold.

"Now." Garrett insisted, inching her toward the stairs.

"Garrett. Leave Jade alone and sit down," Callie chastised. "Breakfast is ready. Honestly. Can't you keep your hands to yourself? I don't know where you get that."

Wyatt snorted into his orange juice. "He gets it from his mother and father."

"I don't think so." Callie looked outraged.

"You and Dad are still at it."

"What's that?" Unknowingly, Caleb proved Wyatt's point by kissing Callie's neck and whispering something in her ear. Something that had her face turning pink.

"I rest my case."

"Oh, eat your eggs," Callie laughed. Seeing Colt, she motioned him to sit. "How many pancakes, sweetheart?"

"Five." He sneered at Garrett. "To start."

"What can I get for you, Sable?"

"Nothing. Thank you."

"Don't be silly. The griddle is hot. Lorena mixed up the batter before she left last night. There's plenty."

"Don't bother, Mom. Sable has a job to do. Mixing with family wouldn't be professional."

The moment the words came out of his mouth, Colt wanted to call them back. He had meant to tease. Instead, he sounded like a petulant child. Before he could apologize, Sable's back stiffened, her eyes turning cold.

"Colton! What a thing to say."

"It's all right." Sable stood. "Excuse me. I'll be outside when you're ready to leave."

Sending Colt a dirty look, Jade rushed after her.

"What the hell?" Nate slapped him on the side of the head. "Stop thinking with your dick, Colt."

"I'm not."

To be honest, Colt didn't know what was wrong with him. One second he wanted to kiss Sable, the next he wanted to push her away. As feelings went, he didn't care for either. The pancakes he'd been looking forward to suddenly tasted like sawdust.

"Do we need another trip to my office?" Caleb asked.

"No, sir. I'm going."

Colt didn't have far to look. Sable stood outside the door, Jade right next to her.

"I can stay," Jade said,

"I think I can handle him."

"No doubt."

Once they were alone, Colt took a deep breath. A simple apology seemed inadequate, but it was all he had.

"I'm sorry."

"You don't have to apologize."

"No. But I want to."

Colt sighed. He made his living expressing his emotions. It was easy when someone gave you the words.

"You spoke the truth, Colt."

"My family thinks of you as more than an employee, Sable." Colt rubbed his head. He could still feel Nate's not so subtle reminder.

"I like your family. However, you're the one who has to be around me all the time. Is this about sex?"

"Partly."

"Fine. Let's go."

Sable headed toward his car.

"Go where?"

"Your place. We have time before you're due on the set. A quick fuck and you'll be right as rain."

"Sable. Stop." Colt grabbed her arm. "Now who's being ridiculous? A quick fuck? Honey, there won't be anything quick about it."

Sable's shoulders shook with laughter, the air draining out of her with righteous indignation.

"We can't keep doing this, Colt." She leaned against his car and wiped the moisture from her eyes. "I appreciate a good laugh, but getting there is brutal."

"I know." Colt joined her, his hand gripping the hood, his hand inches from hers. "Besides, if Dad calls me into his office one more time, I may as well turn in my man card."

"What's the solution?"

"To quote Nate, I stop thinking with my dick." Colt nudged her with his shoulder and grinned. "I know what you're thinking. Breaking a habit I've had since I turned thirteen won't be easy."

"You *are* a mind reader."

"Friends?"

"Let's see how it goes." Sable's lips curved. "Ask me tomorrow."

"Fair enough."

Between the sun and Sable's smile, Colt felt the last lingering tension drain away. It wasn't about his body. He needed a new mindset. Yes, he wanted Sable in his bed. Surprisingly, he wanted her friendship just as much.

Colt liked women, but he rarely took the time to know them. Fun and games and sex. He eased away if he thought his playmate wanted more. He didn't always avoid hurt feelings. But he never made promises he had no intention of keeping.

Asking for Sable's friendship felt right. The rest would take care of itself.

"WHAT'S GOING ON?

"They're smiling. That's good."

Nate wedged himself between Paige and Jade. The window provided the perfect view of the drama playing out in the driveway.

"She didn't knock him on his ass?"

"I don't know your brother very well, and I only met Sable yesterday. I didn't realize they had a history."

"They don't." Nate took Paige's hand in his.

"One kiss."

"What?" Nate turned toward Jade. "When did that happen?"

"The last time she was here."

"No kidding. Still." Nate looked out the window. "That doesn't mean much."

"Sometimes one kiss is all it takes." Paige squeezed his hand.

"Amen," Jade smiled when Garrett joined them.

"Colt isn't ready to fall in love."

"Were you?" Jade touched the stud that pierced his ear. Purple jade, the color his eyes turned when he looked at her.

"I didn't think so at the time. I didn't need a kiss to tell me." Garrett pulled her close. "I was waiting for you."

"Maybe Colt feels the same way."

"He wants her. But love?"

"I agree," Jade nodded. "It's too soon. However…"

"Let Colt and Sable find their way." Garrett nuzzled Jade's neck. "We did."

Yes, thank God. Jade closed her eyes, sighing with pleasure. It hadn't been easy. Maybe love wasn't supposed to be. But she wouldn't change a thing. The pain—the suffering—led her here to the family she always longed to have. And most important, to Garrett.

"I want everyone to be this happy."

"I wake up happy. I go to bed happy."

"Because of me?" Jade knew the answer, but she never tired of hearing him say it.

"You." His eyes turned deep purple. "Only you."

Jade cupped his face in her hands. "And only you, my love."

Chapter Six

A WORLD TRAVELER, there wasn't much Sable hadn't seen. The Great Pyramid, the Taj Mahal, the Eiffel Tower. The list was as wide as it was varied.

After today, she could cross a movie set from the list.

"What do you think?"

"I see cameras and a lot of people who seem to be working at cross purposes."

"Bingo." Colt adjusted his necktie. "Lesson one. Very little time is spent filming a movie."

"Hurry up and wait?"

"There you go."

"Sounds like the Army."

"Who knew?" Colt draped an arm over her shoulders. "We have more in common that you thought."

Falling into her girlfriend role, Sable batted her eyes and giggled. Loudly. It drew attention—which was the point. And made Colt roll his eyes—a nice bonus.

"I never date idiots," he pointed out.

"I beg your pardon. I have a Ph.D. in Pomeranians. I didn't bring my sweet baby because it's her massage and pedicure day."

"Really?" Colt whispered near her ear. "That is how you're playing this? I like brains with my beauty, Sable."

"Come on. The blonde with the mammoth breasts? Which Ivy League school is her alma mater?"

"Remind me. Which blonde?"

"My point exactly."

Sable laughed. Giving Colt a hard time was more fun than she anticipated. However, playing dumb took too much effort. For her sake, as well as his, she needed to tone it down.

Her backstory, the one she and Colt decided on, wasn't complicated. The fewer details, the less chance they would slip up.

Sable was a college student studying art history—and an old friend of the Landis family. Last year while Colt was making a movie in Milan, and she was ending a year of study abroad, romance bloomed. A few weeks ago, she arrived in California, at his invitation, they picked up right where they had left off.

The newness of their relationship made a perfect cover. No one questioned Colt wanting his girlfriend by his side. Sable could watch his back without raising any eyebrows.

"In a week, you'll be bored out of your skull."

"This is nothing. Try lying in the sand for seventy-two hours with only a mid-sized rock for shade."

"Sounds like a story. Can you share?"

Sable smiled. Somehow Colt understood that some missions, no matter how much time had passed, were not for dissemination.

"Dull as dishwater," she assured him. Naturally, he caught the twinkle in her eyes.

"I doubt it." Colt took a deep breath. "You smell good. What is that?"

"Today? Soap and water. Ivory, to be exact."

"No kidding?" Colt touched her hair with the tip of his nose. "I swear there's a touch of lemon."

"My shampoo."

Sable didn't like men who sniffed at her. They came off as overeager dogs. Drooling hounds. She batted them away with ease. Colt didn't drool. He wasn't a dog. Though he made her long to scratch his stomach. And lick every well-defined ridge.

"Colt."

"Hmm?"

"Nothing."

Sable meant to tell him to move away. Honestly. That was her intention. Instead, she kept her mouth shut. A girlfriend didn't push her man away. Why shouldn't she take advantage of the situation? Who could fault her? She was just doing her job.

"Colt? Rene is ready for you."

"Duty calls."

Duty. Interesting way of putting it. Sable grabbed a bottle of water and moved to the director's chair that had Colt's name on it. She knew about duty. To her country. To her job.

Sable couldn't let herself forget what she was doing, or why she was here. Colt had a way of messing up her equilibrium. She needed to focus on her job, not on how the sound of his voice sent shivers down her spine.

"Hey."

An energetic blonde hopped onto the chair next to Sable.

"Hello."

"I'm Janis Mainard."

"Sable Ford," she said, shaking the woman's hand. "I'm—"

"Oh, everyone knows who you are. The girlfriend."

Sable fought the urge to look around. Were people staring?

Janis smiled. "Never dated a movie star?"

"Colt is my first. So to speak."

Sable had no idea if that were something a movie star's girlfriend would say. It seemed lame and not the least bit funny, but it made Janis laugh.

"It's a different world. I'm still learning how to negotiate the curves."

"Are you an actress?"

"You don't recognize me?" she asked, her voice filled with mock indignation. "You missed the critically acclaimed, *Death Ball IV*?"

"Sorry," Sable grinned.

"Hey, it's tough if you missed the first three." Janis shrugged. "I wasn't in any of them, so don't bother catching up. This movie is my big break. I'm the best friend. The second female lead. She cries on my shoulder, and I inject a few witty remarks about love and men. I plan on stealing every scene."

They'd just met. However, Sable didn't doubt for a second that Janis would do exactly that.

"May I ask you a question?" Janis looked around, then lowered her voice. "It's personal."

"You can ask. I might not answer."

"Fair enough. I love your hair. Do you think I should cut mine?"

Sable burst out laughing. It seemed she had made a new friend. Experience had taught her that you could never have too many of those.

"COLT. HELLO?" Rene Longtree sighed. "I can't work with someone who has the attention span of a three-year-old boy."

"Sorry. What were you saying?"

Colt zeroed in on Rene's words. It was embarrassing to admit. The sound of Sable's laughter had distracted him. He had a hard-earned reputation as an actor who focused on his work—he didn't let distractions get in the way.

He hadn't delivered a line and already the director had to chastise him. Not good.

"You used your clout to get me this job."

"I wasn't the only one in your corner, Rene."

"I owe your family a lot."

"You don't owe us anything," Colt assured her.

Rene couldn't do her job if she had to walk on eggshells. Better she established her position right away. If Colt didn't like it, he could have her replaced. The idea made her sick to her stomach. She had worked hard and sacrificed so much to get this opportunity. Was it all going to blow up in her face?

"About your girlfriend."

"Sable?" Colt frowned. "What about her?"

"Is she going to be a distraction?"

"No."

"She already is."

Colt opened his mouth, ready to argue. Then shut it. Right was right, no matter how hard it was to take.

"A momentary slip." Colt looked Rene directly in the eye, unflinching. "You have permission to kick me in the ass anytime you deem necessary."

"Can I have that in writing?"

"We want the same thing, Rene. The best movie possible. I promise. Sable will not be a problem."

Rene soon found that Colton Landis was a man of his word. The moment she called action, he didn't waver. His focus was laser sharp. He gave her everything she asked for and more. Charm. Humor. Sex appeal. The women of the world better watch out. If they weren't in love with him now, after they saw this movie, they would be.

Three hours later, Colt took Sable's hand and led her to his trailer.

"What did you think?"

"There's much more involved than I realized. You worked on one scene all afternoon. So many takes. Don't you lose the, what's the word?"

"Spontaneity?"

Sable shook her head when Colt offered her a bottle of water.

"Exactly."

"Keeping it fresh is part of the job." Colt loosened his tie, letting out a grateful sigh. "You learn where and when to pull back. It's important to reserve your energy and use it at just the right time."

"It would drive me crazy."

"How did you occupy your mind in the desert?"

Sable watched, fascinated, as Colt removed his suit jacket and started to unbutton his shirt. It was worth the price of admission and she was getting a free show.

"Most of the time, I wasn't alone. The same old stories and jokes—but the time together made us a tight unit."

"It sounds like you loved it. Why did you leave?"

Sable hesitated. She rarely spoke of her reasons. And never in detail.

"It's okay, Sable. You don't have to tell me."

"I want to." Amazed, Sable realized it was true. "Not now. But soon."

"I'm here."

Two simple words—and Sable took them to heart.

Trust was a funny thing. In the Army, you trusted your fellow soldiers. Often, your life depended on it. She didn't find it that simple as a civilian. There were a handful of people in Harper Falls that had her back no matter what.

Her father? Yes. She trusted him. Things were tricky there. He wasn't speaking to her or acknowledging her calls, but if push came to shove, she knew he would step up.

Colt Landis. Interesting. She barely knew the man, yet she felt a connection. Sable couldn't put a finger on why. It went beyond attraction. She liked him. The trust wasn't rock-solid. It was new. Fragile. Time would tell how strong the bond would become. Right now, she felt cautiously optimistic.

"I have a dinner date." Colt opened a drawer and pulled out a clean shirt.

"That will be awkward." Sable frowned at Colt's back. "I'm your girlfriend. Remember?"

"Date is the wrong word. I'm meeting a reporter. She's doing a profile for GQ."

"Is this the norm? Dinner with reporters."

"It's show business, Sable. There's no such thing as normal."

Colt slipped off the shirt he had worn all day. Sable licked her lips. Even his back was sexier than an average man. There was no way around it. Colton Landis was sex on a stick, and she wanted to lick every inch.

"Whoa. What are you doing?"

"Taking off my pants?" Colt hesitated, his zipper halfway down. "I need to take them off to put on another pair."

"Really?" Sable could have turned away. She didn't. "I'm not one of the guys."

Colt grinned. "No. You are not. Thank God."

"Have you no modesty? Go in the other room."

"My underwear covers all the private bits." Colt grabbed the jeans. He did as she asked, stepping into the bathroom, out of sight. "Prude."

"Hardly. I was a woman in the Army. I've seen plenty of men without their pants."

"Then what's the problem?"

"Privacy is at a premium in a war zone, pretty boy. Even in the Army, you go behind a bush if one is available."

"Pretty boy? Are we back to that?"

"I call them as I see them."

"I'm not pretty. I'm ruggedly handsome."

Automatically, Sable took the lead. She opened the trailer door, checked right, then left, then signaling Colt to stay, she did a quick jog around the structure.

"Is that necessary?" Colt linked his fingers with hers.

It felt strange—holding hands with a man. Sable searched her memory for the last time it happened. As a teenager? Maybe. She decided she liked the way it felt.

"Yes. It's my job to keep you safe."

"Do you expect to find many desperadoes lurking behind my trailer?"

"Unfortunately, they lurk everywhere, Colt. If they didn't, I would need to find a new line of work."

"I'll keep that in mind next time I use a public restroom."

"Don't worry about it. That's why you have me."

Colt stopped short. "You're going to check out the men's room before you let me use it?"

"Absolutely."

Sable didn't see anything odd in her proclamation. Colt didn't agree.

"Looks like I'll be doing my business here or at home."

"Don't be silly. I do this all the time."

"What about the guys already in there?" Colt shook his head at the thought. "Don't they object to a woman pounding on doors and checking the stalls?"

It had never been an issue because Sable didn't give them time to react. Most were so stunned at her audacity they didn't cover anything that was exposed.

"I'm not there for a peep show, Colt. I get in and out as quickly as possible."

"Has it ever paid off?"

"Once."

"This I have to hear. What happened?"

Sable shared the details while they walked to Colt's car. He was a wonderful audience. He laughed at the appropriate spots, squeezing her hand encouragingly. She enjoyed sharing a part of her life she always kept to herself. Not for security reasons. She didn't think it was interesting. Despite the potential for trouble, she rarely found any. Recounting her day-to-day routine would bore the most tolerant listener.

"My entrance startled the shooter, and he dropped his gun in the toilet. Before he could fish it out, I had him restrained."

"You could have been shot." Colt didn't find that funny.

"No," Sable assured him. Colt snorted. "Maybe. I wasn't, so it's a moot point."

"Your job is dangerous." Colt stopped, his blue eyes shadowed with concern.

"Potentially. It almost never happens."

"Almost? Have you ever been shot at?"

"At?" Sable decided to skirt the question. "No. Never."

"Jesus. Someone shot you?"

Colton Landis was a smart cookie. Too smart. She had to watch what she said around him.

"Grazed." Sable pulled him along. "A little rubbing alcohol and a Band-Aid and I was as good as new."

"Show me the scar."

"No. Like my tattoo, it is in a place you will never see."

Colt took out his keys and unlocked the doors. He already knew the routine. Sable wouldn't let him hold her door. She insisted that he get in the car before she did. He didn't like it, but she wouldn't budge.

"You have a tattoo?" he asked when after she slipped into the passenger seat.

"An Army Ranger insignia."

Colt started the car and shifted into drive. "Tell me where it is."

"Why torture yourself?" Sable couldn't resist teasing him. "It's better if you don't know."

"I don't agree," he grumbled.

Sable sat back and relaxed. She mentioned the tattoo to distract Colt. And it worked. He didn't mention the gunshot wound again. She didn't fool herself. He hadn't forgotten. But he let it slide. For now.

The tattoo was another matter altogether. They both knew why Colt didn't push the issue. He believed they were destined to have sex. He would get her naked and look for the ink.

"It is not going to happen."

"Keep telling yourself that, if it makes you feel better."

"You are impossible."

Sable punched him in the arm. She gave him points for not crying out; she didn't hold back. However, he winced, and that gave her a lot of satisfaction.

"I will never again accuse someone of hitting like a girl."

Delighted, Sable burst out laughing. Keeping her hormones in check would be a challenge. But she looked forward to spending time with Colt. He made her smile, and laugh—and think. A unique combination.

Nope. He was not a vapid pretty boy. He was much more. And Sable couldn't wait to discover the many layers of Colton Landis.

"YOU'RE MY GIRLFRIEND."

"*Pretend* girlfriend. It isn't necessary for us to be inseparable."

"Let me get this straight. You are willing to sit for hours on a movie set, but you won't dine with me? *Trance* has the best ravioli this side of Rome."

Colt's stubborn streak was a mile wide. It was one of those many layers Sable would have happily skipped. They weren't engaging in a discussion. Or an argument. Colt's tone never changed. Nor did his stance. Reasonable and intractable. How was she supposed to deal with that?

"What does the menu have to do with anything?" Sable shifted on the sofa. They arrived home over an hour ago. The only break in this conversation came when Colt took ten minutes to shower.

"Why pass up an amazing meal? Have you been to *Trance*?"

"No."

"Case closed."

"What?" Sable jumped to her feet, rushing after him. "There is no case. You've already told me that this is a working dinner. It makes sense for you to show up alone. My boss has arranged with the owner of *Trance* to let me watch you from the kitchen."

It was the first time Sable had entered Colt's bedroom. It was almost twice the size of hers. Why one person needed so much space, she would never know. However, she liked the soothing tones of green and blue. And she appreciated a good view. Her balcony back in Harper Falls could fit onto the one that overlooked Los Angeles, at least five times. But the principle was the same. It was a getaway space. Surrounded by people, yet isolated.

"I refuse."

"You can't refuse. It is a done deal."

"Why are you fighting me so hard?"

Colt entered his walk-in closet, his voice becoming muffled.

Sable had her reasons. Good ones. Her part as the devoted girlfriend was a great cover. That cover would begin to slip if it appeared that she had leached herself onto Colt. They shouldn't be seen together all the time. Tonight would be a perfect opportunity to shake some attention.

"Why are you?" she demanded. "If our relationship were real, would we go everywhere together?"

"I plan on enjoying my meal," he called out. "How can I do that knowing you're lurking in the kitchen?"

"I don't lurk."

Colt ignored her. He exited the closet carrying a gray suit that sported a stylish thin, black pinstripe. "Think of my digestion. My stomach and I will be happier with you by my side. Give me a good reason you shouldn't join me."

"I'll have a better view of the restaurant from the kitchen."

"Not good enough."

"I need to keep my attention focused on you, not ravioli."

"Try again."

"My wardrobe is limited. I have casual, and I have dressy. It's the in between that's the problem." All true. However, Sable had the knack of making almost anything look fashionable. Call it champagne taste on a beer budget.

"Normally I would have purchased a few things before I arrived, but I didn't have time."

"Why the hell didn't you say so?"

"I just did," she shot back.

Colt dropped his suit on the bed.

"Come on."

He grabbed her hand, pulling her from his room to hers. Colt opened her closet and surveyed the contents.

"You dress well," Colt said. He looked her up and down. "I noticed that when you guarded Jade. Your taste is excellent, and you have a good eye for color."

"Good?" Sable's eyes narrowed. She might not have the money to buy designer originals, but no one could fault her style. "Try excellent."

"Agreed." Colt handed her a simple pale lavender sheath dress and a pair of sling-back heels. "Those will do nicely. Nobody can see the labels, Sable."

"In Beverly Hills? Think again."

"You know the old saying. The clothes don't make the woman. You look fantastic, no matter what you wear."

"Flattery?" Sable smiled, taking the dress and holding it up in front of the mirror. It suited her. "And I think you garbled that saying."

Colt shrugged. "I like my way. It fits. And it's true. Now, about your underwear."

"I can handle the rest," she said, pushing him out the door.

"Party pooper. Things were getting interesting."

"I'll be ready in thirty minutes."

"Really?" Colt looked impressed. "Take your time. It will take me at least an hour."

"To put on a suit?" Sable blinked. He had to be kidding.

"It's a process."

"An asinine process."

Colt grinned. "Welcome to my world where asinine is another word for Hollywood."

Alone, Sable sighed. Wyatt Landis paid her salary, but Colt was her boss. If he insisted on having her by his side, she had no choice but to comply.

Sable began applying her makeup. Perhaps she needed to switch gears—mentally. She had played the girlfriend before now. However, none of those jobs lasted longer than a few days.

Funny how that mimicked real life. Men came and went. Casual. Pleasant. Forgettable. Sable wanted to treat Colt the same and hold him at a distance. Their mutual attraction aside, she knew she didn't have that luxury. Not this time.

Colt couldn't make a move without drawing attention. A live-in girlfriend counted as more than news. As soon as word got around, Sable's face would be splashed all over the internet. Rumors would run rampant. Wedding plans? Babies?

Sable needed to prepare herself for an onslaught from every direction. Including, God help her, her mother.

Hopefully, there would be time enough to worry about the inevitable accusatory phone call. Would there be approval or horror? Either way, Sable knew her mother's reaction was bound to be over the top.

That was a bridge, lined with explosives, that Sable would cross another time. Today, on set, Colt had introduced her as his girlfriend. No one batted an eye. They had jobs to do. Worrying about their star's latest squeeze was far down their list of concerns. Tonight would be different. A new world.

Luckily, Sable loved an adventure. The more it challenged her, the better. It was time for her to hone a new set of skills.

She needed to learn the ins and outs of being the perfect Hollywood girlfriend.

TRANCE WAS EVERYTHING Colt built it up to be—and more. Luxurious, exclusive, and a little obnoxious in the way they slathered Colt with attention.

He took it with good grace and a wink, letting Sable know he understood that it was nothing but bullshit.

Colton Landis, movie star. When his movies made tons of money, he ruled Hollywood. At the moment, Colt was top of the heap. Next year that might change, but for now, people climbed over each other to bow and scrape, hoping some of his luster would run off onto them.

That included the woman interviewing Colt, Sable realized from the moment they joined her at their table. Izzy Clark was young, pretty, and savvy enough not to flirt with Colt when his girlfriend sat inches away.

And she only cared about his glitzy exterior. She couldn't have cared less about the real man.

"Do you mind if I record the interview?" she asked Colt.

"Not at all."

"I feel honored." Izzy set her phone in the middle of the table and beamed at Colt, her eyes occasionally darting Sable's way. "I get to break the news of your new relationship. How thrilling. Tonight is a coming-out party, so to speak."

Sable groaned. Good Lord. Before she could roll her eyes, Colt nudged her leg. *Play the part.* Her lips curved, hiding tightly clenched teeth. This girlfriend thing would be harder than she anticipated.

"When did you meet?"

"Sable and my brother's fiancée are dear friends. Jade introduced us last fall."

The woman had a lousy poker face. Sable could tell she wanted to use the opening to ask about Jade and Garrett. The story was a juicy one. The furor it stirred up hadn't died down. Wisely, she kept her questions to herself. She was ambitious. And smart enough to know what subject matter was off limits.

"Was it love at first sight?"

Izzy directed the question at Sable.

"Love?" Sable shrugged, then proceeded to skirt the word like a pro. She looked at Colt, her smile warming. Time to jump in—full-tilt girlfriend mode. "Not at first. Don't get me wrong. I'm not blind. Looking at Colt is no hardship."

Izzy laughed. And laughed. *Okay*, Sable thought. *Not that funny.*

"I knew I wanted to get to know her. I'm fortunate that she agreed."

Colt raised her hand to his lips. His mouth curved upward against her skin and his eyes sparkled. He knew that Sable was out of her element—swimming hard against the tide that wanted to swallow her under—and he enjoyed every moment. *The bastard.*

"Are you officially off the market?"

"We're living together."

Izzy gasped. Skin flushed with excitement; she checked her phone to make certain she got every word.

Colt's reaction wasn't as obvious, though Sable read him with ease. If they hadn't been in a room filled with eager observers, he would have burst out laughing.

"How long ago did you move in?"

"Yesterday," Colt replied. "It's new."

"What is your family's reaction?"

There was a question behind the question. Izzy hoped the Landis clan hated Sable and disapproved of the relationship. Sable understood that Izzy had a job to do. But did she believe Colt would say such a thing?

Later, Sable asked Colt that very question when they were alone in his loft.

"She can hope. It wouldn't be the first time a celebrity said more than was prudent."

Colt had changed into jeans and a t-shirt. The suit and tie were nice. The pictures taken by the paparazzi as they entered and left the restaurant would make women swoon. Sable had to admit, Colt's impeccably tailored clothing set off his long, muscled frame to perfection—the gray of the material deepening the blue of his eyes.

However, Sable liked him best casual and relaxed. He crossed his ankles and sighed.

"She pushed the champagne. Then proceeded to drink most of it."

"Mmm." Closing his eyes, Colt patted the sofa. He smiled when Sable joined him. "She never recovered from your bombshell. Ms. Clark believed she would interview me about my new movie. Instead, how did she put it? She scooped the world. You can't blame her for falling apart. You made her career."

"That wasn't my intention. But, hey, I'm all for doing my part to advance my fellow woman. Even if I find her job morally reprehensible."

Colt peered at Sable, one eye firmly shut.

"Isn't that a bit harsh?"

"Is it? She almost drooled when you mentioned Jade. She wanted you to throw her and your family under the bus. "

Colt's mouth tightened. "That wasn't going to happen."

"But if you were a different kind of man, one who slipped after a few glasses of wine, she would gleefully write every dirty secret without a single tinge of conscience. I stick with my assessment. In fact, reprehensible might be letting her off lightly."

Sable stretched her legs out next to Colt's, their bare feet inches apart.

"You found your rhythm quickly." Colt tapped her toe with his. "You were a natural in front of the paparazzi."

"They threw me at first, but I reminded myself that they had the cameras. I had the gun."

"Ouch. Literally."

They fell into a comfortable, easy conversation. The tone of Colt's voice, low and soothing was the perfect accompaniment to his stories about growing up with three brothers and high-profile parents.

Colt didn't speak of his mother in reverent tones. She wasn't *Callie Flynn: Superstar*. She was Mom. Loving. Strong. Supportive. Willing to let her boys be who they were meant to be. Surprisingly, Colt painted the picture of a normal childhood—quite a feat, all things considered.

"You've seen how she is. There isn't a pretentious bone in Mom's body."

"I know. Callie made me feel welcome the moment I stepped into her home. Five minutes later, I almost forgot I was sitting next to an Academy Award winner." Sable's eyes widened. "Holy crap," she laughed.

"What?"

"You were nominated."

Colt chuckled. "But I didn't win."

"You will."

Delighted, and a little surprised, Colt turned. "You think so?"

"It's simply a matter of time."

Sable stared out the window at the city lights. From here, they saw only beauty. She knew ugly things happened out there, but while they sat, alone and quiet, none of it could touch them.

"I need to hit the sack." Colt stretched his arms over his head. "We need to leave at four."

"No problem."

"That's A.M."

"Colton." Sable patted his hand before rising. "My father woke me every morning at five. Every day. Rain or shine. Summer, winter, spring, and fall."

"Why?" he asked, obviously horrified.

"Discipline. He tried the same thing with my mother but stopped after their first few years of marriage. She threw things at his head."

"What did you do?"

"Me?" Sable found it an odd question. "I got out of bed."

Colt stayed seated after Sable closed her bedroom door. His body relaxed while thoughts of Sable raced through his mind. She was a complicated woman. A fact that intrigued him. More and more, he wanted to find out what made her tick.

Who was Sable Ford? At times, she seemed open, friendly, and uncomplicated. A beautiful, intelligent woman with no hidden secrets.

Then there was the soldier. Looking at her, Colt found it difficult to believe that she was a warrior. A trained killer. He had seen her in action. Taking down Nate during a simulated fight didn't count as real combat. However, his brother outweighed Sable by over a hundred pounds. And he trained with the best martial artists in the world. It took her less than five minutes to put Nate flat on his back. Then she did it again.

He didn't think Sable realized it, but her comment about her father gave him the first glimpse into her past—and what helped mold Sable into who she was.

The woman was scary tough. Steel—with the softest skin he had ever touched.

Colt groaned. Soft skin, so close and out of reach. It wasn't the best thought to take to bed. On the other hand, he decided with a grin, it wasn't the worst.

Chapter Seven

AFTER THE FIRST day of shooting, Sable wondered how she would stand weeks of the mind-numbing routine. She dreaded another day of sitting and watching nothing happen.

Whoever thought this was a glamorous business was out of their mind.

Sable decided that actors needed the patience of Job. Each scene took forever to prepare and only a few minutes to film. Sometimes, seconds.

Someone always fussed around Colt. If someone wasn't retouching his makeup or styling his hair, wardrobe was there to swap out one shirt for another the second it showed the slightest sweat stain. God forbid if his public found out that the sexiest man alive was mortal. Perspiration was considered rugged in an action flick, not in a romance.

The first sign of a glistening upper lip and everything came to a crashing halt. Sable didn't know how Colt could stand it.

"Want to see how we set up a shot?"

"I would love to."

Grateful for a reason to move around, Sable smiled at Kiki Donahue. Earlier, Colt had introduced her to the assistant director. The number of smart, energetic women working on the movie was impressive. Clearly, the Landis family respected talent and didn't let gender get in the way.

After she had motioned Sable over, Kiki showed her the proper way to look through the camera.

"That is where the big breakup scene is taking place." Kiki pointed to the park bench. "We'll film it later this afternoon."

An hour earlier, the bench hadn't existed. Sable had watched as three crew members built it from stacks of wrought iron and wood.

"I don't understand. We're in a real park. Why not use one of the pre-existing benches?"

"This area has the bush." Kiki pointed to the flowering shrub located directly behind the newly constructed seat. "It will perfectly frame our fictional lovers just as the sun sets. When we leave, the bench stays."

With Kiki's explanation in mind, Sable took another look through the camera. Everything looked different through the lens. Suddenly, she easily pictured Colt and his co-star playing out the emotional scene.

"You love what you do." It wasn't a question.

"It's been my dream for as long as I can remember."

Pretty, with long, coal-black hair, Kiki Donahue had the looks to be on the other side of the camera but not the ambition. She wanted to create images on film that moved people to laughter and tears. And every emotion in between. To do that, she planned to use her brain, not her face.

"Thank you." Sable stepped back. "It gives you a completely different perspective."

"From here, I can make the world as beautiful or as ugly as I choose."

"Power."

"Yes." Kiki turned, her eyes sharpening. "Not many people get that."

"Sometimes the people around us want to push us down. They take advantage of their power to make us feel small and insignificant. When you find a place to be in charge, never let go, Kiki. And use *your* power to help, not hurt."

Sable took a deep breath. She hadn't meant to say those things. The past had a way of jumping up when least expected.

"Wow." Kiki laid a hand on Sable's arm. "Let's get a drink one day soon. You can spill your guts, and I'll spill mine." When Sable hesitated, Kiki shrugged. "Or we can drink a lot of tequila and get shit faced."

"After the movie wraps?"

"It's a date." With a wave, Kiki jogged off.

"I'd like to hear your secrets. With or without the tequila."

Colt. Where had he come from? She wasn't doing a very good job if she lost track of her client.

"My secrets are as boring as I am."

"Then, not boring at all."

Colt moved closer. Close enough for her to see little flecks of silver in his eyes.

"You never know," Sable teased.

"I know more than you think." Colt traced the curve of her jaw, his finger stopping at the corner of her mouth. "You should kiss me."

"Give me two good reasons."

Colt smiled. "Easy. One? That's what couples do. Two? You want to."

"I do?" *Silly question. Of course, she did.*

"Mmm."

Slowly, their eyes locked, Sable took his arms and placed them around her waist.

"No arguments?" Colt asked, his hands settling on her hips.

"No." Sable brushed her lips against his. "I'm your girlfriend. It's time to enjoy the perks."

Colt groaned. Sable's lips were soft, opening against his. She tasted sweet. Like peppermint and Coca-Cola. His tongue slid into her mouth, tasting. Again and again.

"Don't stop," she whispered.

Never. Why would he when he'd dreamed of holding her this way? Slender and strong. Silk and steel. So warm. Colt couldn't get enough. He would never get enough.

"I hate to interrupt."

"Then don't." When Sable tried to pull back, Colt held her tight. "Rene called a ten-minute break."

"It's been eleven."

Colt sighed. Still holding Sable, he turned his head. Nigel Locke, Rene's assistant, sent him a sheepish smile.

"I'll be right there." Kissing Sable's cheek, he reluctantly stepped back. "To be continued."

Sable leaned in and whispered. "That one will have to hold you, pretty boy."

Colt didn't respond, but his smile spoke volumes. He'd had a taste, and he planned on having more.

Shaking her head, Sable lightly touched her lips. They tingled with the lingering warmth of Colt's imprint. Sable watched him leave, a spring in his step. She wasn't fooling him or herself. Why fight it? They would share more than a kiss. And soon. And she planned on enjoying every second.

"His interest never lasts long."

Sable didn't keep up on the latest Hollywood buzz, but she recognized Candice DeMarcco. Colt's co-star had the kind of box office clout that almost equaled his. Dark haired, with chocolate brown eyes, according to Janis Mainard, she was the current rom-com darling. She played sweet, likable women the audience rooted for and cheered as love inevitably conquered all.

Janis hadn't pulled any punches when describing what she called *the real Candice.*

"Vicious," Janis said with no preamble. "Oh, butter wouldn't melt in her mouth if she wants something. She sidles up to new friends like the proverbial snake. Then boom. When she has finished sucking as much from her victim as possible, she moves on. Candice DeMarcco has burned more bridges than Sherman on his way to Atlanta."

Sable took Janis' words with a grain of salt. There were always two sides to a story. No one knew that better than she did. She knew what had been said about her when she left the Army. The rumors that circulated. Rumors that she couldn't completely shake.

She refused to judge anyone based on rumor and innuendo.

"We haven't met. I'm Sable Ford."

Candice ignored her outstretched hand. The actress stepped closer. It was a tactical error. Sable topped her by a good six inches. It was difficult to get the upper hand when she needed to tip her head back to look her adversary in the eye.

"Nice name," Candice smirked. "Are you a stripper or an actress wannabe?"

Okay. Candice was a bitch. Sable felt her open mind closing. Quickly.

"At the moment, I'm Colt's girlfriend," Sable smiled slowly, her eyes cool. She pulled her shoulders back, adding another inch to her height. "Good luck taking my place. The line stretches about ten miles to the rear."

"Oh, now I get it. You're a comedienne. You aren't pretty enough to be eye candy. Colt keeps you around as his court jester."

"I'm a regular Jack Benny."

"Who?"

"Oh, now I get it," Sable drawled, mocking Candice. "You're the brunette equivalent of a dumb blonde."

Sable watched as Candice's face turned an interesting shade of red.

"I could have you thrown off the set like that." She snapped her fingers.

"You could try. But if you want to get into Colt's pants, that isn't the way to do it. Run along, little girl." Sable flicked her hand in the general direction of the park bench. "You bore me."

"This isn't over."

Sable wasn't impressed. The last time someone said that, she had an actual reason to worry. Then again, a major in the Army held more clout than this year's Hollywood sweetheart.

"What burr did you put under Candice's saddle and where do I get one?" Janis watched Candice stalk off, mumbling expletives under her breath.

"Sadly, it appears there are no pajama parties in our future."

"If this were the first grade, the teacher would write, *Candice does not work well with other girls.*"

Sable laughed. "And boys?"

"She's *very* popular—until she isn't. Candice's shelf life is around two months."

"That long?"

"She starts to go bad around week six. By the end, she stinks up the joint."

"Hollywood rumor mill?" Janis seemed well versed on Candice DeMarcco.

"Yes, and a few close friends who she chewed up, spit out, and ground under her heel."

"Isn't it difficult to play her best friend?"

"I'm an actress." Janis winked. "A damn good one."

SABLE KEPT HER encounter with Candice to herself. She saw no reason to tell Colt. He had to work with the woman—pretend to be in love with her. Sable planned on avoiding her, and the subject, as much as possible.

Colt's day ended early. After the big park bench scene, he was free until seven o'clock the next morning.

"Do you want to go out for dinner?" he asked as they walked toward his car, hand in hand.

Casual touching did not come naturally to Sable. To Colt, it was like breathing. Another trait his parents passed down to their sons.

He brushed her cheek, rubbed her arm, held her hand. He wasn't trying to be provocative. The gestures were friendly and casual. And they stirred something deep inside her that Sable couldn't identify.

"Your refrigerator is bursting with food. Shouldn't we eat some of it?"

"Do you cook?"

"No. But I can manage a salad."

"That will do. To start. I'll take care of the rest."

"*You* cook?" Sable didn't try to hide her amazement.

"I do." He paused by his car. "Wanna drive?"

80

Her eyes lit up. Snatching the keys, she pushed him to the passenger side and into the seat. In a flash, she zipped around the car and slipped behind the wheel.

"Hello, you sweet baby."

Colt grinned. He wasn't one of those men who believed his car was a sacred piece of metal and chrome—to be driven by him and him alone. He cared for it, kept it in prime condition, but if he believed someone was capable of handling the powerful machine, he didn't mind sharing his ride.

He didn't hesitate about letting Sable take control of the Maserati. He trusted her with his safety—in and out of the car.

"You're sure?"

"Would it matter?"

"Nope."

They shot out of the parking lot and onto the backroads of Los Angeles. Sable shifted like a pro, taking the corners at speeds that were not strictly legal but a hell of a lot of fun.

"There's a racetrack about half a mile from here. I know the owner. Want to take a few laps?"

Sable's grin widened, her dark eyes sparkling with the excitement of a child on Christmas morning. Colt called ahead, and soon they were racing around the oval in their borrowed crash helmets, Sable's whoops of joy punctuating every turn.

Colt didn't watch the track. He watched Sable. Her face glowed. And all he could think of was how sweet her lips must taste at that moment. Slightly parted and curved, her smile wide and infectious. He knew the one on his face was an exact match.

"I don't think that would ever get old," Sable said an hour later. She drove at a more sedate pace through the downtown traffic, but the excitement still rang in her voice.

"Going in circles?"

"The speed. The power."

"We can go back anytime you like."

"Thank you, Colt. But once was enough."

Colt could see her battling temptation. However, the disciplined soldier in her won out over the daredevil. Now that he knew her weakness, he planned on laying temptation at Sable's feet as often as possible. Speed and power came in many forms. Wait until he showed her a few tricks in bed that would blow her mind.

Sable parked in the underground garage. Patiently, Colt waited while she went through her familiar bodyguard routine.

"No kidnappers under the SUV?" he asked when she opened the passenger door.

"Your smartass remarks can't kill my buzz." Sable followed him into the elevator, her eyes diligently watching the shadows.

"That's good to hear because I'm carrying a major buzz myself."

In a flash, Colt had Sable pinned against the wall. His lips covered hers, and ruthlessly he took advantage of her gasp of surprise by plunging his tongue into her mouth. Hot velvet. Sweet. Colt groaned. No dream could match this kind of reality.

The kiss went on and on. Colt changed the angle to find another spot, another taste. He sighed with pleasure when Sable tugged, freeing her hands. Not to push him away, but to pull his hips against hers. The slow grind of their bodies was a fully clothed sexual act. It teased and excited. Thank God his bed was nearby. He didn't want their first time to be on the floor of an elevator.

"I need you, Sable. Say yes." Colt felt ready to beg. To plead. To fall to his knees and grant any wish just to hear that one little word.

"Yes."

The doors opened, and slowly, they shuffled out, their mouths fused together.

"Lift your arms." Colt slid the hem of her shirt up her body. "I need you naked. Now."

"I—" Sable started to comply, but instincts kicked in. Something felt off. "Someone's here."

"What?" Colt groaned when she pushed him behind her and pulled her gun from her purse. "You're wrong. No one can get in unless they have the—" Then he remembered. "It's okay."

"Stay here." Keeping her gun eye level, Sable checked around the corner.

"Sable, I know who it is."

"Freeze."

The sound of glass crashing to the floor followed a high-pitched squeal.

In the kitchen, hands raised high, blue eyes the size of saucers, stood a tall blonde. The glass of juice she had poured herself smashed at her feet. She didn't move. No one did.

Except for the loaded gun, the scene bordered on the comical.

Feeling something licking her ankle, Sable glanced down. A dog whose paws seemed to get in the way of her every move stared at her with adoring eyes.

"Sable, you remember Paige. And this," Colt picked up the wiggling dog, "is Beauty."

Chapter Eight

COLT LAUGHED WHILE he cleaned up the broken glass. Sable didn't think pulling a gun on his brother's future wife terribly funny. Absurd, yes. Chuckle worthy? No.

"I'm sorry," Sable said, relieved to see the color returning to Paige's face. "Colt didn't warn me that anyone would be here."

"I forgot. I was distracted," Colt snickered.

Idiot. Sable rolled her eyes, grateful that Colt had the sense not to tell them why he forgot to mention that guests were waiting in the loft. That kiss. It reminded her why getting involved with a client never worked. What if there had been an intruder? What if her inattention resulted in Colt getting hurt? Or worse? If she crossed the line into real girlfriend territory, she couldn't do her job properly.

If she couldn't do her job, what good was she to Colt? Or anyone else?

"Is it safe to come out?"

"Jade?"

The redhead poked her nose out of the bedroom.

"I almost called 911."

"No need." Sable hugged her friend. "What were you going to do with this?" She pried Jade's fingers from a wooden hanger.

"Defend myself and Paige. It was the first thing I could find."

"Next time, grab the brass lamp from beside the bed. The hanger might leave a splinter, but it wouldn't stop a flea." Sable tossed it onto the counter.

"You didn't tell her." Jade sent Colt an accusatory look.

"I wanted it to be a surprise."

"Oh, boy." Paige frowned. "Maybe we should leave."

"Maybe someone should tell me what's going on. I almost shot an innocent person. I think I deserve an explanation."

Jade scoffed. "Don't exaggerate." She patted Paige's hand. "Sable wouldn't have shot you."

"Hello. Gun." Sable sighed. "Okay. Chances are that at worst, I would have grazed you."

"Gee, that's encouraging." Paige didn't seem particularly upset. She pushed the fall of blonde hair behind her ear. "Ready for your surprise?"

"I don't know. Am I?" Sable wasn't good at surprises. The few that had popped up in her life from time to time didn't end well.

"You'll love this one."

Sable followed Paige and Jade toward her bedroom. She glanced at Colt, a question in her eyes.

"Go on," he urged. "Beauty and I will finish cleaning up."

Warily, Sable peeked around the door frame. Everything looked the same as she had left it that morning. Neatly made bed. The items on the dresser arranged with pinpoint precision. Some might say it was too organized. If you opened a drawer, you would find straight rows coordinated by color. Light to dark.

It wasn't overkill. It was logical. If Sable needed a blue t-shirt and black socks, she knew exactly where to find them. Her system saved time. Her father, then the Army, taught her that a few seconds could be the difference between life and death for her and her fellow soldiers.

It never occurred to Sable to change her habits now that no one was around to notice. She liked order. Life was filled with too many unknowns that she had no control over. This was a small thing, but it was hers.

"Are you ready?"

"Let me have it."

Jade and Paige exchanged excited grins before throwing open the closet door.

"Ta da!"

Sable's eyes widened. Slowly, she walked into the room.

Before, her clothing took up one little section. They barely warranted a dozen hangers. Now, she couldn't tell where her meager belongings ended and a sea of shirts, jackets and dresses began.

Shoes of every style and color lined an entire wall. Another was reserved for accessories. Purses, scarves, hats. *Who wore hats anymore?* Sable blinked, unable to take it all in. She felt slightly dizzy as though she had walked into a fun house where the mirrors were replaced by Beverly Hills booty.

"Well?" Jade demanded. "What do you think?"

"I think my head is about to explode. Colton Landis! Get your ass in here!"

"Oops," Paige said. "That is not a happy face."

Cautiously, Colt entered the room, his trepidation understandable.

"Before you blow a gasket, let me explain."

"Maybe we should go." Paige edged toward the door.

"Are you kidding?" Jade pulled her back. "I don't want to miss the show. Besides, Colt might need us to call an ambulance."

"I hope you're joking," Paige whispered. She didn't know Sable, but from what little she had seen, the woman seemed volatile. To say the least.

"I am," Jade assured her. "I think."

"Don't worry. Colt can't return these things if they're splattered with blood."

"I'm not returning anything." Colt calmly crossed his arms. He seemed cool, but he planted his feet, ready for battle. "Didn't you complain just the other evening about your limited wardrobe?

"I did not complain." Sable bristled at the implication. "I pointed it out. There is a big difference."

"You want to argue semantics? Fine. The fact remains, you need these things."

"It's too much." Sable picked up a sling-backed pump with a four-inch heel. "Why would I need this? And in six different colors?" She looked closer. "And how the hell did you know my size. Any of my sizes?"

"That's my fault," Jade said. "Colt asked me to check your things. I relayed the information to his personal shopper. I asked Paige to help us put everything away as part of the surprise."

"It all circles back to you," Sable pointed an accusatory finger at Colt.

"You're overreacting."

Colt looked around. Okay, perhaps it was a bit much. He asked the woman who shopped for him to pick out a variety. She may have gotten carried away. However, he stood by the belief that Sable needed these things. He wouldn't apologize.

"I won't touch any of it."

"We are attending an all-star tribute on Friday."

"I have a dress for that."

"Then there's a cocktail party next Monday. A birthday bash for an old friend the Friday after that."

"Fine," Sable huffed. She would bend but she wouldn't be defeated. "Send the bill to H&W. Alex gives me an expense account that I've never used. This will cover it for the next ten years, but he won't argue."

Sable had never seen Colt angry. He was such an easygoing, happy person who let things roll off his back without blinking. It was a trait she admired. She imagined it made the day-to-day frustrations he encountered as a movie star easier to live with if he didn't take them too seriously.

However, everyone had their limits. It appeared Colt had reached his. The warm blue of his eyes turned frosty causing Sable to suppress a shiver. When he spoke, the tone was so quiet and contained, she had to lean in to catch every word.

"Burn the fucking wardrobe if you want. But no one pays for a single item except me. Understood?"

"That's childish and irrational."

Colt held her gaze a moment longer, the tension sizzling between them. Then, without another word, he walked out.

"Wow." Paige fanned herself with one hand. "That was intense."

Jade smiled. "If anyone smokes, now is the time to light up."

"He's angry, not turned on," Sable said, taking a deep breath. The room sizzled with repressed emotion. Silently, she admitted a lot of the tension was sexual. She had another thought. "Colt can't go out by himself."

"I'll go." Paige picked up Beauty. The dog had slept through the drama but was now eyeing a pair of flats that looked very chewable. "If I have to, I'll throw myself in front of the door."

"Right." Sympathetic, Jade rubbed Sable's shoulder. "What's it going to be? Bonfire or capitulation?"

"It seems there's no in between."

Colt had thrown down the gauntlet. Sable could pick it up or be the bigger person and step over it. She wasn't very good at compromise. In the Army, it was a lesson she had learned the hard way.

"These things *are* beautiful."

She ran her hand over a softer than soft gray leather jacket. How many times had she dreamed of owning one item as luxurious as this? Now she had access to hundreds. Not that she owned them. But they were hers as long as she worked for Colt.

"Colt picked the colors and styles. He was very specific."

"Really?"

Sable looked closer. She had to admit, with a few exceptions, the clothing fit her taste and style.

One row consisted of nothing but evening wear. Dresses of varying lengths. Colors in every hue. Sparkles, lace, and satin. Another side trended toward the casual. Jeans, with designer labels, cotton slacks, silk blouses.

Sable had never hung up a t-shirt in her life, yet here they were in every color imaginable.

"Good thing Colt is tall." Jade examined a pair of rhinestone-covered stilettos. "You'll be at least six feet tall in these babies."

"Don't tell Colt, but he has good taste."

"I won't." Jade peered at Sable through a sheer lavender scarf. "But you should. He did a good thing."

"I suppose." Sable felt more and more like an idiot for, as Colt had pointed out, overreacting. "He did this for himself as much as for me."

"Because it feels good to make someone else happy? Sure. What's wrong with that?"

Put like that? Nothing. Sable felt another wave of guilt. Damn. Colt wanted to do a good thing and she did her best to make him feel like crap. *Way to go, Sable.* She gave herself a sarcastic pat on the back. *Once again, you find a way of spreading sunshine wherever you go.*

"Don't beat yourself up."

"I deserve a kick or two in the butt."

"No. Take it from someone who spent most of her life blaming herself for, well, everything. Apologize. Colt doesn't hold a grudge." Jade held a blouse the color of a moonless sky up next to Sable's face. "And he does have good taste. In clothing and friends."

"Is that what I am? His friend? We haven't been doing this very long but the dynamic of our relationship changes daily. My head is spinning. Not a good thing when you're responsible for another person's life."

"Those Landis boys have a way of turning your head," Jade said, her smile sly. "Does Colt kiss as well as Garrett?"

"I've never kissed Garrett."

"But you have kissed Colt." Jade did a little happy dance. "Ha! I knew it."

Sable tried to backtrack. "I admit nothing." Oh, hell. She wasn't fooling anyone, especially herself. She sighed. "Damn it, I'm supposed to be a professional. But you're right, there is something about a Landis."

"Right? They ooze this outrageous sexuality. It's irresistible."

"I'm trying."

"Why?" Jade demanded. "There are no laws stopping you. And if there were, can you think of a better reason to risk arrest?"

"My father would be horrified."

Jade frowned. She could write a book about disapproving fathers. Or rather, one in particular. Unfortunately, it would be long and extremely unpleasant.

"You never speak of your father."

"There isn't much to say at the moment. We aren't in touch. Or rather, I try, he doesn't respond."

"I'm sorry." Jade gave Sable a brief but warm hug. She picked up her purse. "I'm going to go. Sable, I hate giving advice."

"But...?" Sable smiled, letting Jade know she didn't mind a few friendly words."

"Bear with me. I'm going to give you the old life is short spiel. Grab the good when it comes because there is way too much bad. Turn around and something will joyfully rain on your parade. And there. I've reached my cliché limit for the day."

They found Paige and Beauty standing side by side, admiring the view. Colt was nowhere in sight.

"Don't worry," Paige reassured Sable. "Colt grabbed a beer and mumbled something about taking a shower. He is such a sweetheart. He stomped off and slammed his bedroom door. Thirty seconds later, he stomped out, kissed my cheek and thanked me for helping. Then repeated the first part."

"Want us to stay?"

"No." Sable escorted Jade and Paige to the elevator. "Colt will cool off. Or he won't. Either way, we'll pick up our routine in the morning. Nothing has changed."

"Hasn't it?" Jade asked.

"We'll see."

With one last wave at Jade and Paige, Sable watched the elevator door close. Alone, she tried to decide what she wanted. Food or bed. She knew she wouldn't sleep. So instead of subjecting herself to hours of tossing and turning, she headed to the kitchen. After opening the refrigerator, she stood and stared.

"This is ridiculous."

The selection was endless. No one person would be able to eat this much food. Colt had told her that he sent it to a shelter, but honestly, what was wrong with these women? They filled his fridge, cleaned his house. Washed his clothes. And for what? The chance to bask, ever so briefly, in the glow of Colton Landis, superstar?

Ugh. Get a freaking life.

Sable grabbed an apple and a bottle of water. She searched the cupboard, happy to find her favorite standby. Peanut butter. And none of that organic, oil on the top crap. This was good old middle-America Skippy.

The bread in the keeper had a few grains, but it wasn't too bad. Sable slathered on a layer of peanutty goodness, and for good measure, added a couple tablespoons of the strawberry jam.

Sable sat at the table, taking a moment to let her shoulders relax. She said a brief thank you before taking her first bite. Food, no matter how simple, should never be taken for granted.

She had never known hunger, but she'd seen the results. There were entire villages in the Middle East that subsisted on a few crusts of bread a day. The water, if they had any, needed boiling before it could be drunk. Sable knew how lucky she was to be warm and safe. It made that refrigerator full of food all the more obnoxious.

The last bite of sandwich sat on her plate. The apple, juicy and crisp, was nothing but a core wrapped neatly in a paper napkin. Sable downed the last of her second bottle of water. She felt better with a full stomach. She always did. Her current perspective on her inconvenient attraction to Colt was a work in progress. But she was getting there.

Sable put the few items she had dirtied into the dishwasher and decided she should be able to sleep. She closed her bedroom door just as her phone rang. One glance at the screen and the tension began seeping back into her shoulders.

"Mom. How are you?"

"Me? Me?"

Sable held the phone away from her ear, convinced the speech was loud enough to travel three thousand miles without the aid of modern technology.

"Why didn't you tell me?" Iris demanded. "Did you quit your job? My friends are having a field day, laughing behind my back. My daughter, the kept woman."

"I didn't quit my job and Colt isn't *keeping me*. Your friends need to update their terminology."

"You think this is funny? A joke?"

Sable wished she could laugh. Unfortunately, her mother didn't inspire joviality.

Dutifully, Sable listened to the litany of imagined woes her mother suffered daily because of her ungrateful daughter. It went on and on. Long enough for her to brush her teeth, wash her face, and change her clothes. Sable left the drawer filled with sexy nightwear untouched. Instead, she slipped on her usual t-shirt and boxers.

"What will your father say?"

That refocused Sable's attention.

"He doesn't know?"

"I certainly haven't told him. God knows what he's heard. As you know, when it comes to gossip, an Army base is worse than a beauty parlor."

Oh, she knew. Better than most.

"If he says anything, ask him to call me."

"So you can explain?"

Yes. But she wasn't going to tell her mother that.

"There's nothing to explain. I'm living with Colton Landis."

"Oh, Sable." Disappointment. It seemed like the only reaction her mother could manage. "You didn't listen to me when you were a teenager. Why should I expect that to change? Men chew you up and spit you out. It's in their DNA. What will you do when he gets tired of you?"

"Maybe I'll get tired of him."

"Please," Iris scoffed. "The glamour? The money? I'll bet he's bought you a bunch of expensive clothing."

Sable hesitated a moment too long.

"He's seduced you with luxury. You'll never willingly give that up."

It took Iris another twenty minutes to wind down. She ended by reminding Sable that the clothing belonged to her.

"When he dumps you, don't be a fool. Take everything that isn't nailed down."

Words to live by. With that kind of twisted morality, Sable wondered why she didn't make a living wrapping herself around a stripper pole.

Because in the Ford household, her father's words always rang loudest. Whether she was in a dirt poor, war-ravaged village in Afghanistan or a luxurious multi-million-dollar Los Angeles loft, Mathias Ford kept Sable on the straight and narrow.

No matter their personal situation, he was, and would always be, her moral compass.

Sable hung up. She closed her eyes and took a deep, cleansing breath. She was tempted, but she couldn't turn off her phone. So she plugged it in and set it on the nightstand.

Time to unwind. Music. The best cure for the Nagging Mother Blues. Sable put in her earphones, hit her favorite playlist, rested her head on the pillow, and let her mind shut down and blissfully drift away.

COLT FELT LIKE an idiot. Holing up in his bedroom like a petulant three-year-old. He hadn't accomplished a thing.

He was hungry and tired. And instead of spending the evening with Sable, he'd wasted it sulking. He should have apologized immediately and saved himself the added embarrassment of having to do it hours after the fact.

A bit of anger lingered. When he set up the surprise, Colt imagined a different outcome. In his fantasy, Sable threw her arms around him, excited by the new wardrobe. She rushed from item to item, exclaiming over each one, holding it up and twirling in a giddy circle.

Colt lowered his head to the marble counter, knocking his forehead against the surface several times. He felt it, but it didn't knock any sense into him.

Did he know Sable at all? Apparently not. How many times had he said she was different? She didn't giggle or flutter or lavish him with extravagant compliments. She didn't care about fame or money. At least, she didn't care about his.

From day one, Sable treated his family like regular people, not Hollywood royalty.

In his defense, he hadn't been trying to buy her. He wanted to give her a few nice things to wear and enjoy. In his enthusiasm, he must have made it sound like he was outfitting Sable for the next year, or five. The items were beautiful and perfect, but there were too many of them. Way too many.

Colt glanced across the room. Sable's door was shut. No surprise. It was after eleven. Had he expected her to wait up on the off chance he came to his senses? She would be asleep—not worrying about him.

Colt put together a sandwich, making a mental note to send the extra food to the shelter first thing in the morning. After that, he needed to call Paige and Jade. It seemed he had apologies to make all around.

The roast beef and cheddar tasted like cardboard, but he finished it and the glass of milk. The idea of going back to his big, empty bed depressed Colt. Damn it. He didn't want to wait. Maybe Sable was still awake. He would sleep much easier if he cleared the air between them right away.

Taking a deep breath, Colt lightly tapped on her door. When she didn't answer, he knew he should leave her alone. But something made him push on. Slowly, trying to be as quiet as possible, Colt turned the doorknob. He peeked inside, hoping to find her reading or watching television.

The lamp on the end table glowed, the light low.

Sable wasn't under the covers. She lay on her back, her head turned away from him. Colt smiled. He knew the dresser contained three or four lacy nightgowns. Naturally, Sable left them where they were. Instead, she wore a well-worn Seattle Mariners t-shirt and a pair of men's boxer shorts.

Seeing her long, smooth legs stretched out on the quilted blanket, Colt decided he preferred her choice. God, she was sexy. Her toned body made his mouth water. The slight swell of her breasts, the curve of her jaw. The short dark cap of glossy hair framed by the white pillowcase.

Sable Ford was the exact opposite of every woman he'd been with. Yet, for some reason, simply looking at her moved him more than all of them combined.

Colt noticed the earphones. No wonder he hadn't disturbed her. Sable could hear a pin drop in a hurricane. He wondered what kind of music she liked. He sighed. One more thing he didn't know about her.

He took a blanket from the bureau and lightly draped it over Sable. Beginning tomorrow, he would ask questions. He wanted to know about her childhood. Where had she lived? Any pets? Had she worn braces? What caused the shadows that occasionally crept into her beautiful eyes?

"I'm not sleeping."

Sable whispered the words, but Colt heard them clearly. He settled the blanket over her shoulders, then lightly brushed her skin with the back of his fingers.

"Are you still mad?"

"No." Sable opened her eyes. In the dim light, the color looked like rich, warm chocolate. "Are you?"

"No. I'm sorry. I—hey." He noticed the drying tears. "You've been crying."

Colt watched as Sable did her best to rein in her emotions.

"I'm a little sad."

"I'll send every last stitch of clothing back, first thing in the morning."

Sable's lips curved. "Not because of that." She hesitated, her eyes clouding over. "I miss my father."

"Want to talk about it?"

"Not right now."

"Slide over." Colt lifted the blanket and joined her on the bed.

"Colt. This is a bad idea." But Sable moved enough to let Colt lie beside her.

"Shh." Colt removed one of her earbuds. "Relax."

He put the bud in his ear and settled beside her. Colt didn't recognize the tune. It was smooth and bluesy. The kind of song that spoke to your soul.

Colt closed his eyes. He didn't sleep with women. They played. Sex and games. They dozed. But sleep? No.

For the first time in his adult life, he wanted nothing more than the comfort and warmth of a body next to his. Sable's body.

Colt didn't touch her. The connection came through the music. However, when Sable slid her hand into his, he felt something stir in his heart. It wasn't something to worry about or analyze. It—this—felt good. Right.

The notes of the song and the sound of Sable's breathing lulled him, pushing him closer to sleep. The feel of her hand sent him over the edge.

SABLE TURNED OFF the iPod. She didn't look at the clock. Her body told her it was an hour or so before dawn. Colt's chest rose and fell in a steady, easy rhythm. She listened to his breathing, looked at his slightly parted lips, and wondered at having him in her bed.

The circumstances were nothing like she had imagined. She had pictured something more X-rated. They were fully clothed and hadn't shared as much as a kiss. Did holding hands count as getting to first base? Not in her book.

Women all over the world dreamed of Colton Landis spending the night. Sable would bet almost anything those dreams included a lot more than sleep. But she wouldn't have changed a thing.

Colt could have taken advantage of her vulnerability. She wouldn't have objected. One kiss. She would have melted into his arms, happy to feel something other than the heavy sadness that pushed down on her chest. However, instead of seducing, he comforted. Somehow he understood that she didn't need sex, she needed him.

Gently, Sable removed the earbuds and set the iPod on the end table.

"Hi," Colt smiled and Sable's heart turned over.

"Hi." Without thinking, she brushed the dark, wavy hair from his forehead.

"How did you sleep?"

"Great."

"Me too."

"Colt?" Sable met his gaze. The light was at his back but she could see the tenderness in his eyes.

"Hmm?"

Slowly, deliberately. So there could be no doubt of her intent, Sable kissed him.

Colt opened his mouth, his tongue lightly bathing her bottom lip. It was sweet. The kind of kiss shared at the end of a first date. They weren't in a hurry. There was no desperation. Their hands, the ones that had remained clasped as they slept, prevented their bodies from touching.

"Thank you."

"My pleasure," Colt grinned.

"Not for the kiss. Though that was lovely. Thank you for last night. For staying with me."

"You never have to be alone, Sable." Colt kissed the corner of her mouth. "I like sleeping with you."

"This must be a first."

"I was thinking the same thing."

"I would hate to ruin your reputation." Sable sat up and pulled off her shirt.

"Sable." Colt swallowed. Her breasts were perfect. Better than he imagined. High and firm. Her hard nipples the color of ripe cherries. It took all his willpower not to reach out. "This isn't necessary."

"If it were, I wouldn't be here." She smiled, slow and seductive. "You can say no."

"No, I can't."

In one fluid motion, Colt threw off the blanket and pulled her leg over him until she straddled his hips.

"So you like what you see?" she asked. It was a rhetorical question.

Colt's expression, the heat in his blue eyes, told her everything she needed to know.

Colt cupped her breast with his hand, his thumb rubbing the tight bud of her nipple. Sable watched the movement, almost hypnotized. She was a visual person. Imagining his hands on her was exciting. Seeing the reality sent a wave of pleasure shooting through her body.

"So soft," he murmured. "Every time I touch you, I think of silk. Only better. Infinitely better."

"Years of copious amounts of lotion. It's my addiction."

"I approve." Colt's eyes darkened. He ran a finger over her other breast. "I can't decide which would be sexier. Watching you smooth the cream over your body or doing it myself."

"Why not both?" She moaned.

"Sounds perfect." Colt whipped his shirt over his head. He rose until his mouth was even with her breasts. "*You* are perfect."

Sable's head fell back. God, one touch of his tongue and she felt ready to come undone. So much anticipation. Every moment, every look, every brush of his hand. It led to this moment. Endless foreplay.

She had tried to be good. She had meant to resist. The attraction was there before she came to Hollywood. It started months ago with a scorching kiss. She hadn't expected to see him again, let alone spend every waking moment in his company.

One week of watching Colt. Laughing with him. Teasing and taunting. The world believed they were lovers. Her friends encouraged her to make it true. Even her boss had given her the green light.

Colt made it clear from day one that he wanted her. Considering the bounty of temptation, Sable's holdout was admirable. She had done all the right things.

And now she would get her reward.

"I've been good." Her eyes blazed, matching the heat in his. "Now I want to be bad. Be bad with me, Colt."

Sable's fingers slid into his thick, soft hair, tugging until his mouth was inches from hers. She paused, a mere second. Sable swore a spark flew, then she stopped thinking and kissed him.

Endless. She never wanted it to stop. Sable didn't know why Colt made her feel so much more than any other man. Or how he seemed to make time stop. Who cared? She was in his arms. Right now, that was all that mattered.

"I need to taste you, Sable. Every inch. Honey and spice."

Colt bit the side of her neck and Sable almost shot out of her skin.

"What was that?" she panted.

"You mean this?" Colt found the same spot with his teeth. At the same moment, he slid his hand between her legs.

Sable didn't know what happened. It wasn't an orgasm. She knew how those felt. This was something else. There wasn't a gentle rise. There was no reaching or anticipation. The pleasure crashed over her. Unexpected. Relentless. She stopped breathing. Colors, new and bold, flashed in front of her eyes. Her heart pounded, almost bursting from her chest.

At any second, she felt she would break into a million pieces. Somehow, Colt's strong arms held her together.

"I have you," Colt crooned. "I won't let you go. Ride it out, Sable. I'm with you all the way."

Colt's words, knowing he meant them, allowed Sable to free fall the rest of the way. Arms wide. There was no danger. He was her safety net.

When Sable opened her eyes, she was surprised to find herself on her back. She didn't remember moving.

"There you are." Colt leaned over her, his smile warm. He caressed her cheek with the lightest of touches.

"Did I pass out?" The possibility was real—and a bit embarrassing.

"No." Colt brushed his lips over hers. "Zoned out would be a better way of putting it."

"I'm sorry." Sable settled onto the mattress. She sighed. She was no longer flying, but at least, her landing pad was soft. "I don't know what happened."

"Do you want the biological or emotional answer."

Colt's grin contained a touch of self-satisfaction, mixed with pure male arrogance. All things considered, Sable supposed he was entitled.

"That was a new one for me."

"Your first orgasm?"

God, now his smile bordered on *King of the World* territory. He deserved some credit, but there were limits.

"No, Tarzan. This isn't Jane's first rodeo." Sable smiled then laughed. He got her. His sense of humor was as sexy as the rest of him. "I like sex. I get great pleasure from it. But that wasn't a normal orgasm."

"Want my opinion?"

"Please."

Colt settled next to her, his head resting on the pillow. Sable turned so they faced each other.

"You're carrying around a lot of emotion." He gently tapped her temple. "Eventually, something has to give."

"I cried." And that almost never happened.

"Did you sob?"

"Colt." Sable shook her head. Honestly. Cry. Sob. What was the difference?

"There's a big difference."

"When was the last time you did either?" She added quickly, "Not on screen."

"Never," Colt admitted. "You won't want to hear this, but men and women aren't the same."

Sable grasped his erection. The thin cloth of his pajama bottoms couldn't mask the heat or the size. "No kidding."

"Careful," Colt warned, but he didn't move her hand. "I plan on using that."

"When?" Slowly, with a teasing touch, she measured his length.

"Soon," he groaned. "Very soon. Don't change the subject."

"I prefer to think of it as shifting down, and a little to the right."

"It's okay to cry, Sable. I would if I were on the outs with my parents."

Sable swallowed. It wasn't easy. A lump formed in her throat. It happened every time she thought about her father.

"Things are fine with my mother." Nothing ever changed with her. Unfortunately. "Dad and I haven't spoken in almost two years."

"Are you close?"

Tears formed in her eyes. Damn it.

"He's my hero."

Colt gathered her close. His strong arms comforted her in a way she hadn't known possible. It wasn't sexual. It went beyond friendly. It was deeper. Sable wanted to hold on—and be held—forever.

"Does it have to do with why you left the Army?"

"He doesn't care why. As far as Dad is concerned, I betrayed the trust of my fellow soldiers and my country."

"Jesus." Colt rubbed her back. "Betrayed? That's harsh."

"I entered the service intending to make it my career. Dad decided I would be the first female head of the Joint Chiefs of Staff."

"And what did you want?"

"I was ambitious." She still was. "I wanted to be the best soldier possible. I never said it but, deep down, I shared Dad's dream."

"What happened?"

"Not tonight, Colt. Please?" Sable pushed his t-shirt up, kissing his chest. Then the top of his gorgeous abs. "It's an ugly story. I don't want it to taint something so beautiful."

"When you put it like that." Colt hesitated. "You will tell me? Soon?"

"Yes," Sable promised.

"I'm a good listener." Colt grinned. Her teasing lover was back. "I'm an even better lover."

"How can I accuse you of bragging when I've already experienced your skills?"

"Could have been an anomaly." Colt took her lower lip between his teeth, biting just enough to send shivers down her spine. "You need multiple orgasms before you can truly judge."

"Multiple?" She thought it was an urban myth. Like Bigfoot or politicians who kept their campaign promises.

"Let me show you."

"But it's your turn."

"Don't worry about me. If I'm as good as I claim, and I am, neither of us will have any reason to complain." He took her hands, carrying them to the headboard. "Hold on."

"But—"

"Relax," he whispered. Colt licked the curve of her ear. "Let me take control. I promise you won't regret it."

Sable grabbed a metal bar in each hand. There it was again. Trust. Did she only believe in Colt when it was easy? Or could she let him in when she was at her most vulnerable? Naked—physically *and* emotionally.

It was time to find out.

"I love your breasts." Colt flicked her nipple with his finger and grinned when she gasped.

"That hurt."

"Did it?" A second later his mouth covered the bud, easing the sting. "Pleasure and pain. A little of one, a lot of the other."

Sable had to admit, Colt knew how to walk that razor's edge between one and the other.

"No whips or paddles."

"You've been reading some naughty books."

"Maybe."

"Close your eyes." While he verbally teased, Colt continued to play with her body. Sable followed his command. If she couldn't see him, she couldn't anticipate his next move. It heightened her other senses. The sound of his breathing. The barely there feel of his hand brushing against her stomach. And taste. Colt kissed her. Long and deep. She wanted more. More kissing. More touching. More everything.

"What did you think?"

"Hmm?" Sable tried to focus. "Oh. The books? Hot but not my thing."

"Better on paper than in reality?"

"Yes."

Colt nudged her knees. The mattress shifted under his weight. Sable smiled. She didn't need her eyes to know his next move.

"Lift your hips." Colt removed her shorts in the blink of an eye. "So pretty. Wet. Just for me. And what do we have here?"

She smiled. Colt found her tattoo.

"Like it?" she asked. She moaned when he ran his finger over the Army Ranger's insignia. The spot at the top of her inner thigh was extremely sensitive. Especially when she was already sexually stimulated.

"Who did it?"

"A sweet man in Atlanta. He and his boyfriend have the hottest parlor in the city. I was on leave before my first tour overseas. A few shots of tequila and it seemed like a good idea."

"Why here?" Colt kissed the spot.

"Mmm." Sable licked her lips. "It isn't for anyone but me."

"And your lovers."

There weren't many of those. And fewer who had seen her from Colt's current location. She didn't think that bit of information was any of his business.

"I should have known," she teased. "All talk and no action."

That got him going. Sable arched her back. God, his mouth! How could anything that good be legal?

"I hit a sweet spot," Colt declared with satisfaction. "Again?"

"Please."

"Since you asked so nicely."

Colt lowered his head and Sable screamed. Loud and long. When his fingers joined the party, Sable wondered if she would survive the onslaught. Death by orgasm? What a way to go.

However, she had a strong heart and a stronger will to live. If only to find out what delight he would throw at her next.

"Are you keeping track?" Colt asked, kissing his way up her body. "Three. I count three orgasms."

"Nobody likes a braggart." Unless he had a magic tongue. And supernatural fingers.

"Want me to stop?"

"It wouldn't be fair."

Sable rotated her hips. Colt's erection lay in an interesting spot. Just below her belly button. She appreciated the hardness and the heat. She knew from her earlier exploration that the size was impressive. However, it wasn't doing either of them any good in its current location.

"Basic biology tells me you have that thing pointed at the wrong hole."

Colt sputtered, then broke out laughing.

"I took that class. I don't remember the teacher mentioning that."

"If you were confused you should have asked. Teachers like questions."

Sable caressed Colt's firm butt. The skin was smooth—taut. Mentally she began a to-do list. Number two? Bite Colt's ass. Number one involved getting his clothes off and cock inside of her.

"I didn't plan on this, Sable."

"Sure you did. You let me know from day one that we would wind up in bed. And naked. Speaking of which." Sable pushed at Colt's pajama bottoms. "Why are you wearing so much clothing?"

Sable loved the feel of Colt's big, hard body lying on top of her but it made getting his clothes off a tad difficult. However, she was a gamer. She inched his t-shirt up his body.

"It would be so much easier if you helped."

Colt took pity on her and removed the shirt.

"Happy?"

"You have no idea."

Catching him off guard, Sable flipped Colt onto his back. There wasn't a person in the world with access to a computer who didn't know what he looked like without a shirt. Pictures. Videos. Thousands littered the internet. But, oh, baby, nothing compared to the real thing.

"You could make a fortune selling tickets." She spread her fingers over Colt's drool-worthy chest. Eyes twinkling, Sable's gaze met his. "Oh, that's right. You already do."

Happy to let her explore, he gripped the headboard. Symbolically, he placed his hands exactly where Sable's had been. "Hello. Thespian. There's more to me than my muscles."

"I appreciate that you are an artist. But at the moment, I couldn't care less if you can act your way out of a paper bag."

"You only want me for my body?"

Sable looked him up and down, then let out a long, expressive sigh. "Can you blame me?"

Colt's laugh turned into a groan when Sable licked his nipple. She admired his fortitude. After several orgasms, she felt loose and ready to play. Colt was still on edge. It wasn't fair. It was time to make him feel good.

"Off with these." Sable finished removing his last piece of clothing, tossing the pajama bottoms onto the floor.

"As I was saying before you distracted me, I didn't expect this to happen tonight." Colt hissed when Sable wiggled her hips. "No condom."

"Ah. Sexy movie star and a Boy Scout. No wonder women find you irresistible."

"Not a Boy Scout. They kicked me out after only a week."

"That's a story I'd like to hear." Sable leaned over, opening the end table drawer. "Later."

"You keep condoms by the bed?" Colt's eyes widened. "You swore you wouldn't sleep with me. Who were those for?"

"Deep down I knew you and I would end up right here." Sable opened the packet. "I wasn't a Girl Scout, but I know it's important to be prepared."

"Thank God," Colt sighed when she slid the condom into place. "I was five seconds from begging you for a hand-job."

"Really?" Sable moved over him, teasingly rubbing the tip of his erection with her slick folds. "If you prefer, I can do that."

"I'm dying here, Sable. Do you want to be the one who has to explain to my mother what happened to me?"

"It's an erection." Sable began her slow decent. "Can you die from that?"

Colt grabbed her hips, pulling until she was fully seated. In unison, they gasped.

"Shut up and move. Please."

"Since you asked so nicely," Sable laughed, repeating his earlier words.

"Sable... "

"Shh." She kissed Colt, her tongue running along his. "No more waiting. For either of us."

Colt was in no condition to take it slow. And Sable wasn't in the mood for any more teasing. The ride was hard and fast. There was no build. One. Two. Three strokes and Colt shouted his release. Sable tumbled with him, moving her hips in rhythm with his.

It couldn't be called smooth or perfectly choreographed. It was raw and intense. Wild. Heart-stopping. And infinitely satisfying.

Sable had no words. Neither did Colt. She slid into his arms. Boneless. Spent. She had just enough energy to brush his chest with her lips before she collapsed.

Colt's breathing slowly returned to normal. Sable rested her head on his chest. With no wasted movements, he disposed of the condom and pulled the covers over them. In seconds, he drifted off to sleep, but not before he settled Sable into his arms.

Out of habit, Sable checked the clock. The alarm was set to go off in less than two hours. Christ. She didn't know how Colt would be able to function on so little sleep. He would be dragging by mid-day. But she would bet almost anything he wouldn't have a single regret.

Sable felt the same. What would be the point? From day one, this had been inevitable. Fighting it was counterproductive. Now, they could enjoy each other. They could play out the attraction and when her job was finished, part as friends.

Sable ignored the twinge in the region of her heart. Colt had no room in his life for anything permanent—nor did she. They *would* say goodbye. There would be no happily ever after Hollywood finale.

The ending of this story had already been written.

Chapter Nine

COLT WASN'T FOND of days off. When he started a film, he liked to stay immersed in the story and the character. Colt believed in working hard and playing when the work was done. He had plenty of time to rest between projects. As the saying went, he could sleep when he was dead.

However, now there was Sable. She made the thought of a day off appealing. When an unexpected rainstorm washed out the day's shoot, Colt didn't curse as he normally would have. He looked up at the sky and thanked the weather Gods.

Instead of fake canoodling, he planned on staying in bed all day. With Sable.

"You'll get tired of me."

"Not going to happen."

Colt grabbed Sable's hand, preventing her from getting out of bed. It was early. Seven o'clock. Normally they would be at the set. As they were heading out the door, Colt received the surprising news. They were washed out for the day.

It took another hour for the rain to hit downtown Los Angeles. By then, he and Sable were resting up from a particularly vigorous round of sex.

"An entire day? Your dick will be crying for mercy."

"My dick is a big boy."

"I'll say." Sable waggled her eyebrows.

"Thank you. But you didn't let me finish. Big boys don't cry. A day? I can do that standing on my head, with my hands tied behind my back."

"I told you. I'm not into ropes."

"Bet I could change your mind."

Sable appeared to be considering the idea. Colt wasn't surprised when she shook her head.

"Nope. But if you stand on your head, I'll give you a whirl."

"Why don't we save the acrobatics for another day." Colt nuzzled her warm, soft neck. "Today, all I want is some good old-fashioned sex."

"I need food."

"The fridge is empty."

"Right." Sable sighed. "We need to hit the grocery store. Now that your groupies aren't making their weekly pilgrimage, the coffers are getting bare."

Colt put the word out that he no longer required food deliveries. Or cleaning services. Or laundry pick-up. After a week, he realized how much he had come to depend on those things *magically* getting done. He would leave the house, go to work, and when he returned, there was fresh food to eat, his bathroom sparkled, and his underwear was neatly folded and put away.

For years, his brothers teased him about his harem of household helpers. Colt accepted the ribbing with careless good grace. He didn't think twice about the arrogance it took to allow these things to be done on his behalf. He appreciated it. He made sure his assistant sent each woman flowers once a month and gave them tickets to his movie premieres.

And then what? The names and faces changed. For almost six years, a club had existed for the sole purpose of making Colton Landis' life easier. Now, it was over. He hoped it ended without hard feelings, but he didn't know. Because he didn't want to.

The truth wasn't pretty, but Colt didn't mind looking it straight in the face. If it weren't for Sable, he didn't know if it ever would have stopped. Colt chuckled. He imagined himself at ninety, still being cared for by a bevy of... Seventy-year-olds?

"What's so funny?"

"Do you think my fans will age as I do?"

"Your fans will get older. And younger." Sable understood the way the world worked. "Look at your father. He's a fox. Unless you let yourself go to pot, women will drop at your feet until the day you die."

"Either way, I need a housekeeper. And a laundry service. And a place that delivers groceries."

Sable rolled out of bed.

"Hey," he protested.

"Unless you want me to tinkle on your designer sheets, I need to go to the bathroom. While I'm gone, order some takeout."

"What are you in the mood for?"

"Chinese? No, a juicy hamburger. Check that. Macaroni and cheese." Sable paused to pull on Colt's t-shirt. "You decide. When I'm hungry, everything sounds good."

"Why do you bother with clothes?" he called out.

"Habit. For years, I lived around thousands of men. I forget I don't need to cover up for one."

Good answer, Colt decided. They hadn't shared a bedroom for very long. He couldn't expect her to get used to him in only a week. But she would. Colt was determined to have her walking around, naked as a jaybird, in no time at all.

It had been a good week. Better than good. After that first night, there was no question of going back. Sable kept her things in the other bedroom, but she slept with him.

Sable was slowly adjusting. He was over the moon.

The lovely Sable. His to play with anytime he wanted. And Colt wanted to play often. Luckily for him, so did she.

They played in bed. In the shower. On the sofa. The cement counter in the kitchen turned out to be the perfect place for a little post-breakfast fun. For the first time since he had moved here, Colt made regular use of the hidden window blinds. The last thing he needed was some industrious member of the paparazzi taking pictures of Sable and him as they enjoyed the benefits of living with his lover twenty-four hours a day, seven days a week. At one time, Colt wouldn't have cared. But this was different. Sable was different.

Colt frowned. There it was again. Why did he keep thinking that way? Yes, Sable wasn't like the other women he had known. So what? What did it mean? Colt didn't want to worry about it. He had a day of nothing but Sable ahead of him. He wasn't going to let unsettling thoughts ruin their fun.

Food. He'd promised Sable something to eat. Colt picked up his phone, but before he could scroll through his list of go-to delivery places, it rang.

Wyatt.

"Hey. What's up?" Colt asked. He turned on the speaker phone and began scrolling. Instead of picking one thing, he decided to order a variety. "That place with the amazing egg rolls? Do they deliver?"

"Yes. But forget it. You have the day off and Mom wants the whole gang there for lunch."

"How did you know I wasn't working?"

"I'm a producer. I know everything."

Wyatt's explanation was simple and true. Not much happened on a Landis production without his brother knowing about it. Usually seconds after the fact.

"Come right away. Lorena made guacamole. Once Nate arrives, there's no guarantee anyone else will get any."

He did love Lorena's guacamole. There was no chance of leftovers. Not with Nate, the human vacuum cleaner around. "I've already made plans."

"Cancel them."

"But—"

"Mom wants you here. Need I say more?"

Colt hesitated. No one said no to Callie Flynn. Especially her sons.

But he was tempted. He didn't know how many opportunities he would have to be alone with Sable for an entire day.

"You can't get out of it, so don't bother trying."

"I didn't say anything." Damn. It wasn't easy to get anything past someone who had known him all his life.

"Who knows the way your mind works better than I do?"

"We'll be there." Colt sighed. The best-laid plans, etc. "And Wyatt? Just so you know? I'm giving you the finger."

Wyatt ignored the verbal jab. "Your beautiful bodyguard must be sick of you by now. She can use a change of scenery."

Sable. Well, shit. The second they walked in the door, everyone would know things had changed. After the dire warning to keep his dick to himself, his father wouldn't simply call him into his office. He would give him *the look*.

Caleb Landis never raised a hand to his sons. He could metaphorically flail off a layer of skin with one laser-sharp, blue-eyed gaze. His didn't use it often. Which made it all the more effective.

He loved his family. But come on. He wasn't a child. Neither was Sable. What two consenting adults did in private was nobody else's business. And it was a damn good thing they didn't know. Some of the things he and Sable had done were likely illegal in some states.

"That's quite a grin. I didn't know calling for takeout was so entertaining. What did you decide on?"

Sable hopped onto the bed and into his arms. Colt wrapped his arms around her, breathing in her scent. A blend of his soap and her shampoo. And something he couldn't put his finger on but it drove him crazy. He would forever call it simply, Sable.

"You'll love the food. But we won't be eating in."

"No?" Sable took off his shirt. "Naked Lunch would take on a whole new meaning."

How could he resist a woman who was so beautifully natural and had read William S. Burroughs? He never should have answered the phone. Next time he would know better.

"We've been summoned to the old homestead."

"Your parents' house?" Sable scrambled off the bed, searching for his t-shirt.

"They can't see us, Sable."

"You can laugh. My job is to watch your back, not suck your— "

"Hey." Colt put a hand over mouth. "One is your job. The other is between us. Never insinuate otherwise."

"I hope your family feels the same way."

"They like you. If anyone gets some flack, it will be me."

"Yes. They like me. But they love you. I'm replaceable."

Colt stopped himself from saying the first thing that popped into his head.

Replaceable? Not as far as I'm concerned.

"Let's hit the shower."

Colt grabbed Sable's hand. Stray thoughts had a way of freaking him out. He couldn't think of a better way to clear his head than hot, steamy, shower sex. With Sable.

"MORE FRIED CHICKEN, Sable?"

"Yes, please." Sable took the plate from Garrett. "This has the Colonel beat by a mile."

"Wait until you try Lorena's pizza. She could start her own restaurant."

"Shh." Nate piled his plate with a second helping of mashed potatoes. "Where would I get my enchilada fix?"

"I'll teach Paige." The longtime Landis family cook smiled at Nate. She had a basket filled with hot rolls just out of the oven.

"I wouldn't dare try, Lorena. Your food is legendary. When I spoke with Dad last week, he was still raving about your cooking. I think he and Irene are flying in from Montana next month just for your waffles."

"Sable." Jade took a roll and slathered it with butter. "I've been working on those self-defense moves you showed me, but I can't seem to get them right. Will you give me a refresher course after lunch?"

"I'd like to get in on that," Paige said.

"Me too."

"You?" Sable looked at Nate in surprise. "Why?"

"My ego is still bruised from that beat down you gave me. I want a rematch."

"Give it a rest." Garrett winked at Sable. "Do you want Paige to witness a repeat of your humiliation?"

"My fiancée loves me."

"I do," Paige assured Nate. "And I won't think any less of you when Sable kicks your ass."

Colt smiled as Sable easily fell in with his family's banter. It helped that they already knew each other. But it was more than that. Sable was a warm, open person. She liked people and they liked her. His family welcomed everyone with open arms. Garrett and Nate had the good sense to fall in love with intelligent women with big hearts. It made the meal, and every gathering, a joy to attend.

"Who wants dessert?" Lorena called from the kitchen.

"Who doesn't?" Nate responded.

Laughter filled the room. Colt looked from smiling face to smiling face. A man would be a fool to take this for granted, and one could call him many things. Arrogant. Pampered. A bit spoiled. Definitely catered to. But he was not a fool. Above everything else. The money. The fame. The multitude of perks that came with his life. Most of all, he was a lucky son of a bitch.

"Colton."

Over the din, his mother's whispered word caught Colt's attention. Smiling, he leaned closer. Good Lord, she was beautiful. In her fifties, she looked twenty years younger. Good genes and a happy life. According to Callie, that was the secret. She passed those genes to him. That and a basically sunny personality. They expected the best from the world.

However, cross them, or someone they loved, and the rose-colored glasses came off. They could be vicious if pushed. Just ask the small list of people stupid enough to push once too often.

"Are you getting younger?" he asked. Taking her chin between his fingers, he turned her head from one side to the other. "Is there a portrait in the attic that I don't know about?"

"Silly boy." Callie's famous gray eyes sparkled. "All women should have sons. You see us as we were when you were little boys. Forever young."

"We love you. *And* you never age." Colt kissed her cheek. "Tell me what's worrying you."

"You always know, don't you?"

"Sometimes I think we share a brain."

"Please, spare me that. I would be a wrinkled crone if I knew everything you got up to."

"Probably."

"Mmm. For instance. Sable?"

"Is that what this is about?" Colt rubbed a hand over his face. "I wondered when someone would say something, but I expected it to be Dad or Wyatt."

"I imagine your father will have a few words with you before you leave. I want to talk to you about Wyatt. Have you spoken to him lately?"

Colt watched as her eyes darkened. There was no mistaking the sign. Callie was worried about her oldest son.

"He called this morning. He sounded fine."

Colt glanced at his brother. Then he looked. Really looked. Wyatt seemed a bit quiet. Almost removed from everyone. His eyes seemed tired—weary. And his hands were restless, arranging his silverware and fussing with his napkin.

Colt recognized the signs and it made his stomach clench. He did a quick mental calculation. Damn it. He had been so distracted with the movie and Sable, Colt had lost track of time.

"I forgot all about it."

"Four years next week." Callie kept her voice low. "That bitch wasn't happy to torment him while they were married. She had to die— on their anniversary. Wyatt relives it every year."

The truth was, Wyatt lived with the guilt of his wife's death every day. It was a constant companion that he couldn't shake no matter how much time passed. The bloom left the marriage early on. Stephanie was a manipulative, self-obsessed harpy. On top of that? She was a secret

114

drinker who, the longer they were married, stopped hiding it. She came out of the proverbial alcoholic's closet. Loud and proud.

Her death had been ruled accidental. A car accident, in the mountains, on rain-slickened roads. But knowing Stephanie, she chose the day Wyatt married her to end it. The perfect way to make certain he never forgot her. One last punch to his already battered gut.

"If I thought it would work, I would hire an exorcist to chase that she-devil from his soul." Callie sounded close to tears.

Colt squeezed her hand. He knew better than anyone the pain and suffering Wyatt went through. Most days, he seemed fine. No. He was fine. But Stephanie was like malaria. Once in his bloodstream, one never knew when the disease would reappear. Only, in Wyatt's case, there was no treatment. He couldn't shake her, no matter how hard he tried.

"I'll talk to him before he leaves. I hoped this year would pass without a problem."

"It might," Callie said. "I want to make sure someone is there for him. Just in case. When I ask, he claims that everything is fine. You're the only one he opens up to, Colt."

"I won't let him close down, Mom. Please, don't worry."

"I'm a mother."

"Right," Colt nodded. He had heard this before. "Worry becomes part of your DNA."

"I've been lucky. Your father and I have raised four strong, decent men. However, the world likes to throw all of us the occasional curve ball. It threw Wyatt a big, crap-covered one." Callie shrugged. "He hurts. I hurt."

"I have his back."

"Then I can worry a little less."

Callie sent him a smile, one he knew very well. This time, when Colt's stomach clenched it had nothing to do with Wyatt. *Oh, boy,* he thought. *Here it comes.* "How are things with you?"

"Great. The movie is on time and under budget. That should help Wyatt's spirits."

"And Sable? Are you adjusting to a permanent bodyguard?"

"Temporarily permanent," he reminded her.

"I like that jacket she has on."

"It's okay."

"Colton."

Callie patiently waited for him to tell her everything. She could afford patience. When she turned that sharp, silver gaze on them, her sons never held out long.

"Fine. I bought Sable a few things."

"Really?"

"A lot of things," he admitted sheepishly. "She needed them."

"Twelve pairs of running shoes?"

Jesus. That many? Colt didn't care about the money, but who needed twelve?

"Sable let me know I'd messed up, Mom."

"I should hope so." Callie smiled. Warm. Loving. Understanding. "I want you to think long and hard about why you found it necessary to buy her all those things, Colton."

"Mom—"

"Long and hard. Understood?"

"Yes. Understood."

"Good." She patted his hand. "Here is Lorena with dessert. Lemon icebox cake. Stop frowning and dig in. I know who much you love it."

Colt ate his dessert and it was excellent. As always. But his mind was on his mother's words. He didn't want to think long and hard about clothes or motives. Or for that matter, Sable. They were having fun. Wasn't that enough?

He looked across the table at Sable. She and Jade were laughing over something Garrett had said. As if sensing his gaze, she turned her head, her eyes meeting his.

The zing in the region of his heart didn't mean squat. Too much rich food. As soon as he hit the gym, he would work off the calories and everything would be back on an even keel. He and Sable had a limited amount of time together. One movie shoot. At the most, five or six weeks left. He didn't want to ruin it by *examining his feelings*.

Sable was his friend. His lover. He treasured her as both. But when they parted, he would move on. And so would she.

Shit. There it was again. Not a zing. This time, it felt like a vice tightening around his heart.

Colt shook it off and finished his dessert. He didn't do long-term relationships. His career wasn't suited to them. And he wasn't ready to fall in love. Not with Sable. Not with anyone.

Chapter Ten

FILMMAKING WAS A mystery to Sable.

She had known the basics before she began spending her days on the set. Scenes were not shot in order of the story. The climactic reunion was already being edited. While today they were filming the first time the lovers met.

It seemed odd, but it worked. It had since the beginning of movies over a hundred years ago. Colt explained that most days he didn't think about the story arc. He focused on the moment. The words. The emotions or actions he needed to convey right now. If he did his job, the movie would fit together seamlessly. With the help of a skilled, and often underrated, editor.

Sable understood all of that. What she couldn't grasp was the outrageous waste of time. The soldier in her hated inactivity. In the Army, there was always something to do. Cleaning and repairing her gear. Working out. Tactical meetings. Or a few minutes of much-needed shut-eye. She never let time slip away without accomplishing something.

After a few weeks of observation, she concluded making a movie consisted of two things. Bursts of frantic activity. And hours of standing around.

"Today has been a bitch. For a nickel, I would chuck the business. Want to run off to Tahiti?"

Sable blinked in surprise. Colt never complained. Well, sometimes he grumbled about his co-star. In spite of her efforts, Colt hadn't succumbed to the charms of Candice DeMarcco. If she really wanted him, she was going about it in the wrong way.

On a good day, Candice was temperamental. She treated the crew like crap, making demands that sent them running in every direction except the right one. She often flubbed her lines, or worse, hadn't learned them. Today's major delay had been caused by her complaint that her blouse wasn't the right shade of pink. She refused to come out of her trailer until fuchsia was replaced by peony.

"Tahiti sounds great. When do we leave?"

"As soon as you change. I'm already dressed for island living."

At the moment, Colt wore nothing but a pair of board shorts and flip-flops. Sable could see the goosebumps on his arms. Apparently his anger kept him warm. Knowing that wouldn't last long, she motioned for his assistant to get him a jacket.

"You wouldn't make it to take-off." Smiling her thanks, Sable took the jacket. "Stand up."

Colt obliged. This was the first time Sable had fussed over him. He liked it. When she fastened the last button, he tipped her chin and gave her a sweet thank you kiss.

"I'm serious."

"I know. And I don't blame you. America's sweetheart needs a firm kick in the butt."

"Are you volunteering for duty?"

Sable leaned close, adjusting his collar.

"Trust me, it would be a pleasure, not a duty."

Colt pulled Sable in for a hug, his arms slipping around her waist. He swayed, almost dancing, enjoying how easily she adjusted to his rhythm.

"We aren't going to Tahiti." He felt a touch of regret.

"No. Face it, pretty boy. You aren't the type to skip out. This is a job, but more than that, it's a promise. You made a commitment. Think of all the people you would put out of work. Nope. It doesn't matter if you never joined. You, Colton Landis, are a Boy Scout at heart."

"Mmm." His breath tickled her ear. "Sounds boring."

"There is nothing boring about a good man."

Colt felt his chest puff out. He heard it in her voice. She handed him the ultimate compliment. In Sable's world, good men were few and far between. He was proud to be added to that short, but precious list.

"Rene is at her wits' end."

Sable tried to pull away, but Colt muttered, "Nope." And held her firmly in place. He knew she could get away in a heartbeat, but she understood. He needed comforting. She stayed put and turned her head.

"You look pretty frazzled yourself."

Kiki Donahue flopped onto one of the chairs.

"What the fuck is the difference between fuchsia and peony?"

"Peony is a paler shade of pink."

Sable and Kiki gave Colt matching stares of amazement.

"My mother loves her garden," he said with a grin. "Real men love flowers."

"No question. You are without a doubt a real man."

Kiki made a gagging sound. "Give me a break. Rene is giving me grief because she has no recourse to deal with Candice. I broke up with my boyfriend over a month ago, so I'm in the middle of a sexual drought. Do me a favor? Keep the lovey-dovey crap to a minimum. At least, when I'm around."

"That's it." With a kiss on her cheek, Colt set Sable away from him. "I gave the bitch a long piece of rope and now she's hung herself. I'm going to remind her that she's supposed to be a professional. And if that doesn't work, I'll call in the big gun."

"Should we be worried?" Kiki asked Sable as they watched Colt stride toward Candice's trailer.

"No. Colt won't hurt her."

"I know that. I meant should we worry about his threat? The big gun? Whatever it is, it sounds dangerous."

"Not what. Who. Candice needs to pay attention to Colt. Because from what I've heard, nobody wants to get on the bad side of Wyatt Landis."

IT TOOK HIM an hour. Sable didn't know what Colt said to Candice, but when she returned to the set, she was all sweetness and light. And she was wearing the original blouse. Bright fuchsia. Not a peony in sight.

The beach scene went off without a hitch. They wrapped it up in only two takes. Rene called cut, and the crew began breaking down the set. The privately owned oceanside property was rented until sundown today. If they hadn't finished on schedule, the overage costs would have been astronomical.

Colt saved the day, artistically and financially.

Sable waited while Colt conferred with Rene about tomorrow's schedule. He had a producing credit in the movie. At first, Sable had been surprised by how seriously he took the title. He never left the set without making sure everything was set for tomorrow. It made his day longer, but he never complained. It wouldn't have occurred to him. He grew up learning every end of the family business. Sometimes through osmosis. Mostly by asking questions and doing his homework.

The more Sable learned about Colton Landis, the more she admired him.

"Hi, Janis," Sable smiled. She hadn't seen the actress for over a week. She only had a handful of scenes with Colt, so they were always missing each other.

"Promise me you won't shoot the messenger?"

"That sounds ominous."

"I say it's a ball of crap, but…"

"Spill the beans, Janis." Sable preferred that everything was done in a straight line—including gossip.

"Candice is telling anyone who will listen, and around here, that's just about everyone, that Colt talked her around the old-fashioned way. Horizontally."

"She claims they had sex?" Sable shook her head. "That is sad and pathetic."

"I agree. Unfortunately, juicy gossip has a way of spreading. Each retelling is embellished. Tomorrow the rags will have Candice pregnant with Colt's love child."

"It can't hurt me, Janis. I know it's a lie."

Sable meant every word. Her skin was tough. Forged by the kind of maliciousness that Hollywood could never come close to matching. Once you had survived the military grapevine, you could survive anything.

"I admire your attitude. But remember. When a lie is juicy enough, nobody cares about the truth."

"The truth is the only thing that matters. Even if you're the only one who knows what that is."

"God! I want to be you." Janis laughed when Sable snorted in disbelief. "Honestly. You have your shit together. And I wouldn't mind taking over your body for a few hours. What's it like to look like a supermodel?"

"It's the clothes."

Sable lovingly ran a hand over the teal-colored cashmere jacket. Every morning, because she knew she couldn't be seen, she danced around her closet deciding what to wear. She discovered something new every time. It was like her own personal designer outlet.

She would never let Colt know, but it was going to be torture to leave it all behind. For now, it was hers. And she reveled in wearing something different whenever she went out.

"Please." Janis scoffed. "You would look good in a gunny sack. It's the long legs. And the cheekbones. And the attitude."

"Attitude?" Sable asked, puzzled. "I have an attitude?"

"You said it yourself. You don't care what other people think."

"That's a loose interpretation of what I said, Janis."

Sable didn't care what strangers thought. But there was one person whose opinion meant more than anyone else. At one time, her father was her biggest supporter. Now, she didn't know what he thought. Until he answered her endless messages, she would never know.

"Nope. I stand by my words." Janis hopped off the chair. She fluffed her blonde hair before giving Sable a quick hug. "I have to run. There's a certain hunky sound man with killer blue eyes who claims to make a mean margarita. Tonight I'm going to find out. If all goes well, I'll get a little tipsy and have my way with him. See you later."

"Is it me?" Colt slung a friendly arm around Sable's shoulders. "Janis is always rushing away whenever I arrive."

"It isn't you." Sable turned into his embrace. "As far as I can tell, she rushes everywhere. Tonight she's rushing to get laid."

"I can't think of a better reason."

"Me either." Sable brushed her lips against his. "I'll race you to your trailer. First one naked wins."

"How about this? You take your clothes off while I watch and I will do anything you want."

"Anything? Careful what you promise. I can be very demanding."

Grinning, Colt took her hand, leading her toward his trailer.

"We have all night. Demand away."

COLT HAD WAITED a few days to speak with Wyatt. He knew from experience that his brother wouldn't appreciate his interference. When he began to slide into his personal black hole, he wanted to do it alone. Colt loved him too much to let that happen. He made sure he was always around to pull Wyatt out.

Once it meant flying in from the Australian Outback. He looked like a Yeti and smelled like the underside of a koala, but he made it. And he would do it again. Any time. Anywhere.

Since he was shooting his current film in and around Los Angeles, keeping an eye on Wyatt was simpler. Colt called his brother as he was getting ready to leave for the set.

"Why don't you stop by after work? We'll order a couple of pizzas and catch up."

"I've been expecting your call." Colt could hear the impatience in Wyatt's voice. "Mom put you on my scent."

There was no point in denying it.

"Come over, Wyatt. If you don't, I'll track you down."

"You can try."

Great. Colt sighed. Wyatt was in one of *those* moods. His brother went to work every day in a suit and tie. He presented a polished, sophisticated image to the world. However, when the mood hit, he could be the toughest badass in town.

This time? Colt had a secret weapon.

"I'll send Sable."

At first, Wyatt didn't respond. Then Colt heard a deep, heartfelt sigh.

"You don't play fair, little brother."

"I learned from the best."

"Fuck you," Wyatt grumbled.

"I love you too," Colt shot back. "I'll see you at seven. Sharp."

COLT WATCHED AS Sable dabbed a bit of color on her lips. Red. It matched the dress that caressed the creamy skin of her shoulders and hugged the swell of her hips.

His view from the bed was prime. Every time she bent to pick something up, her short skirt tightened across her gorgeous ass. As a bonus, it crept up her thighs, exposing an extra inch or two of her long, shapely legs. He reclined on one elbow and smiled.

"Promise me you won't leave the loft."

"We went through this already. Wyatt is coming over. Unless the place catches on fire, we won't budge."

"Fire. I should have thought of that. I can't go."

"Sable." Colt hopped off the bed and took her hand. "You deserve a night out. Jade and Paige will be here any minute. You can't disappoint them. Besides, you were looking forward to this."

"I still am."

Sable wrestled with her conscience. It was her job to make certain nothing happened to Colt. She wasn't here to have fun. When he told her that Wyatt was coming over, he suggested a girls' night out. After all, he reasoned, what could happen to him here at the loft?

124

In Harper Falls, she often met her friends for lunch or drinks. They got together whenever the mood struck. It had been a new experience for Sable—friends who weren't in uniform. However, it hadn't taken her long to get used to the luxury, and she had missed it since coming to Los Angeles.

Sable made a token argument, but it didn't take much for Colt to persuade her. Now she had second thoughts.

"You have the sexiest brain." Colt kissed her temple. "I can see it working away, trying to figure out how danger might infiltrate the loft."

"It is my job."

"And you're very good at it."

"Damn straight. Hey," Sable pushed at Colt's wandering hands. "I get to be girly when I'm off the clock. Don't mess up my hair."

Colt grinned. He knew she was teasing. Sable was all woman, but she wasn't the least bit girly. He cupped her head, his fingers gently massaging her scalp. Slowly, he kissed the line of her jaw, ending on one of his new favorite places—her lips.

"Men will try to pick you up."

"Mmm." The pleasure was too much. Sable closed her eyes and parted her lips. "With Jade and Paige along? It's inevitable."

God. What had he been thinking? What were Garrett and Nate doing, letting their women out on the town alone? Alone, each turned heads. Together? Three smoking hot women, a brunette, a blonde, and a redhead, walk into a club. It sounded like the first line of a joke. Colt wasn't laughing.

"Maybe this isn't such a good idea."

"Don't go all caveman on me. We can take care of ourselves."

Frustrated with the delay, Sable closed her lips over his. She sank into the kiss, sighing when Colt, his hands still buried in her hair, slanted his mouth. His tongue teasing hers. When he pulled back, they were breathing hard and smiling.

"You make me forget my good intentions."

"Which are?" Sable slid her arms around his waist. She nuzzled his neck. Unable to resist, she took his earlobe between her teeth and tugged.

"Sable." Colt groaned. "Jesus. You're driving me crazy."

"Sorry." Unrepentant, Sable stopping biting. Instead, she licked the outline of Colt's ear. She knew the area was particularly sensitive.

"That's it." Colt ran his hand up her leg and under her skirt. "These aren't underwear," he proclaimed when he touched a barely there scrap of lace.

"They are perfectly respectable." Sable thought for a second then amended her statement. "I won't be flashing anyone. Besides, you purchased them."

"I'm an idiot. Sable— "

"Hold that thought. You have company."

Sable gave him a quick peck on the lips before she hurried from the room. It was just as well. Colt had no idea what he had been about to say. *Don't go. The idea of a room full of men ogling you makes me jealous.*

Colt shuddered. Him? Jealous? It was such a horrifying thought. Nope. It wasn't possible. Besides, Sable wasn't going to fall for any smooth talker's line. She wasn't going to jump into bed with the first charming, handsome man who tried to buy her a drink.

Sable was going out with friends for some fun, not trolling for a one-night stand.

"Colt. Wyatt is here." Wyatt. That was where his mind should be. Colt headed for the living room. Spending some time away from Sable was a good idea. One day soon, he would reach for her in the middle of the night and she wouldn't be there. Tonight would be a good reminder that she wasn't a permanent part of his life.

"I'm constantly amazed," Sable said. She was in the kitchen where Wyatt was pouring himself a cup of coffee. "Colt loves making movies. It would drive me crazy."

"It takes a great deal of patience and dedication to be an actor. Colt knew what he wanted at a young age and he's never wavered."

"I admire that." Sable shook her head when Wyatt offered to pour her a cup. "Was it the same for you? You have followed in your father's footsteps. Did you ever want to do anything but produce?"

Colt peered around the corner but stayed out of sight. He was curious to hear what Wyatt would say.

126

Their parents never pushed him or his brothers to work in the business. They let each of them take their own path. They would have been happy with a dentist or a lawyer or a lumberjack. All they wanted was for their sons to follow their passions.

Colt wanted to act. Period. There was only one restriction put on him. He had to wait until he graduated from high school.

His parents knew the statistics and they didn't want him to become a burned out has-been before he reached his eighteenth birthday. At the time, Colt resented the restrictions. There were offers coming in almost daily. Commercials. Television. Movies. He wanted to work—immediately.

Hindsight was a wonderful thing. The longer he was in the business, the more he realized his parents had made the right choice. He hadn't been ready. The stumbles he made early in his career were minor. If he hadn't been held back and allowed to mature away from the spotlight, Colt shuddered to imagine where he would be today.

It was one more example of how important it was to have loving, supportive parents. They wanted what was best for him in the long run. As a result, his happiness wasn't predicated on how his latest movie performed at the box office. He was in this for the long haul. That meant searching out roles that meant something to him. One hundred, two hundred years from now, no one would care how many polls named him the sexiest man alive.

It was the work that survived the test of time. Colt was determined to be remembered for his body of work—not his body.

His brothers felt the same way. Garrett already had a reputation as a perfectionist. He was a director every actor dreamed of working with. Nate couldn't keep up with the job offers. If he and his stunt team worked on a film, one knew every car chase and fight scene would be first rate.

Wyatt's job was harder to explain but just as important. If you asked him, he would tell you no one made a move without him. And, Colt had to admit, his brother was right. He gathered the money. Made the negotiations. Smoothed ruffled feathers. If a problem arose, Wyatt fixed it.

He assumed Wyatt became a producer because he couldn't imagine doing anything else. But Colt had never asked and he was interested in what Wyatt was going to say to Sable.

"When I was five years old, Mom was pregnant with Colt. Very pregnant. Can you imagine? She worked until her seventh month. Garrett and Nate were toddlers and getting into everything." Wyatt laughed. "I didn't understand why Mommy couldn't play with me. She made up the best games. Not girly games, but tough little boy games."

Colt grinned. Wyatt was right. Callie always got down in the mud with her boys. She would joke that women paid hundreds of dollars to have their skin slathered with muck. She got her treatments for free. And it was a lot more fun than going to a stuffy old spa.

"Grandma was visiting. She liked to be there when her baby was having a baby of her own. I had no idea what that meant, but I remember thinking it was stupid. Dad likes to remind me that, at that age, I thought everything was stupid."

"You were five," Sable said.

"And I had no patience for a baby I couldn't see."

"You love him now." Colt heard the smile in Sable's voice.

"The first time he peed on me, I decided he might not be so bad."

Sable burst out laughing. "God. Little boys are odd creatures. I don't know how your mother survived."

"I've wondered that myself. Dad helped. Which brings me back to your question. Did I ever want to do anything but produce?" Wyatt took a drink of coffee and shook his head. "Mom needed a lot of rest. The twins were fine with Grandma, so for about a month, Dad took me to work. I didn't understand what was going on, but I felt the energy. And I knew Dad was in charge. That was it. A job where I could tell everyone what to do? For a five-year-old boy, that sounded like heaven. I still feel that way."

"No acting aspirations? I'll bet the camera loves you."

"Is that your way of saying you like the way I look?"

"I think the term is drool-worthy."

There was a long pause.

"Wyatt Landis. Are you blushing?"

What? Colt didn't think anything could fluster his brother. He couldn't wait any longer. This he had to see.

"Smile." Colt took Wyatt's picture, then studied the image on his phone. "It's true. Wait. Garrett and Nate have to see this."

"Damn it, Colt."

Wyatt made a grab for the phone but Colt backed out of his reach.

"Don't you dare—"

"Done," Colt exclaimed triumphantly.

"That's it. You, little brother, are a dead man."

Deftly, Sable put herself between Colt and Wyatt. She wasn't trying to stop them. In fact, she wished she could stay and find out who came out on top. But Jade just sent her a text. She and Paige were parked in a tow away zone. She had to get going.

"I'm off." Sable's hand was on Wyatt's chest, holding him back. "I'll see you soon?"

"Just say the word. We'll get a babysitter for this guy and I'll show you my Los Angeles."

When Wyatt winked, Sable smiled and kissed his cheek.

"Don't fall for that line, Sable. Wyatt's Los Angeles is boring."

"Somehow I doubt that." Sable turned and planted a big, enthusiastic kiss on Colt. "See you later. If Wyatt wants to leave before I get home, call me."

"Be safe."

"Always." Sable stood in the elevator and as the doors began to close, she called out, "Have at it, boys."

Before Colt could react, Wyatt tackled him. Sable was still laughing when she walked out of the building.

Chapter Eleven

SABLE SAT IN the limousine sipping a glass of champagne. She recognized the label. One bottle cost as much as a month's rent on her place in Harper Falls.

Her life was unpredictable. Last month she ran recruits through drills at the H&W compound. Sweaty and dressed in a t-shirt, shorts, and scuffed tennis shoes, she bore little resemblance to the woman who wore designer clothes and smelled of expensive perfume.

However, she was the same person. Two sides of the same coin. Comfortable in both worlds and able to slip from one to the other in a blink of an eye.

Sable's life was unpredictable. And she wouldn't have it any other way.

"In Montana, a night on the town meant beer and peanuts at Basic's one and only watering hole," Paige crossed one long leg over the other. "I'll always prefer jeans. But there is something to be said for getting glammed up Hollywood style."

The blonde clinked glasses with Jade and Sable then downed the last of her champagne.

"More?" Jade offered.

"Why not?" Paige held out her glass. "I have a big, strong man waiting at home. He won't have any problem pouring me into bed."

"Before I started seeing Garrett, I never did this. I went to a million parties, but I hated every one of them. Now, when I go out, it's because I want to, not because it's expected of me. Oops." Jade laughed when she emptied the last drop from the bottle. "That went fast."

"Here's to living life on our own terms."

With that declaration, Sable popped the cork on a fresh bottle.

"Well done." Paige laughed, not because it was funny, but because the night was meant for laughter. "Tell us about Colt."

"What do you mean? Colt is Colt."

Paige coughed, her champagne coming precariously close to covering her lap.

"No. He's Colton Landis. Movie God."

This time, it was Jade who almost lost control of her drink.

"Do not say that in front of him. Colt is a love, but his ego barely fits through the door as it is."

"He's a Landis," Sable said.

"Amen," Paige sighed. "Ego is stamped on their DNA. So is charm and killer good looks. Luckily, they all possess the kind of self-deprecating humor that makes them irresistible."

"I love Nate. As far as I'm concerned, he is the sexiest man to ever walk the face of the Earth." Paige's blue eyes sparkled, her smile wide. "But before we met, I had a major crush on Colt."

"You and every woman with a pulse. What?" She asked when Jade and Paige exchanged surprised looks.

"It can't be easy," Jade shrugged. "Women make passes at Garrett. But it isn't constant. Colt is a walking target."

"I'm a trained bodyguard. A few rabid fans are nothing I can't handle."

"You're jealous?" Paige inquired. "Nate had his brush with fame, but we were in Montana at the time. All I had to contend with were a few hormonal teenagers."

Sable suddenly understood. And she quickly set Jade and Paige straight.

"Colt and I aren't dating. Or involved. I'm here to keep him safe."

"And you're sleeping with him."

"Paige."

"It's okay," Sable assured them. "I'm sleeping with him. And there is a lot of sex in between. It's great. Better than great. I like him. We're having fun. I don't have the right, or the inclination, to be jealous."

"Do you believe her?" Paige asked.

"Not for a second," Jade replied.

"Just a second." Sable filled her glass and emptied it in one gulp. "I will say this only once and you can never repeat it. Agreed? Before you answer, keep in mind that no matter where you are or how far you run, I'll find you."

"Agreed." Jade crossed her heart.

"Absolutely," Paige promised.

"The thought of Colt touching another woman makes my stomach churn. Look," she held out her hand. "My palms are damp and my heart is racing. Apparently I've caught a rare and potentially deadly disease."

"Or you're in love. The symptoms are amazingly similar."

Sable's hand wasn't as steady when she filled her glass.

"That would be foolish."

"Yes." Jade took the bottle. She covered Sable's wobbly hand with her steady one. "Love is foolish. And terrifying. And splendid. And a journey like no other you will ever embark upon."

"It brought me to Nate," Paige smiled, her eyes a little misty.

"And I found Garrett. Or maybe he found me." Jade shrugged. "It doesn't matter. We arrived at the same conclusion. We love each other."

"What happens if you jump and find out you've taken the journey alone?"

Neither woman had an answer to that. Sable didn't expect them to. They loved and were loved in return. They hadn't given their hearts only to have them ripped out and crushed into a million pieces.

God, what a scary thought. Sable wasn't in love with Colt. Not yet. But if she were headed in that direction, she was afraid it was too late to put on the brakes.

The car pulled to a stop. The building looked deserted and a lone man stood by a smooth metal door.

"Are you sure this is the place?" Paige asked.

The driver held the door open, helping the women out, one by one "According to my sources, this is the hottest club in town."

Jade handed over a card that the doorman scanned. A second later, the door slid open and he motioned for them to enter.

"I've seen this movie," Paige said. "And it didn't end well."

"Don't worry," Jade whispered, adding to the eerie atmosphere. "Sable will kick any and all ghoulish butt."

Sable smiled. She could hear the din of voices competing with bass-driven music. This was what she needed. A few hours of mindless fun and a shot or two of something stronger than champagne.

"I want to dance and that music is calling." She linked arms with Jade and Paige. "Come on, ladies. The tequila is on me."

"WHEN WAS THE last time you got laid?"

"None of your business."

"That long?"

Wyatt let out a long suffering sigh and Colt hid his smile. This wasn't the first time they'd had this conversation. Wyatt, unlike Nate and Garrett, kept his personal life close to the vest. It wasn't anything new. When the brothers used to sit around and shoot the breeze, the conversation inevitably turned to women. They would laugh and tease. Names were dropped. But Wyatt rarely shared that part of his life. And though there was some good-natured prodding, generally, his brothers respected his privacy.

Colt worried that since his disastrous marriage, Wyatt had stopped looking at women as anything but a temporary outlet. Wyatt didn't do one-night stands. He hated to make that much of a commitment.

"You have a beautiful woman in your bed. Concentrate on her and stop worrying about my sex life." Wyatt shot a throw pillow at Colt's head when he turned to pick up the remote.

"Hey. Watch it."

Colt threw it back, but Wyatt was ready. He caught it and put it behind his head.

"You could share Sable."

"Excuse me?"

"Share, little brother. You remember the concept. Mom and Dad were big on it."

"Sable isn't a toy." Colt ground out the words. He felt a streak of heat rising up his neck and over his face.

"No?" Wyatt bit back a smile. "Perhaps not. But I like her. More than any woman I've met in a long time. When you get tired of her, let me know."

"Fuck you." Colt couldn't believe what he was hearing. It wasn't like Wyatt. Then it hit him. It *wasn't* like Wyatt. "Asshole. What's the deal?"

"What do you think?"

Colt knew. It was Wyatt's round-about way of making Colt consider his feelings for Sable. The hell with that.

"We played some old school video games and ate some damn fine pizza. We consumed exactly one beer each and ran through half a dozen episodes of Seinfeld. Overall a good evening. Don't ruin it by playing amateur psychiatrist."

"Like you do with me?"

"I'm allowed," Colt grinned. "Don't forget. You're fragile."

"My ass. Do I seem fragile?"

To his relief, Colt had to admit that Wyatt appeared to be in good spirits. He hadn't fallen into a dark funk this year. More like a shady introspection.

"You look good."

"I am good. But it still hurts, Colt. My child would have been five years old this year."

"Wyatt... "

"Enough." Wyatt took a deep breath. "I'm sick of my family treating me with kid gloves. It's time to stop dwelling on the past."

"I agree. Did you hear that?"

"What?"

Wyatt looked around, giving Colt the perfect opportunity to bounce a pillow off his head.

"Just paying you back. Wyatt." Wyatt advanced, a pillow in each hand. Colt realized he was out of ammunition and held up his hands. "I was getting even."

"I'll show you even."

Wyatt pummeled Colt with a double-barreled assault. Fast and furious.

"I thought you would have gotten this out of your systems by now."

"Sable."

Wyatt used the moment of Sable claiming Colt's attention to give him one last shot to the head.

"And that is why you never win. You're too easily distracted."

"Poor baby." Sable patted Colt on the head as she passed by on the way to the kitchen. "Are you bleeding?"

"No." Colt reached for her hand but missed.

"Is your life in imminent danger?" Sable removed a bottle of water from the refrigerator, opened it, and took a sip.

"Not at the moment," Colt muttered.

"Then stop whining."

Wyatt laughed at Colt's disgruntled expression. "For once a woman isn't fawning over you. Boo hoo." He put on his jacket. "Sable, you are a breath of fresh air."

"Are you leaving?" Sable walked Wyatt to the elevator.

"I've had all the Colt I can take for one evening."

"I love you, too," Colt said, giving Wyatt the finger.

"Mom would be proud."

"Again." This time, Colt shot him a double middle-finger salute.

Wyatt ignored him, turning his attention to Sable.

"I'm sorry you have to deal with him, but I live with the happy knowledge that if he gets out of hand, you can kick his ass." Wyatt gave her a friendly hug.

"How are you?" Sable asked in a voice only he could hear.

Surprised, Wyatt was touched by her concern.

"Spending time with Colt always helps." Wyatt's tone matched hers. "But don't tell him I said so."

"Your secret is safe with me."

"Did you have a good time?" Sable asked Colt after Wyatt left.

"Same old. We mostly hung out. He says it's better this year."

"You don't believe him?"

Sable slipped out of her shoes. The four-inch heels looked great but her feet were beginning to scream for relief. She sighed and flexed her toes, then sat next to Colt, curling her legs under her.

"Yes and no." Colt took her hand, his thumb absently rubbing the back. He liked touching Sable and did so as often as possible. "Most of the time Wyatt is good at keeping his emotions in check. Too good. I believe he's doing okay but I wish he had someone."

"Someone?"

"Okay. A woman. He works crazy hours. Wyatt's idea of leisure time is more work. He's either in his office downtown, or the one at his house. If Mom didn't insist he spend time with the family, I doubt he would ever take a break."

"I know this isn't any of my business." Sable hesitated. "Is Wyatt celibate?"

"No. He has sex."

Colt didn't add that he suspected Wyatt paid for it. He never asked his brother for confirmation. But the signs were there. It made sense. Wyatt wanted to stay emotionally detached. What better way than treating sex as a business transaction.

Not that Wyatt would pick someone up off the street. There were plenty of high-class operations if you knew where to look. Colt doubted he did it often. But despite the image he presented to the world, Wyatt was only human.

"Enough about that." Colt leaned close and gave Sable a kiss. "Mmm. I missed you."

"I was only gone a few hours," Sable reminded him. But it was nice hearing Colt say it.

"Was that all?" When he looked at her, his eyes were a warm shade of blue. "It seemed like longer. Did you have a good time?"

"Yes. But," Sable sighed. "Something happened."

"What? Why didn't you say something sooner? Are Jade and Paige okay?"

"Slow down." Giving Colt a reassuring smile, Sable patted his leg. "I wouldn't have waited to tell you if it were anything serious."

"Right. Tell me."

"We arrived at the club. Had a drink. Danced. With each other," Sable added before Colt could ask. "It was fun."

"How many guys hit on you?"

"Not many."

Colt didn't respond but his look told her he didn't buy what she was selling.

"Honestly. We made it clear that we weren't there to be picked up and after a few lame attempts, we were left alone."

The truth was, the men kept coming, but they were good sports, taking the rejection well. Until they were getting ready to leave.

"After a few hours, we decided we'd had enough. On the way out, a man made a pass at Jade."

"Shit."

"He had too much to drink and got handsy. I was about to step in when she used that move I taught her. She had him on the floor, sobbing for mercy, before I could react. Didn't even break his finger."

"Great." Colt was impressed. Jade was nobody's victim. Not anymore. She had come a long way in a short time.

"Not great. But not bad," Sable said in a rush. "The car was waiting for us. I'm here and Jade and Paige are on their way home."

"Then what's the problem?"

Sable sighed. She handed Colt her phone. "See for yourself."

The video wasn't the best quality, but there was no mistaking Jade. Her long red hair stood out in any crowd. Colt watched as someone stopped her by putting a hand on her arm. Jade tried to push him away, but when the man tightened his grip, she grabbed one of his fingers, twisted, and quickly had him on his knees. It was an impressive move. Especially considering that Jade was in a dress and heels and the man outweighed her by close to a hundred pounds.

"Who the hell filmed this?" Colt asked, watching the clip again.

"According to the post, someone called Musiclover666."

"These days you can't fart in the wind without it hitting the internet."

"That's a lovely analogy," Sable laughed.

"And accurate." Colt set the phone down and pulled Sable into his arms. "Paige would have done the same thing."

"Probably. I taught her the move."

Colt nuzzled her neck, smiling when she stretched her head to the side, giving him better access. He breathed deeply. The night spent in a crowded club couldn't mask her unique, heady scent. The smell shot a jolt of desire through his body.

"You have turned my brothers' women into fierce, take no shit, warriors."

"If I had my way, I would give every woman in the world the ability to take care of themselves. Do you have a problem with that?"

"Are you kidding? That is so damn sexy."

Colt slowly unzipped her dress, his hands sliding under the material to caress her warm back. So strong and so soft. The combination drove him crazy.

Sable melted into his touch. "You like that I'm able to take care of myself?"

"The world can be a scary place, Sable. You never know what you're going to find when you step out your door. Hell, sometimes you don't have to leave your home. Shit can find you anywhere." He took her hand and kissed the palm. "Your strength is beautiful."

She didn't know whether to laugh or cry. To solve her dilemma, she kissed him.

Sable had traveled the world. Seen sights both breathtaking and horrific. She had rubbed elbows with heads of state and goat farmers. Who would have guessed that, in the middle of a town that dealt in make believe, she would find a man who accepted her for her true self?

"Let's go to bed," Colt whispered.

"Later."

Hitting the switch by the sofa, the room went dark. Sable picked up the remote that worked the window shades. Slowly, the city lights came into view.

"Here?" Colt asked when Sable straddled his legs.

Sable pulled Colt's shirt over his head and rested her hands on his chest.

"Here."

She wrapped her arms around Colt, her lips meeting his.

Hollywood was all about dreams. For a little while, she wanted to let herself believe that a wish could come true. Sable looked into Colt's eyes and suddenly she felt the possibilities were endless.

For a few hours, deep in her heart where no one else could see. Where no one could guess what she wanted more than anything else, she would let herself dream.

It was crazy and impossible. But she didn't care. Here, in his arms, she didn't want to be sensible. There would be time enough for practicality tomorrow. Tonight, she would let herself dream of Colt's love.

Chapter Twelve

SABLE COULDN'T REMEMBER laughing so much in her entire life. Colt had a way of telling a story, no matter how mundane, and bringing it alive. Sometimes he acted it out. But he was equally gifted when he only used words.

Today he expounded on the hazards of a screen kiss.

"I've encountered everything from an overabundance of saliva to stubbly upper lips. But the worst is bad breath. God knows I've kissed my share of garlic-laden leading ladies." He laughed. "Try saying that three times fast."

Sable proceeded to do precisely that.

"Nice." Colt was impressed.

"Back up. Do you really expect me to believe that an actress would eat garlic before a love scene?"

Sable stuck her head out of her closet. Colt was in what had become his usual spot. At least, when she was dressing. Reclining on the bed, his head propped up on his hand. His feet hung off one side, the double mattress wasn't made for a body that long.

Most of the time, like now, he wore nothing but a pair of jeans. No socks. No shirt. It made Sable think of a restaurant though she couldn't imagine anyone denying Colt service.

Dark hair. Laser-bright blue eyes. A killer smile. Not to mention a body that would make the dead drool. Lord, he was gorgeous. And for now, all hers.

Colt would stretch out while she dressed, talking the entire time. Sable loved these moments. She learned more and more about him. He spoke of his childhood. His love of acting. Why he thought cottage cheese was creepy and the difference between brands of root beer. Colt preferred Diet Barq's. And the reason he always hung up his car keys on the caddy on the wall by the elevator the second he walked into the loft. Because his father taught him to do it that way.

"It happens. Talk about acting."

"How do you prepare?" Sable pursed her lips and made a smacking sound.

"You laugh, but I have a set routine. I floss. Mint flavored. Then I brush. Followed by mouthwash. Right before the camera rolls, I pop half a dozen Tic Tacs."

Sable shook her head and muttered, "I was right. Boy Scout."

"I think you mean that as a compliment," Colt called out after her.

"I think you're right."

Sable took a dress from the long row. Mint green. It had a flirty skirt that would hit her just above the knees. Perfect for a casual Saturday. Colt was free until Monday when his schedule would get crazier. Longer days and a lot of night shooting. He wanted to take advantage of the downtime. A leisurely lunch. A drive through the hills. Lots and lots of sex.

If they were staying in, Colt would have the dress off her in five seconds, but for lunch it was perfect.

"What do you think?"

Sable turned in a circle, the skirt twirling around her long legs. She held her shoes in one hand. As much as she loved the strappy sandals, she didn't want to put them on until they were about to leave. Her feet would thank her later.

"The last time I was in Rome I had some gelato. It was exactly that color." Colt pulled her onto the bed. "And delicious. I'll bet you taste better."

"If we're going out to lunch, you'll have to wait to find out." Sable scooted out of his reach. "Go get dressed. I'm hungry."

"I could make you change your mind."

"No, you couldn't. I'm definitely hungry."

"Har, har, har." Colt weaved right, then left, before swatting Sable on the butt.

"I take it back," she called out as he zipped from the room. "You aren't a Boy Scout. You're a dickhead."

"Really?" Colt leaned through the bedroom door. "Want to kiss my," he wiggled his eyebrows, "head?"

"Go."

Chuckling, Sable took a purse from the shelf. A lemon yellow cross-body bag that complimented her dress perfectly. She added a few items and was debating what else she needed when her phone rang. The ring tone, *Big Boss Man*, letting her know who it was before she looked at the screen.

"Alex. Did you check out that list of names I sent you?"

"Hello to you, too." Sable could hear the smile in his voice. "And yes, I did. They all checked out. Your boy can feel safe hiring any of them."

"He isn't my boy." Sable didn't know why she said it. Or why she sounded so defensive.

"It was a figure of speech, nothing more," Alex assured her. "Is there a problem I need to know about?"

"No. Everything is fine. Boring." Sable slipped her gun into the purse. It was such a part of her everyday routine, she did it automatically. The way some women would carry lipstick or a comb. "Colt was right. He doesn't need a bodyguard."

"As you know, it isn't always about need. The money people behind the movie feel better if their investment is protected."

"They're worried about money, but they waste it hiring me. Does that make sense?"

"No. But it is our bread and butter, Sable." There was a pause. "What's wrong?"

Sable had no idea. Before Alex called, she felt great. Terrific. She had been getting ready for a day out with her… Crap. She was thinking of Colt as her boyfriend, not her client. Alex was a reminder of who and what she was.

Opening her purse, she looked at the gun. *That is your life, Sable. It was before you came here, and it would be again after you leave.* She could dress it up with pretty clothes and fancy meals. Colt could take her in his arms and make her feel things she never knew existed and hold her close while she slept. But it didn't change the facts. Nothing would.

Sable was hired muscle. And Colt was her client.

"Nothing is wrong. Honestly."

"I'm always here if you need to talk. No subject is off the table and it stays between us."

Once or twice Sable had been tempted to spill her guts to Alex. It wasn't easy keeping why she left the Army bottled up and he understood the military and how it worked as well as anyone. But even though she trusted him and knew he would sympathize, she held her tongue. He couldn't fix what happened. No one could.

But Sable didn't think Alex was speaking about her past. He was concerned about the here and now.

"I'm doing the job, Alex."

"I don't doubt it for a second. I'll let you go. But remember. It's okay to let your guard down, Sable. No one will think less of you."

Sable put down the phone. She sat on the edge of the bed, her mind working furiously as she calmly slipped on her shoes. Alex was right. At this point, who was going to care if she enjoyed her time with Colt— guilt free?

One minute she would tell herself sleeping with him was wrong. Unprofessional. The next, she grabbed him and tore his clothes off. Sable waffled between embracing their temporary affair and worrying about it ending.

The facts were simple. She was Colt's bodyguard. At the moment, she was also his lover. Crossing that line hadn't been the end of the world. Crowds weren't gathering with torches and pitchforks. The tar and feathers were nowhere to be seen.

Sable was the one making something out of nothing. Why couldn't she have fun? Tomorrow—the future—was coming no matter what she did. One day soon, she would kiss Colt goodbye and wish him well. She hoped they would part as friends. If she had to deal with a slightly broken heart, so what? She wouldn't be the first or the last woman to live with that affliction. They survived and so would she.

Sable opened the purse. She lay her phone next to her gun which lay next to her lipstick. Three items. Seemingly incongruous. But in her world, they were part of her everyday life.

Sable Ford. Woman. Bodyguard. Friend. Lover. From the outside, the pieces may have seemed odd. But every day she found a way to make them fit.

She had two choices. Pull back and be miserable. Or stop worrying about the future and embrace every moment. Here. Now.

When put like that, there wasn't a choice. Sable wanted to be happy. With Colt.

DINING OUT IN Hollywood often was more about business than pleasure. Executives met to finalize deals. Others sat in trendy restaurants, picking at their overpriced meal, desperate to be noticed. *The Shack* was not the place to go to do either.

The small, family-owned café served rib-sticking fare. It was bright and cheery and filled with loud voices, laughter, and the aroma of spicy tomato sauce. It attracted a working-class crowd. And it was one of Colt's favorite places to eat in the world. He wanted to share it with Sable.

There was no valet service, which suited Colt. Every now and then he liked the challenge of finding a parking space on a crowded Los Angeles street. It took talent and perseverance. Giving in was not an option.

"There was a spot on the last block."

"It wasn't close enough."

"This is the third time you've circled around." Sable watched as they passed another empty parking space.

"That would be giving in." Colt maneuvered the car between a delivery truck and van pulling a horse trailer.

"Giving in to what?"

"The parking Gods. If you show weakness, they won't shine on you. And there." Colt pointed triumphantly at a car pulling away from the curb. "I kept the faith and I was rewarded."

Sable kept her thoughts on the subject to herself. Colt seemed so proud. She didn't want to burst his bubble by pointing out the amount of gasoline they had wasted looking for a parking space that was half a block closer than the one they drove past two loops ago.

Colt neatly parked next to a hulking black SUV and mud-caked Ford pick-up that on better days might have been dark green. The larger vehicles dwarfed his Maserati, but it stood out in any crowd. Colt's car gleamed in the California sunshine. Polished to a bright red perfection.

"Not bad." Colt shifted into park. "What do you think?"

"I think that you are wonderfully weird and absolutely adorable."

Sable leaned over and kissed him and with a hum of pleasure, Colt kissed her back. Slow and easy, she teased his lips with her tongue until he opened for her. On and on. Sable would have gladly skipped lunch if she could stay right here, like this, all afternoon.

"You taste like wild cherries." Colt sucked on her bottom lip then.

"Lifesavers. It's my favorite flavor. Want one?"

"I'm happy sampling you."

Sable was happy letting him. She wound her arms around Colt's neck, her hands sliding into his thick dark hair. She loved touching him. So many textures. Silky hair. Hard muscles. Firm lips that softened perfectly when they kissed. And that bit of scratchy perfection when his cheek rubbed against hers.

"Necking in the front seat of my car. The last time that happened I was a sophomore in high school. All I could think about was trying to talk my date into the backseat."

Sable turned her head, to look at the seat, and give Colt better access.

"This backseat?" There was barely room for a small suitcase. How two full grown teenagers could fit back there, she had no idea.

"I had borrowed my father's Mercedes sedan."

"Ah. How did the evening end?"

"I hate to brag." Colt's lips curved against her neck.

"You love to brag," Sable smiled back. "Go for it."

"I'll say this. That condom in my pocket didn't go to waste."

Sable laughed. She wanted to ask how many young women gave into his adolescent charms but decided she didn't need to know. The number had to be high. Who in their right mind could resist?

"You must have beaten the boys off with a stick. Any backseat shenanigans in your past?"

"Nope."

"That's it? Nope?" With his right hand, Colt linked his fingers with her left one. He brought them to his lips. "Any particular reason?"

Sable watched as Colt lightly kissed the back of her hand, rubbed his lips across her knuckles. It was a surprisingly erotic gesture.

"My mother put the fear of pregnancy in my head from the cradle. I carried around visions of broken condoms and a life of dirty diapers."

"Scary." The more Colt heard about Sable's mother, the more he wondered how she got away without being totally screwed up.

"Scary is putting it mildly. That kind of fear is the best birth control ever invented. I had plans and they didn't include a baby or a husband."

"That meant staying pure until when?"

"I didn't say that I stayed pure." Sable kissed the side of Colt's neck. She liked giving as well as receiving. He always smelled and tasted amazing. "But if you were asking when I lost my virginity? After high school."

"That's vague."

"It's honest. How about you, hot shot?" Sable sent out the challenge. She should have known Colt wouldn't hesitate to pick it up.

"It was summer. We were in London where Mom was shooting a film. She was older and experienced."

"Naturally."

"Laurell was the leading man's daughter. Seventeen and built like a brick shithouse."

"Charming." Sable sat back to listen, but she kept hold of Colt's hand.

"I call them as I see them. And to a fifteen-year-old boy, breasts that size are a dream come true. Not to mention the rest of her."

"The hussy. Did she know she was breaking you in, so to speak?"

"The way I remember it, I was sophisticated and worldly," Colt grinned. "Laurell might have a different tale to tell. Either way, I studied. Putting my nose to the proverbial grindstone. By the end of the summer, I put a smile on her face."

"And she put one on yours. I'd say it was a fair trade."

"Mmm. You never forget your first. And if you're lucky, it's worth remembering."

Colt waited, his eyes locked on hers. Finally, Sable shook her head and gave in.

"Behind the barracks in North Carolina. The mosquitoes were fierce but Jubal Crowe was sweet. We dated for a few months. And yes, it was worth remembering."

"I'm glad." Colt squeezed her hand.

Sable lightly kissed Colt. "Our experiences have been very different."

"Yet they brought us here."

"In the front seat of a Maserati?"

"Together," Colt added.

He pulled her close, deepening the kiss. And bright lights went off in Sable's head.

"Shit."

The lights weren't clicking in her head. They were from the flash of a camera. Three men surrounded the car, furiously taking pictures. One caught Sable just as she turned toward the windshield, making her blink in surprise as the flash momentarily blinded her.

Colt started to get out, but Sable stopped him. It only took a second for her to shake off her role of girlfriend. Bodyguard mode kicked in and she was all business.

"No, Colt. Stay there until I get around the car."

"Hell no. I'm not sitting here while you wrestle your way through a sea of paparazzi."

"Three men isn't a sea. But it doesn't matter. I'm here to protect you."

"You're my girlfriend. Or so they think," Colt added when she would have argued. "How will it look if you open my door and shield me with your body?"

"Like I'm doing my job." But she understood what he meant. "You're right. The chances of this happening were always there. I'll drop my cover. From now on, I'm your bodyguard. Period."

"Fuck that. Buckle up."

Colt started the car and laid his hand on the horn. Startled, the men jumped back, opening a clear path and he took it, quickly merging into traffic. Sable watched in silence as Colt turned down a side street, cut down an alley, then headed back the way they came—toward the loft.

"Lost your appetite?"

"We'll order in."

Colt had a white-knuckle grip on the steering wheel and his jaw was clenched so tightly Sable worried about his teeth. Sable had never seen him react this way. Colt was so easy going, so laid back. This was such a complete one-eighty, it was almost shocking.

"Relax."

Colt took the turn into the garage. He was traveling way too fast and he missed clipping the corner of the building by mere inches. They approached his parking spot at the same pace. She couldn't stop him. And jumping wasn't an option. Taking a deep breath, Sable closed her eyes, gripped the seat, and prepared for impact.

"You can open your eyes.

"Nope."

"The car is stopped. We didn't hit anything. And here." The engine died. "Hold the key. I promise we aren't moving another inch."

Colt pried her fingers loose and put the key in her palm. Carefully, Sable opened her eyes. She looked at the key, then at Colt. His jaw was relaxed but he still vibrated with tension. They were safe.

"What the hell?" Sable slapped the key onto Colt's lap, barely missing the bulge.

"That was too close for comfort."

"If I'd wanted to hit your dick, I would have. Asshole."

Sable unbuckled herself and threw open the door.

"And if I had wanted to hit the wall, I would have." Colt was by her side before she was out of the car. "I was in complete control."

"No, you weren't." Sable shoved him aside. When he grabbed her arm, she froze. "That's a bad idea."

"I'll take my chances."

Amazed at his gall and curious to see how far he would take it, Sable let Colt pull her toward the elevator. That was fine. As soon as they were in the loft, she planned on locking herself in her room. If he wanted to apologize, he would have to do it through the door.

However, Colt didn't stop at the security panel. Instead, he went around the corner to a secluded area out of sight from the rest of the garage. It was dark and dusty and smelled slightly of gasoline.

"I don't know this game, Colt, but I don't want to play. Let go of my arm before you force me to hurt you."

"No games. And nobody gets hurt."

Colt took her mouth with his, pushing her until her back was flush with the wall. This kiss was savage. Primal. Completely different than the sweet, teasing ones they shared in the car less than twenty minutes earlier. Colt put his hand behind her head, cushioning it from the hard brick. The other trapped her wrists, holding them high and out of the way.

For a brief moment, Sable thought about breaking the hold. Colt was strong and he had her at a disadvantage. But it wouldn't take much to have him on his knees. She could grind her heel into his foot. Bite his lip. Knock her forehead against his. Or simply knee him in the groin. They were effective weapons and she was proficient at administering all of them.

But the brief moment passed and all she wanted was to kiss him back.

Colt wasn't thinking about Sable retaliating. His blood pounded and he wanted one thing. To screw her brains out. He felt her body relax. When she began to return his kiss, he let go of her wrists, freeing his hand. Colt reached under her skirt to rip off her panties, but Sable was already there. She slipped them down her legs, kicking them away.

He took care of his belt while Sable unbuttoned his pants. She had his zipper down and his dick out while Colt dug a condom out of his wallet.

"Are you ready?" he panted against her lips.

"Shut up and fuck me."

Sable wrapped one leg around his hip, opening to him. With one clean stroke, Colt buried himself deep. He groaned. She gasped. Their rhythm was awkward, their pace fast—almost desperate. Neither cared about making it last. This was about achieving release, not technique.

It didn't take long. Sable grabbed Colt's butt, urging him on. Their breath was harsh and ragged. A few thrusts of his hips and she soared over the edge, the orgasm hitting her hard and fast. A second later he joined her.

Colt straightened his clothing, watching as Sable smoothed her skirt.

"Are you okay?"

"Yes."

She looked for something. Colt saw what it was and picked up her discarded panties.

"I'm not going to apologize," he said, handing her the garment.

"I'd punch you if you did."

Colt grinned. Damn, she was something. He held out his hand.

"Hungry?"

"Starving."

They walked to the elevator. When the doors opened, they entered, fingers laced. And as they began the ascent, they burst out laughing.

"I COULDN'T EAT another bite."

Sable pushed her plate away.

"I could." Colt took the rest of the sandwich and downed it in one bite. "I love corned beef."

"I never would have guessed."

Colt picked up her plate on his way to the sink. Sable toyed with her napkin, pleating and unpleating the edges. One bare foot swung back and forth. They had eaten at the counter, sitting on the barstools that lined the far side.

They had showered before ordering from the deli just down the street. This time, the sex had been slow—unrushed. But just as passionate. Colt's soap-slickened hand touched every inch of her body. He lingered when he found a spot that he particularly enjoyed. Her breast received most of his attention.

When Sable's breath would catch, telling him he'd found a spot that gave her pleasure, he was just as thorough.

Sable happily took her turn. She stood behind Colt, exploring his strong back, the curve of his spine. The slope of his ass. Then, staying where she was, she ran her hands over his chest and down the hard planes of his stomach. Colt's palms flattened on the wet tile, his head falling back as her fingers gripped his erection.

Slowly, she slid up and down, loving the feel of him. His hard, smooth heat. Sable kissed Colt's shoulder blade. And as he reached his peak, she bit down, leaving her mark as he shot his seed onto the wall.

Without a word, Colt turned and dropped to his knees. His mouth tasted her as water ran over him, making his skin glisten like molten gold. Sable held him close, letting her fingers run through his hair, massaging his scalp as his tongue urged her higher. She came, calling out his name and sinking next to him, her legs no longer able to support her weight.

Colt kissed her cheek, reaching around her to turn off the water. Helping her to her feet, he grabbed a towel and quickly dried her skin. He set the towel on the counter before settling her on it.

Then he did the sexiest thing of all. He took a jar of cream and applied it over her body. When he was finished, Sable felt warm and utterly relaxed.

"Would you like a cup of tea?"

"Please."

Sable smiled. She couldn't fault the view. Colt wore nothing but a pair of Snoopy pajama bottoms that rode low on his hips.

"Where's the top?" she asked.

"There isn't one. I bought these in Aspen. The gift shop at the hotel had all kinds of Peanuts merchandise. Snoopy is my favorite so I couldn't resist."

Colt carried their cups to the sofa. Sable had on a nightshirt made of silk. It was the color of amber honey. She sat, curling her legs underneath her and took a sip of the hot liquid. When Colt was settled beside her, she finally addressed the elephant in the room.

"Want to tell me what happened earlier?"

"I was hoping you would let that slide."

"You frightened me, Colt."

He took her hand. "I never would have hurt you."

"I know that, you fool. You acted completely out of character. I was worried about you, not me."

"I'm sorry." Colt sighed, running a hand through his hair. "I wish I had an answer because, to be honest, my reaction took me by surprise, too.

"Was it the paparazzi?"

"No. I've dealt with them most of my life. They're parasites, but for the most part, harmless. At first, I was angry for letting them find us. As much as I enjoy playing with you in the car, I know better. I should have taken you inside the restaurant as soon as we arrived. Instead, I made us sitting ducks."

"I'm the one who fell down on the job, Colt."

"That's another thing. I didn't like the idea of you putting yourself at risk."

"You said yourself, the photographers were harmless."

"Okay. God." Colt groaned. "I'm not proud of it but my ego got in the way."

Sable frowned. "I don't understand."

"When you were about to get out of the car, I had this flash of how the headlines would read. *Girlfriend shields movie star.*"

"You're kidding."

"I know. I make a big deal of how erroneous publicity doesn't bother me. It turns out I'm not completely immune."

"It was your idea to have a woman bodyguard. What did you think would happen if I actually had to guard your body?"

"I didn't think that far ahead."

Colt looked so distraught. She couldn't help herself. Sable burst out laughing.

"I'm glad you find my feet of clay amusing."

"Please." Sable wiped the moisture from her eyes. "Your feet are fine. You're human, Colton. There's nothing wrong with that. And," she laid a hand on his thigh, "the sex was smoking hot."

"It was," Colt chuckled ruefully. "I can't believe you let me get away with the caveman routine."

"It won't fly very often," Sable warned. Then she grinned. "I guess I was in the mood."

"You certainly were." Colt took her cup and set in on the coffee table. "Think you might be in the mood again?"

"Maybe. But let's use the bed this time."

"Sounds good."

"Colt." Sable held out a hand when he reached for her. "A situation could arise where I have to protect you."

"I know."

"Can you handle it?"

"Honestly? I don't know." Colt shook his head. "I'm sorry. I know it's your job. I know you're trained to put yourself at risk for your client. But in the heat of the moment, I can't guarantee that instinct won't take over. I'm a man."

"Oh, please."

"Evolution only goes so far, Sable. In the heat of the moment, I don't think I could let you shield me."

"You wouldn't have a choice."

"It's a moot point. Nothing is going to happen."

"Colt." Sable sighed.

"Can we let it go?"

"Yes."

Colt took her hand and led her to the bedroom.

Sable would let it go. Not because he was right. But because there wasn't any point in arguing. Her job was to protect Colton Landis. The world thought she was his girlfriend and chances were excellent that when she headed back to Harper Falls, her cover would be intact. However, if the day came that she had to take a punch or a bullet, to keep him safe, she would. Without hesitation.

Chapter Thirteen

SABLE HAD NEVER been grocery shopping in Beverly Hills. If it had been up to her, she never would. Colt decided it would be fun, and no amount of persuasion would sway him. Since she went where Colt went, Sable had no choice.

"I have a list of people who will do this for you. They were vetted and approved. Pick one and let them do their job."

They hadn't arrived at the store. There was no harm in making one more attempt at getting Colt to see reason.

"This will be fun." Colt pulled into the parking lot.

"Have you ever been grocery shopping?"

"Once. Lorena took me when I was a little boy."

"And the experience was so life changing it's taken over twenty years for you to do it again."

Colt found a spot near the store entrance. It seemed the parking Gods were with him today.

"Why are you so opposed to buying a few essentials?"

"Call it bodyguard intuition. You can't go anyplace without drawing a crowd. I have images dancing in my head of me peeling women off you in the middle of the produce department."

"You heard what Mom said. The Beverly Hills *Custom Foods* gets celebrities all the time. No one will give me a second look."

That wasn't exactly what Callie had said. She told them that she shopped at the store. As did several of her friends. The regulars were used to her stopping in for a loaf of bread or a jar of Caleb's favorite olives. No matter how blasé the Beverly Hills consumer, they were not accustomed to glancing up and seeing Colton Landis testing the ripeness of a cantaloupe.

Even in his faded jeans and dark blue t-shirt, Colt did not look like your average shopper. Unless that shopper was over six feet tall with dark wavy hair, bright blue eyes, and had a body that would tempt saints to turn in their halos. If men like that walked the aisles on a regular basis, then yes, they might breeze in and out of the store without incident. Somehow, Sable had her doubts.

"If you fill all of those, where are we going to put it all?"

Colt had borrowed some reusable, environmentally friendly grocery bags from his mother. Sable thought two or three would be plenty. Colt took eight. Just in case.

"The trunk is surprisingly roomy."

Sable couldn't help but grin. He had the enthusiasm of a little boy and it was contagious. If this was how he wanted to spend part of his day off, she would play along. But she wouldn't let her guard down in case a rabid fan hid behind a box of cereal or under the random bag of potatoes.

Fifteen minutes later, Sable realized Colt's fans were not the problem. He had no self-control. Every item was irresistible. Twinkies. Frosted Flakes. Spam.

"What are you going to do with that?" Sable asked when he added a dozen cans to the cart.

"Eat it."

"Have you ever tasted Spam?"

"No." For good measure, he added another can. "Did you know that Hawaii is the number one consumer of Spam? There must be thousands of recipes. I'll look some up when we get home."

Colt wasn't shopping, he was storing up for the apocalypse.

Sable gave him an indulgent smile. Then, while he read the back of a can of Chef Boyardee, she put all but one can back on the shelf. Six boxes of Cap'n Crunch turned into two.

This continued aisle after aisle.

"You will weigh three hundred pounds if you eat all this junk."

"I have a stellar metabolism."

Colt leaned over to get something on the bottom shelf.

"That isn't the only thing that's stellar."

"Are you checking out my ass, Ms. Ford?"

"Of course not." Sable sent him an innocent smile. "And when you put that jar of pigs' feet back, I promise not to check you out again."

"I thought I might get them."

"No. It's like someone was trying to cover up the smell of spoiled meat by splashing it with vinegar."

Colt cringed. He replaced the jar.

"How do you know that?"

"My mother loves them. Grandma Freed sends some every year for Christmas."

"You didn't acquire a taste for them?"

"No," Sable said emphatically. "Mom says it's a southern thing."

"Where was she born?"

"Treetop, Tennessee." Sable shook her head when Colt offered her a sample of apple pie from the bakery counter. "Mom is a walking, talking contradiction. She'll go on for days about how much she hated Treetop. Her goal was to get as far away as possible. She didn't want anything to do with it ever again."

"That's kind of sad."

"I agree. She lost her accent and tells people that she was born in Georgia."

"Why is that better than Tennessee?" Colt took another bite of pie.

"Beats me. Dad calls it Iris logic. Meaning there is no logic at all. And those pigs' feet? She hides them in the back of the cupboard and eats them when she's certain no one will see her. I only know about them because late one night when I was eight, I wandered into the kitchen to get a glass of water. She was at the table stuffing these gelatinous globs into her mouth as fast as possible."

Colt tossed the rest of the pie into a nearby trash can.

"Full?"

"No. You paint quite the picture, Sable. Gelatinous globs?" Colt shuddered. "I've lost my appetite."

"Sorry." Sable hid her smile. That hadn't been her intent when she started the story, but it was a nice bonus. "Are you ready to hit the checkout line?"

"Are you tired of emptying the basket as soon as I fill it?"

"You stinker!" Sable recognized that particular twinkle in Colt's eyes. "You were doing that on purpose."

"Not at first." Laughing, Colt blocked her playful punch to his midsection. He held onto her hand. "After the first few times, I couldn't resist."

"I followed you around for an hour." Sable shook her head. Instead of hitting him, she slid her arms around his waist and squeezed. Hard.

"You should have caught on sooner. Geez, Sable. I'm not a little boy who can't control my impulses."

Sable kissed his neck, breathing in his spicy scent.

"No, you aren't a little boy. Thank you, God. But I'll argue the impulse bit. Your control," she lowered her voice, "outside of sex, is questionable."

"Sable, honey, this is not the place to tease. Let's hit the produce department and head home. I'll give you a sample of my infinite control."

"Sounds like a plan I can get behind."

"I thought I would get behind you."

"And?" She loved when Colt explained in great detail what he was going to do to her. Mental foreplay. It drove her crazy.

"I'll go into detail in the car. Now, tomatoes."

"And apples. You are completely out of apples. What?" Sable asked when she noticed his frown.

"Why do you always make a point of saying *you* instead of *we*?"

"Do I?" Sable wasn't going to pretend she didn't understand. Nor was she going to explain that, for her own piece of mind, she needed to remind herself that she wasn't a permanent part of his life. "It *is* your place."

"Not at the moment."

"It's yours." Sable wouldn't waver. Not on this point. "I'm your employee. And your guest."

"Okay." Colt began pushing the cart. "Come on. Tomatoes and apples." He winked. "And anything else that looks good."

Sable followed, not certain what just happened. Colt never gave in that easily when it mattered to him. Which meant, her status wasn't important. Bodyguard? Friend? Lover? She kept reminding herself that she didn't belong. And it was obvious that Colt agreed.

Wasn't that what she wanted? When it was time to leave, didn't she want the break to be clean, easy, and as painless as possible? Sable felt a lump form in her stomach. Funny how getting her way wasn't always as satisfying as she would think.

Sable saw the movement out of the corner of her eye, followed by a sharp, high-pitched squeal. Both were directed at Colton. Without thought, she positioned herself to ward off the threat. Automatically, her hand reached for the gun in her purse.

"Colton Landis. Oh my gosh, oh my gosh, oh my gosh."

A woman in her fifties reached out to touch Colt, then pulled back her hand at the last second, blushing like a teenager. She shuffled from one foot to the other, her breath coming in large gulps. Dressed in khaki pedal pushers and a bright lime green shirt, she had tourist written all over her. She probably came to Beverly Hills to see some movie stars. Boy, she hit the jackpot.

A fan. Sable relaxed and zipped her purse. She didn't think pointing a gun at a woman whose only weapon was a ballpoint pen would go over well with the store management, the press, or Colt.

From the moment they entered the store, Sable had known a fan attack was a possibility. One quivering, exuberant woman wasn't bad. It could have been worse. As she soon found out.

"Denise. Denise." The woman frantically waved her hand in the air. "Over here. It's Colton Landis."

"OMG!"

Sable cringed. Fan number one's squeal was nothing compared to Denise and her high-pitched screech.

"Dolly! Where did you find him?"

Twins. It had to be. Dolly wore the same pedal pushers and shirt though instead of green, it was an eye-searing neon pink. The women had the same short, round figures and teased out blonde hair. They even bounced from foot to foot with the same disarming twitchy rhythm. Sable hoped it was because they were excited. If they needed to pee, things might get messy.

"Sisters?" Colt asked, giving them his best movie star smile.

"Twins," they answered jointly.

"You don't say? My older brothers are twins."

"We know."

Sable wondered if they always spoke in stereo. Probably. A lifetime habit she doubted they noticed.

With easy grace, Colt accepted the pad and pen that Denise shoved in front of his face.

"Where are you from, Denise?" Colt's smile went from heart pounding to dazzling.

When Colt said her name, it was almost too much for Denise. She fanned herself furiously and giggled.

Sable couldn't blame her. She knew how it felt to be the focus of Colt's attention. She was just an observer and her heartbeat had kicked up a couple of notches.

"Birmingham, Alabama," Dolly answered. Denise tried to roll her tongue back into her mouth.

"Beautiful area. Most of *Sinner's Paradise* was filmed there. What was it? Three years ago?"

"Four. We watched you film the duel."

Colt handed them the autographed pad.

"Did you enjoy the movie?"

"We love all your movies. Colt." Dolly drew out his name, savoring the moment. "Especially your nude scenes. May we get a picture?"

"I insist." Colt took Dolly's phone. "But I'm keeping my clothes on."

As jokes went, it was lame, but Dolly and Denise laughed as if it were the funniest thing they had ever heard. Colt put an arm around each woman and somehow managed to take a selfie at the same time. He handed Dolly the phone. The sisters, still giggling, scampered off. They would have quite a tale to tell when they got home. All because Colt took the time to be charming and kind.

It wasn't an act. Sable watched Colt as he dealt with the sisters. He loved every second. Not because his ego needed petting. Because he liked people. He loved his fans. He didn't hurry them along. He took the time to make them feel special. They adored him before. Now, if Sable was any judge, they worshiped him.

The sisters started the ball rolling. It wasn't a flood. More like a constant trickle. For the next hour, Colt greeted his fans. Signed autographs and posed for pictures.

Sable watched with growing admiration. Colt's enthusiasm never flagged. He didn't hurry them along or count heads, anticipating when he could get away. Each person was treated with the same courtesy and respect. She didn't know how he did it.

"Miss?"

Sable turned. A man wearing a shirt with the store's logo on the front stood to her left. The badge clipped to his shirt pocket read Ben Freedman, Manager.

"Yes?"

"I noticed you earlier. Aren't you with Mr. Landis?"

"That's right. Is this a problem?"

Sable motioned to Colt. There were three people still waiting for autographs. At one point, the line circled around the produce department and the canned foods aisle.

"Not for me." Ben seemed a little uncomfortable. He gripped his hands together, squeezing tightly. "I should have broken it up right away. We get a lot of celebrities. We pride ourselves on giving them a stress-free shopping experience. A place where they can buy their groceries without being mobbed."

"I can see why that would be appealing."

"I was out for lunch when this started. I—"

"Mr. Freedman. Relax." Sable gave the man a reassuring smile. "Look at him. Colt enjoys meeting his fans. No harm done."

"I don't want his mother to be upset."

"What does she have to do with this?"

"I, well," he fidgeted. "She shops here and I wouldn't want to jeopardize that."

Sable hid her smile. Now, she understood. The manager had a crush on Callie Flynn. It was hard to hide and Ben Freedman had all the signs. The telltale flush. The way he stammered. He wasn't worried about losing Callie's business. He was worried he would miss out on seeing her, in the flesh, on a regular basis.

It didn't matter if the name was Landis or Flynn. This family was like catnip to everyone they met.

"Don't worry, Mr. Freedman. Callie understands. Besides, look at Colt. He's having a great time."

As though sensing her attention, Colt looked up from signing his last autograph. His blue eyes brimmed with good humor. When he winked, Sable felt it down to her toes.

The man wasn't catnip. He was hundred-proof whiskey. Dangerous and highly addictive. A woman with an ounce of self-preservation would run for the hills. Sable had always been good at protecting herself. But she wondered if this time she may have met her match.

Chapter Fourteen

"THIS IS CRAZY."

"Not crazy, practical. I won't need another trip to the grocery store for a month."

"Try a year."

"These are staples." Colt added a can of tuna fish to the cupboard. "Now when it's three in the morning and I have a craving for water chestnuts, I'm all set."

"Is that a problem you've run into? Desperate Chinese condiment cravings?"

"No. But it never hurts to be prepared."

"Boy Scout," Sable whispered under her breath.

"I heard that." Colt spun her around. His kiss was sweet and playful. "I'll finish putting these things away. Why don't you pick some music? Something happy."

"I can do that."

Happy sounded good. Right. After Colt's marathon autograph signing session, it took them another forty-five minutes to go through the checkout line, load the groceries into Colt's car, drive to the loft, and lug the bags inside.

Seven bags. Filled to the top. Colt was flushed with success. Sable was amazed.

The success of her efforts to cut down on his purchases was debatable. True, there weren't a dozen cans of Span—only two. And two boxes of Twinkies. And two bags of salted in-shell peanuts. Sable had no idea when Colt had acquired those. Or why he would want them.

Two of everything. Colt Landis. The *Custom Foods* Noah. Sable grinned, listening to him hum as he stocked his kitchen shelves. She wouldn't worry unless he began plans for an ark.

Colt's iPod was hooked up to a state of the art sound system. The bells and whistles would be intimidating to the uninitiated, but Sable had plenty of experience with high-end electronics. Her bosses at H&W were techno-geeks. They were constantly updating anything and everything. If she wasn't savvy before she joined the company, she soon was. Or went crazy. Luckily for Sable, she was a fast learner. She scrolled through several playlists, the titles making her laugh.

Most began with *Songs For.* Songs for a rainy day. Songs for chilling out. Exercising. Dinner party. Seduction. The last one made her pause.

"You need mood music to get a woman into bed?"

"Goddamn, Garrett. He put that on there as a joke. I delete it, but it keeps popping back."

Amused, and intrigued, Sable looked at the titles.

I Changed Her Oil, She Changed My Life. I Wanna Whip Your Cow. I've Got the Hungries For Your Love and I'm Waiting In Your Welfare Line.

"These can't be real."

"They are. Play one."

It was a tough choice. In the end, Sable closed her eyes and did a musical version of pin the tail on the donkey. Her *pin* hit *Bridge Washed Out, I Can't Swim and My Baby's On the Other Side.*

"That might be the god-awfullest song ever recorded."

"At least one of the top five. The rest of the contenders are on that list."

"Garrett had way too much time on his hands. Tell him to get a hobby."

"Tormenting his brothers is his hobby. Want a glass of wine?"

Sable glanced over her shoulder. Colt held up two bottles. One red, one white.

"White, please."

Colt opened a drawer. He rummaged around until he found the corkscrew then deftly opened the bottle.

"These days Jade fills up most of Garrett's free time. But he hasn't given up completely. Last week I received an email inviting me to join the next cast of *Dancing with the Stars*."

"Was it fake?"

"Completely legit." Colt joined her, two glasses in hand. "Garrett had his agent contact the show's producers."

"Were they pissed off when you turned them down?"

"Who said I turned them down?"

Sable took a sip of the cold, fruity wine. Her eyes met his over the rim of the glass. She expected the blue depths to be brimming with humor. There wasn't a trace. Either Colt was serious or he was a damn good actor.

"I can't wait," she said, playing along. "Gold glitter and spray on tan. The ratings will soar."

"It would have been a challenge."

Colt took her glass, setting it with his on the table. With a push of a button, the song changed. The clunky country became smooth, bluesy rock and roll.

"Unfortunately, my schedule wouldn't permit my participation."

"What a shame."

"Mmm." Colt easily swung Sable into his arms. "I told them Garrett would be happy to take my place."

"You didn't."

"No." The teasing glint was back in his blue eyes. "It wouldn't have been fair to the producers. But Garrett didn't know that. I had a friend spread some fake publicity. It gave *Dancing with the Stars* some extra exposure and made Garrett sweat. So, win-win."

"I don't know how your mother survived four boys," Sable laughed, following Colt's strong, sure lead. They danced in a slow, swaying circle.

"Don't let her fool you. Callie Flynn is an instigator. More often than not, she encouraged us."

"Whatever she did, it worked. It's obvious you love your brothers."

"I do." Colt's breath warmly caressed Sable's ear, sending a shiver of pleasure down her spine. "They are my best friends. They have my back. No matter what. This business can eat you up and spit out your bones without a second thought. Family—people who love you unconditionally? There's no substitute for that."

Sable lay her head on Colt's shoulder. Family. She had her mother. That relationship was so complicated it would take a slew of shrinks years to chip away at the source. Sable shuddered at the thought. No thanks. The problem with her father was easy to diagnose. However, unless he agreed to speak to her, the solution was just as impossible.

"You're quiet."

"I was thinking about family."

"Your father?"

Sable nodded. "The movie industry is your family business. The Army is mine. My father was thrilled when I joined up."

"And your mother?"

"Horrified. But resigned. I wasn't able to visit my parents very often. Especially the first year or so. The Army—the soldiers around me, became family. When I quit, I lost them and my father."

"I'm sorry." Colt's arms tightened around her waist.

She loved that Colt didn't ask her to explain. Instinctively, he seemed to understand she wasn't ready. Sable didn't know if that day would ever come. The words always stuck in her throat. Her stomach would churn.

Sable prided herself on her strength. She refused to be a victim. It was why she left the Army. If she had stayed, it would have meant giving into someone else. Someone who used his power to make others bend to his will.

It wasn't a decision she had made lightly. She weighed her options. Considered every avenue open to her. In the end, she walked away. She kept her dignity and her self-respect. But she lost the most important person in her life. Her father.

The song changed. Hearing the first few notes, Sable smiled. It reminded her of when she was a little girl. A good memory and at the moment, exactly what she needed

"*Moondance* is my father's favorite song."

"Would you like me to put on something else?"

"No." Sable held Colt close. "Dad loved vinyl records. He didn't care about material things, but his collection went with us wherever we moved. He had an old portable turntable and the sound was terrible." Sable laughed. "God, I loved it. After dinner, on the nights he was home, he would make us a milkshake. Chocolate. Mom warned that it would give me acne and make me fat, but we didn't listen. She would close the bedroom door and Dad would play Van Morrison. He let me stand on his feet and we danced."

"How old were you?"

"Five? Maybe six? The last time was just before my tenth birthday."

"What happened?"

"Mom." Sable sighed. "She didn't think it looked right."

"A father dancing with his daughter? What's wrong with that?"

"You would have to ask my mother. Or crawl inside her head, and I wouldn't wish that experience on anyone."

As much as she loved and respected her father, Sable never quite forgave him when he didn't put his foot down. Mathias Ford was a born leader of men. However, when it came to his wife, he almost always gave in rather than deal with her. Sable understood. There was no reasoning with Iris. She formed her opinions quickly and they were set in stone.

Still, she wished, just that once, her father would have put his foot down.

"We didn't dance again until the night of my high school graduation. I can't remember the song. Something formal that my mother picked out."

"It wasn't the same." It was a statement, not a question.

"No."

The song faded. Holding her with one arm, Colt picked up her glass and handed it to her.

"I tell you what. Finish that while I cook us dinner."

Sable followed Colt to the kitchen. She sat on a barstool, ready to be entertained.

"FYI? I'm not a big fan of canned ravioli."

"Please. Your doubts wound me."

Colt took a carrot in one hand and a long, dangerous-looking knife in the other. With dazzling skill, he sliced and chopped until there was a pile of small, uniform pieces.

"Impressive," Sable admitted. "But I'm not a rabbit. This woman needs stick to her ribs fare. Why don't we have something delivered?"

"I took a course." Colt opened the refrigerator. "T-bone or Chateaubriand?"

"T-bone."

"Good choice."

"A course?"

"Cooking."

He whipped out an apron that had a big turkey on the front, it read, Butter my balls, *and I'll follow you anywhere*. God, he was adorable.

"I assumed."

"A few years ago I was in negotiations to play a classically trained chef. To prepare, I spent a month at the Cordon Bleu."

"Naturally." Sable sipped her wine. "There are some very good schools in this country."

"True. But they aren't in Paris."

"It's a beautiful city. The food is spectacular."

"You've been?" Colt sliced a pile of mushrooms in record time.

"Join the Army, see the world."

"How does that song go?" He thought for a second. "*I joined the Navy to see the world. But what did I see? I saw the sea. I saw the Atlantic and the Pacific, but the Pacific ain't so terrific, and the Atlantic ain't romantic anymore.*"

168

"Not bad." Sable applauded. Colt had a fine singing voice. And he knew how to sell a song. "Fred Astaire. *Follow the Fleet.*"

It was Colt's turn to be impressed. "Wow. I didn't think you would get that."

"The women I hang out with in Harper Falls are movie fans. Before I moved there, I probably saw one or two movies a year."

Colt gasped in mock horror, making Sable laugh.

"Now, it's more like two or three a week. Sometimes more. They have themed weekend marathons. A few months ago it was Fred and Ginger."

Ever the showman, Colt entertained Sable while he prepared their meal. She was so busy listening and laughing, he was ready to plate the meal in what seemed like record time. In truth, two glasses of wine and forty-five minutes had passed.

"Aren't we eating at the counter?"

"This is the first time I've cooked for you." Colt took two silver candle holders from the cupboard. "First times should always be special."

Sable met his gaze. Colt's lips curved in a slow, sexy smile. She could tell what Colt was thinking because his eyes were so easy to read. And because she was thinking about the same thing. The first time they had sex. Special didn't begin to describe it. She would cherish the memory until the day she died.

Setting out candles on a lace tablecloth with silverware and china was Colt's way of giving her—them—another shared memory. It made her heart ache a little, but Sable refused to dwell on the future and all the things they wouldn't share. She kept telling herself to live in the here and now. And, for the most part, that was what she was doing.

"If you'd asked, I would have set the table." She felt pampered and a little odd, sitting while Colt took care of everything.

"You did your part. You kept me company."

"I watched," Sable corrected, then shook her head. "I don't know how you stayed so calm and focused. No performance anxiety?"

"That's never been a problem for me."

"Thank God," Sable grinned.

Colt leaned over, his mouth covering hers. The kiss was hot and much too brief. "Hold that thought for later."

"You don't know what I was thinking."

"Bet I do. Just as you know what I have on my mind."

Sable swallowed. The blue heat from the look he gave her sent shivers down her spine. It made her hungry for more than food.

"No." Colt backed away. "Dinner," he winked, "then dessert."

"It looks amazing."

Sable brought their glasses to the table. The loft had a designated dining area. It was toward the back, almost hidden from the living room. She was aware of its existence, but until now, they hadn't used it. They either stayed at the counter or used the coffee table and sat on the floor or the sofa.

This was nice for a change. Intimate. Romantic.

Colt seemed to agree. He held her chair out, seating her with a flourish. Not something he did when they ate cold cereal or takeout pizza. The kiss he left on the side of her neck was a nice touch.

The bank of windows let them enjoy the city with their meal. It was beautiful. Perfect.

"Cooking is an art form." Colt refilled their glasses before bringing their plates from the kitchen.

"It's temporary. A painter or a sculptor creates something that potentially will last forever. This, though admittedly beautiful, with be gone in minutes. All that work forgotten."

"I didn't make the meal for the world, or generations to come, to appreciate. I did it for you. Will you forget?"

Sable smiled. "No. Never."

"Then this artist is happy."

The meal lasted more than a few minutes. They lingered. They talked movies and music and art. What they liked. What moved them. What made them laugh. What made them cry.

"The end of *Love Story*. Every time." Colt rolled his eyes. "Come on. Ali MacGraw in the hospital bed? It was the only time I bought Ryan O'Neal except as window dressing. How could that not destroy you?"

"She didn't look sick," Colt exclaimed. "And what disease did she have?"

"Leukemia."

Adamantly, Colt shook his head. "I defy you to find one reference to leukemia. It isn't there."

Sable opened her mouth to argue, then changed course when she realized something.

"How many times have you watched *Love Story*?"

"It only takes one time to see a plot hole that big."

"How many times?"

Sable watched Colt squirm. He fiddled with his napkin. Rearranged his knife and fork. Took a sip of wine. Her gaze didn't waver. She knew the second she won. Colt didn't prevaricate when he looked her directly in the eyes.

"Six times. But," he added when she laughed, "In my defense, it's one of Mom's favorite movies."

"I see. You poor baby." Sable patted his hand with mock sympathy. "She strapped you down and forced you to watch it with her? Should I call Child Services?"

"Smart. Ass."

"*Love Story*. Lover."

Colt held out a few moments longer. Then he grinned. The full-on smile that made her heart beat a little faster.

"Guilty." With a sigh, he threw his hands up in surrender. "When I was ten, Ali MacGraw was my dream girl."

"That's sweet." Tongue firmly in cheek, Sable asked, "How old were you when you discovered big breasts?"

Colt didn't dispute her statement.

"Remember the girl I told you about? The one I talked into the backseat of my dad's car?"

"I do."

How could she forget? The teasing in the car. The paparazzi. The wild sex in the garage. It made her smile. It always would. Colt returned her smile. Another shared memory. The list grew on a daily basis.

"She had large breasts."

"Men and mammary glands. It's a mystery."

"We're simple creatures, Sable. I like women's breasts. Big, small, and everything in between." Colt's eyes lowered to her chest. "I've become particularly fond of yours."

"The in-between variety?" Sable teased.

"Perfect." Colt licked his lips. "Ready for dessert?"

With studied calm, Sable dabbed her mouth with her napkin. She kept her eyes down, hiding the spark of interest. "Dinner was delicious. And filling. I couldn't eat another bite."

"I had something non-caloric in mind."

"Sugar-free?" Sable wrinkled her nose.

"But very, very sweet." Colt pushed his chair back from the table. His deep blue eyes teased, the heat in them building.

The sound Sable made was somewhere between a laugh and a gasp. He wanted to play? She couldn't have eaten another bite—but her mouth watered. She stood, backing away. She didn't turn. Or run. However, she maintained a fair distance between them. If Colt wanted her, he would need to put some effort into it.

"It was a heavy meal, Colt. I wouldn't want you to get a cramp."

"We won't go swimming."

Colt stalked her. Sable couldn't think of a better word to describe his movements. Slow. Relentless. His gaze never wavered. She was his willing prey. Nowhere to hide. But plenty of room to evade.

Sable began by putting the sofa between them.

"Tell me what you have in mind. I may not be in the mood."

Colt raised one eyebrow. *So that's how you want to play this? A little cat and mouse? Fine. I don't mind. In the end, we both get what we want. We both win.* It was an extremely expressive eyebrow.

"The longer you tease, the more I'll have to pay you back."

"Is that a threat?" If it were, he would have to do better. Sable liked his form of retribution.

"A promise." Colt's eyes narrowed, a sure sign he meant business. "Take off your shirt and I'll go easy on you."

Sable had never heard a better argument for staying fully clothed. Easy? No thanks. She wanted everything he had to give. The harder and more intense, the better.

"You first."

Colt's shirt flew through the air before Sable could blink. Then she didn't want to. No one in their right mind would close their eyes if it meant they would miss a second of the view he presented.

"I didn't say anything about your pants."

"It will save time," Colt reasoned. He sent his jeans in the same direction as his shirt. "I'll be naked when I catch you so I can concentrate on ripping off your clothes."

"Rip?"

Sable ran a finger down the buttons of the silk blouse. She was fond of her wardrobe. Technically the items didn't belong to her, but that didn't mean she was careless in her treatment of them. If she removed it from a hanger in the morning, it was replaced that evening—with gratitude. Almost reverence.

It wouldn't be right to let Colt destroy a single item. No matter how good the cause.

"There you go." Colt nodded when Sable slowly unbuttoned her shirt. "Cooperation is always appreciated."

"I'm doing it for you, you idiot. This is silk."

"So?"

"You don't rip silk."

"I do." Colt fainted right, faking a move in her direction. "But if you hurry, I'll have mercy. The worms will not have toiled in vain."

"Did I say idiot? Correction. You, Colton Landis, are a first class asshole."

"First class?" Colt folded his arms over his puffed out chest. "Thank you."

"First class *asshole*."

"Eh?" He cupped a hand to his ear. "I didn't hear that last bit."

Sable neatly folded the blouse and set it on the arm of the sofa. Next, she unzipped her black jeans and shimmied them down her legs.

A few moments later, they sat next to the blouse. She wore two small scraps of lace. Pale pink. Feet planted firmly, hands on her hips, she faced Colt.

"Ass. Hole. Still can't hear me? Come closer. I dare you."

"Jesus. My own warrior princess." Colt hissed the words, his breathing harsh. "You are the sexiest woman I have ever seen."

"Take me down and you can have me." Sable circled him. She crouched slightly, preparing for battle. "Any thing. Any way. But you have to beat me to get it."

Colt's eyes flared with desire. The deepest, brightest blue Sable had ever seen. The determination she saw written on his face took her breath away. He wanted her.

"More than my next breath."

Sable didn't question how he read her mind. She knew what he was thinking. It made perfect sense that he could return the favor.

"I won't let you win."

Colt's stance mimicked hers. His smile slowly widened. "I wouldn't have it any other way."

Chapter Fifteen

SABLE OPENED HER eyes. She didn't want to do it. *Keep them closed. You're warm. Relaxed. Half asleep. Colt's arms are wrapped around your waist, holding you close. There is no place on Earth you would rather be.*

Instincts were great. Sable followed hers more often than not. But habit ruled. The light on her phone flashed. The slight buzz woke her and there was no going back until she checked to see who was texting her at two in the morning.

Colt was sound asleep. One glance told her he was out for the count. Nothing short of an earthquake, or a blow job would wake him. On second thought, nix the blow job. Been there, enjoyed that.

She came out on top of their little skirmish. But they both won the battle. They started in the living room. Then the hallway. Then up against the door. When they finally hit the bed, Sable happily let Colt take the lead. His stamina amazed her. The hell with that little blue pill. Pharmaceutical companies would kill for whatever magic flowed in his blood. On the open market, it would be worth billions. Alone in this bedroom, it was priceless.

For a brief second, Sable considered ignoring the text. Colt was worn out and so was she. They had a few more hours before he was due on the set. The idea of spending them sleeping in his arms sounded like heaven. Then she glanced at the screen and froze.

Sable checked it again. No, her eyes weren't deceiving her. Heart racing, she carefully eased away from Colt and slid out of bed. She grabbed the first thing in sight, Colt's shirt, covered herself, and quietly padded to the door. She took a glance behind her to make certain Colt hadn't stirred. Her heartbeat pounded in her ears. It wasn't loud. It was cacophonous. Like cymbals crashing against her head. She wondered how Colt slept through it.

Dad.

Sable feared the word would suddenly disappear. An illusion. A trick. But there it was. Finally. After almost two years, her father had gotten in touch. She had hoped for a phone call, but at this point, she would take whatever she could get.

Sable's hand shook. Deep breaths. Calm. That didn't work. Instead, she gripped the phone and hit the screen. Any hopes she had for a reconciliation were dashed after she read the first sentence.

What are you doing with your life?

Sable closed her eyes. She should have known better. Her father would have called if he wanted to speak to her. This was another condemnation. Cold. Emotionless. He delivered the blow in a text because he couldn't bear to hear her voice or see her face. And it sliced right at her heart.

Taking another breath, Sable forced herself to read the rest of the message.

You left the Army. Your career. There was no explanation and you refused to listen to reason. A bodyguard to the rich and pampered? That was bad. But this? Your mother tells me you've moved in with this movie star. He's paying your bills? Making you the butt of jokes all over the base. I can't ignore it because I'm not allowed to. The pictures. The gossip. I repeat. Where is the young woman who dreamed of impacting the world in a positive manner? Think long and hard, Sable. I repeat. What are you doing with your life?

Carefully, Sable set the phone on the coffee table. There was no need to read the message again. The words were stamped on her brain. Hard and with deliberation. Her hands were no longer shaking. She didn't want to cry. In truth, she felt nothing.

Once, when Sable told her father that she was resigning from the Army, he asked her why. And for the first time in her life, she lied to him. It hurt, but the truth would have hurt him more. It hadn't occurred to her at the time that the day she told her lie would be the last time she saw him. All she could see was the disappointment etched on his face.

Would it be different if she had told him the truth? Sable didn't know. At the time, it seemed like the only thing to do.

Mathias Ford loved three things. His daughter, his country, and the Army. The Army came first. He showed his loyalty to his country by doing his job to the best of his ability—and beyond. Sable understood that. And she respected it. After all, it wasn't simply his career. It was his life. Before Sable understood what it meant, she witnessed the sacrifices her father made to do his duty. He couldn't understand walking away.

Because Sable loved him more than anything. Because she refused to be responsible for putting a crack, no matter how small, in his absolute faith that the Army was always right, Sable kept her secret.

With a sigh, Sable leaned back. She rested her head against the sofa and closed her eyes. Was she wrong? A seed of doubt crept past her staunch belief in her decision.

Since the day she left, Sable had refused to rehash the series of events that led up to her decision not to re-up and hand in her resignation. Why put herself through the pain of remembering all the dirty details? What good would it do?

Tonight, she needed to rethink it all. For her peace of mind. And to figure out her next move. Should she let the past stay buried? Unless he had a drastic change of heart, that meant a life without her father. If she spoke out, would he believe her? Or would his faith in the infallible Army be so strong, he would throw her words—her accusations—back in her face.

Sable needed to make a decision. She let her mind wander. Back. To where it began.

THREE YEARS AGO

"THEY SAY HE'S tough but fair."

"We can't ask for more than that."

Sable high-fived her friend and fellow soldier, Doreen Mayfield. The other woman was five inches shorter, had bright blonde hair and was built like a playboy bunny. But as she said on the day they met, *Don't let my looks fool you. I'm a tough bitch with eyes in the back of my head.*

They hit it off immediately. Their backgrounds were as different as could be. Sable grew up an Army brat. Doreen came from old New England money. Debutante balls and tea sandwiches. Doreen shuddered when she spoke of it. She joined the Army as an act of rebellion. To her surprise, she found her vocation. Their jobs threw them together. The love and pride they found doing those jobs bound them as sisters.

After an intense workout, they had cleaned up and were dressing for a much-needed evening out. Maneuvers had kept them on the base for the last month. Tonight it was time to let loose.

Gossip ran rampant at the best of times, the arrival of a new C.O. amped the stakes. They were all curious who would be replacing Colonel Maxwell. He had run Camp Allenby with a firm hand. But if a soldier had a problem, his door was always open. It was easy to celebrate his promotion to adjutant general. It was a huge honor and no one deserved it more. But they were anxious for any news about the colonel's replacement.

The locker room buzzed with movement and conversation. It wasn't a large group. Of the four thousand plus soldiers on base, only a fraction of them were women. The Army did its best to make everything co-ed. The more the sexes mingled, the less friction when they worked side by side. The theory worked—for the most part. That afternoon the weight room had a ratio of about six-to-one, men to women.

Naturally, the post-shower conversation rolled around to the new C.O., Colonel Baker Montgomery. Sable imagined it was the same on the men's side.

"He's old Army. Married. Two sons, both at West Point."

Geri Frain worked in the administration office. The brunette was a whiz on the computer but as a soldier, she was expected to stay in shape and liked to work out with Sable and Doreen. She wasn't privy to personnel files but she kept her ears open. Geri liked nothing more than getting the scoop before anyone else. Except passing it along to a rapt audience.

"He and his wife arrived sometime yesterday. There will be a big *Meet the C.O.* assembly tomorrow morning. The meet and greet, cocktails and hors d'oeuvres, is scheduled for next week."

"Think your pops will come?"

"If he can."

Sable didn't try to hide the fact that her father was an Army colonel. What would be the point? Nothing remained a secret for long.

On the day she enlisted, her father made it clear that he was just that—her father. But once she donned her uniform, he was her superior and he would not give her special treatment. If she had a problem, he expected her to handle it through the proper channels. There was a chain of command and it didn't include her father.

In three short years, she had risen from private to corporal. As far as she was concerned, the sky was the limit. But she would get there on her own merit, or not at all. And that was the way she wanted it.

"Drinks at *Shooters*?" Sable called out to the room. The invitation was open to anyone who could make it. It was more fun with a crowd.

"I'm in." Geri buttoned her jacket. "Can I get a ride with you?"

"Sure. Six thirty at the gate." Sable picked up her duffle bag, slinging it over her shoulder. "Doreen's boyfriend is chauffeuring us there and back, so we don't have to worry about a designated driver."

"God, Doreen. You are so lucky to have a steady guy. I'm so horny Hillbilly Will is starting to look good."

"He's an MP," Doreen pointed out.

"And *loves* to brag. I don't care about the size of his sidearm."

"From what I hear, it's a tiny caliber and goes off without any warning."

"Poor Will," Sable said.

Doreen and Geri looked at Sable. A second later, the three women burst out laughing. You learned fast in the Army, or you didn't survive. Near the top of the list, especially for a woman? Watch out for would-be players. Men like Hillbilly Will thought that female soldiers were there for one reason. To hit on. He expected them to fall on their backs, grateful for the opportunity.

Men like Hillbilly Will did not represent the majority. However, they were often a vocal minority. The best way to handle it was to stay as far away as possible. And laugh. God, if one didn't have a sense of humor, Army life could be brutal.

"When do you think we will get our orders to redeploy?"

"Soon." Sable held the door for Doreen and Geri.

"Afghanistan?"

"That would be my guess."

"I don't know how you do it." Geri's job kept her in an office hooked to a computer.

"What? The dirt? The heat? Crapping behind a rock? Who would turn down that kind of glamour?"

Sable chuckled. Doreen had hit it on the head. Add dehydrated food rations and bugs the size of her fist, and it got better and better.

"I meant the bombs and bullets. I joined the Army because I didn't want to spend the rest of my life in Humble, Missouri." Geri pushed back a stray strand of dark brown hair. "I've seen a nice chunk of the world and I hope to see more. But when I signed those enlistment papers, it was with the express understanding I would never see combat. I admire your bravery."

"Hell. We aren't brave. We're stupid as posts." Doreen winked at Sable. "Why else would we ruin our manicures cleaning guns? If I had half a brain, I would be married to a very rich lawyer. I could spend my days lounging by a pool with a drink in one hand and the gardener in the other."

Sable's eyes sparkled with humor. She knew her part in this routine. When Doreen started waxing on about what could have been, Sable's job was to play straight woman.

"What about your husband?" she asked, her tongue planted firmly in her cheek.

"He would be too busy with his secretary to worry about my extra-curricular activities. We would meet up once a week at the in-laws for cocktails—there are always cocktails—and perhaps in a few years, I would pop out an heir. Ah, the good life."

It was Geri's first time hearing Doreen's patter, but she had no problem playing along.

"If you had all that to look forward to, why are you here?"

"I joined for the waters."

"Waters?" Sable frowned, clearly puzzled. "What waters? Afghanistan is in the desert."

"I was misinformed," Doreen said, using her best Humphrey Bogart deadpan.

"Oh, my God." Geri looked between Sable and Doreen, her brown eyes wide with admiration. "Casablanca, right? I love that movie."

"How many times did we watch it during basic training?"

"Too many." Sable rolled her eyes.

"Perhaps I was a bit obsessed," Doreen conceded. "You were a good friend to sit through it over and over again."

"It's a good flick. Besides, now you owe me. When I collect, it will make it worth all those, *here's looking at you kids*."

"Name it and I'll pay. But for now?" Doreen slung an arm over Sable's shoulders, then did the same to Geri. "Drinks. The first round is on me."

THE MUSIC WAS loud and the alcohol flowed freely. Sable and her friends made the most of their night off.

The number of bodies at their table ebbed and flowed throughout the evening. At the moment, six women laughed and yelled over the music. They danced when the mood hit them, not waiting to find a partner. It wasn't that kind of evening.

They moved around the other bodies, letting the pounding beat, and a few drinks, help them relax. Tonight was about forgetting their responsibilities back on the base. They weren't worried about their next deployment or keeping their country safe. It was all about the booze and the pounding beat.

A few of them, Geri included, looked to pick up a local hottie for an unencumbered one-night stand. But most of them simply wanted to have fun. That meant shots, laughs, and good company.

Sable made her way across the crowded room. It was her turn to buy a round and their server was missing in action. The area around the bar was three bodies deep, but she was good at slipping through tight spots. A push here, an elbow there and she was at the bar, right in front of the bartender.

He looked a little like Tom Cruise in *Cocktail*. Taller. Tattoos circled both muscular arms. And his skin was a rich chocolate brown. But he sported the leather vest and his moves were smooth. Bottles flew, spinning in the air and caught nearly behind his back. *A gorgeous man putting on a show.* Very nice.

"I need four drafts and two shots of tequila."

"And I need four more hands. Wait your turn, honey."

"No hurry. I like the view."

The bartender sent her an impatient glance. He must have women hitting on him all the time. But when he looked at her, his gold-flecked eyes warmed. It seemed she wasn't the only one who liked what she saw.

"Hello."

His voice was like warm, thick honey. And his smile. Wasn't this ironic? She hadn't met a man who interested her in a long time. Her last relationship had left a sour taste in her mouth and she didn't do one-night stands. But, oh, brother. She could feel temptation sitting on her shoulder.

"Hi. Four beers and two shots of tequila."

"Coming right up."

"Hey," a man called out. "I was here first."

"But you're ugly."

"So?"

The bartender gave Sable a knowing smile.

"So, I would rather look at this beautiful lady's smile. Shut your mouth and I'll get to you when I get to you."

"Here you go."

"You're fast." Sable handed him some money.

"At some things. I can be nice and slow when I want to be. Why don't you meet me after this place closes and I'll prove it?"

"Sorry." Sable picked up the tray of drinks. She sighed and shook her head. "Not tonight."

"When?"

"Will you be around in six or seven months?"

"Probably not. I move around a lot."

"Me too."

Their eyes met. Sable felt a twinge of regret and saw it mirrored in his. She headed back to her friends without asking his name. What was the point? But it had been a nice moment. All the women jockeying for his attention and he noticed her.

Sable spent her days playing down her femininity. In the Army, she was a soldier—not a woman. Having a sexy man notice her—hit on her—was a great ego booster. Hopefully, it would last her until she returned from her next deployment. If he were still around? She might take him up on his offer.

"We wondered if you were coming back." Doreen took her beer. "That crowd eats people up. See?" She pointed out two empty seats. "They danced away with a couple of townies and haven't returned."

"It wasn't the crowd that got them. It was lust," Geri said. She licked the salt off the back of her hand before downing her tequila. "Speaking of which. There's a tall hunk who's been giving me a come-hither look all evening."

"Come hither?" Sable craned her neck to the left. A tall blonde who barely looked old enough to shave walked toward them. "Cute."

"Mmm. I'll settle for that." Geri grabbed her purse. "Don't wait up, girls."

"Why do I suddenly feel old?"

"Because you have a good man waiting for your call. Last year that would have been you."

"Unfortunately, you're right." Doreen frowned at the thought. Then she smiled. Thank God for Robbie. He's saved me from sad one-night stands."

"Not to mention the next morning's walk of shame."

"Two things you wisely avoid."

Sable sipped her beer. She was no sainted virgin. She avoided pickups but she had made a few mistakes. Her one consolation was that she had never fallen in love. For her, it didn't go with the uniform. Or her ambitions.

"Would you like to dance?"

The man was handsome. Older than Sable went for but the gray in his short hair would qualify him as a *silver fox*. He dressed casually. Jeans and a polo shirt. His arms were muscled and there was no visible paunch when he bent over. Not bad. But he wasn't her type. Not tonight or any night.

"No, thank you." The smile Sable gave him was the opposite of the one she shared with the bartender. "I'm here for a few drinks. Nothing more."

The man rubbed Sable's arm. "I bet I can change your mind."

Sable's smile quickly morphed from pleasant to feral. "Bet you can't."

"Listen, fella." Doreen recognized the look in Sable's eyes. "My friend doesn't like to be touched by strangers. Take your hand away. Unless you want to lose the use of it for a couple of weeks."

Sable didn't think the man was going to heed Doreen's warning. Briefly, his fingers tightened, as did the line of his mouth. She could tell he wasn't a man used to hearing no. She tugged at her arm, hoping he would be smart enough to let go. Again, he tightened his grip, but only for a second. He dropped his hand and straightened, his lips curving slightly. But his eyes stayed cool.

"Perhaps another time."

Sable didn't watch as he disappeared into the crowd. *Not in this or any other lifetime.*

"Thank God he came to his senses," Doreen said with feeling. "The last thing we need is to scuffle with a townie on the eve of our new C.O.'s arrival."

"Amen." Sable drained her beer in two gulps.

"Time for another?"

"Mmm. But this time, make it the hard stuff."

"A tray of shots, coming up."

"YOU DRANK AS much as I did. More. Why aren't you writhing in pain?"

"I was blessed with a stellar metabolism."

"I hate you."

Sable took pity on Doreen and handed her a steaming cup of black coffee. It was seven o'clock. A late start on most mornings. But the assembly introducing the new commanding officer pushed everything back. Instead of their usual duties, they were in the mess, grabbing a quick breakfast. Well, Sable ate. Doreen had her elbows on the table and her head cupped in her hands.

"You hate me this morning. And I don't blame you. But you'll love me this afternoon."

"Why?" The sound Doreen made was more of a groan than a growl.

"I switched places with you on the duty roster."

"You mean...?" Doreen's bloodshot eyes lit with hope.

"That's right. I will be teaching the self-defense class while you take care of housing inventory."

"If I could move without making my head explode, I would kiss you."

Sable laughed. "I'll take a raincheck. Drink up. We're due at the compound in fifteen minutes."

SABLE STOOD AT ease, feet shoulder-width apart, hands clasped behind her back, along with most of the troops stationed at Camp Allenby. They were dressed the same. Everyday gear, clean and neat as a pin. There were a few murmured conversations as they awaited Colonel Montgomery.

"How are you holding up?" Sable glanced at Doreen. Her color was better. Less green.

"I'll live. A handful of aspirin and a gallon of coffee made all the difference."

"A gallon?" Sable gave a low whistle. "How's your bladder holding up?"

"Why did you have to bring that up?"

"What are friends for?"

"I give you—"

"Attention!"

As one, the unit dropped their casual stance. Head up. Shoulders back. Chest out. No one spoke, their eyes pinned on the platform.

The second in command, Captain Todd looked over the troops. Satisfied with what he saw, he began.

"Soldiers. It is my pleasure to introduce your new commanding officer. Colonel Baker Montgomery."

Sable's training and iron will were the only things that kept her from reacting. Holy shit! What were the odds? The idiot who had hit on her the night before was the new C.O.

IT TOOK TWO days, but Sable wasn't surprised when the order came calling her to Colonel Montgomery's office.

"He can't know it was you," Doreen reasoned.

"He knows."

"How?"

Sable hadn't told Doreen. At the end of the assembly, just before they were dismissed, Colonel Montgomery looked at her. It was only for a second but it sent a chill racing down her spine.

"It was bound to happen." Sable checked her uniform. "It's better to get it out of the way. Hopefully, he'll turn out to be reasonable."

"What are the chances of that?"

"In this *man's* Army? Not great."

Sable waited in the outer office, her cap in her hand. She didn't sit or pace. Her face was calm, portraying not a flicker of emotion. But inside, her heart raced and she had a vague desire to vomit.

"The colonel will see you now."

Sable entered the office. It looked the same as when Colonel Maxwell occupied it. The man behind the desk had his head down, reading. She stood at attention. The energy felt different. Of course, this was the first time she visited feeling nervous and uncertain. Her relationship with her former C.O. had been one of mutual respect.

She didn't know this man, but because of the bar incident, she was afraid things were going to be very different around here. At least for her.

Finally, the colonel looked up. Sable didn't meet his gaze. But as the seconds passed without a word, she felt that chill again. It traveled from her spine to the rest of her body.

"Corporal Ford?"

"Sir."

Sable raised her hand to salute. Again, he made her wait. She knew what he was doing. It was a power game. He wanted to remind her at every turn that her future was his to manipulate. It gave her insight into the man and the kind of C.O. he would be. Colonel Baker Montgomery was a petty dick. And she was stuck with him.

Intimidation didn't work with Sable. She kept her expression blank and her thoughts to herself. Colonel Baker wanted to play games? Fine. Let him. She could stand there all day if need be.

Finally, he snapped off a return salute.

"At ease." He opened a file. "You have an impressive record. Top marks from basic training to your first deployment and everything after."

"I do my duty, sir."

"So it would seem." He closed the file, neatly setting it aside. His desk was immaculate. Nothing the slightest out of place. "Tell me, Corporal. How long until you're on your knees?"

"Sir?" Sable had no idea what he was talking about.

"According to the notes Colonel Maxwell left behind, you're up for promotion. In fact, his last official act before handing over command was to sign the papers."

Sable blinked. She hadn't known. But it was gratifying to know her hard work and dedication had paid off. She had taken another step. And she planned to take many more before her career ended.

"Sergeant First Class. What did you do to earn it? Interesting. Why you?"

"I hope Colonel Maxwell appreciated the job I did under his command."

"Interesting choice of words," Montgomery sneered. "Job? Hand or blow?"

"No, sir." Outraged at the suggestion, Sable's shoulders straightened. "My relationship with the colonel was completely above board."

"Don't give me that. I watched you last night. The way you came on to that guy. You like your men with some color? Colonel Maxwell? The black stud behind the bar? All I wanted was a dance. But I guess my skin was too white."

Sable took long, steady breaths trying to calm her racing heart. Jesus. It was unbelievable. Montgomery was a sexist and a racist. It was like being in combat. The next bombshell was going to fall. It was inevitable. You could only brace yourself and hope for the best.

"I can't stop your promotion."

Sable kept her eyes glued to a spot over Montgomery's shoulder. A small bug climbing up the window. Valiantly, the creature gained a few inches only to lose its grip and slide down, farther than where it began. It kept trying, but it wasn't intelligent enough to understand that forces were at work against it. Unless it changed course, it would never reach its goal.

Sable was smarter than the bug. But changing course wasn't an option for her. Montgomery had her career in his hands. He could lift her up, or squish her into oblivion. He knew it and so did she.

"It's easy, Corporal. You treat me right, and you'll have those lieutenant bars in no time."

"And if I'd rather not?" Sable gritted out. "Sir?"

"Enjoy life as a sergeant."

THE ARMY WAITED for no man—or woman. Sable's unit received their orders three days later, effectively putting her problem with Colonel Montgomery on the back burner.

"Maybe he'll drop dead. A man his age? His heart could go like that." Doreen snapped her fingers.

"He's only fifty-six and in good shape. But a heart attack *would* be a convenient solution."

Sable had considered keeping the details of her meeting to herself. Involving her friend meant endangering Doreen's career as well as her own. But she had to talk to someone or go crazy.

Doreen looked around. No one was in earshot, but to be safe, she wisely lowered her voice. "I'd like to castrate the bastard and hang his balls out for the buzzards."

"God, I love you, Doreen."

Doreen hadn't doubted Sable's word. Not for a second. She listened, her face a mask of increasing horror. As women in a man's world, they had experienced minor harassments. But this was so far over the line you wouldn't be able to find it with the Hubble Space Telescope.

"I need to focus on the task at hand." Sable zipped her duffle. "Montgomery isn't going anywhere, but we are."

"Afghanistan."

"Six months. By the time we get back, I have to have a game plan."

"We'll figure something out."

Sable hoped so. Beyond giving in to his demands, her options were limited. She could report him. The chances of winning a he said/she said battle with her superior officer were zero. Her career would effectively be over. Or she could turn him down flat. The results would be the same.

Another solution slipped in and out of her subconscious. One she didn't want to consider. The last resort that she wouldn't think about unless all else failed. Sable couldn't imagine a life outside the Army. Hopefully, she wouldn't have to.

SIX MONTHS LATER

THE BASE LOOKED the same but everything had changed.

"Welcome home!"

A group of wives, husbands, and sweethearts greeted them as they left the bus. Reunions were exuberant, especially after a six-month deployment. Kisses. Hugs. And buckets of joyful tears.

There was never anyone there to welcome Sable home but she always enjoyed the show. Getting home in one piece was a victory worth celebrating. Even secondhand.

"Sable? Sable!"

A pair of arms enfolded Sable, the grip tight—almost desperate. She heard weeping. *God, please no.* The last thing she wanted was more tears. Hers or anyone else's.

"I couldn't believe it." Geri wiped at her cheeks but didn't let Sable go. "When word reached us last month, I was certain it had to be a mistake."

"There was no mistake."

Sable remained stiff and unresponsive. She held herself and her emotions in check. If she gave in, she was afraid she would break into a million unmendable pieces.

"I keep asking myself why. Why Doreen?"

"The risk is part of the job."

Sable grew up hearing those words. From her father. From fellow soldiers. She had lost count of the times she had said them. It was an easy way to justify the unjustifiable. They rolled off her tongue with little thought. But this time, she could barely spit out the phrase. It left her throat dry and her tongue felt like it was coated with sawdust.

"You look worn out. No wonder." Geri blew her nose. "Come to my place. I have an unopened bottle of pure Kentucky bourbon. We'll break the seal, drink to Doreen, and get shitfaced."

"Another time. I have an appointment."

"Already? You just got back."

"It was scheduled before I left."

Sable left Geri gaping at her retreating figure. The world had changed while she was in Afghanistan. It changed the day Doreen and six other soldiers didn't return from a routine patrol. The roadside bomb that took out their truck didn't leave much behind to identify. But there was no mistake.

Doreen was dead. No more delays. No more games. It was time to end this. Once and for all.

"I don't have you in my book, Sergeant Ford." A dark-haired, bespeckled man who appeared to be in his late twenties gave her a sympathetic look. It was the same one she had received on the way over here every time she passed a fellow soldier. It was a tight-knit community. They knew that she and Doreen had been close. "Is the colonel expecting you?"

"No."

Sable reminded herself that the corporal was only doing his job. And that she was a soldier. There was protocol to be followed at all times. She couldn't punch out the corporal or barge into Montgomery's office, no matter how satisfying it would be.

"Please tell him I would appreciate a few minutes of his time." Sable plastered on a fake smile. "I'll wait. Or come back whenever he's free."

"I can't guarantee anything." He picked up a stack of papers. "Let me see what I can do."

Sable paced the outer office. Her uniform was dusty and a coating of dried sweat covered her body. She didn't exactly smell like a rose. And she didn't give a damn.

Another time, she would have showered and changed. Perhaps waiting a day or two for this inevitable confrontation. But her temper was on a low but steady burn. It began six months ago. The death of her best friend only added to the flame.

"Colonel Montgomery will see you now, Sergeant Ford."

"Thank you."

"Welcome back, Sergeant." Montgomery looked her up and down. "Never again enter this office looking like that. Understood? Good Lord, you smell like a locker room. Worse."

"I wanted to settle things immediately, Colonel. There wasn't time to get cleaned up."

"There is always time." He wrinkled his nose. "Stand back."

Ever the good soldier, Sable moved two paces to the rear.

"Don't get me wrong. I'm glad you're anxious to see me. But you won't be touching me until you've showered. And a light perfume. Something spicy."

"No." Sable gritted her teeth. It caught in her throat but she pushed the word out. "Sir."

"I beg your pardon?"

Sable was certain it wasn't a word he heard often. It made her sick to think of how many women he had forced into this untenable situation. How many caved under the pressure? She refused to think of how many would come after. Right now, she had to think about herself. Her survival. Because no one else would.

"I came here to find out one thing. If you had changed your mind—your terms. I see now that you haven't."

"Don't be a fool. I can give you everything you want. A future with no limits."

"At what price?"

"Women fall to their knees every day, Ford. It's natural. You were made to service a man. Many men. Be grateful that I'm willing to reward you for it," Montgomery sneered. His attractive features morphing into a living, breathing embodiment of the devil.

Behind her back, Sable's hands clenched and unclenched. The urge to wipe the grotesquely smug expression from his face was almost too much. But she respected the uniform, if not the man. Perhaps another time and another place. But not today.

Without a word, she pulled some papers from her back pocket. Calmly, she handed them to him.

"What's this?"

"The term of my enlistment ends on Friday. I will not be re-upping."

Montgomery read the papers, tapping his fingers on the desk.

"Does Colonel Ford know about your decision?"

Sable hadn't expected the colonel to bring up her father. It took a lot of nerve. Even for him.

"It has nothing to do with him."

"No." He sat back in his chair, his eyes cool. "It's best for everyone that it stays that way."

The threat was clear. There was more at stake here than Sable's career. A scandal would have far-reaching effects. All the way to her father. It was the only thing that kept her silent. If it were only about her, Sable would have pressed charges—damn the consequences. But nothing—not even the satisfaction of putting a stain on Colonel Baker Montgomery's record—would make her endanger what her father had worked so hard to build.

"May I be dismissed? Sir?"

"You're a fool, Sergeant Ford."

"If you say so. Sir."

Again, Montgomery's eyes narrowed. He couldn't call her out on insubordination. But that little pause every time she called him sir? Sable could tell it grated.

"Dismissed."

Sable gave him one last salute. And head high walked out of his office.

SABLE BLINKED. IT took her a few seconds to remember where she was. *When* she was. Los Angeles. Colt's living room. Present day. Sometimes the Army seemed a lifetime ago. Then in the blink of an eye, she was back there. Reliving it all over again.

"I wondered where you were."

Colt. God, his voice sounded good. He looked even better. Sable held out her hand.

"Your hand is like ice." Colt sat beside her. He kissed her icy fingers, one by one. "Why are you sitting out here when you could be curled up next to me? All toasty warm."

"I'm an idiot." Sable met his gaze. So blue. So kind. Suddenly, more than anything, she wanted to curl up in Colt's arms and cry.

"Hey." Concerned, he gently pulled her close. "What happened? What's wrong, Sable?"

Sable handed him her phone.

"Read this."

She rested her head on Colt's shoulder, waiting for him to finish her father's brief text.

"I know you love him," he growled, his lips brushing her forehead. "And I'll take your word for it that he's a good man. But, honey, your father is an asshole."

"Yes." How could she argue? "But he's my asshole."

"Fair enough. Want to go back to bed? There is still a good hour before we have to get up."

"That sounds good." Her lips curved when Colt lifted her and carried her to the bedroom. She wasn't the type to be swept into a man's arms. But Colt didn't seem to know that. And she wasn't in the mood to tell him. "But I don't want to cuddle."

"Music?" He slid in next to her, tucking the covers around them. "We can listen *and* cuddle. I promise I won't get handsy."

"No music. Not tonight." Sable turned to face him. "I've never told anyone why I left the Army. But if you wouldn't mind, I'd like to tell you."

"I wouldn't mind a bit." Reaching for her, Colt tucked Sable against his side, his arm holding her close. "You go right ahead. I can listen and cuddle at the same time."

Chapter Sixteen

COLTON KNEW WHAT he wanted to do with his life for as long as he could remember. He hadn't gone through the fireman or cowboy stage. There were no dreams of shaping young minds as a teacher or saving lives as a heart surgeon.

Acting. It was his passion before he understood what that meant.

Dressing up. Losing yourself in a character so different from the real you that you forgot your name—your life—outside of that moment. You became the character—fully. It was exciting. Thrilling.

Colton loved the craft. He studied to hone his skills. Watched the masters at work. Olivier. Tracy. Davis. Hepburn. Hoping to find something—anything—he could use to make himself a better actor.

He would have done it for free. Luckily, he didn't have to. Producers threw ridiculous amounts of money at him. They threw in perks. Private jets. Villas in the south of France. An island off the coast of Greece. One even offered to put his supermodel wife at Colton's disposal for the duration of the shoot. Colt turned down the offer—and the movie.

The life he lived was a dream. A fantasy world few people would ever experience or fully understand. Hell, sometimes *he* wondered at it. He was loved by successful, smart, take no shit parents. His brothers were his best friends. Nothing bad had ever touched him. The closest was Wyatt's marital drama, but that was a secondhand hurt. He could never understand what it felt like to experience that kind of betrayal and loss.

Some might say he lived in a velvet-lined bubble. Protected from the real world. Until a few days ago, Colt would have ignored it. Shrugged off the accusation with his usual ease and good humor. Now he wondered. Sable had lost so much all at once. She was such a strong woman. Funny. Intelligent. Brave. God, she was brave. Colt didn't know how he would have handled what she went through.

The death of a friend was hard enough to fathom. But Sable walked away from the life she loved because she was given no other palatable choice. As a result, her father cut her from his life. Not a clean, merciful break. It festered. Her mother periodically gave a jab with her ego-riddled rants.

Admiring Sable had always been easy. His family adored her. She made friends easily and was loyal to her core. But now his admiration had taken on a new, deeper tone. And, if he were completely honest, the little corner of his heart that already belonged to her encroached on the rest.

"You're quiet."

"Am I?" Colt smiled at his mother. Sunny as always, both in temperament and wardrobe, her yellow dress brightened an already cloudless California day. "Maybe by comparison. Between the ruckus raised by Nate's dog and the beautiful women chasing her around, anyone would seem subdued."

"I love a noisy, happy house." Callie sat beside him. She smoothed her skirt, then settled back with a sigh. "Are you happy?"

"Aren't I always?"

"Yes." Callie kissed his cheek. "I swear you were born that way. No crying for my Colton. You greeted the world with a smile and that's the way you've continued."

"There you go," Colt said absently.

Following his gaze, she wasn't surprised when she discovered what, or rather who held his interest.

"You and Sable have caused quite a stir."

Colt looked at his mother and shrugged.

"It goes with the territory."

And when he thought about the text Sable's father sent her, he wanted to rip the territory to shreds.

"What's wrong, Colton?"

"Everything is good."

"Then why do you have those armrests in a death grip?"

"Gas." Colt relaxed his fingers.

"Colton."

"Mom."

When it came to stare-downs, Callie always won. Her sons were no match for her Mom powers.

"It isn't my story," Colt sighed.

"Sable." Callie's gaze shifted to the lawn where Sable, Jade, and Paige were playing with Beauty. "She looks happy."

"She's—"

Colt almost said perfect but caught himself at the last second. His mother would read too much into that one little word. Though it certainly described Sable to a T.

It had been a week since her father's text. Colt's feelings were mixed. He wanted to ream out the man for treating his daughter so callously. But it was the catalyst that let her finally open up. He was humbled that she trusted him. And sick that she had to go through something so traumatic.

Sable was perfect. Colt was the one reevaluating his life.

"Sable is fine. Mom." Colt hesitated. "I'm kind of worthless, aren't I?"

"Where did you pick up such an asinine idea?" Callie's eyes flashed indignantly. "Did Sable tell you that?"

"No! Of course not."

Callie relaxed. "I didn't think that sounded like her, but you never know." She looked closely at Colt. "What's going on, baby?"

"I want to make more of an impact on the world." Colt had thought about this but putting it in words was harder than he expected. "I'm proud of my work. You've always said not to diminish the worth of a good movie."

"That's true. Shutting off your brain for a few hours is amazingly beneficial. How many times has a fan thanked you for giving them a laugh, or making them cry, exactly when they needed it most?"

"That feels great. But I want to do more."

"Charity work?" Callie poured herself a glass of iced tea. "You never turn down a good cause."

"It's time for me to find something of my own. Something that I feel passionate about. I have a name and a face that gets attention. It's time to use that for something important."

"I think that's a wonderful idea. Your father and I have our foundation and we sit on the board of several charities. We have always encouraged you and your brothers to give back." She squeezed his hand. "You, all of you, make us proud. Do you have something in mind?"

A shout followed by a burst of laughter caught his attention. Across the lawn, Sable held the end of a thick piece of rope. On the other end, Beauty tugged with all her might. He didn't know who was winning the battle, but it was obvious they were having a great time.

Colt's lips curved when Sable threw down the rope and picked up the exuberant dog. When Nate and Paige brought Beauty home from Montana, she was a growing puppy. How big she was going to be when the growing stopped was anyone's guess.

At the moment, Colt estimated the dog weighed close to seventy pounds, but Sable lifted her with ease, laughing when Beauty tried in vain to swipe her face with a big, wet tongue.

Colt had known the answer to his mother's question before she asked it. But looking at Sable reinforced his choice.

"Something for returning soldiers."

Callie couldn't hide the tears that welled up in her eyes.

"I had hoped that would be good news." Colt handed his mother a napkin.

"It's perfect."

"Perfect?" Colt frowned. Why would she pick that word?

"For Sable."

"I—"

"Are you going to try and deny she's the inspiration?"

"I suppose spending time with Sable has made me think seriously about our military and what they face when they return home."

"You're falling in love with her."

"Mom."

Jesus. What was he supposed to say to that? How could he admit it to his mother when he wasn't ready to admit it to himself? Colt shook his head. And there it was. He didn't know if she had done it on purpose, but she made him face the facts. He *was* falling in love.

"I have an Academy Award nomination."

"I know. I popped the cork on the celebratory champagne."

"Then why can't I hide my feelings from you? I'm not as good an actor as I thought."

"Sweet boy." Callie's eyes crinkled at the corners. "Turn on a camera and you can fool the world. But here? In real life? You can't hide your emotions. You never could. Those eyes of yours give you away. Just like your father. Transparent as glass."

"Great."

It was too soon. Sable wasn't ready for declarations and he wasn't ready to give them. According to his mother, his eyes were big expressive pools of goo. Colt couldn't think of a better way to make a skittish woman hightail it out of town.

Callie grinned. "Don't worry. It takes time and experience. Right now, Sable isn't looking. She won't until she's ready."

"What if that never happens? What if I'm in this alone?"

The thought made his stomach do a sickening flip. Unconsciously, Colt's fingers tightened their hold on the chair. He couldn't make Sable love him.

"I used to dream of days like this." Callie rubbed the back of his hand. Slowly, Colt relaxed. But his insides weren't as quick to settle.

"We visit all the time."

"Look." Callie inclined her head. "In love. Settled."

Garrett and Nate had joined the fun on the lawn. It seemed to Colt that they were more interested in flirting with their women than playing with the dog. But who could blame them? Jade and Paige were more than beautiful. They were the whole package. Smart. Funny. And more important? In it for the long haul. They wouldn't wilt at the first sign of trouble. Or run when things got hard. His brothers loved, and were loved, by women of character and strength.

"Sable fits."

"Yes."

Callie laughed. "Is that surprise I hear?"

"She's not what I expected."

"Let me guess. You wanted delicate. Sweet. Uncomplicated."

His mother's description wasn't far off. Colt didn't have a type per se. He knew what he liked. The type of women he gravitated toward. Easy to be with hit the nail on the head.

Not that Sable was high maintenance. Far from it. But she *was* complicated. She came with a truckload of baggage. Big, heavy pieces that had a tendency to shift at inconvenient moments. If a man weren't prepared, it could send him careening off the road and into a tree.

Until the other night, Colt hadn't thought he wanted to deal with the kind of drama Sable brought with her. He was wrong. For the right woman—for Sable—he was willing to take on anything.

"Tastes change."

"SABLE? MAY I speak with you for a minute?"

"I should hope so. If you don't speak to me, how will we pass the time?"

Sable handed Jade a washed crystal goblet. She, Jade, and Paige had volunteered to clean up the kitchen. After another amazing meal, it only seemed right. Callie demurred, but the Landis men had no problem with the suggestion.

"We'll be in the game room," Garrett called out as he and Nate hustled their mother along.

Chuckling, Caleb and Wyatt followed.

"Where did Colt disappear to?" Paige handed Sable two more glasses.

"He was the first one out the door. The man loves to cook, but he hates the cleanup."

"Colt cooks?" Paige and Jade asked. Shocked didn't begin to describe their expressions.

"I had the same reaction. He's very good at it. Excellent, in fact."

"Garrett can open a can. Barely."

"Nate does a mean scrambled egg." Paige put the last of the plates in the dishwasher.

"Neither of you are marrying them for their culinary skills." Sable dried her hands. She pumped out a dab of lotion from the bottle by the sink and smoothed it over her skin. "Let's sit down and you can tell me what has you looking so serious."

"It's nothing bad," Jade assured her.

When they had first met, Jade was fifteen pounds underweight and unnaturally quiet. Now, she glowed with good health and had no problem speaking her mind. She found the strength to change her life and Sable admired her for it.

"We need a favor." Paige joined them, bringing three cups and a full pot of coffee.

"We?"

"I told Paige about an idea that I've been mulling over for a while now. And she suggested talking to you."

"So talk."

"I belong to a group." Jade took a deep breath. "A domestic abuse survivors group."

"That's wonderful, Jade."

"It's been a big help."

"Tell her about the video," Paige urged.

"A few of the women in my group saw the video from the other night at the bar."

"The one where you had that creep crying for mercy?"

201

Jade smiled sheepishly. "That's the one. I can't understand why it caused such a fuss."

"Can't you?"

Paige's name drew attention. Plus, she was a beautiful redhead. That always drew attention. Those things coupled with her high-profile fiancé tended to up the interest factor.

"Fine. By now I should be used to it."

"Nate says you never get used to it. You simply learn to tolerate it."

Jade nodded. "Paige is right. But never mind the attention. It's died down, thank goodness." She laughed. "I was about to say, *to make a long story short*, but that train left the station long ago. Sable, the women in my group wanted me to teach them the move."

"You should."

"I'm not qualified to do it."

"It doesn't take any special training." Sable took a sip of coffee. "Take it step by step. The way I did with you."

"I was hoping you would show them."

"Me?"

"One class." When Sable hesitated, Jade hurried on. "When I was frightened and unsure of myself, you gave me confidence, Sable. You made me believe I could take care of myself. That I didn't have to be a victim ever again. That's what these women need."

"I'd like to learn a few moves, too," Paige said. She pushed her blonde hair over one shoulder. "Nate has tried to teach me, but every time he puts his hands on me, we end up doing other things. If you know what I mean."

"He's a Landis." Jade's green eyes sparkled. "Of course we know what you mean."

Sable didn't want to go there. It might be common knowledge that she and Colt were sleeping together, but she felt a little uncomfortable talking about it. Even with Jade and Paige.

"I have a job. I can't promise anything until I talk it over with Colt. His schedule changes from day to day. Next week, the movie is shooting in San Diego. Then Las Vegas for three days."

"We understand. But if we can coordinate everything, will you do it?"

Jade's expression was almost comically earnest. How could she say no to that?

"Okay. One class."

"Thank you, Sable." Jade jumped up and hugged her from behind. "This means the world to me. And to my friends."

"I hope I can help."

"I know you can. You have no idea how much it means to take control of your life. To stop being a victim."

Sable understood exactly what that meant. No woman should ever feel as though she had no choices. Knowing how to defend herself was one more way to take back her life. Her power. She would do this. For Jade and her friends. And for herself.

SABLE HADN'T exaggerated about Colt's schedule. To save time and money, the majority of the night scene shoots were bunched together over one week. It meant getting to the set around five in the afternoon and working until dawn. It threw everyone's body clocks out of whack.

Everything was flipped. Or as Colt put it, cattywampus. It was strange eating dinner at five in the morning, trying to sleep through the afternoon, and catching breakfast just as the sun was setting.

Handling the change took some creative measures.

Colt dealt with it by increasing the length of his workout routine. Drinking plenty of water. And having sex as often as humanly possible. In his case, that meant every chance he got—no matter the location.

"I should say no." Sable buttoned her shirt.

"Okay. Next time say no. I promise to stop."

"Mmm."

"You don't believe me?" Sable could tell that bothered him.

"I believe you. I was trying to imagine a scenario where I would want you to."

In lieu of a comb, Sable ran her fingers through her hair. Another benefit of keeping it short. Quick post-coital grooming after heated sex in a potting shed.

"You like my improvisational style?"

Sable tried not to smile. Why encourage him? But God, he was adorable. And gorgeous. And sinfully sexy. Colt needed a comb more than she did but on him, messy hair simply added to the allure. The rumpled shirt, the crooked grin. He looked like a man who had women falling at his feet—all day, every day. And he did. Sable could attest to the fact that he did.

"I'm an enabler," she declared. "My actions have turned an arrogant, cocky bastard into a mega-arrogant, cocky bastard. Sex. Sex. Sex. We can't keep up this pace. Can we?"

Colt pulled her into his arms. His lips nuzzled her ear, sending a familiar tingle through her body.

"First. I'm not arrogant or cocky. I'm confident. And charming." His chuckle told Sable that he knew exactly how that sounded. Cocky *and* arrogant. "Second. Do you want us to cool off? For the pace to slacken?"

"No." That was the last thing she wanted. The sex was amazing and she couldn't get enough of Colt.

"As long as we're enjoying ourselves, does it matter where?" He kissed the side of her neck. "Or how often?"

"No." Sable moaned. Automatically, she tipped her head to give him better access. Then she realized what Colt was doing. "No!" she said firmly. "You need to get back to work."

"We're on a thirty-minute break. We still have," Colt looked at his watch, "three and a half minutes."

Sable thought about pushing Colt out the door. But when his lips brushed her ear, her knees went weak. His touch made her ignore the fact they had done this just minutes before.

"Condom?"

Colt's lips curved. "Front pocket."

Sable fished out the packet. "Three minutes and counting."

He unsnapped his jeans and took the condom.

"I love a challenge."

"I love an orgasm. Think you can pull it off?"

"You mean, can I get you off?"

Flipping up Sable's skirt, Colt pushed her panties to the side and entered her without missing a beat. The breath left her lungs in a fast whoosh.

"Are you counting?"

She couldn't remember her name. How was she supposed to count? Her head fell back. Her body tensed. The orgasm hit and the world went black. Seconds later, Colt joined her.

"Thirty seconds to spare."

"Don't gloat."

"I wouldn't think of it."

Sable couldn't move. She was limp. Worn out. Completely, wonderfully spent. Luckily, Colt's reaction was the opposite. Somewhere he found a hidden source of energy. He cleaned them up and straightened their clothing. When a voice called out, *'Mr. Landis. You're wanted on the set,'* he looked at his watch.

"Three orgasms for you and a big fat one for me. Not bad."

"Smug."

"Happy." Colt corrected. He waited for Sable to open the shed door and check for lurking boogie men before taking her hand. "And very satisfied."

"Me too."

Sable smiled when he kissed her palm. Colt was always doing things like that. A little touch. A light kiss. She was getting used to the casual affection. No. It was more than that. She looked forward to it. Craved it. If she weren't careful, it could become a full-blown addiction. What would she do for her fix when she was in Harper Falls and he was a thousand miles away?

"Okay?"

Sable pulled her thoughts from the future and something she couldn't control. She had the here and the now. And she was determined to enjoy it.

"How do I look?"

"Fantastic."

"Not like I've had sex in a potting shed."

"You look like you've had sex. No one would guess the location."

"Idiot."

"How do I look?" Colt paused. He put a hand behind his head, making his best beefcake pose.

So good. Sable hid her smile, giving him the once over.

"You'll do."

COLT DIDN'T ASK the cast and crew what methods they employed to get through the odd hours. He kept his secrets and let them keep theirs. Whatever they did, on the whole, everyone adjusted nicely. Experienced professionals, they behaved as such. But there always seemed to be an exception who was determined to prove the rule.

In this case, it was Candice. DeMarcco.

The diva wannabe decided the night schedule was the perfect time to assert her power as the movie's female lead. In other words, *if I choose to flub my lines and pout through every scene, so what? You can't replace me. You can't ruin me. I'm a star. Live with it.*

"There is a woman who needs to spend a whole lot of time in a potting shed," Colt grumbled. They were on another break while Candice looked over her lines.

Sable raised an eyebrow.

"Sex." Colt flopped onto the chair next to hers. "I meant she needs to have lots and lots of sex."

"I know what you meant." Sable held up her hands, her eyes filled with mock horror. "Don't look at me. I wouldn't touch her with a ten-foot pole."

"You could shoot her."

"No. Too much blood. Besides, I really like that dress she's wearing. It would be a shame to ruin it."

"Then I'm at a loss."

Colt had her hand in his. Sable wondered if he knew he'd done it, the gesture was becoming second nature. So was the little ping she felt around her heart when he rubbed his thumb against hers.

"You know what you have to do."

"*I* have to shoot her?" Colt shook his head, blue eyes filled with mock regret. "Nah. I've never discharged a gun outside of a firing range or an action movie. I might miss and hit someone important."

"Or," Sable playfully jabbed Colt in the ribs. His grin was her reward. "You could use that famous Landis charm. A few words of encouragement might get this party started."

Colt sighed. "Fine. But I still say your gun is more effective."

"We'll keep it in reserve—just in case."

Watching Colt drag his feet as he walked to Candice's trailer was as entertaining as any scene in the movie. He paused outside the door. Took a deep breath and pulled his shoulders back. Before he knocked, he turned toward Sable, pointing at his huge, plastered-on smile.

Colt had barely made one rap when the trailer door opened. A hand with long red nails appeared, grabbed him by the arm, and pulled him inside. The door shut with a resounding snap.

"I don't know how he does it." Janis, made up for the scene Candice couldn't get through, joined Sable. She had a wry smile on her face and a cup of coffee in each hand. She gave one to Sable before hoisting herself onto Colt's vacated seat. "No one else has the nerve to beard the barracuda's den."

"He feels a responsibility to the cast and crew."

"And Candice knows it. Her little tantrums are all about manipulating Colt."

"How so?"

"Do you mind some gossip?"

"Do you mind if I take it with a grain of salt?"

Sable had lived most of her life on one Army base or another. Gossip was the fuel that powered many a backyard barbecue or weeknight poker game. Her mother had lived for every tidbit, taking it as gospel—unless it reflected poorly back on her. Then it was all petty lies and backstabbing.

Her father used to say, *Listen if you must, Sable. But always remember. Gossip never benefits anyone but the teller.*

"Hell. You can take it with a whole shaker full," Janis laughed good-naturedly.

"Then gossip away."

"Well," Janis leaned closer, her eyes sparkling with the excitement of being the bearer of less than reliable news. "One of the grips overheard Candice on the phone. It seems she is not happy with the state of her romantic relationship with Colt."

"What romantic relationship?"

"Exactly. By now, she thought they would be hot and heavy. The darlings of the internet. Splashed on the cover of every checkout line celebrity magazine. Colt is everywhere, but not with Candice on his arm. There's one major problem standing in her way to the top of the trending charts."

"That Colt is too smart to be dragged under by a publicity-hungry bitch?"

"There's that," Janis nodded. "But the answer is more succinct. The problem, according to Candice, is you."

"The problem is that Colt isn't interested. If he were, he would be with her."

"Logic." Janis tapped the side of her head. "Not Candice's long suit. She sees you as her only obstacle. Eliminate you, and Colt will fall at her feet like the proverbial piece of ripe fruit."

"Delusional," Sable whispered under her breath.

She knew the type. Her mother was a prime example. Once Iris Ford convinced herself something was true, there was no reasoning with her. Apparently, Candice suffered from the same affliction.

"And then some." Janis tapped a packet of artificial sweetener against her hand. She opened the packet and added it to her coffee, absently stirring it in.

"For the sake of crazy, let's say she was right. What's her plan? Because I'm not going anywhere."

Until the movie wraps. Sable couldn't help silently adding that for her own benefit. After that, Colt was free to get involved with all the nitwits his heart desired. It left a sour taste in her mouth, making it hard to swallow her mouthful of coffee. With a grimace, she set aside the cup.

"Plan? Candice? She doesn't strategize. She leaves that up to her management team. They've pulled some crazy stunts to get some attention for her. But the latest tantrum has Candice written all over it. Poorly thought out and destined for failure."

Before Sable could respond, the trailer door burst open. She and the entire production crew heard Colt's voice before they saw him.

"That's it," Colt yelled. Sable's brows rose in surprise. Angry Colt was rare. Especially on the set. She edged off the chair, poised to step in if Colt appeared to be in danger.

"Colt... "

Though out of sight, the whiney voice obviously belonged to Candice.

"No. I've had enough."

Colt jumped from the trailer. His hair was messed up, standing in multiple directions. But it was the state of his shirt that had Sable on her feet. It was torn, leaving his chest exposed. And if she weren't mistaken, there were scratch marks, red and angry-looking, marring his skin.

"I'm fine." Colt held up a hand, keeping Sable in her seat. She didn't move, nor did she relax.

"Colt." Candice stood in the doorway, wearing nothing but a skimpy piece of lingerie and a pout. "Come back. We were just getting started."

"Listen to me. If you ever pull something like this again, I will have you thrown off the set. The hell with the movie."

"You don't mean that."

Sable wondered at the woman's lack of self-preservation. An idiot could see Colt wasn't just angry. He was livid. His face was red, his fists clenched. And the vein on his temple throbbed with alarming intensity. Yet Candice, entrenched in her own cuckoo world, approached Colt without an ounce of caution.

Sable prepared to intervene. Not to protect Colt from a pending attack. But to keep him out of jail. If he strangled Candice, the cast and crew might cheer, but not even his famous charm would get him out of a murder rap—justifiable or not.

"Stop," Colt commanded.

"I can make you feel good." Unbelievably, Candice kept on coming. "That skinny rack of bones won't keep you warm for long."

Skinny rack of bones? Sable had been called many things, but that was a first. She was lean, not skinny. And snapping Candice like a dried twig would be a piece of cake.

"Listen, and listen good." Colt sidestepped Candice's grasping claws. "Candice." His tone was sharp, finally getting her attention. "Get your ass in your trailer. You have exactly forty-five minutes to be on the set. In costume and makeup. And you better know your lines. I will shut this movie down and recast, no matter what it costs, if you don't begin to behave like a professional. Understood?"

"But—"

"Forty-four minutes, fifteen seconds."

Candice looked around, desperate for support. What she found were people, fascinated by the show, but firmly on Team Colt. The only support she had was from her pushup bra. And even that was showing signs of wear and tear.

Taking a deep breath. Then another, Candice stomped her foot in frustration. She turned and flounced to her trailer, accompanying herself with a long, ear-piercing wail.

"OMG. My hero." Janis threw her arms around Colt. "I better freshen up. I'm in the next scene."

"If she shows up," Colt grumbled.

"She'll be there," Janis said with absolute conviction.

"How can you be so sure?"

"As we speak, little Candice is getting her makeup retouched. And calling her agent. He'll stroke and soothe and tell her, in nicer language, to get her ass on the set. She's his meal ticket. A big fat cash cow. No way he'll let her derail that."

Janis jogged off, a sprightly bounce in her step.

"Why did I become an actor?"

Sable took Colt's hand. "Come with me."

Without protest, Colt let Sable guide him over cables and around cameras. No one approached or tried to waylay them with the usual endless questions and requests. They wouldn't have dared. After his confrontation with Candice, everyone looked at Colt with new respect, and a touch of fear. As far as Sable was concerned, that wasn't a bad thing.

Because of his inherent good nature, the cast and crew came to Colt with every little problem. He wasn't a pushover by any means. But he tried to smooth troubled waters. Perhaps now they would think twice before dumping their messes in his lap.

Sable gently pushed Colt into his trailer, shutting the door behind her.

"You became an actor because you love your mommy."

Colt paused in the middle of opening a bottle of water.

"Excuse me? Are you saying I have mommy issues?" Colt wasn't upset by the accusation. He was appalled.

Wide-eyed, Sable bit her cheek to keep from laughing.

"Don't you?"

It took him a second, but Colt's eyes narrowed when he saw the twinkle in her eyes.

"Why, you little—"

Colt tossed the bottle on the floor. He grabbed Sable by the arms, pulling her close. All she saw was a flash of bright blue eyes before he kissed her. Hard. Without preamble. Hours of pent up frustration and anger surging out of him, into her.

Sable welcomed it. Gladly. She let him back her against the door and take whatever he needed.

"I don't want to hurt you."

"You never could." *Not physically.* "It isn't in you, Colton. If you want to play a little rough, I don't mind. I can take it."

"Turn around," he growled in her ear. "Palms flat on the door. Don't move a muscle unless I tell you to. Got it?"

Sable didn't answer. She let Colt position her the way he wanted. With one foot, he tapped the side of her ankle, an indication he wanted her to spread her legs. He bunched the skirt of her dress up around her waist.

"Are you ready for me?"

"Yes."

"Show me."

Sable didn't think—she reacted on instinct.

"May I move my hand?"

"Mmm." Colt bit her earlobe, making Sable hiss, then moan.

Licking her lips, Sable slid her hand between her legs. She was wet, moisture seeping through the silk of her underwear. But she wanted more than a trace. She pushed the material aside and coated her fingers with the proof Colt demanded.

"See?"

Colt took her wrist, his grip firm. She wouldn't have pulled away, but he wasn't taking any chances.

She heard his deep intake of breath. "You smell like heaven." He drew one of her fingers into his mouth. Colt's tongue made sure there wasn't a drop left. "But, God, the way you taste. There are no words."

Sable's nails scratched at the door, finding no purchase on the cold metal surface. Her heated skin sought relief, searching for something to cool it down. But it was no match for the flame burning in her. The second her cheek made contact, the metal burned as hot as she did.

Though she couldn't see him, Sable heard every move he made. The crinkle of foil as Colt prepared a condom made her breathing deepen. He nudged her entrance with his erection. Once. Twice. Sable closed her eyes—frustrated. Now he wanted to tease? When his every move until now had been designed to make her as hot and ready as possible?

"Colt?"

"Yes?"

He licked the curve of her ear. Sable shivered.

"*Please!*"

"That's what I wanted to hear."

Before she could say, *fuck you*, he entered her. One sure motion.

"Say it."

Sable groaned. She needed to move. She needed it hard and fast. She needed it now.

"Say it, Sable."

"Fuck! Me! Now!"

"My pleasure."

One hand around her waist, Colt cupped her between her legs. He urged her higher, stroking with his fingers. Sable cried out his name. Her orgasm had barely begun when Colt joined her, riding the wave with her.

"Thank you," he whispered when he could find the breath.

Sable managed a small, but happy smile. "My pleasure."

Chapter Seventeen

"LAUREL CANYON IS beautiful."

"It's a great place." Colt agreed. He shifted to a lower gear. The turns were not meant to be taken in anything higher than second. "Perfect for someone who wants a slower pace. Funny. When Garrett and Nate bought their places, neither had any intention of settling down. They were on location so much of the time. When in town, Garrett stayed at the downtown loft, and Nate usually crashed with our parents. The properties in Laurel Canyon were more of an investment in the future."

"The future came faster than they expected."

"Twins," Colt laughed.

Sable turned from looking at the view. "What does that mean?"

"It's something about sharing a womb. Nate and Garrett aren't identical twins, but I can't count the number of times they've acted as one. They think the same way. It makes sense that once Garrett had fallen for Jade, it would only be a matter of time for Nate. The way he tells it, he and Paige clicked almost immediately."

"I was surprised when Jade told me Nate was engaged."

"Because deep down you wanted him to wait for you?"

Deadpan, Sable said, "Yes. From the moment I kicked his ass, I was a goner. Months of pining. He broke my heart."

"But it was me you kissed, not Nate."

"Who says I didn't kiss him?"

Colt's head whipped around. "Did you?"

"Eyes on the road, Colton."

"Answer the question, Sable." But Colt did what she asked.

"You have kissed every inch of my body. Would it matter if Nate got to my lips before you did?"

"Yes."

"Paige doesn't care."

"Paige knows?" Colt's fingers tightened on the wheel. "Why do women tell each other everything?"

"Beats me. I've never understood it."

Colt glanced at her, then the road. Then back at her. When she grinned, he let out a big, expressive sigh.

"Jesus, Sable. You were kidding? About everything?"

"Yes." Sable patted his leg. "I couldn't resist. Though for the life of me, I can't figure out why it matters. I've kissed plenty of men. Let's not start on the legions of women you've locked lips with. One kiss, Colt? Come on."

What Sable said was true. He didn't care who she had kissed before him because they were anonymous faces that he would pass in a crowd without a second thought. But his brother was different. Not the end of the world. Simply... disconcerting.

"I was never very good at sharing my toys."

The second the words were out of his mouth Colt wanted to pull them back. If the car weren't moving, he would have pounded his forehead against the steering wheel. *Stupid, stupid, stupid.*

"What did you say?"

"I don't know where that came from, Sable." Colt pulled to a stop, but it was too late to knock himself unconscious.

"Sounded to me like you knew exactly what you meant."

Sable was out of the car before Colt could apologize. Or figure out how. She walked to his door and opened it.

"Get out. I can't leave you here like a sitting duck. No matter how tempting the prospect."

"Sable…"

"Move."

Colt hated feeling like a chastised little boy, but there it was. He walked ahead of Sable toward the house, his hands shoved in his front pockets and his shoulders slightly slumped.

"Are you going to let me apologize?"

"Right now, I don't want to hear the sound of your voice."

"But—"

"You made it."

Frustrated, Colt watched as Jade ran down the front steps to greet them, enveloping Sable in a warm hug. The look Sable gave him over Jade's shoulder made him feel about an inch high.

"I count nineteen cars. How many people are here?"

Here was Nate and Paige's home. It was big and sprawling. Too big for one person. But now that Paige lived with him, there never seemed to be enough room. She took care of animals. It was her gift and her passion. Most of them were there temporarily until she could heal their wounds—mental and physical. Then they moved on to permanent homes

Paige started small. A few horses. Then a couple of dogs. But it didn't take long for the numbers to grow. There always seemed to be another animal in need, and Paige hated turning one away.

Nate had plans to add two more corrals and another barn. He liked living the life of the gentleman rancher. But more than that, he loved Paige. If she were happy, he was happy.

After some deliberation, it was decided it made sense for Sable to teach the self-defense class somewhere more private than the room where the support group usually met. Besides, it didn't have the proper equipment.

Jade and Garrett were in the middle of a huge remodel—including the in-home gym. Since Nate and Paige already had a state of the art facility, they volunteered to play host.

"Most of the women carpooled. I'm afraid word spread to some other groups. Callie wanted to take the class. With her and Paige? Forty-six."

216

Sable couldn't hide her surprise. It was depressing to think of that many women, in such a small area, needing support. And of all the others trapped in abusive relationships, who had no idea how to get out.

"If there's room, I don't mind the number. In the Army, I taught bigger groups."

"Mostly men."

"True. Men can show a lot of stupidity when a woman is in charge." Sable gave Colt a long look. "Comparatively? This crowd should be a piece of cake."

Colt began to wander off. The idea of checking out the horses seemed more appealing than entering a house filled with people.

"Are you trying to get on my last nerve?"

Colt sighed. What now?

"I didn't say anything."

"For which I am extremely grateful. But you can't go out there by yourself."

"For fuck's sake, Sable. It's a corral. With horses. What do you think is going to happen?"

"Nothing is going to happen, you idiot." Sable grabbed Colt by the ears, pulling him to eye level. "Because I won't let it." Then she planted a kiss on his mouth.

Colt didn't have time to do more than enjoy the ride. When Sable dropped her hold, both of them were breathing hard. The anger lingered, but most of the heat had mellowed—at least on his side. Sable's eyes held his for a second longer.

"Understand?"

"I think so." Sable held duty above all else. The problem was, it was easy to forget that she wasn't his girlfriend. And too easy for her to remember she was his bodyguard. He couldn't help it. It pissed him off—logical or not.

"Let's go in the house." Jade took Colt's arm. "Nate is going to give Garrett a tour of the place during Sable's class. You can go with them."

"Am I allowed out of your sight?" Colt asked, not looking at Sable as he passed her and escorted Jade up the steps.

It was just as well. He wouldn't have appreciated the double *fuck you* fingers Sable shot at his back. But Nate saw them. He stood on the porch, grinning.

"What's so amusing?"

"You, little brother." Nate winked at Sable.

Suspicious, Colt glanced between them.

"You kissed her."

"Oh, for God's sake." Sable rolled her eyes.

"What?" Nate had no idea what was going on. "Kissed who? Sable?"

"Ignore him, Nate. He put his head up his ass. Which is appropriate since he's full of shit."

"I don't know what you did, Colt. But trust me. Quit while you're behind. The hole can only get deeper."

"In the house." It wasn't a request. Colt wanted to tell Sable to go to hell, but Nate enjoyed the show way too much. This could wait for later.

Nate waited until Colt and Jade were inside before putting a friendly arm around Sable's shoulders.

"You're good for him."

"How so?"

"You don't simper and moon over him."

"I should hope not," Sable scoffed.

Nate let out an appreciative laugh. His eyes, so like Colt's, crinkled at the corners. He was bigger than his brothers. Taller, with thicker muscles that were necessary for his job. He made his living as a stuntman. And was damn good at it. But his temperament belied his size. Sweet to the core. But get him mad. Threaten anyone he cared about, and Nate Landis wasn't a man to tangle with.

"What was that kissing thing about?"

"I suggested that I might have kissed you. Before you met Paige. I was teasing him. Something we do to each other all the time. Suddenly, he lost his sense of humor."

"Mmm."

"What?" Sable put her fists on her hips. "He was completely unreasonable."

"No doubt."

Nate understood where Colt was coming from. His temper would have flared if one of his brothers had made a move on Paige. Even if it were before they fell in love. There was no statute of limitation on that kind of thing.

"Then there was the *I don't like to share my toys* crack. Try and justify that one."

He groaned. That hole Colt dug himself was deeper than Nate imagined.

"There is no argument for that one."

"Exactly," Sable nodded.

"Except—"

"Go on."

Nate loved the thrill of jumping from a plane at twenty thousand feet or crashing a two hundred thousand dollar sports car into a building. Controlled danger was one thing—Sable was another. She had the skills to kick his ass—something she had proven on one very memorable occasion. The spark of heat in her eyes had him holding up his hands in surrender.

"I was going to say I understand the impulse. A man in—" Nate almost slipped and said *a man in love*. It wasn't his place to put that out there. No matter how obvious Colt and Sable's feeling were to anyone with eyes. "Colt isn't used to a woman like you, Sable."

Sable crossed her arms. Her stance was a little too combative for his liking. "A woman like me? Who am I, Nate?"

"Independent. Non-clingy. You don't care about his money or his celebrity. Colt is used to women who want to be seen on his arm as much, or more, than they want to be with him."

Sable didn't speak for several seconds. But her eyes softened from a hard brown to a mellow gold.

"Why does that make me sad?"

Nate wanted to give Sable a shake and say *because you love him, you beautiful idiot.* Instead, he smiled and gave her a hug. *Why was it so hard to admit something so wonderful?* Nate wondered. If he knew the answer, he would have said it to Paige weeks sooner. He supposed that love made idiots of them all. Hopefully, Colt and Sable would wise up and put themselves out of their misery.

"Colt knows the score, Sable. He's not a victim. Call it tit for tat."

"In other words, they let him play with their tits in exchange for his tat."

Nate threw his head back and laughed. Hard. It made Sable smile and drew Paige from the house.

"Want to share the joke?" she asked with a grin, her eyes sparkling.

"Yes." Nate wrapped his arms around her. "Later. When we're alone."

"Oh." Paige winked at Sable. "It's that kind of joke."

"No. But I don't want to show you my *tat* in public."

Chuckling, Sable slipped into the house, giving Nate and Paige some privacy. As she closed the door, she saw Nate cup Paige's face so sweetly it made her heart ache a little. A woman would give up a lot to have a man look at her like that.

"Hey." Colt gave her a tentative smile.

"Hey." Her smile wasn't the least bit cautious.

Talking to Nate had helped settle things in her mind. It gave Sable a new perspective on Colt's life. Yes, women catered to him. Pampered him. Built him up to almost God-like status. And Colt reveled in the attention. But those women were often users. Taking advantage of his fame and power to advance their own agendas.

Colt knew the score. He wasn't a babe in the woods. No one took what he wasn't willing to give. However, it had to prey on his mind. Occasionally, he had to ask himself the question. Do they like me? Or are they only interested in *Colton Landis, Movie Star?*

"Still pissed?" Colt asked.

"A little." She wasn't going to lie. "Are you?"

"A little." Colt sent her a half-grin instead of a whole one. It didn't matter. It only took a fraction of his smile to make her stomach flip-flop. "Want to kiss and make up?"

"In front of all these people? Not on your life."

"When did you get shy?"

"Not shy. But, Colt." Sable lowered her voice. "Your mother and father are over there."

"Who? Them? They hug and kiss all the time. No matter who's looking. They wouldn't blink an eye."

"My parents barely spoke. Or touched." Sable let out a happy sigh when Colt took her hand. "Honestly, I can't remember them kissing in front of me. Not even on the cheek."

Colt loved when she unintentionally gave him another piece to the Sable puzzle. She wasn't a toucher. Hugging didn't come naturally. For Colt, it was like breathing. Second nature. The longer they spent time together, the more she was at ease with it. Every now and then, much to his delight, she would rub his back when he leaned over to look in the fridge. Or brush her fingers across his cheek after she handed him a beer. Little things. But, as time went on, they added up to so much more.

"No kissing in front of my parents," he promised. *For now.*

"Good. Would you like a clean slate?"

The look in Sable's eyes turned from friendly to cagey, putting Colt on red alert. He knew he would regret it, but he couldn't resist the offer.

"Sure. What can I do?"

"Nothing strenuous. All you have to do is stand around and look pretty."

AS IT TURNED out, Colt didn't do a lot of standing. When he wasn't on his back, he was trying to avoid landing on it. Nothing was injured. Except his pride. But the laughter that followed his every defeat wasn't malicious. At first, the chuckles were muted. A bit reluctant. But soon it filled the room. Loud and unrestrained. Colt didn't mind a slightly bruised ego if it meant he was helping to bring these women out of their shells.

"Remember. Your first and best defense is to find a way not to engage your would-be attacker. Run. Scream. Draw as much attention as possible."

"I heard yelling fire is more effective than calling for help." The comment came from the back. Colt tried to see who it was, but she was hidden by several other women.

"Unfortunately, that's true." Sable kept her gaze steady and her voice even. She was there to help empower these women. That meant giving them the truth. No matter how brutal.

"It's easier to look the other way. Some people are afraid to get involved. Others figure, if it isn't me, I couldn't care less. But." Sable looked around. "And this a big one. Most people *do* care. They want to help."

It was a hard sell to women who had been brutalized by so-called loved ones. Boyfriends. Husbands. Fathers. Men whose first instincts should have been to protect—not hit.

"*They* are the weak ones. *You* are strong. You got out. You survived. Gradually. A little bit at a time, *you* are thriving. I'm here to help you take one more step in that direction."

Colt noticed a few of the women nodding. There were a few tears. And a few curses. But they all held their heads up with pride. Sable couldn't have put it better. Survivors. Each and every one of them.

"Hands up. Who wants to knock the *Sexiest Man Alive* on his ass?"

More laughter. Sable grinned at him. Colt silenced a groan. She knew she had him. He couldn't refuse.

As the women lined up for the pleasure of manhandling Colton Landis, he started a list in his head. One hundred and one ways to get even with Sable Ford. It was such a satisfying mental exercise, he couldn't help but laugh.

"What's so funny?" Sable asked so only he could hear.

Colt held her gaze. "I'll tell you later. With pleasure."

HOURS LATER, THE last thing Sable was thinking about was Colt's thinly veiled promise.

After she had finished the class, most of the women lingered to ask follow-up questions. Some stayed to rubberneck.

It wasn't every day they met so many famous people. The chances of it happening again were zero to none. Sable couldn't blame them for taking advantage. Especially when Colt and the rest of the Landis clan were so friendly and gracious.

"When is the next class?" The question came from a pretty woman with shoulder-length auburn hair. She spoke in a soft, hesitant voice as though she wasn't used to speaking for herself.

It wasn't the first time one of the women had asked. Sable realized that she should have made an announcement that this was a one-time thing before she dismissed everyone, but she thought they already knew.

"I'm sorry. What's your name?"

"Marta." She looked around furtively.

Sable smiled, wanting to assure Marta that no one was going to fault her for asking a simple question. She admired the woman for making the obvious effort to step up and make herself heard. For most people, it wouldn't seem like a big deal. But something told Sable it was a big step for Marta.

"I wish I could continue the classes, Marta. But I have a job that takes up most of my time."

"Oh." She seemed to melt into herself. Part embarrassed. Part afraid. "Sorry. I didn't mean to… I mean…"

"Marta?" Colt gave her a gentle smile. "Would you like a glass of my mother's world-famous lemonade? I usually keep it all to myself but I would be happy to share a glass with you."

"I don't know." Marta looked around, then down at the ground.

"Please," Colt urged. He spoke as he would to a frightened kitten. "You would be doing me a big favor. If you're with me, I won't gorge on cookies." He patted his flat stomach. "The camera picks up every extra pound."

"Okay."

Colt held out his arm. The gesture surprised Marta so much, Sable thought she was going to faint. Instead, she smiled shyly, tentatively letting him escort her to a table laid out with refreshments.

"If I didn't adore him already, I would now," Jade said, joining Sable. They watched as Colt kept up a casual conversation with Marta.

223

"She's a new member of the group. It took a lot to persuade her to come today. Talking to you took every ounce of courage she possessed. Now look at her. Colt has her blushing and answering his questions. The man is a sweetheart."

Sable agreed. Colt was irresistible.

"I don't know how this works." Sable frowned. She didn't want to step on any sensitive toes. "May I ask what happened to Marta or is it confidential?"

Jade shook her head. "We share our stories—when we're ready. Talking about it helps. The point is to get abuse out of the shadows. Even now, there's a stigma attached. If someone punches you, you must have done something to deserve it. If you're raped, you led them on. You asked for it so you deserve what you got."

"I wish I could say that surprises me."

"You understand better than most, don't you?"

Sable frowned, her eyes puzzled. "I empathize. But no one has ever abused me, Jade.

"What about your commanding officer?"

"What about him?"

Sable's stomach clenched. What did Jade know? Had Colt said something? She refused to believe he would betray her trust, but there was no other explanation.

"You don't remember, do you?" Jade's green eyes filled with concern. "I'm sorry. You mentioned it in passing. You were packing your things and the car was waiting to take you to the airport. I wouldn't have brought it up if I'd realized."

Suddenly, the memory of that day came back to her. Jade had asked why she left the Army and Sable made an almost joking reference to her C.O. asking her to get on her knees. It had been stupid to make light of it, but sometimes it was either laugh or cry. Sable preferred laughter.

"I'm the one who's sorry, Jade. It's something I try not to think about. I forgot that I'd said anything to you."

"I know you walked away," Jade said. "It was still abuse. It does help to talk about it, Sable. The women in my group are there if you need us."

"Thank you for the offer." Her gaze wandered to Colt. "But I have someone who's a very good listener."

"I see." Nodding, Jade smiled when she saw where Sable was looking. "There's something about a Landis boy. They make opening up easy."

"Why is that?" It was something that had puzzled Sable for some time. She wasn't the type to confide her problems. Yet she told Colt everything. About her strange relationship with her mother. How painful it was to be cut off from her father. And the ugly business that made her resign from the Army. He knew it all.

"Colt didn't pry. He let me tell him in my own time—in my own way."

"It felt good, didn't it?"

"Yes."

"And you knew your secrets were safe with him. That he would never spread them around or use them as a weapon against you."

"Is that how it was with Garrett?"

Jade's eyes turned a misty green. "It wasn't easy. But trusting Garrett, and myself, healed me."

On the other side of the room, Garrett was talking to his father. As if sensing her gaze, he looked up. Jade smiled when their eyes met— Garrett grinned. Without words, their feelings were clear. Trust. Deep, unwavering love.

Sable couldn't help but feel an ache of envy. Love and trust. It was easy to live without either when she didn't know what they looked like. But now? Sable wondered what her life would be like when she was back in Harper Falls. Away from the Landis family. Away from Colt.

"Sable." Callie waved her over to where she and four other women were gathered. "We were saying how much we enjoyed your class."

The others nodded. Sable wasn't surprised that they no longer seemed in awe. Callie had a way of drawing people in. It was easy to forget they were in the presence of true Hollywood royalty. She was down to Earth, lacking the slightest trace of artifice. In minutes, she had them feeling like they were old friends.

"We plan on practicing those moves you demonstrated at our next meeting."

"That's smart," Sable nodded. "Practicing them is important. Eventually, you'll get to the point where you can do it without thinking."

"I don't know about that." A plump woman in her forties held out her hand, giving Sable's a strong, firm shake "Annie Moore. It's been twenty years since I divorced my scumbag husband. The fear has lessened, but it's still there. Regaining our confidence takes a lot of work. This, what you did today, helps a lot."

"You seem a bit overwhelmed," Callie said later when the women had left.

"I'm not used to hearing thank you. Not for this. In the Army, or with H&W, I taught classes. But it was part of the job. This was different. It felt more important. Like I made a difference." Sable groaned, followed by a small, self-deprecating laugh. "Wow. Did that sound as pompous as I think it did?"

"Not at all." Then Callie laughed when Sable raised an eyebrow. "Fine. Stating a fact can often come off as a bit pompous. But I knew what you meant." Callie's gray eyes grew thoughtful. "Do you find working as a bodyguard unfulfilling?"

"Maybe."

That was the last thing Sable meant to say. It came off as disloyal. Alex Fleming had given her a job—a home—when she had none. The money was excellent and her services were in high demand. All that said, today had opened her eyes to the possibility that she was wasting years of training. Her skills were rarely needed. Most of the time, she was nothing more than a babysitter to the rich and famous.

"Colton doesn't need a bodyguard."

Sable shook her head. It was as if Callie read her mind. Now she knew where Colt acquired that talent.

"No."

Sable didn't add that she felt like a fraud taking a salary under false pretenses. She wasn't guarding Colt. She was sleeping with him. And getting paid to do it. Sable refused to think of herself as a hooker. She knew better. But if the details got out, others wouldn't hesitate. And hooker would be kind compared to the names they would call her.

"Never be afraid to reevaluate your life, Sable." Callie rubbed her arm. "The path we take in life isn't a straight line. It veers off in many directions. When I was young and filled with ambition, I put on blinders. Nothing was going to get in my way. Straight to the top."

"And here you are."

"True." Callie handed Sable a glass of lemonade and a napkin. "But *here* isn't where I imagined it would be. Not then. Sandwich or cookie?"

Always the nurturer, Sable thought. "Chicken salad, please."

"If it weren't for a stubborn man who didn't know the meaning of the word no, I doubt I would have married. Can you picture me without Caleb? Without my boys?"

Sable shook her head. It was inconceivable.

"I was twenty-two years old and determined not to fall in love. Marriage and children were for ordinary people. How mundane— boring." Callie grinned. "Talk about pompous. If I hadn't taken a chance and stepped off the path that I was focused on, I wouldn't be here. And *that* would be *my* tragedy."

Sable's breath caught in her throat. Callie's eyes. One second they were a crystal clear gray. Then in a heartbeat, they changed to a bright, iridescent purple. It was literally the color of love.

"Caleb."

Callie held out her hand. The big man linked his fingers with his wife's. With a sigh of contentment, she went into her husband's waiting arms.

"Choices, Sable. Sometimes you have to open your eyes and take a leap. If you're lucky, the right person will be there to catch you."

Caleb gave Callie a lingering kiss.

"Always, my love. Always."

Chapter Eighteen

ONE WEEK. MAXIMUM.

That was all the time Sable had left with Colt. Though it was probably an optimistic estimate. Lately, it seemed nothing could go wrong on the set. Candice had become a perfectly behaved professional. She showed up on time. Delivered her lines with flawless precision.

The weather was a dream. Temperate, with clear blue skies and mild breezes. The movie equipment ran with well-oiled precision. No one suffered from an unexpected illness. Not even a bout of hay fever.

In other words, the movie was ahead of schedule. Smooth sailing all the way.

The production would wrap and the happiest time of Sable's life would come to an end. It wasn't right and she felt a little guilty. She found herself hoping for a minor, bloodless, catastrophe that would delay the inevitable. But nothing would slow it down.

Sable would miss Los Angeles. She hated to leave Jade and Paige. She ran her fingers over the silk of her blouse. Every day, she reminded herself that the beautiful clothing wasn't hers. Callie and Caleb. Nate. Garrett. Wyatt. They had become dear to her. Like, family. But thanks to technology, it wasn't hard to keep in touch. She would miss the

Landis clan. The city. The clothes. But she wouldn't be leaving her heart with them. It belonged to Colt.

"It was a good day." Colt collapsed onto the sofa. He leaned his head back, closed his eyes, and took a deep breath. "Want to hear a confession?"

Sable had told herself from the beginning to enjoy what she had and live for today. That axiom had never been truer than right now. Falling into a funk. Worrying about tomorrow. What good would that do? It would ruin the precious time she had left.

Sable shook off her thoughts of doom and gloom. If she had a week, or an hour. She planned on savoring every second.

"Now I'm your priest?" she teased. Sable kicked off her shoes then curled up next to Colt.

"Only if there were female priests. And they weren't celibate." Keeping his eyes closed, Colt pulled her close. "Nope. Don't go there. It conjures up all kinds of strange and disturbing thoughts."

"All of your thoughts are inappropriate."

Sable nuzzled his neck. The heat of his skin. His scent. The little prickle of beard that made her shudder with pleasure when he rubbed his cheek against her breasts. She wanted to remember everything. Not that there was a chance that she would forget.

"You bring out the worst in me." Colt thought for a second. "Or is it the best?"

"It's something all right." Sable laughed. She was happy around Colt. Her spirit felt light. Lighter than she could ever remember. "Now, about that confession."

"I didn't think we were going to get this movie made."

Surprised, Sable looked him in the eye. "I know Candice was a pain in the ass but was it really that bad?"

"Okay." Colt took a deep breath. "Here's the real confession. I hate touching her. I've been doing this for almost ten years and this is the first time I can honestly say, my leading lady... repulses me."

"Why haven't you said something before now?"

"What was there to say?" Taking her hand, he kissed the back then kept it in his. "I made my bed—so to speak. There was no way to change actresses mid-movie."

"You threatened it."

"It was a bluff. And I'm damn lucky she didn't call me on it."

"What would have happened?"

Colt made a chopping motion toward his balls.

"Ouch."

"That might be a bit of an exaggeration." With his lips, Colt smoothed the frown from her brow. "I had no real leverage. Other than scrap the movie—"

"Which you also threatened to do."

"God. I can hear Wyatt if I had made that suggestion. *Cut the movie star crap, Colton. This is about money, not your ego.*"

"Ego, my ass!" Sable straightened, her eyes flashing. "You coddled that bitch. Wyatt needs to get out from behind his desk and see what you have to deal with on a daily basis."

"Calm down. That was my interpretation of what he might say. It didn't happen."

"Hmm." Sable let herself relax. "He's your brother. He's supposed to have your back."

"Trust me. He always does. Unfortunately, if it came down to it, he would be right."

"But—"

"Landis Productions isn't a vanity project, Sable. When one of us makes a commitment to a project, we see it through. No matter what. Wyatt won't make an exception for me. Not over a temperamental actress."

"Temperamental is a kind way of putting it."

"Candice has talent." Colt laughed when he heard Sable's snort. "Be fair. You've seen the dailies."

Sable had to admit Colt was right. The camera loved Candice. She projected a wholesome, perky image. She glowed on screen. Sable didn't know how she pulled it off, but sitting in a darkened room, Candice's image projected onto a screen, the actress had… What was the word?

"Spunk." That was it.

"I suppose that describes her screen persona as well as anything

"I hate spunk," Sable muttered.

Colt looked at her for a moment, seemingly puzzled. Then, his blue eyes lit up and he grinned, delighted.

"*The Mary Tyler Moore Show.* I can't believe I almost missed the reference."

"Mom has the entire series on DVD. VHS when I was a kid. We watched those episodes over and over again." Sable smiled, her eyes a little sad but still a warm brown. "It's a good memory."

"I like making good memories. With you." Colt curled his legs around hers, making it so his knee ended conveniently pressed against a very intimate spot.

"Want to make some more?" Sable purred the words. The way Colt petted her, she felt like a soon to be contented cat.

"Let's take this to the bedroom."

"What's wrong with here?"

When Sable moved her head to the side, giving him access to the long, sweet side of her neck, Colt obliged her silent request. He left a trail of soft kisses all the way to the curve of her ear.

"There's more room," he whispered. "I'm going to start here."

Sable let out a long sigh. Colt was the first man to spend time finding her body's many, many erogenous zones. Or perhaps he was the first who left her breathless, no matter where he touched.

"You've persuaded me. The bedroom it is."

Wrapping her arms around his neck, she gave him a slow smile, waiting to be lifted into his arms.

"You like this." With ease, Colt wrapped one arm around her waist and the other under her legs, and stood.

"So do you. Besides, it keeps you in shape. Better than bicep curls."

"And a lot more fun."

Sable started to close her eyes—to enjoy the ride—when her phone rang.

"Ignore it."

Colt knew better. By now, he recognized the ringtone. He felt Sable stiffen. Instead of putting her down, he kept his arms around her, settling them both on the sofa.

Sable met his gaze and shrugged. She could have let it go to voicemail, but she would have paid the price later. There were some forces of nature that refused to be pushed aside.

"Hi, Mom."

"Where are you?"

Her mother never said a simple hello. Somehow, she began every conversation with an accusation.

"I'm exactly where I should be at quarter to twelve on a Thursday night. Getting ready to go to bed." Sable didn't know why, but suddenly she had a terrible thought. "Where are you?"

"At the airport. I need you to pick me up."

Sable slid off Colt's lap. When a disaster was in the works, she needed to be on her feet.

"The airport? Which airport?"

"LUX of course."

"Do you mean LAX? You're in Los Angeles?"

"LUX. LAX. What difference does it make? You know what I meant." Iris let out a long suffering sigh. "I've been here for almost an hour and I don't like it, Sable. Come and take me to my hotel."

Hotel. Thank God for that. Sable thought her mother was going to insist on staying with her. And Colt. It was a small miracle—one she took with gratitude.

"It would be faster if you took a cab."

"Are you crazy?" Iris shrieked. Sable held the phone away from her ear. "Those things are death traps. Not to mention what happens to single women who are foolish enough to get in one at this time of night. Do you want me to end up a statistic, Sable?"

"What airline did you fly in on and what was your flight number?" Sable took down the information. "Find a place to wait. I'll call you when I get there."

"How long will you be?"

"I don't know, Mom."

"Well, hurry. There's a very strange man by the magazine rack. I think he followed me off the plane."

"The plane landed, Mom. You can't blame the guy for getting off."

"You're just like your father—an answer for everything."

Sable knew there was no reasoning with her mother.

"If you feel threatened, call airport security. I'll be there as soon as possible."

"I take it you didn't know she was coming."

Shaking her head, Sable scrolled through the numbers on her phone.

"She never goes anywhere. When Dad got a permanent assignment in Florida, she swore that was it. No more traveling. This can't be good."

Colt rubbed her shoulders, his eyes filled with concern.

"Are you all right?"

Sable understood what Colt meant. Her mother's phone calls tended to send her into a tailspin. Surprisingly, the usual melancholy that seeped into her bones with the sound of Iris' voice wasn't there. Huh. Something had changed—and she had the feeling it was because of Colt.

"Other than wondering what sort of destruction Hurricane Iris is bringing with her? I'm fine."

"Want me to come with you?"

"Are you crazy?"

Horrified couldn't begin to describe how Sable felt about his suggestion. Colt and Iris in the same space? Her mother had no filter. She suffered from chronic verbal diarrhea. Who knew what she would say or do? No. Not now. Hopefully never.

"It's better if I go alone. The problem is finding someone to stay with you."

Colt sighed. "Sable. Honey. Sweetheart."

"It's my job, Colton."

"And you do it very well." He turned her to face him, both hands on her shoulders. His blue eyes were clear and steady. "Diligence is your middle name."

"Actually, it's Amaryllis."

"No." Colt's lips twitched. "Really? Sable Amaryllis Ford? What was your mother thinking?"

"She named me after a pelt of fur and a flower that blooms once a year. I hope that gives you a little more insight into what I'm dealing with. You stay here. I'll call Wyatt."

"Sable." He took the phone from her hand. "This is a secure building. No one is getting up here unless I let them. Go get your mother."

"But—"

"Now."

Sable knew Colt was right. There hadn't been a whiff of a threat since she had been here. Not even hate mail. Leaving Colt alone for a few hours wouldn't hurt. Unless it did. She couldn't help it, that was the way her mind worked.

"Give me a second."

Snatching back her phone, Sable made a quick call.

"Problems?"

"Do you think we will ever get to the point where we don't think the worst when the phone rings?"

Alex laughed. "Depends on who's calling."

"Good point. My list tends to bring trouble. Which leads me to the reason for my after-hours interruptions."

"There's no such thing as after hours in this business. Besides, my wife is a night owl. Unless I want to go to bed alone, before midnight is early. What's up?"

Sable quickly outlined her dilemma.

"I know I shouldn't leave him alone but... "

"But it's standard procedure to stay with the client at all times."

"Right."

"Colt's okay with you going?"

"He insists."

"I do," Colt called out.

"I checked out the building's security. It's top notch. Go, Sable. You have my blessing."

"It feels odd." More than odd. It was one thing when Colt had his brother with him, but leaving him alone? Sable had a hard time with that.

"Too much military training. We look for trouble around every corner."

"That sounds like a good thing to me."

"Most of the time it is. But not tonight. Go. Relax."

Alex hung up before Sable could get another argument in. She looked at Colt, who was doing a lousy job of hiding a self-satisfied smile.

"I guess I'm going," she grumbled.

"Was there any doubt?"

"Don't gloat."

"I wouldn't think of it."

Sable looked down at her jeans and t-shirt and sighed. She looked fine. L.A. chic. But *fine* wasn't good enough. Not for Iris Ford. She had to take time and put on something her mother would consider a proper airport greeting outfit.

She headed for the bedroom, Colt right on her heels.

"There's no need to change. You look great." He flopped onto the bed. "Better than great. Now that I think about it, I'll send a car for your mother. Too much chance of some foreign gigolo hitting on you at LAX."

"If it were anyone but my mother I wouldn't bother. And what in God's name would I do with a foreign gigolo?" Sable held up a silk dress and stood in front of the mirror. The red looked good with her dark hair and lightly tanned skin.

"Kick him in the balls? That I would like to see. Are you sure I can't come?"

"You live in a beautiful, lollypop-lined world where mothers are Callie Flynn. Iris Ford isn't just different. She comes from another planet. Save us both the trauma and stay home."

Sable walked out of the closet and did a twirl.

"What do you think?"

"Have I seen that dress before?"

"No." Sable frowned. Colt's blank expression wasn't the reaction she had hoped for.

"Have I seen whatever you're wearing under it?"

Ah. Sable sent him a sly smile.

"What makes you think I'm wearing anything?"

"You can't leave without underwear."

He jumped off the bed, but Sable was too far ahead of him. The heels of her slate gray pumps clicked across the hardwood floor.

"Let's see." She checked the contents of her small black bag. "Comb. Lipstick. Gun. Just the essentials."

"Sable."

"Look." Sable held up her skirt. "Black lace. The bra matches but you'll have to take my word for it."

"I was going to say, take my car. But I'm fine with the peep show."

"You," Sable grabbed the keys from his hand, "are an idiot."

Colt simply held out his arms. Shaking her head, Sable walked into his embrace.

"Drive safe."

"Always."

"Text me when you get there."

"Promise me you're in for the night. And no visitors outside of your family."

"I promise. I'll wait up for you."

Sable kissed his chin, then lingered a little longer on his mouth, before stepping into the elevator. As the doors closed, she sent him a little wave and took a deep breath. She had no idea what mess was waiting for her at the airport. But knowing Colt would be here when she got back made the dread a little easier to bear.

PARKING WAS A little easier at night—but not much. Sable found a spot in the lot next to LAX that was only a football field length from the entrance.

Before getting out of the Maserati, she considered her options. Take the gun with her and deal with all the airport security hassles that would entail. Or leave it here—safely locked in the car.

The choice was simple. Better to err on the side of caution. Sable looked around, making certain no one was near the car before slipping the gun from her purse. Opening the glove box required a scan of Colt's thumbprint—or hers. He made that little addition at the same time he changed the security at the loft.

On the walk to the terminal, she sent Colt a text.

Made it safe and sound. Your car is guarding my gun. With a click, she set the alarm. *But if I need a weapon, my stilettos should work nicely. See you soon.*

Sable could make a twenty-mile hike through mountain terrain with a full pack strapped to her back. But walking across pitted asphalt in four-inch heels was another thing altogether. She longed for her Keds and a bottle of water. She had to settle for the air-conditioned din of LAX.

The sights and sounds of an airport rarely changed from city to city. Especially the large ones. People coming and going. Hurrying from here to there. This was not the destination. It was a necessary pit stop. A way out. Or a way in.

Before security became the battle cry, loved ones could escort you to the boarding gate and watch as your plane took off. Now it was more of a waiting game.

Sable stood to the side, out of the flow of bodies, and phoned her mother. She expected Iris to pick up after the first ring. When three went by, Sable felt a twinge of annoyance. When the call went to voicemail, she started to worry.

Wandering around trying to find one lone woman would be a waste of time. Instead, Sable went to a courtesy counter and asked them to page her mother. It took fifteen minutes during which Sable's imagination ran the gamut. The least she expected was for Iris to be upset.

Once again, her mother refused to do the expected.

"Sable."

The sing-song voice drew the attention of everyone at, or near, the courtesy desk. Relieved, Sable turned, prepared for anything. Except a smiling, laughing Iris on the arm of a handsome man.

Iris looked fit and trim as always. But her hair was different. *Very* different. Her mother always wore it long. Once or twice a year, she would get no more than an inch or two trimmed off.

The change involved more than a few inches of hair. Iris looked like a different woman with the flattering shoulder-length bob that bounced as she walked. And it was red. Eye-popping would be a good way of describing the color. It shouldn't have worked. On anyone. But Iris managed to pull it off.

"Mom. I love your hair."

"Thank you." Iris gave the ends a practiced flip. "I felt like a change. When my cousin Tessy—you remember Tessy—well, she won a trip to Hawaii. Can you imagine? Her husband can't get away from work so she insisted that I go with her."

That explained a lot. Tessy and Iris were as close as sisters. Though Tessy still lived in Tennessee, they kept in touch. These days they would Skype at least once a week.

Sable accepted Iris' hug but her eyes were on the smiling stranger. The man looked prosperous, but didn't all con men? Easy marks like her mother were drawn to charming men in well-tailored suits. And if they had a big white smile, a nice physique, and dimples, it didn't hurt.

"Sable, I want to introduce you to Wade Fairfax. This nice man was kind enough to keep me company while I waited for you." Iris fluttered her lashes. "Even though there were plenty of younger women his own age giving him the eye."

"Younger?" Wade turned his blinding smile on Sable. "I couldn't believe it when Iris told me that she had a grown daughter. I would have taken you for sisters."

It was all Sable could do to contain the groan that wanted to burst from her mouth. That old chestnut? Naturally, her mother ate it up with a spoon. The guy was young enough to be Sable's brother. And Iris, while a very attractive woman, looked her age.

"You won't believe what this kind young man did for me, Sable."

Oh, I'll believe it. The question was, how much had it cost and could she recover the money.

"It was nothing," Wade grinned, his dimple getting alarmingly bigger. "I know some people at the airline. When your mother mentioned that her connecting flight to Honolulu wasn't leaving until late tomorrow morning, I called a friend and got her on an earlier flight."

"Wasn't that nice of him, Sable? I leave in two hours." Iris bubbled with excitement. A new emotion to go along with the hair. Again, it looked good on her.

"Excuse me for a minute. I want to make sure Iris' luggage is transferred to the proper plane."

"I can't believe my luck." Iris sighed with pleasure. "I was bored to tears waiting for you so I struck up a conversation with Wade. Boom. He offers to take care of everything."

"Why?"

"Because he's kind? Oh, I see that."

"What?"

"The way you rolled your eyes. You think this is some kind of scam, don't you?"

"Mom," Sable kept her voice calm and reasonable. "It doesn't make sense for a stranger to do this out of the goodness of his heart. He's too smooth to ask for anything yet, but wait until you're halfway across the Pacific. He's after something."

"You think you're *so* smart. For your information, Wade isn't going to Hawaii. In fact, he had only stopped to check the messages on his phone. He's thirty-one years old, single, and owns a very successful construction business."

Sable had to admit, she might have jumped to the wrong conclusion. But for her own piece of mind, she planned on doing a thorough background check on Mr. Wade Fairfax.

"He sounds like a peach, Mom."

"Did I mention that he doesn't have a girlfriend?"

"No. Why would you?"

"I told him all about you and he seemed very interested. I'm so glad you wore a dress. Your legs are your best feature. I'm certain that Wade noticed."

This time, Sable couldn't keep her groan from bubbling out.

"What?" Iris demanded.

"Let's sit down, Mom."

"I don't need to sit."

"I do. My feet are killing me."

Reluctantly, Iris let herself be led to a row of seats that were out of the path of impatient travelers.

"I know what you're going to say." Iris took a compact out of her purse. Her makeup was perfect but she powdered her nose just to be safe. "You aren't interested in Wade because you already have a boyfriend."

Actually, it hadn't occurred to Sable to mention Colt. She had planned to tell Iris that she wasn't interested in Wade, or anyone else—period. But since her mother believed the relationship was real, she used it as a convenient buffer.

"Colt does exist, Mom." No lie there.

"But for how long?"

"He's healthy and has excellent genes. Hopefully, he'll be around for another sixty-plus years."

"You know what I meant. He's a movie star, Sable. How much longer do you think you can hold his interest?"

About two weeks.

"This isn't about Colt, Mom. Picking up strange men at the airport is bad enough. Picking one up for me? Unacceptable."

"Time is no woman's friend, Sable."

"I don't know. Have you seen Sophia Loren? I would do her in a heartbeat." The joke missed its mark by a mile. The only thing her mother heard was the possible admission that Sable's interest lay with women—not men.

"Is that why you left the Army?" Looking around surreptitiously, Iris lowered her voice. "Don't ask, don't tell?"

"They repealed that piece of crap policy before I resigned." It was obvious that answer hadn't satisfied her mother. Sable sighed and gave in. "No. I am not gay. Or bisexual. I like men. Straight up." Sometimes with a twist. If she were playing with Colt.

"I don't know why you're smiling. No matter how much fun you provide to Colton Landis, it's temporary. You can't afford to throw away a perfectly good man."

"You don't know that Wade Fairfax is a good man. Maybe he kicks his dog. Or cheats on his income tax. Do you know how much prison time you can do for that? That's how they got Al Capone."

Iris sent her a blank stare.

"I have no idea what you are talking about."

To be honest, neither did Sable. She was rambling in the off chance her mother would get the hint and drop the subject.

"Oh. There's Wade." Iris rummaged through her purse, triumphantly pulling out a tube of lipstick. "Here. A bright color draws a man's attention to your mouth."

Dumbfounded, Sable couldn't think of a single comeback. Then to her, and Iris' surprise, she burst out laughing.

"Mom."

Iris raised her chin. "Yes?"

"I love you."

Iris blinked once, then twice, before smiling.

"I love you, too, sweetheart."

Chapter Nineteen

IT WAS AMAZING what the passing of a few hours could do for a person's outlook.

When Sable left for the airport, her emotions had been all over the place. She didn't know what she would find or how she would deal with it. Now, her mother was safely on a plane to Hawaii and for the first time, Sable felt hope for the future of their relationship.

Not that she expected miracles. Iris would never change. Nor would Sable. But she saw her mother through clearer eyes. Vain. Self-centered. Clueless. Also warm, caring, and loving. No. Neither of them had changed. It was all a matter of perspective. *That's* what was different."

The elevator dinged. As the doors opened, Sable took a moment to lean against the wall and remove her shoes, then padded into the loft. She sighed with pleasure when her soles hit the cool hardwood floor.

It was half past four. Sable listened, not expecting to hear anything. Colt had to be on the set at seven o'clock. She hadn't called to tell him she was on her way. She hoped he did the smart thing and went to bed. Something she planned on doing. With luck, she could get an hour of sleep. It wasn't the ideal amount, but she had survived on less.

Sable made a quick detour to the kitchen and grabbed a bottle of water. She was at the bedroom door when she heard the faint sound of the running shower. Change of plans. The hell with sleep when she could rub up against a wet and warm Colt.

She reached for the zipper on the side of her dress. It was halfway down when a voice from the bed froze her in her tracks.

"Hello."

The light was low, but there was no mistaking the identity of the naked bleached blonde in Colt's bed.

"Candice?"

"This is awkward." The actress made a show of adjusting the sheet over her breasts. "Colt said you were supposed to call before showing up. A bit of advice. Always follow the script. Bad things happen when you try to improvise."

Sable looked at Candice. Then at the open bathroom door. Colt's voice rang out as he sang a snappy rendition of *Crocodile Rock*.

"Interesting choice of tunes," Sable mumbled.

"He sounds happy, doesn't he?" Candice purred the words. "*Good sex* will do that to a man."

With a sigh, Sable rubbed her eyes. Rumpled sheets. A naked woman. A singing man in the shower. It all added up to one obvious conclusion—if this were a bad romance novel. She was tired. But she wasn't a fool.

"Honestly, Candice? This is straight out of bad plot ploy one oh one."

"I have no idea what you're talking about." Candice made a poor attempt at turning her nose up in a dismissive manner.

"What did you hope would happen?" Sable set her purse, and her gun, out of reach. It was tempting. But the pleasure of scaring the crap out of the blonde wasn't worth the trouble it would cause.

"Was I supposed to recoil in horror? Run into the early morning with tears streaming down my face—never to be heard from again?"

"What is wrong with you?" Candice pounded the bed with her fist. Splotches of angry red burst onto her cheeks. "I had sex with Colt. Don't you have any pride?"

"Don't you?"

Colt stood in the bathroom door, a towel wrapped around his waist.

"Colt," Candice gasped. "I—"

"Save your breath." He grabbed Candice's clothes from the chair and tossed them at her. "Get dressed. This was low, Candice. Even for you."

"Why don't you want me?" she wailed, tears welling artfully in her eyes. In Sable's opinion, it was the best performance of her career. Then she ruined it by going one step too far. "I love you."

"Oh, boy."

"Bitch." Candice launched herself from the bed, her claws drawn and aimed at Sable.

Colt rushed forward, putting himself between the women. He held Candice back, his hand on her forehead.

"Let her go," Sable said calmly. She watched with growing amusement while Candice tried to push past Colt, her arms flailing like a cartoon character. "I won't hurt her—much."

"I would love to oblige. But I still need her in one piece. If she's crazy enough to hang around after the movie wraps, she's all yours."

"Fine." Sable ambled toward the bathroom. "Five minutes. If you haven't put the trash out by then, it will be my pleasure to kick her to the curb."

Shutting the door with a firm snap, Sable could still hear Candice's pleading wails. Which was fine—great. She didn't want to drown it out. It lent a certain symmetry to her evening. On one hand, she had dealt nicely with her ditzy mother. On the other, Colt's loony tunes co-star.

Another screech from Candice put a smile on Sable's face. Humming, she slipped out of her dress and into the shower.

COLT WASN'T WAITING for her when she exited the bathroom. Not that Sable was surprised. She gave Candice a five-minute deadline, but because she felt all loose and relaxed from the multiple jets of hot water, Sable didn't push the issue.

Ten minutes had passed. Whistling, slightly off tune, Sable stripped the bed of the actress-contaminated sheets. A quick spin through her brain told her the housekeeper Colt had hired would be here later today. She would send the laundry out and make the bed.

Tightening the belt on her robe, Sable walked into the living room. Colt wasn't in the kitchen or on the sofa. Sable felt a slight spike in her temper. He wouldn't have been crazy enough to drive Candice home?

"Colt?"

"Over here."

He was standing out of sight, just off the kitchen, staring out the window and dressed in a pair of pajama bottoms—nothing else. His hands were wrapped around a steaming cup of coffee.

"Want some? I just made a fresh pot."

"Mind if I take a sip of yours?"

Sable took the cup, sighing with pleasure as the strong flavor hit her taste buds.

"You can't be too angry if you're willing to share my germs."

"That ship sailed long ago. If you've got it, I've got it."

"And vice versa." Colt shook his head when she tried to hand back the cup. "I have a good reason why Candice was here."

"You *think* you have a good reason." Sable wasn't angry, but she wasn't letting him off the hook that easily. "What did I say before I left?"

"Christ, Sable. I'm not a child. It isn't necessary to chastise me."

She simply took another sip and met his gaze over the rim. When she raised her eyebrows, he sighed.

"Candice called a couple of hours after you left. She was outside the building and was drunk."

"Or claimed to be."

"Yes," Colt nodded. "But I didn't know that. She swore she was going to drive home. I couldn't let her do that."

"You should have called her a cab."

"She wouldn't wait. And since, per your instructions, I couldn't go out and stop her, I let her come up."

"And then invited her into bed?"

"Fuck that." Colt searched her face. Sable let him off this particular hook and smiled. His shoulders relaxed. "I thought she had passed out on the sofa. I put a blanket over her and called her assistant to pick her up. The ETA was an hour, so I decided to take a shower. I didn't know when you would get back. I planned on getting dressed and ready to leave for the set."

"Let me take it from there." Sable set the cup on the counter. "As soon as you were naked—"

"And in the shower," Colt reminded her.

"And in the shower," Sable conceded. "Candice miraculously sobered up. She dropped her clothes and climbed into bed."

"That about sums it up."

"Except how did she know I wasn't here?"

"You don't think she had someone watching the building?"

"Creepy, but it's the only thing that makes sense. When they saw me drive away, they called Candice. Obviously, it took her awhile to get here. From the look of her, she took the time to do her hair and makeup. Since I hadn't returned, she took advantage of the situation. She once told me she didn't like to improvise but in a pinch, she's pretty good at thinking on her feet."

Colt frowned. "She couldn't have known how long you would be gone."

Patting his hand, Sable shook her head. The poor guy still hadn't grasped the entire situation.

"She didn't care. No matter when I showed up, her plan was to make it look like the two of you had or were about to have, sex."

"You didn't buy it." It wasn't a question but a statement.

Sable wasn't immune to the most basic human emotions. When she saw Candice in Colt's bed, she felt a myriad of emotions. Surprise. Hurt. Anger. Disgust. But they came and went in a schizophrenic flash. It was too staged. Too obvious. And most of all—it wasn't Colt.

Candice had badly miscalculated. She had spent too much time reading her own planted publicity. She believed herself to be irresistible. What man in his right mind would turn down a chance to have sex with America's Sweetheart? And what woman wouldn't believe it? Especially with the evidence right in front of her.

The answers to those questions were simple and succinct. Colt and Sable—that's who.

Colt wasn't the kind of man to jump from one woman to another with no explanation. And Sable wasn't the kind of woman to run away in tears—with no explanation. Even if she had believed the setup, she would have waited for Colt's confirmation.

However, it didn't change the fact that Colt broke rule number one. Do not let anyone other than Sable and his family through his door.

"I know what you're thinking."

"I doubt it. Not this time."

"Go on," Colt said, confident and ready to take his medicine. "Call me a Boy Scout."

"I'll call you an idiot. Not even a Boy Scout would let a barracuda cross his threshold. You welcomed her with open arms—and wrapped her in a blankie for good measure."

"In my defense—" Colt held up a hand when Sable started to interrupt. "It's the only one I have, so let me finish."

"Fine. Go on."

"You would have done the same thing."

That stopped her. She had all kinds of comebacks planned—one for every scenario she anticipated him using. But *this* she hadn't expected. It was short and to the point. And, much to her consternation, he was right.

There was no argument for the truth.

"You didn't follow orders." Lame. Sable knew it and so did Colt. "Don't you dare grin at me. I'm giving you this one. You don't get to gloat."

"No gloating." Colt tempered his grin, downgrading it to a smile. "We have time before we have to leave. Breakfast or a nap?"

"Breakfast," Sable said emphatically. "A nap won't be enough. I'm better off staying awake."

"Me too." He took eggs and butter from the refrigerator. "A cheese omelet. Bacon? Toast?"

"Cholesterol alert?" Laughing, Sable poured more coffee, grabbing another cup. "Why not? If you promise to eat a salad for lunch. And not one drenched in ranch dressing."

"No problem." With the skill of a man at ease in the kitchen, Colt broke the eggs with one hand and whisked them with the other.

Sable settled on a stool to enjoy the show. Food? Cooked by a sexy bare-chested Colton Landis? Sounded like the perfect way to start her day.

"IT'S THE LAST day."

"Mmm."

"We made it."

"Yes, we did."

Colt looked at Sable's reflection in the mirror. She thumbed through a copy of *Architecture Digest* while he sat through another session in the hair and makeup trailer. She looked cool, breezy, and relaxed in a pair of cotton drawstring pants and sleeveless silk blouse. Her hair, which Gilda, the same woman working on him at the moment, had trimmed last week, was flawlessly messy—and sexy as hell. She wore just the right amount of makeup, giving her a natural look that drove him crazy.

Colt knew the truth. It wasn't what Sable wore, or how her hair and makeup were done. It was her. And he couldn't get enough of her.

He knew how he felt. He loved Sable. For him, it was as simple as that. But getting a handle on how she felt wasn't as easy. Hell, he would have settled for not easy. Sable was harder to read than ancient Sanskrit.

Tell her how you feel. That made the most sense. All she could do was— What? Laugh? No. Sable wasn't a cruel person. She would let him down with kind words. And it would kill him. Laughter he could react to. He could rail. Call her names for her callous treatment. But kindness? It left a man with no alternative. He had to be kind in turn— even while dying a little inside.

There had been times over the past few weeks when he thought Sable felt the same as he did. The look in her eyes. Her smile. The way she touched him. Not when they made love. The relaxed moments. A natural brush of her hand against his. Or how she curled up next to him when they were watching television.

It felt like love. It didn't seem possible that he could be in this alone.

Then she would talk about what she planned on doing next month. Or a trip she wanted to take over the Christmas holidays. It was done with a casualness that made Colt uncomfortable. As though she had already moved on. Left him behind. He didn't like the way she spoke of the future. Her future away from him.

"Mom wants us to stop by after we wrap. No matter how late."

"I know." Sable lowered the magazine. "She called me yesterday. I know I'm new to all of this, but isn't there usually a wrap party?"

"We'll pop some champagne, but there's something a bit more formal planned for next week."

"Okay."

Okay? Colt ground his teeth in frustration. *Thanks for the resoundingly underwhelming interest.*

"Hey, gorgeous." Gilda tapped his cheek with the brush she was using to smooth out his skin tone. She was forty-six, as wide as she was tall, and hands down the best makeup artist in the business. "Relax those pearly whites, honey. That smile of yours won't be nearly as appealing if you grind your teeth down to nothing but nubs."

Sable straightened, a frown marring her normally smooth brow.

"Is something wrong?"

"No." Colt's retort was harsher than he intended. Sable didn't want to know the kind of thoughts swirling around in his brain. Too bad. It might clear up a few things if she did. Because he couldn't bring himself to ask the questions plaguing him, he made up an excuse. "I was thinking about the final scene with Candice. Things have been a bit tense."

"With good reason," Gilda snorted.

Surprised, Colt glanced at Sable. She simply shrugged, apparently as baffled as he was.

"What reason is that?" he asked.

Three people knew about what happened between them and

Candice. He hadn't said anything. Neither had Sable. That only left Candice. Since she came out looking like a ridiculous crazy woman, it didn't make sense for her to say anything.

Gilda laughed. "You grew up on movie sets. Did you honestly think something that juicy could remain a secret?"

"Who told you?"

"Kirk."

"The catering guy?"

"Who heard it from Willie, the assistant grip, who heard it from Flubber."

"Flubber? Who is Flubber?" Sable asked. She looked as bewildered as Colt felt.

"FX," Gilda replied.

"Special effects," Colt clarified.

"I get what he does. How did he find out?"

"Let me cut to the source."

"Please."

"Word has it, Candice cried all over her assistant. Sparing none of the details. You didn't come off very well in the original version."

"Shocking," Sable chuckled.

"Don't laugh. You were the true villain. Candice painted you as a clingy, foul-mouthed witch. I'm paraphrasing, but you get the idea."

"I embrace foul-mouthed witch. But clingy?"

Sable looked at Colt for vindication and he gave it. Sable, much to his annoyance, didn't cling. Especially not to him.

"You're very independent."

"Damn straight," Sable declared.

Colt mentally rolled his eyes. Then he asked Gilda, "You said the *original version?*"

"The assistant didn't buy Candice's version. When she relayed the story, and since she was telling it in the strictest of confidence, she tacked on what she thought was most likely the truth."

"And everyone ran with it." Colt wasn't surprised. "What about the assistant?"

"Do you mean is she still among the living? Yes. But not the employed. Candice fired her ass the second the whispers started."

"That was a week ago. How have I missed all the drama?"

"For once, discretion reigned. Everyone decided that you've had enough to deal with. I'm telling you now because it's the last day. I thought you might like to know that the crew had your back." Gilda made one last stroke with her brush. "There. Perfection." She winked. "But I say it's gilding the lily."

"That was nice," Sable said as they made their way to the set.

"Gilda is a peach."

"I agree." Sable patted her hair. "But I meant her and the crew. They shielded you from one more shit storm. And since I haven't heard from my mother, didn't spread the story to the press."

Sable was right. His crew was a good bunch. And it humbled him to know they thought so highly of him. Without conscious thought, Colt took Sable's hand. It had become a habit, walking around, connected. A habit he didn't want to break.

"There she is." Sable nodded to where Candice sat. "The fictional love of your life."

Colt shuddered. "I know that was meant to be a joke, but seriously, Sable. I don't know if I will ever be able to watch this movie. I kissed that woman."

"It's a shame. Until you write your memoirs and spill every detail, no one will know that this could be your finest acting job ever. But I know." Sable kissed his cheek. "And so does everyone who worked on the movie."

Sable left him, walking to her usual chair. Surreptitiously, Colt touched his cheek. The gesture was small, but it sent a warm feeling through his body. He didn't want to get used to living without Sable. She was a part of his life. Big—and small.

He took his place in front of the camera, freeing his mind of everything but the final scene. Sable wasn't going anywhere. Not right away. And if he had his way? Not ever.

"Are you ready, Colt?" the director called out.

Colt glanced at Sable. Ready? Absolutely. For today. Forever.

Chapter Twenty

"CONGRATULATIONS. YOU MADE it through another shoot." Callie hugged Colt.

"There were times when I had my doubts if we would get it done."

Callie laughed. "You faced some unique and unusual challenges. But believe me. You aren't the first actor who had problems with his co-star."

"I'm just glad it's over."

Colt had taken a quick shower in his trailer before he and Sable left the set. His hair was still damp and he was bone tired. But for the first time in days, he felt like he could finally relax. The last week had played havoc on his nerves. He hadn't known if Candice would go completely off the rails. She was unstable on a good day. After the debacle at his loft, she became a true wild card.

But they made it. Somehow. Someway. It appeared at first glance that they had a damn good movie on their hands. Time would tell how the critics, and more importantly, the public received it. That was out of Colt's hands. He had done his part—above and beyond.

"Sable is ready to bolt."

"What makes you say that?" Callie glanced across the room where Sable was talking to Wyatt and Nate. "Did she say something?"

"There isn't anything to say. The job is over. Time to get back to her real life."

Callie sighed.

"What?" Colt knew that look of exasperation. He saw it on a regular basis. They all did. And deservedly so. Dealing with the five Landis men took the patience of Job. However, Colt had no idea what he had done this time.

"Have you said anything?"

"For instance?"

"Oh, Colton." Callie cupped his face with her hands. Her expressive eyes were filled with impatience—and a touch of laughter. "A woman's heart is her own. You can't force her to give it away. But, my dear, sweet baby boy. You have to say it. Three little words. Is it really that difficult?"

Colt swallowed nervously, his eyes darting to Sable.

"I plan on telling her, Mom. After the party."

"Ah."

"Ah?" Colt's lips curved. He loved this woman dearly, but sometimes he needed an interpreter. "Is that code for something? Because if it is, I'm lost."

"Of course, you are. Your father was the same way. Instead of simply telling me how he felt, he planned this big elaborate spectacle. Always the producer, he thought of everything down to the most minute detail. Except he forgot one thing."

"What was that?"

Colt had heard it a thousand times—and never tired of the telling. The big party. The big declaration. A heart-melting happily ever after. Suddenly he was finding out that the night hadn't been the perfect fairy tale? It was a new twist to one of his favorite stories.

"I didn't want to play Snow White to his Prince Charming. I wanted simple words. Said from the heart. The whole thing almost blew up in his face—and mine. Luckily for all of us, he figured it out before it was too late. The party was wonderful. But the moment I always hold dearest came before. He took me aside, away from prying eyes. It was those three little words—*I love you*—that sealed the deal."

253

"What if she doesn't want to hear them?"

"You want guarantees?"

"Do you have any to spare?"

"The sun will rise. The sun will set." Callie's smile and her eyes turned warm—filled with unconditional love. "It's the best I can do, Colton. But even that isn't set in stone. "Don't take it for granted. Not the sun. Or that, because you're young, time is on your side."

"Tell Sable what's in your heart."

"I love you, Mom."

"See, that wasn't so hard."

"You have to love me back."

"No, baby. Unfortunately, not even a mother's love is guaranteed."

Colt kissed her cheek, breathing in her familiar, comforting scent.

"Then I'm a very lucky man," he whispered. "Not once, even for a second, have I ever doubted that you love me."

Tears in her eyes, Callie hugged him close.

"Thank you." And because she knew the words were important, she added, "I love you."

SABLE CHECKED THE hallway before slipping into the bathroom. It was ridiculous to hide, but she didn't want to answer any questions—especially from Colt.

She sat on the closed toilet seat and took out her phone, hitting speed dial. What she was about to do was the coward's way out. And she was just fine with that.

"Sable."

"Alex."

There was a pause.

"Should I guess why you called or is something wrong and you don't know how to tell me?"

"Everything is fine."

"Good. If our client were in the hospital, I would have heard by now. An injured Colton Landis would break the internet."

"I returned him to his family unbroken."

"Interesting choice of words." Sable held her breath, waiting for the next question—a personal question, but to her relief, Alex let it pass. "What's up?"

"Today was officially my last day."

"I know. I have it marked on my calendar with a big, red circle. As events go, it's right up there with Dani's birthday or our anniversary."

"Sarcasm? Really? What did I do to deserve it?"

"You tell me?"

Sable breathed in, then out. Her words came in one long, uninterrupted rush. "I need another job. Something quick. Two or three days. Please?"

"I spoke with Wyatt earlier today The family is very happy with H&W Security. And you in particular."

"That's good."

"He mentioned a party. Some big shindig wrapping Colt's movie? My understanding is that you've been invited."

"I'll be there." Sable hadn't known how to decline. "It isn't until next week. Monday. Since today is Thursday…"

"You have three whole days to fill."

"Right."

"When was the last time you took a vacation?"

Sable frowned. What did that have to do with anything? "I'm always taking time off."

"A day here. Two there. I'm talking about a real vacation. A week or two—completely away from work."

What do you think this was? Sable almost asked. For all intents and purposes, her time in Hollywood had been nothing but fun and games. And a lot of amazing sex. She didn't need a vacation. She needed to get away from Colt. To think and clear her mind. Sable couldn't think of a better way to do that than working a *real* job.

"Alex." Sable hated the catch in her voice. She swallowed and tried again. "A couple of days. Please."

"There's a job in San Francisco. It's only one night. You follow a guy around on Sunday night. In and out. I was going to send Baxter but if you want it, it's yours."

"Sold." Sable had never been as grateful to her boss as she was right now.

"I'll text you the information. It won't hurt to get up there a few days early. Check in with the client. Get the lay of the land."

"I can leave right away."

"Tonight? Jesus, Sable. What are you running from?"

Myself. But she didn't want to open that can of worms.

"Call it a breather." Sable rolled her eyes. She used to be a better liar. "I've spent too much time with one client. It's time for a change of scenery."

"If you say so. I see there's a flight out of LAX in three hours. Can you make it?"

"Not a problem."

"Sable."

"I know what you're going to say, Alex. I can't talk about it. Not now."

"Okay. But remember. You have a lot of friends who are good listeners."

Sable hung up, thankful that she had an understanding boss. And a friend who understood when to back off. He could have pushed. Instead, he gave her what she asked for with few questions asked. Those would come later when she was home in Harper Falls.

Sable didn't have the answers. Not now. In a week? A month? Ever? Only time would tell.

SABLE PACKED ONLY the things she had brought with her when she arrived in Los Angeles.

This wasn't a glamorous assignment. It would be her job to ride shotgun with a nervous scientist while he delivered some papers from one lab to another. It seemed silly, but a lot could happen from point A to point B. Especially when it involved something experimental and potentially worth millions of dollars.

This wasn't her first such assignment—and it wouldn't be her last. Alex called them their bread and butter. Small, fast, and profitable.

"This doesn't make any sense."

"It's my job. It doesn't have to make sense to you."

Colt paced the bedroom floor, a scowl marring his forehead. It formed when she had told him about the sudden assignment and hadn't eased. Not on the ride to the loft nor while she packed.

"Why now? Why you?"

"I told you. The client is jumpy. I've worked with him before and he specifically requested that I take the job."

It was a lie. Bold-faced and obvious. At least to her. But Colt didn't comment. Maybe she hadn't lost her touch after all.

"Sounds fishy."

Okay. Her prevarication skills needed some work. Damn Colt. He was such an open, straight to the point kind of guy. Apparently some of that had rubbed off on her.

"You should have stayed at your parents' house. There was no need for you to interrupt the party. I could have called a cab."

"Are you coming back?"

"Of course. I'll be here for the party." Sable plastered a bright smile on her face before exiting the closet.

Colt gave her a long, searching look. She didn't know what he saw, but to her relief, he kept it to himself.

"At least let me drive you to the airport."

"And cause a stampede? If one fan gets a glimpse of you, thousands will follow."

"Thousands?" Colt smiled for the first time in almost an hour. For him, that had to be a record.

"Hundreds?"

It felt good to tease him. Almost as good as when his arms slipped around her waist.

"Try again." Colt nuzzled her ear.

"At least ten," Sable grinned. One brush of his lips and her body relaxed. His kisses were so much better than Xanax. Unfortunately, they were highly addictive.

"Now you've wounded me. A shot," Colt made the sound of an arrow hitting its target, "straight to my ego."

"It, and you will survive." Reluctantly, Sable backed away, picking up her bag. "The taxi will be here at any moment."

"Sable."

"Yes?"

She held her breath. There was something in Colt's eyes. Something anxious. Intense. Frightening. Suddenly, she wanted him to speak more than she wanted to breathe. Her phone buzzed. Glancing down, she released the air from her lungs. Whatever he had been about to say would have to wait.

"That's my ride." When Colt started to follow, Sable held up a hand. "Stay here."

"You're off the clock." Colt took her hand, kissing the back. "I can come and go as I please."

"What will you do without me to keep you out of trouble?" she asked lightly.

"I have no idea."

Four words. Simple. Brief. But Colt's answer—and the look in his deep blue eyes as the elevator doors closed—would stay with her all the way to San Francisco—and back.

UNEVENTFUL AND BORING. There was no other way to describe the last four days. Not even a hilariously awkward sexual proposition could lift her trip from anything but what she had to call drudgery.

Her cute nerd scientist client didn't know the first thing about talking to a woman. He stammered and blushed. Sable found it adorable. Another time she might have kissed him and seen where it would lead. But that was B.C. Before Colt. No man, not even one as sweet as Dr. Joshua Lowenstein, could measure up. The bar had been set at a very high level. Too high.

Sable spent most of her time kicking herself for not being with Colt. She had panicked. There was no other way to put it. She saw her time with him ending and she didn't have the guts to say what she wanted to say.

I love you. How difficult could it be? People said it every day. But not

Sable. No. Rather than act like a reasonable adult, she begged her boss for a lame-ass job that anyone with half a brain and a license to carry a gun could have done. And from what she could tell whenever she went to the local range, there were plenty of gun owners who fit that description.

Sable shook off her wandering thoughts. She was in Los Angeles. In a car. Watching the buildings go by. Not exactly full circle—but close enough. Seven weeks ago, she had no idea how her life was about to change. She had thought that acting as Colton Landis' bodyguard would be fun. A breeze. She pictured a little flirting. Maybe a few easy kisses. If she decided to take the leap and Colt was amenable? A brief, no-strings affair.

Fun and breezy? Absolutely. Colt made her laugh. He was the least negative person she had ever known.

A few kisses? Hardly. It would be fruitless—but pleasurable—to try to count how many they had exchanged.

As for the no-strings affair? The person who said, be careful what you ask for, would laugh his ass off if he could see Sable now. She wasn't dealing with strings. They were ropes. Tied in big, intricate knots. Just like her stomach.

The taxi pulled to a stop outside of Colt's loft. She paid the driver, exiting with her case in one hand and her metaphorical heart in the other.

Sable breathed deeply. The Los Angeles air wasn't quite as clear as Harper Falls. It didn't have the river view or the pine trees lining the road she took to work each day. But the city had its charms. Number one being the man who lived twelve flights up.

Instead of walking into the lobby, Sable went around the side of the building and down the ramp to the garage. It felt natural entering this way, and it meant she avoided any prying eyes that she might encounter in the lobby. She laughed at herself. Thinking about her privacy was another offshoot of spending so much time with Colt.

The elevator doors were in sight when a disturbing thought suddenly crossed her mind. What if Colt had the security updated while she was gone? Not likely. But it would certainly alert her to his feelings. A man didn't lock out the woman he loved.

Heart racing, Sable leaned in, letting the light scan her retina. When she heard the familiar beep, and the doors slid open, she let out a sigh. One hurdle out of the way.

The ride to the top seemed to take forever. Until she was staring at the living room sofa and couldn't make her feet move. Then it seemed like it had taken a few seconds. She wasn't ready. When she thought of it later, Sable was embarrassed that she had reached for the button. But before she could do it, Beauty stood before her, half in the loft, half in the elevator.

Tail wagging with the force of a small engine, the dog cocked her head to one side as though asking, "Well? What are you waiting for?" Then she plopped on her back and offered a very furry tummy for Sable to scratch.

"You took the decision out of my hands," Sable laughed. She gave Beauty a thorough pet—head and stomach—then whispered, "Thank you."

"She is such an attention hound. No pun intended."

Sable looked up to see Paige walking from the kitchen. She carried a bowl of water in her hand. Carefully, she laid out a towel on the hardwood floor, before setting the bowl on top.

"There you go, Beauty." Done with Sable, Beauty trotted over to the blonde who patted the dog's head.

Paige smiled at Sable. "She spills as much on the floor as she swallows."

"So I see."

The sounds of a big, enthusiastic tongue lapping water filled the room. Sable didn't know why, but she felt awkward and unsure what to say.

"Colt isn't here," Paige told her.

"He isn't?" Frowning, Sable looked at her watch. "It's only four o'clock. It's too soon for him to be at the party."

"There were some last minute details he wanted to go over with

Callie." Paige shook her head at Beauty, who had finished drinking. "I know what you want. What did Nate say? No snacks between meals. Remember?"

Beauty turned her head one way, then the other. Her big, brown eyes pleading.

"Fine," Paige sighed, but there was a twinkle in her eyes. "One biscuit. But don't tell Nate."

Beauty delicately took the treat between her teeth, trotting to the rug. She plucked down and happily began eating.

"Sorry about that." Paige stood. She and Sable were almost the same height—without heels. Today, Sable wore flats with her jeans. With the strappy sandals that went perfectly with the body-hugging coral-colored dress, Paige topped her by four inches. "We have a daily routine. A little more polish and we're taking it on the road."

Sable had questions—lots of them. But she didn't know where to start. Not without sounding a little crazy. Sorting through and discarding most of them, she picked one that seemed relatively innocuous.

"Why are you here?" She added quickly, "Not that it isn't great to see you."

"But I wasn't who you expected," Paige smiled knowingly. "Colt didn't want you to come back to an empty loft. I, along with Beauty, volunteered to be your official greeters.

"Was I wrong to hope he'd be here?"

"No." Paige gave her an understanding look. "When you left, Colt wondered if you were coming back."

Sable wanted to have this conversation with Colt. But she understood. If the tables were turned, she wouldn't be here either. On the other hand...

"I texted."

"ETA between four and five? Be still my beating heart."

Well, crap.

"I love that the Landis family is close," Sable sighed. "But do you have to share everything?"

"Not everything," Paige assured her. "Colt was a bit... incredulous. He passed his phone around asking, 'What the hell? She's been out of touch for almost four days and this is all I get?'"

Sable frowned. "I have things to say."

"And?"

"And I want to say them to Colt. Not with a text. Or on the phone. *To* him. Face to face."

"Why didn't you say so?"

Paige grabbed Sable's hand, pulling her toward the bedroom.

"All of a sudden, we're in a hurry?"

"I feel energized. The party starts at seven. It is now," Paige scanned the room for a clock, "ten to five. Two hours to get you ready, drive to Callie and Caleb's where my dress is waiting. Then off to the *Four Seasons.*"

"I thought this was a wrap party for Colt's movie? You're going? *The Four Seasons?* It sounds like a big deal."

"You know the Landis clan," Paige said with a wave of her hand. "The bigger, the better."

"It's a wrap party."

Bewildered, Sable followed Paige into the closet. A small party meant a few drinks. Casual. Friendly. A place where she could ply Colt with some liquor, coax him onto the dance floor, and find a cozy place to be alone. But no one gathered at the *Four Seasons* for beer and chips.

"Colt decided to use the occasion as a charity event. You know how people are. The more celebrities and champagne, the looser they get with the purse strings."

"Stupid. Why not save the money they spend on a new dress and give to charity?"

"I agree, in theory. But this is a time-honored method—because it works. And speaking of new dresses. Ta da!"

"Wow."

Dazzled, Sable stared, unable to take her eyes off the garment draped over Paige's arm. The color was hard to describe. It was a shade she didn't recognize.

"What shade is that?" she mused.

"That's what I asked. Promise you won't laugh? Colt calls it *Sable blue.*"

Laugh? Sable wondered how she would keep from crying. Sable blue. The man knew how to go straight to a woman's heart. Hope. It started down deep, warming her from the inside out.

"You have to hand it those Landis boys." Paige handed Sable the dress. "They know how to knock a woman for a loop. In a good way."

"Very good."

Sable ran her hand over the material. It shimmered—iridescent in the light and slipping like water through her fingers. There wasn't much to it but what there was, was spectacular. She couldn't wait to put it on.

"Leave that with me." Paige laughed when Sable reluctantly let go of the dress. "I promise it will still be here after your shower."

Sable took one last look before heading for the bathroom. Funny. Her stomach was calm. Her nerves under control. Maybe the dress possessed magic powers. Soothing qualities. Or maybe the jolt of hope it had provided was all the magic she needed.

Sable reached into the shower and turned on the taps. As she undressed, she suddenly realized she was humming. *Crocodile Rock.* Interesting choice. She thought about Colt singing the same song. The man's influence seeped into all aspects of her life.

Grinning, she walked under the falling water. She belted out the chorus, singing about a Chevy and some old blue jeans. Sable's voice didn't compare to Colt's, but if she played her cards just right, she might be lucky enough to hear him serenade her from the shower every day for the rest of her life.

Chapter Twenty-One

THE LOBBY OF the Beverly Hills *Four Seasons* was always a busy place. However, tonight it was overflowing with more glitz and glamour than usual.

The management was used to hosting celebrities, dignitaries, heads of state, and a few minor royals. It was their job to make them feel that, while guests of the hotel, they were the most important people to ever walk through the doors.

Sable imagined that if she had arrived by herself, the greeting would have been gracious. But she wasn't alone. She was surrounded by the top of the Hollywood food chain. The Landis family was as close as it came to royalty in a country that had decisively disposed of the monarchy close to two hundred and fifty years earlier.

Caleb and Callie led the procession. They drew stares as much for their good looks as for who they were. Evening clothes suited the big man. His broad shoulders filled out the perfectly fitted suit. The streaks of gray in his hair didn't age him. Caleb was the definition of a silver fox.

Callie Flynn, dressed in a gold gown that showed her youthful figure to perfection, walked next to her husband with regal grace.

Garrett and Jade. Nate and Paige. The next generation. Handsome. Beautiful. And obviously, head over heels in love.

No, Sable thought with a smile, it wasn't her arrival that had the hotel manager fawning with more enthusiasm than usual.

"We are honored that you chose the Four Seasons to host your gala."

Gala? Now it was a gala?

Sable looked around as they entered the ballroom. It was almost full. Groups of people stood around visiting, accepting glasses filled with sparkling champagne from nattily dressed roaming waiters. To her surprise, Sable recognized many of the faces.

"When did a simple wrap party become a gala?" she whispered.

Jade smiled. "This is Hollywood. There's an old saying. I went to a party and a gala broke out."

Sable laughed.

"You got the joke," Jade said, obviously pleased. Her hair was piled into an artfully messy bun. Her dress hit her mid-thigh, showing off her toned legs. Pink seemed like an incongruous color for a redhead, but on Jade, it worked.

"It was a good one."

Jade gave Garrett a light jab with her elbow. "I told you so."

"Jade. Love of my life. That is, what, the fourth time you've told that joke? How many laughs have you gotten?"

"Counting you? Two," Jade conceded. "But that means I'm batting five hundred."

"A baseball reference." Garrett groaned. "God, that is hot! Let's dance so I can hold you in my arms."

"Since when do you need an excuse?"

"Public place, sweetheart."

Garrett swung Jade in a circle and onto the dance floor.

"You look gorgeous."

Sable's breath caught in her throat. Colt. She turned, her eyes going straight to his.

"So do you."

Actually, gorgeous didn't begin to describe how good he looked. In a room filled with handsome men, a good portion of whom were directly related to Colt, he stood out. She would accept that she was biased, but in Sable's opinion, it wasn't a close race. The blazing blue eyes. The dark wavy hair. The tall, leanly muscled frame. And she knew every inch of it—intimately. She would be a fool to willingly walk away from that.

"I'm not a fool."

"No. That is the last thing you are."

Oh, and she couldn't forget that killer smile. It made her stomach do a back flip—every time.

"I'm sorry I wasn't at the loft when you got there."

"Paige explained."

"How was your trip?"

"Good." *Small talk? Really?* "Uneventful."

"Did your client hit on you?"

Sable could tell that Colt meant it as a joke. And that he expected her to laugh it off accordingly. When she hesitated, his eyes narrowed. Light blue to dark in only a few seconds.

"Well, fuck me," he growled under his breath. "Did you rip his balls off? Please tell me you left him singing soprano."

"He was very sweet."

Colt rolled his eyes. "Unbelievable. We see a woman and boom. Our brains go into neutral and our dicks take over. We can't help rooting around like a pig searching for truffles."

"He asked, Colt. That's all. We touched exactly twice. Shaking hands when I arrived and when I left. Wait." Sable's eyes sharpened. "Did you just call me a truffle?"

"And men pigs. Besides, truffles are rare and sell for a lot of money. Scratch that last part."

"It's hard to un-hear something, fella." But Sable knew what he meant so she decided to give him a pass.

"What's his name?"

"Why?" Sable sighed when Colt pulled out his phone. "Are you planning on calling him?"

"No. I want to look him up."

"He's a sweet, shy, science nerd."

"Not so shy if he bucked up the courage to hit on you."

"Colt." Gently, but with intent, Sable took his phone. "I wasn't interested."

"Jealousy." Colt frowned. "It's been riding on my back since you left."

"I ran."

That got her his full attention. The frown was replaced by a look of surprise. Colt took her hand. He began purposefully weaving through the crowd, not giving anyone time to waylay them.

"Come with me."

"Where?"

Colt didn't answer and she didn't argue. She let him lead her out of the ballroom and to a bank of elevators.

"You have rented a room?"

"I always do. You never know when you'll want to get away for some peace and quiet."

"Or sneak off with a sexy partygoer."

Colt turned his head, his eyes filled with mischief. "In my misspent youth. These days I'm more likely to take a nap. Alone."

"Interesting."

"Hmm?" Colt waited until the car emptied before pulling her in.

"Elevators. We've spent a lot of time in them."

"One of my best memories happened behind one."

"Mine too."

"Stand over here." Colt left her against one wall. He walked to the other. "I've missed you."

"You have a funny way of showing it." Sable took a step his way but stopped when Colt held up a hand. "What?" she asked, batting her eyes as though butter wouldn't melt in her mouth.

"*You* know what," he told her. "Look at that smile. I haven't touched you in four days. I'm not getting arrested for public indecency because you enticed me into having elevator sex."

"Could I?" Sable's smile widened. She ran a finger along the neckline of her dress, drawing his attention to the creamy expanse of bare skin.

Colt swallowed. "What?"

"Entice you?" She paused at her breast, lightly caressing the slope. "Could I entice you?"

"In a heartbeat." The elevator dinged and Colt sighed with relief. "Thank God. That had to be the longest ride in history."

"Thirty seconds. Forty-five max."

"It felt like an eternity." Pulling her into the hallway, Colt checked right, then left. Seemingly satisfied, he put an arm around her waist. "I think we can risk a kiss."

Sable rubbed her cheek against his palm. She loved when he cupped her face, smoothing the skin with his thumb. It felt wonderfully intimate. His eyes only a few inches from hers. She felt as though they were the only two people in the world.

"One kiss?"

"To start."

Her gaze dropped to his mouth, willing it to touch hers. Had it only been four days? It felt longer.

"The hell with this."

"Wait," Sable protested when Colt pulled away. "Nobody likes a tease, Colton."

"You'll get your kiss." He pulled a keycard from the inside pocket of his jacket. "And more. But not out here. I want you away from prying eyes. And cameras."

Following closely behind, Sable felt a wave of embarrassment. Security was her business. More than anyone, she should be aware of the eye in the sky. There were few places you could go anymore where you weren't watched.

For Colt, it was even worse. He had fans and paparazzi dogging his heels at every turn. She knew that. And yet she, the so-called expert, forgot the second he tempted her with a kiss.

"I didn't think about the cameras. I'm sorry."

"Don't beat yourself up. I've dealt with this my entire life. And remember. Tonight you're a guest."

Colt opened the hotel room door, standing aside for her to enter.

Sable's first instinct was to insist he go first. With a clear head, her bodyguard training kicked in. But Colt shook his head.

"You're off the clock." He gently pushed her over the threshold. "It's you and me. A man and a woman. Not a man and his bodyguard."

"I'll always carry a gun."

Colt glanced at her purse, then at her. "I can live with that. But forgive me if I balk at you for always taking the lead."

"No more checking the area before I let you leave your trailer?" She set her purse on the bureau.

"I hated that." Keeping his eyes on hers, he unbuttoned his jacket and began to pace. "No more sitting in the car while you rush around to open my door."

"Sounds fair."

"No more..." he tossed up his hands, "any of it."

Colt seemed agitated. At the rate he was going, he would wear a hole in the carpet. He put his hands behind his back. Then ran one through his hair. This was the first time Sable had seen him like this. Unsure of his next words.

It had a calming effect on Sable. They were in the same boat. She liked thinking of it that way. The same boat meant, no matter what the problem was, they would figure it out—together.

"Stop." Sable laid a hand on Colt's arm. "Take a deep breath. We're getting ahead of ourselves."

"Right."

Colt breathed in—held it—then slowly let out the air. He tilted his head, looking directly into her eyes and smiled.

"Hello," she whispered. The moment felt too important. Almost reverential.

"Hi." Colt brushed his lips over hers. Once. Twice. He pulled back a bit. "Did I tell you that I missed you?"

"You did."

Sable sighed when he deepened the kiss.

"Did I tell you that I haven't been able to sleep without you next to me? That I would lie awake, certain you were never coming back."

"I didn't sleep very well, either." She rubbed her cheek against his. "And I always planned on coming back."

"To me? Or to say goodbye?"

This time when she sighed it was deeper—heartfelt.

"I had no idea." Colt stiffened. Sable wound her arms around him, rubbing his back—soothing. "I missed you. I wanted to be with you. But I didn't know if our lives fit. If I wanted them to. Or if you did."

"Sable—"

"You have a pretty sweet setup, Colt. You're young and rich. Saying the world is your oyster is putting it mildly. Why settle for one woman when you can have a different one every day of the year? Every hour of every day, if you were so inclined." Sable's words were serious, but she couldn't help teasing, "And had the stamina."

"No one has ever questioned my stamina."

"Certainly not me."

"I love you, Sable."

"I love you, too." Funny. The words weren't so hard to say—not to the right man.

"Our lives will fit if we want them to. I do."

"So do I. But—"

Colt put a finger to her lips. "Give and take." When she kissed the finger, his blue eyes sparkled. "Nothing is perfect. God," he shuddered. "Who would want it to be? Isn't it the little imperfections that make life interesting?"

"I have plenty of those."

"Me too. You've seen them."

She had. But at that moment, she couldn't think of a single one.

"My mind's a blank."

"Give it time," he grinned. "They'll come rushing back. As for other women? I played that game when I was younger. And enjoyed every minute."

Sable gave him a look that told him she didn't doubt it for a second.

"I. Love. You." He punctuated each word with a kiss. "We Landis men don't take those words lightly. You don't say them unless you mean them. And once you say them, you're all in."

"*All* in?"

"For life."

"That's a long time."

"I certainly hope so." Colt took her hand. Slowly, with great deliberation, he went down on one knee. "I want forever, Sable. Will you marry me?"

Sable never jumped. She thought things through. Weighed her options. Researched the pros and cons. She didn't believe in making hasty decisions—especially when it involved the rest of her life. She listened to her head, not her heart. However, now and then, when everything aligned just right, her head and her heart were in complete agreement.

"I love you. Now. Tomorrow. Forever."

"Is that a yes?"

"Yes, Colton. I will marry you."

"One of us should cry." Colt lifted her, swinging her in a circle. "Isn't that the normal reaction?"

"I don't feel like crying." She was too happy. All she could do was grin. A big goofy grin, if the one on Colt's mouth was at all like hers.

"I could." He set her on her feet. "I am an actor after all."

"Fake tears don't count."

"Agreed. Sex." If possible, Colt's face lit up even more. "Let's celebrate the old-fashioned way."

"Of course. There's nothing as traditional as pre-marital sex."

"We'll make our own traditions."

Shaking her head, Sable slowly backed away. She recognized that glint in Colt's eyes. If she didn't move fast, her beautiful dress would be in a heap on the floor.

"There's a party going on, Colton."

"Ten minutes. No one will miss us."

"Add on the time we've already been gone? Nope. You'll have to wait." Sable laughed at his look of disappointment. He wasn't alone. She wanted him just as much. "Anticipation. And," she added, "We will be able to take our time."

"There is that." With a resigned sigh, Colt took her hand in his and headed for the door. "Besides, the whole family is waiting to find out if you said yes."

"Now he's in a hurry." Sable tugged, but Colt had her hand and wasn't letting go. "I need to use the bathroom, Speedy. And I want to check my makeup. You—" Her eyes widened. "What did you say?"

"A lot." Colt batted his baby blues. "But I imagine you mean my comment about my family?"

"They knew you were going to propose?"

Sable felt her cheeks heat. She didn't know why, but it was embarrassing to think that everyone had been in on the secret. God, what if she had said no? She liked the Landis family. Considered them friends. How would she have faced them after turning down Colt's marriage proposal?

"It's a good thing I said yes. Callie never would have forgiven me for breaking her baby's heart."

"Sure, she would have." Colt paused to think about it. "In thirty or forty years."

"Give me a second." Sable grabbed her purse. "Then let's go. I want to stay on Callie's good side. Besides, I'm suddenly in the party mood."

She unzipped the bag. Sable sighed. The big disadvantage of having to carry your gun this way was that it was always on top of something. Usually, the one thing she needed right away. Setting the gun on the bureau, she looked again. There it was. Her tube of lipstick.

"Why don't you leave that here?" Colt said when she started to put the gun back.

"In the room? I know I'm no longer your bodyguard, but if my gun isn't locked up, it's with me. I want to have fun. I won't if it's unsecured."

"I meant, don't take it into the bathroom." Colt pried the purse from Sable's fingers. "I have something to tell you and I'd rather you weren't armed."

"I would never shoot you," Sable assured him, leaving the bathroom door open. "Or hit you."

"What about my balls?"

Sable paused, the lipstick halfway to her mouth. "Did you sleep with someone else?"

"No," Colt said emphatically. "You don't have to worry. I will not cheat. Never."

"Then your balls are safe. Come on. Spit it out. What could be that bad?"

"Your father is here."

Sable waited for her hand to start shaking. In anticipation, she kept the lipstick far away from her face. Moonlight Blush was her favorite shade. On her mouth—not her chin.

But as the seconds passed, her hand remained steady as a rock. Not even a tremor.

"Sable? Did you hear what I said?"

"I assume you mean he's downstairs in the ballroom. Not here with us."

"Yes. Damn it, say something."

"Why?"

Colt looked up from where he sat on the bed. She knew what he saw. A woman with perfect lipstick and freshly fluffed hair. On the surface, she looked calm, cool, and collected. Inside, she didn't know how she managed to place one foot in front of the other.

"I asked him."

"Again. Why?"

"Sit down and let me explain."

Sable sat. Hands neatly folded in her lap. Her eyes were trained on Colt as she waited.

"I didn't want to have one more meaningless party. I wanted it to do some good. Mom helped me organize a gala to benefit returning soldiers. All of the proceeds will go to help the men and women of our armed services integrate into their regular lives. If someone is struggling—physically, psychologically, financially—they can get help."

273

"Why didn't you tell me sooner? I think it's wonderful. I would have helped—any way I could."

"I wanted it to be a surprise."

"You succeeded." Sable closed her eyes for a moment. "That explains why my father agreed to be here. He works hard on the behalf of veterans. He wouldn't turn down the invitation. Not for this."

"But he did."

"What?" Sable's eyes whipped open. "I don't understand."

Colt sat next to her. "Mom called him personally. He said he wished he could attend, but his schedule was full. He couldn't make it on such short notice."

"He's here." Sable was confused. "What made him change his mind?"

"She told him you would be here."

"Me?"

"You." When she began to shake, Colt took her in his arms. "He wants to see his little girl. His words, not mine."

He held her while she cried. Two and a half years of pent up hurt, anger, and frustration poured out. Because, for the first time, she had someone she trusted enough to let down her guard.

"I was afraid you would be angry," he said several minutes later, when she was able to pull away.

"No." Gratefully, Sable took a tissue from the box Colt held out. "I was stunned. Now," she gave a watery laugh, "I'm a mess."

"Your eyes are a little red. I'll get you a cold washcloth.

"There's my Boy Scout."

"Lie back."

Sable sighed when he placed the cool cloth across her eyes.

"That feels good."

"We'll give it five minutes and you'll be as good as new."

"Thank you." She smiled when she felt the bed sag and Colt curl up next to her. "For the cloth. For my father."

"I love you."

"And most of all, for that."

"It works both ways. Next time I feel like crying my eyes out, you can hold me."

Sable reached for his hand, knowing without a doubt that it would be there. Smiling, she rested her head on Colt's shoulder.

"It's a deal."

Chapter Twenty-Two

COLT WAS RIGHT. Five minutes and Sable's eyes were ready to face the world. Her makeup and his suit jacket were another matter.

"That's what you get for letting weepy women cling to you."

"And like any good Boy Scout, I'm always prepared." Colt opened the closet. "Black or white?"

Incredulous, Sable set down her mascara and looked around the bathroom door. "You brought not one, but two spare jackets?"

"*The Lady Eve.*"

"I don't know what that is."

"Only one of the greatest screwball comedies ever made." When Sable pointed to the jacket in his right hand, Colt slipped on the black double-breasted. "Barbara Stanwyck. Henry Fonda. Slapstick at its finest."

"Next movie night."

Walking to the full-length mirror, Sable looked at herself—top to bottom. Miraculously, her dress had been spared. Not a tear stain or wrinkle in sight. Magic material, indeed. Her face, with the help from judiciously placed concealer, was none the worse for wear.

Colt stood behind her, a hand on each shoulder. "Gorgeous. As always."

"I'm ready." She wanted to go before her nerves got the better of her.

"One more thing."

"I swear, Colt. If you make me cry again, I *will* kick your ass."

"I'll take my chances," he chuckled. "I forgot something before."

"Can it wait?"

Impatient, Sable looked at the clock. They had been up here over an hour. She didn't want her father to think she was avoiding him.

"After spending most of one day helping me pick it out, my mother will never forgive me if you show up without this."

Sable gasped.

Colt held an open ring box in his hand. Square cut, set on a platinum band—and a deep sparkling blue. As stones went, it wasn't the biggest diamond, but as far as she was concerned, it was perfect.

"Should I get down on my knee again?"

She shook her head. She held out her left hand. Colt slid the ring on her finger.

"What do you know? A perfect fit."

Sable met his gaze and smiled. Her thoughts exactly.

THE PARTY WAS in full swing and as far as Sable could tell, their absence hadn't been noticed. The free-flowing alcohol and rocking band might have had something to do with that.

Laughter and music greeted Sable and Colt as they stepped into the ballroom. Surreptitiously, Sable looked around. As much as she wanted to see her father, she couldn't control her nerves.

"It will be fine," Colt reassured her.

Sable nodded. She wanted to believe him. But her stomach wasn't cooperating. Taking a deep breath, she pulled back her shoulders. No matter what, tonight was the beginning of a new chapter in her life. And she was determined to enjoy the party.

"I take it back," Sable said over the noise. "We could have stayed in the room for a private celebration. No one down here would have cared."

"Now you tell me." Colt squeezed her hand. "Thirty seconds ago, we could have made our getaway. Not anymore."

Callie was the first to reach them with Caleb close behind.

"Is it good news?" she asked. "Of course, it is. You're smiling. You wouldn't be smiling if it weren't good news."

"Take a breath, sweetheart." Caleb laughed. "Give them a chance to speak."

"Right." Callie looked from Colt to Sable then back again, her gray eyes wide and anxious. "Well. Tell me. I'm dying to know."

No matter how tempting it was to tease his mother, Colt loved her too much to draw out the moment. Besides, he wanted to share his happiness with his family.

"You want to show her?" he asked Sable.

Sable held out her hand.

"Oh," Callie sighed. "It's perfect."

"Don't you dare cry," Sable warned when she saw Callie's eyes begin to fill. "I don't think I can take another round."

"No tears," Callie promised as they began to roll down her cheeks. "I'm sorry. My baby is in love. And getting married." She took the handkerchief Caleb wisely tucked into his pocket before they left the house.

Callie was crying. Caleb beaming. But Sable had to ask.

"You approve?"

"You were already part of the family," Caleb enveloped her into a big, warm hug. "Now I have another daughter. I couldn't be happier."

"I have a hankie if you need it," Colt told her.

"She can share mine." Callie dabbed at Sable's eyes before the tears could spill over, then pulled her into her arms. "I knew from the moment we met that you would be important to this family. I love when I'm right."

"If you wanted to keep this a secret, you can forget it. I was washing my hands in the men's room when somebody asked me for confirmation on your engagement."

"What did you tell him?" Colt asked as Wyatt hugged him.

"What I always say in that situation. I never discuss family business in the bathroom."

"Did that discourage him?"

Wyatt nodded to where a thin man in a burgundy tuxedo alternated between taking pictures of them with his phone and frantically typing on the tiny keyboard.

"The internet is blowing up as we speak."

"Great. It will save us from having to put out a press release."

Wyatt's bark of laughter had the reporter lifting his phone to snap another picture. It was a good one. And would turn out to be profitable. All the major news services used it. It showed Wyatt and Colt Landis grinning, with a glowing Sable sandwiched in between.

"Here is the champagne," Callie declared. "And the rest of our family."

Garrett and Jade had arrived with a tray filled with sparkling wine. Nate and Paige were with them.

"A toast." Caleb held up his glass. "To the happy couple. May this be the saddest day of the rest of their lives."

"Hear, hear."

The clink of crystal and sips of the excellent vintage was followed by more congratulations. Sable accepted more hugs which she warmly returned. She was floating. Only one thing could have made this moment better.

"Sable."

An arm around her waist, Colt felt Sable stiffen. He looked around, recognizing the source of her sudden tension.

"Colonel Ford." Colt held out a hand. The colonel automatically returned the gesture, but his eyes didn't move from Sable.

"Sir."

Sable's heart raced. She took in every detail of her father's appearance. To her relief, he looked exactly the same. Tall. Lean. Perhaps a bit grayer sprinkled in his dark hair. The strong, handsome lines of his face were wonderfully familiar—the same face she had watched with pride so many times as he commanded the soldiers under him.

She loved him without reservation. No matter their differences. Or any harsh words he had spoken. But until he made the first move, her feet were glued to the floor.

Then, his eyes softened and his arms opened wide.

"Sable?" The little hesitation. The trace of uncertainty—that she had never heard before loosened her reserve.

"Daddy." With a sob, Sable raced to him.

"Come on," Caleb gently moved his family along. "Let's give them a little alone time." He smiled indulgently when he saw tears in the women's eyes, then realized he had shed a few of his own. "We need more handkerchiefs."

"I'll be around if you need me," Colt told Sable.

Her head still on her father's shoulder, Sable smiled at him and mouthed, *"Thank you."*

"I'm sorry, Sable. For everything. That text." Frowning, he shook his head. "I'd had a God awful day and your mother was going on about you and your movie star. I regretted it immediately, but once I hit send, there was no bringing it back."

"Let's forget it." Sable didn't want to rehash the past. "All I care about is that you're here."

"No." Mathias Ford lifted her chin and looked her in the eyes. "Don't let me off the hook that easily. I let you down. As a father." He swallowed, his shoulders straightening. "And as a superior officer."

"What did Colt tell you?" Sable took a tissue from her purse. "Here."

Surprised, her father stayed still as she wiped his cheeks.

"Should I frame this?" she teased. She slipped the damp paper into her purse. "When was the last time Colonel Ford cried?"

"The day you were born."

"Oh, Daddy."

The music changed from up-tempo to something slower. Sable recognized the song immediately. Her eyes flew to her father's. Would he remember? Mathias smiled.

"Moondance." He took her right hand in his left, and placed his other hand on her waist. "May I have this dance?"

Unable to speak, Sable nodded. They were content to move silently to the rhythm, letting the old memories circle around them. When the last notes faded, her father took her hand and led her toward the balcony.

"I need a little fresh air."

"That sounds good."

The night air was wonderfully cool. Sable took a deep breath, lifting her face to the gentle breeze.

"It's my turn to apologize." She said, turning her head to meet her father's gaze. "I was a coward."

"Never!"

"Hear me out before you make such a definitive declaration."

"From what your young man told me, you left the Army because you weren't given a choice."

"At the time, I didn't think I had an alternative." Sable sighed. "But by not speaking out, I lost you. And I betrayed female soldiers who came after me. It's been over two years. How many women do you think Colonel Montgomery has harassed in that time?"

"It was your word against his."

"That's what I told myself. But Dad," Sable gripped his hand. "I should have tried. At least, I could have raised some doubt. Then the next time a woman filed a complaint against him, it might have counted for something."

"That was up to you. But you shouldn't have let him use me as a weapon against you."

"Damn, Colton."

"I need to thank him. You weren't going to tell me that part."

"Colonel Montgomery has powerful allies, Dad. He would have tarnished your reputation."

"He could have tried." Mathias sighed. "I have a few friends of my own. But that's beside the point. It wasn't up to you to protect me."

"No, sir."

"But I love that you wanted to." He pulled her close, brushing her temple with his lips. "I love you, Sable."

"I love you, too, Daddy."

GOD, WHAT A night.

Sable looked at herself in the bathroom mirror. Considering all the tears, her eyes were in pretty good shape. A little puffy and a touch red. But she didn't care. She was in love. Engaged to marry the most amazing man in the world. And her father was back in her life.

After their talk, Sable felt closer to him than ever. She had told him everything. And he believed her—without reservation. Mathias reminded her that it wasn't too late. She could press charges against Colonel Montgomery and he would stand behind her.

Sable promised to think about it. Tomorrow. Tonight, all she wanted to do was celebrate.

Sable patted her nose with the pad from her compact, not looking when the bathroom door opened. She was searching her purse for her lipstick when someone jabbed her arm with a long, sharp fingernail.

"You," Candice DeMarcco slurred.

"You got it in one." Sable sighed. The last thing she needed was a drunk crazy actress killing her buzz. "Why don't you stay in here for a few minutes, Candice?" Sable tried to steer the woman to the sofa in the corner. "You aren't very steady on your feet."

"I don't need your help."

Candice pulled away, stumbling backward. The marble vanity kept her from falling on the floor. She caught a glimpse of herself in the mirror and smiled.

"So pretty." Awkwardly she patted her image. "Prettier than you."

"Okay. I'll leave you to it."

Sable turned to leave, but Candice grabbed her arm.

"Why you?" She lurched to the side when Sable removed her claws. This time, she hit the marble with greater force, causing her swept-up hair to fall over one eye. "You get the guy?" Candice frowned. "That's wrong. *I'm* the lead. He's supposed to fall in love with me. *I* get the happily ever after."

The booze, and a healthy dose of delusion, made Candice sound crazier than usual.

Resigned, Sable took out her phone. She couldn't leave Candice alone. The woman would probably stumble into a stall and drown in the toilet. Colt could send someone to take the actress off her hands.

"Not that you'll get one." Candice snorted. "Cock-sucking bitches don't get happily ever afters, do they?"

Great. Now it was deteriorating into foul-mouthed name calling. Candice looked a little green around the gills. In self-defense, Sable took two big steps back.

"If you plan on throwing up, aim for the garbage can."

"Not sick. But you will be." Candice pushed her hair off her face, but it fell right back. "I spoke with an old friend of yours. *Conel Mongomry.*"

Candice slurred the name but Sable understood her. A chill ran down her spine. Followed closely by a surge of heat.

"Colonel Montgomery is here? Colonel *Baker* Montgomery?"

"Mmm." Candice sneered. "He had a fine tale to tell about you. How you spent most of your time in the Army on your knees. The press will eat it up. Good luck getting Colt to the altar after that shit hits the fan."

Sable didn't want to turn her back on Candice. There was no telling what the woman would do. Keeping an eye on her, she hit speed dial.

"Sable? Did you get lost on the way to the bathroom?

"No. I'm still there."

"What's wrong?" The humor had left his voice.

"With me? Nothing. But Candice is in here and she's a mess."

"Alcohol or drugs?"

Sable had no idea. Though Candice's pupils were a little off.

"Maybe both. She can barely stand up and her speech is slurred." Though when she wanted to, she had no problem making her point. Sable kept that, and Candice's revelation, to herself.

"Someone is on the way."

"I'll stay until they get here."

"I figured you would," Colt said warmly. "I'll meet you outside the door."

"Don't bother. There's something I need to do."

"What's going on, Sable?"

"Nothing to worry about." Sable hoped. "I won't be long."

As soon as help arrived, Sable left the bathroom. She knew Colt would worry. And she knew he wouldn't stand around and wait for her. She loved him, but she didn't want to deal with him at the moment. As she searched the crowd, she made another call.

"Wyatt?"

"What's up?"

"Find Colt and keep him busy."

"How long do you need?"

Sable smiled. She appreciated that he trusted her enough not to ask questions. There would be plenty later, but not now.

"Twenty minutes?"

"I can do that with one hand tied behind my back."

"Thank you."

"Sable? Is this dangerous?"

Spying her quarry, Sable's smile turned feral.

"Not for me."

Chapter Twenty-Three

SABLE HAD PICTURED this moment a thousand times. Confronting her former commanding officer was one of those fantasies she believed would never come to fruition. That it would happen—and on tonight of all nights seemed like destiny nodding its head in her direction. For too long she had lived without closure. This was the perfect way to put it behind her—once and for all.

Playing it just right was the key. Sable didn't want to walk up to him, filled with self-righteous indignation. To get exactly what she wanted, she had to play it cool.

Sable wound her way through the groups of partygoers. Close enough for Montgomery to notice her, but so it didn't seem as though he was her destination. She wanted him to approach her—not the other way around. She understood how his mind worked, at least well enough to know he wouldn't be able to resist oozing his oily smarm all over her. His ego wouldn't let her get away. And that was what she counted on.

Keeping him in her peripheral vision, Sable didn't glance his way. He stood alone. Exactly how she wanted him. He held a glass, now and then sipping the liquid as he arrogantly surveyed the room. When she was almost directly in his line of sight, Sable stopped, making a show of searching through her bag.

She knew the instant he saw her. He raised his chin. His eyes narrowed. And he smiled. Slowly. Like a predator spying its dinner. She didn't mind playing Red Riding Hood to his Big Bad Wolf. She knew the story. The wolf ruined many lives, but in the end… Thwack! Off with his head.

The middle of the room wasn't the place for this showdown. Sable zipped her bag and walked away. Certain he wouldn't let her get away.

"Sable Ford. I was hoping I would get a moment with you."

It was the perfect spot. Crowded, but removed from the main flow of people. She and Montgomery would be seen but not heard.

Wiping the smile from her face, Sable turned. He wouldn't see the steely glint in her eyes—because he didn't believe women had backbones. Sable's expression was blank. For his benefit, she added a touch of wary.

"Colonel Montgomery. This is a surprise." *No lie there.*

"When I heard about tonight's gala, I was anxious to attend."

"It's a good cause."

"Yes. The poor, disenfranchised soldier." He lowered his voice so only she could hear the sneer in it. "Weak-willed. There's always a name for it. Shell shocked. Battle-fatigued. Post-traumatic stress disorder. A new generation, a new excuse."

"Soldiers aren't machines, Colonel. PTSD is real."

"Because a doctor says so? Bullshit." He took a long drink, emptying his glass. From the way he smelled, Sable guessed it wasn't his first. He flagged a waiter. "Get me a whiskey. Neat."

"I'll leave you to enjoy your evening."

"Not so fast."

Sable didn't object when Montgomery grabbed her arm. Instead, she gave him a look that she hoped passed for fear. He smiled again, rubbing her skin with his thumb.

Keep going, Sable silently goaded him. *You're playing your part perfectly.*

"Please, Colonel. My fiancé is waiting for me."

"That's right. Good for you. You nabbed a rich pretty boy with more dimples than sense. Once again, you landed firmly on your back."

"Colt is a good man." The quaver in her voice was anger, but as she hoped, Montgomery heard fear.

"Meaning I'm not? My offer was made in good faith." He looked at her finger. "I couldn't give you a ring. Tell me, what did you have to do for that?"

"I don't know what you mean."

"Yes, you do. Tell me." Montgomery pulled her closer. "I want details."

"You're drunk." Sable made a poor effort at trying to get away.

"Not drunk. More like feeling no pain. I have a room upstairs. I've always preferred showing to telling."

"I said no when you were my commanding officer. My answer hasn't changed."

"But a few well-placed words from me, and everyone will believe you came on to me."

"It's a lie."

"I know it and you know it. But when a full bird colonel in the United States Army speaks, the world listens."

"But you admit that you tried to force me into a sexual relationship? I quit the Army because it was either give in to your demands, or you would have ruined my career."

"Sure, I admit it. To you. You weren't the first. Or the last. But no one would have listened to you then. And they sure as hell won't listen now."

"They won't have to." Sable took her phone from her purse. "I have it all right here. In your own words."

"I DON'T CARE if you paint my ass blue and call it the Pacific Ocean. You take care of the publicity. I need to find Sable."

Wyatt had been yapping about PR for what seemed like an eternity. Colt didn't know what bee had gotten in his brother's bonnet, but enough was enough.

"I don't find the idea of your ass, no matter the color, appealing. But for some reason, the rest of the world does. I'll keep the ocean idea in mind," Wyatt called after him. He looked at his watch. Twenty-four minutes, thirty seconds. Not bad. He hoped it had been enough time for Sable to finish her business.

Frustrated, Colt searched the room for Sable. It didn't take him long to spot her. She was engaged in an animated discussion with a man in an Army dress uniform. They were too far away for him to make out the insignia, but from his age, and the number of medals and other hardware on his chest, Colt guessed he was fairly high ranking.

"I seem to have lost my daughter." Mathias Ford said, stopping by Colt. "Does that frown mean you're in the same boat?"

"She's over there." Colt nodded. "Do you recognize the man she's with?"

"Son of a— I didn't know that bastard was here."

"Who is it?"

"Colonel Baker Montgomery."

Colt heard the anger. It echoed through him. But when Mathias started over, Colt stopped him.

"I know you want to save her. So do I. Sable can take care of herself. She needs to do this, sir. On her own."

Reluctantly, Mathias gave a short nod, but he kept his eyes glued on his daughter. As did Colt. He would let Sable finish with Colonel Montgomery. If there were anything left, he would take his turn.

"GIVE ME THAT, you cunt."

Montgomery made a grab for her phone. Sable was way ahead of him. She had no intention of taking any chances. Before putting it in her purse, she quickly sent a copy of the recording to her boss, Alex Fleming.

"I kept silent once. It was a mistake. This time, you're going to pay, Colonel. For what you did to me. And every woman you've ever harassed."

Montgomery sputtered. Sable had knocked the perpetual smirk off his face. In its place was a look of disbelief—and growing rage. She needed the last nail in the coffin. To get it, she poked the bear one more time.

"Don't take it so hard, Colonel. It isn't the end of the world. Oh wait," Sable slowly smiled. "In your case, I guess it is."

Sable knew it was coming. Had planned for it. She used her training to move at the last second. Even so, Montgomery's punch hurt. When she staggered back, clutching her face, it wasn't entirely an act. But falling to the floor was. She could have easily stayed on her feet. But the effect on the crowd wouldn't have been as dramatic.

She lay in a heap, covering her face with her arm as though afraid he would hit her again. Gasps echoed through the room. Shouts of outrage followed a brief shocked silence.

"Sable!"

Colt pushed his way through the crowd, her father close behind. Going to his knees, he pulled her close.

"How badly are you hurt?"

"He's dead," Mathias growled. "If he's breathing tomorrow, I'll know the reason why."

This had gone on long enough. Baker Montgomery had shown his true colors. In front of a crowd filled with high ranking military officers, reporters, and flashing cameras. She didn't want her father getting into trouble because she overplayed her part.

"I'm fine." She let Colt help her to her feet, whispering under her breath, "If my father goes for Montgomery, hold him back."

"Is this an act?" Colt whispered back.

"Yes."

Colt's eyes met hers as if to say, *I got this*. Sable saw the moment it happened. When Colt Landis, fiancé, became Colton Landis, movie star. He turned, the fury was real, but the actor in him knew how to sell the emotion.

"Someone arrest that man. You saw it. He hit my fiancée. What kind of monster punches a defenseless woman?"

"Careful," Sable warned. No need to overdo it. But Colt knew his audience and the crowd was with him. The outraged voices grew in volume and as if on cue, two men dressed in Army MP uniforms appeared beside Colonel Montgomery.

"Will you come with us, sir?"

"I will not." The alcohol was wearing off, but Montgomery's arrogance was bone deep. "Remember who you're addressing, soldier. I can have you stripped down to private before you can cry for your mommy."

"Take him away, Sergeant." Mathias Ford stepped forward in full colonel mode. "And if he resists, you have my permission to use force."

"Yes, sir."

Montgomery seemed to weigh his options. He looked around for support, finding none. His best course of action was to cooperate. He had friends, damn it. Important men who had his back.

"You think this is over?" He directed the words at Sable. "Burn me down, I will rise from the ashes."

Head held high, Colonel Baker Montgomery walked from the room, flanked by military police.

"I'll go with them." Mathias took Sable's hand. "You're going to have a shiner. Not your first, but I'll bet the most memorable."

Sable hugged her father. "You won't leave town without saying goodbye."

"No. I've been invited to breakfast with the Landis family. Do you think I would miss the opportunity to sit across the table from Callie Flynn? Take care. I'll see you in the morning."

Mathias marched across the ballroom, stopping to speak with several Army officers, one a general. Whatever he said had the men nodding in agreement. After the brief conference, they left as a united force to be reckoned with.

"Ladies and gentlemen." On the bandstand, microphone in hand, Caleb Landis drew everyone's attention. "This shocking event will stay with us for a long time, but as you can see, my future daughter-in-law, Sable Ford, is going to be fine. Please, honor the cause we are supporting this evening by staying and enjoying the party. And," he winked, "opening your wallets."

The light laughter Caleb's words generated seemed to do the trick. The band played an up-tempo tune and the crowd began to disperse. Some toward the bar, others the buffet. But the gossip ran rampant.

"Our PR team has already put out a statement," Wyatt assured Sable.

"That was fast." Sable was impressed.

"It's what they do," Wyatt shrugged. "It was only a few lines—just to get ahead of the inevitable demands for information. They will take care of everything. If you want to do an interview at a later date, that will be up to you."

That was the last thing Sable wanted. She would have to give a statement to the Army. If there were a trial, or court martial, her testimony would be read. She was no longer military. They kept things as internal as possible. Sable wasn't adding fuel to the fire by making public declarations. What happened was now between Colonel Montgomery and the United States Army.

"YOU GOADED HIM into punching you."

They were in the hotel suite. He had whisked her away as soon as his family had made sure Sable was all right. The party would continue—without them.

"I goaded him," Sable admitted, sighing with pleasure when Colt placed a cool cloth on the darkening bruise. "But I expected a slap. Bastard. Who punches a woman?"

"I wanted to kill him."

"Me too."

"In which case, we would be the ones in prison." Colt had removed his jacket and tie, draping them over a chair while he unfastened the first two buttons of his shirt. "Will there be justice?"

Sable reached to remove her shoes, smiling when Colt did it for her. He kept one foot in his hands, massaging the sole. With a grateful sigh, she reclined on the bed.

"I can't guarantee anything. However, the Army can't ignore one of their colonels punching a woman—in public. Nor will they be able to sweep the recording I made under the rug."

"So smart." Colt joined her on the bed, pulling her close. "Sending it to Alex. The way your mind works fascinates me."

"I spent a lot of time picturing a confrontation with him. I wasn't going to let the opportunity slip away. He dug his own grave. I made certain he was too deep to climb out."

"You're still a soldier at heart."

"Part of me always will be."

"Sable—"

"I know what you're going to say." She rested her hand on Colt's cheek. She looked into his blue eyes and smiled. "That life is over. It was over the day I turned in my papers. I had my regrets, but they weren't because I left the Army. It was *how* I left. Leaving Colonel Montgomery free to abuse other women has eaten at me, Colt. It won't anymore."

"They would take you back."

"Maybe. But I don't want it. Not anymore."

"You'll be happy here? Hollywood can be a bitch."

"So can I," Sable grinned when Colt laughed. "Can you live with an ex-Army Ranger who carries around a bit of an attitude? One who can kick your ass?"

"I came to grips with that reality the first time you knocked me off my feet."

"Then kissed you."

"Best day of my life. Until now." Colt unzipped her dress, caressing her warm, silky back. "I love you, Sable. Attitude and all. If you promise to kiss it and make it better, you can kick my ass anytime you like."

Epilogue

"**W**HO WANTS TO knock the sexiest man alive on his ass?"

"When I said you could do this anytime you wanted, I meant you and me, in the privacy of our bedroom." Colt lowered his voice. "You know. Foreplay? These women mean business."

Damn straight, they did. This was Sable's new business. When a woman signed up for a class, she was taught how to take care of herself against all comers. When Colt volunteered to help, he knew what he was getting into.

"Fine." Sable turned to the class. "Ladies. Mr. Landis will be starting production of a new movie next week.

There was a squeal of excitement from several women, followed by a buzz of conversation.

"Ladies." One word from Sable and they quieted, but the hum of energy remained. "This is a multi-million-dollar face." She took Colt's chin between her thumb and forefinger, turning his head for the women to admire. "No damage, please. Besides, I'm rather fond of it. So for my sake, be careful."

"I love you, too," Colt muttered as he waited to play attacker. But the twinkle in his blue eyes took the edge off his words.

Sable wasn't worried about Colt. He knew how to take a fall. One woman. One demonstration. Then he would leave. He was meeting his mother for lunch and had stopped by to say hello. Commandeering his services had been a spur of the moment impulse. And Colt, no matter what he said, was happy to oblige.

Lord, he was beautiful. And so sweet with the women in her class. Colt took the time to speak with each one—drawing them out with his trademark charm. Her heart melted when he shook the hand of a shy fan, bringing a blush to the woman's cheeks. If Sable hadn't already been in love, that would have done it.

The decision to start teaching self-defense classes full time had been an easy decision. The response from the one Jade had organized had been overwhelmingly positive. With some help from her friends, Sable had put out feelers—to get an idea if there was interest. She had to turn away applicants. Plans were in place to hire more instructors—women Sable knew from her Army days. But for now, she was happy to start small and build a solid reputation.

Colonel Montgomery resigned his commission. End of story. Sable's father had kept them up to date. At first, Montgomery tried to bluster his way through, convinced he was too important—too well connected. He soon discovered there was no support to be had. He was left with two choices. Leave with a full pension, or face charges. In the end, there was no choice. He retired. Scandal averted.

The story died down in Hollywood because Sable refused to speak out. Requests for her to tell her side stopped when they realized no meant no. She wasn't waiting for a better offer. Money wasn't the issue. As far as she was concerned, it was over—and she wanted it to stay that way.

Colt graciously let the volunteer send him to the mat. Applause followed, and Sable ended the class. Reluctantly, the women gathered their things, talking excitedly as they exited the room.

"Thank you." Sable handed Colt a bottle of water. The small refrigerator was one of the reasons she had chosen this space to rent. Another plus was the convenient location. Sable liked being able to walk to work each morning. There was room to expand when she was ready, and the owner was open to making renovations.

"My pleasure. I got to spend part of the day with you, and look." He did an impressive pirouette. "No bruises."

"Are you sure?" Sable wrapped her arms around his waist, snuggling close. "Tonight I better check. Just in case."

"Now that you mention it, there's a spot right here." Colt pointed to his inner thigh. "Want to see?"

"Yes." Sable laughed when Colt's hands went for the waistband of his sweats. "Later. You don't want to keep your mother waiting."

"No. And we're meeting Alex and Dani for dinner, right?"

Alex and his wife, Dani, were in Los Angeles on business. He had taken Sable's suggestion about hiring more women to heart and wanted to get her input. The couple used it as an excuse to visit. Sable looked forward to seeing her friends.

"He's going to ask you to come back to work."

"And I'll tell him the same thing I have every other time. I'm willing to do the occasional freelance job. A day or two at most. But not full time." Sable gave Colt a lingering kiss. "I'll miss Harper Falls and my friends. But this is my home. With you."

"Because you love me." Colt rubbed his cheek against hers.

"With all my heart."

Sable looked into his eyes, the blue deeper than usual. This was home. Right here, in Colt's arms.

Coming Soon

COMING IN JUNE
After the Fire (One Pass Away Book Three)—Gaige's story

COMING IN JULY
Dreaming Again (Hollywood Legends Book Four)—Wyatt's story

COMING IN AUGUST
An exciting new series.
Flowers on the Wall (Hart of Rock and Roll Book One)

And in December look for Callie and Caleb's story
Dreaming of a White Christmas (Hollywood Legends Book Five)

An Excerpt from

After The Rain

(One Pass Away Book One)

*L*OGAN. *LOGAN. LOGAN.*

Logan Price closed his eyes, taking it all in.

"Hear that, kid?" Starting quarterback Gaige Benson slapped him on the back. "Two games under your belt and you're a star. Now let's go out there and add super to the front of it."

The announcer for the team set them in motion down the tunnel with his familiar introduction.

"And now, let's hear it for your division champion *SEATTLE KNIGHTS.*"

The roar of the crowd. There was nothing like it. A packed stadium. Fans chanting his name. Few people would ever experience what it was like to take the field in a professional football game.

Logan Price had been working for this his entire life. He could still remember in exact detail the first game he ever saw. Too small to climb onto the stool in his father's bar by himself, his old man had lifted him onto the seat.

Stay and be quiet.

Not an easy order to follow for an active, inquisitive little boy. One glance at the game and for once, Logan had no problem following his father's command. The old TV transported him to a foreign world filled with bright lights and shiny helmeted warriors. Logan didn't know what he was watching. He did know he wanted to be one of those men.

A Sunday afternoon in rural Oklahoma. *Lefty's Pub* was filled with after-church drinkers who figured they had done their duty to God and family. The rest of the day was their time. A beer. Or two. Or six. Cronies who understood a man's need to unwind before the start of another workweek.

And football.

If the Friday night high school game was their true religion, the Sunday afternoon games were a close second. As Oklahoma boys, they hated anything Texas. The men of Denville gathered every week to root for whichever team was playing the Dallas Cowboys.

No matter how the games ended. Whether the crowd was happy or disgruntled. It meant more drinking. Hours later, husbands, boyfriends, and sons would stumble out, pile into beat-up trucks, and weave their way home to frustrated wives, girlfriends, and mothers.

As he grew older, Logan's view changed. He moved from the stool to behind the bar. And he promised himself one thing. He would never become one of those men. He wouldn't spend the week at a job he hated. His home wouldn't be a semi-wide trailer filled with hand-me-down furniture and a wife to whom he couldn't face going home.

His Sundays were going to be spent playing football, not watching it.

"Ready to take down this vaunted Arizona defense?" Gaige yelled at him, butting helmets.

Vaunted. Good word, Logan thought. His QB liked to use what his granny called highfalutin talk. Must have been that Ivy League education. He knew that Gaige Benson didn't grow up with a silver spoon in his mouth. He came from the mean streets of Brooklyn. He had the scars to prove it.

Like Logan, Gaige had vowed to get out of the life into which he was born. In the process, he polished himself up like a new penny. He took advantage of his full-ride scholarship to Yale. He didn't spend all his time on the football field. Fancy vocabulary. Fancy clothes. Fancy women. They were all part of the package Gaige purposefully fashioned for himself.

Seventeen years after clawing his way out of the tenement that he grew up in, very little of that borough-rat remained. Until game time. No one was tougher than Gaige Benson. Three-time league MVP. Considered one of the best ever to play the game. No one stood in his way when he was playing the game. He had the scars to prove it.

"Gather round."

Knights head coach Harry Coleman gathered the team close. He had to yell over the crowd, but he had the voice to do it. Booming was putting it mildly. The first time Logan heard it, he stood right beside the man. The ringing in his ears didn't go away for three days.

"Divisional game. If I have to say any more than that, you shouldn't be out here. Go kick some ass."

The defense took the field to start the game. Arizona had a rookie quarterback drafted in the second round from a small college in the Midwest. The only reason he was out there was because the regular starter suffered a concussion in last week's game and the regular backup had food poisoning. Thrown into action at the last minute, Logan swore he could see the guy's hands shaking before he took the first snap. When the ball went sailing between his legs, Logan shook his head.

The moment was too big for some people. For Logan, it wasn't big enough. He aimed for the biggest stage of all. The Super Bowl. It wasn't a matter of *if* he would get there, but when.

"Three and out." Gaige grinned, pulling on his helmet. "Come on, kid. Let's go show them how it's done."

Logan ran onto the field. *Kid.* He shook his head, grinning. From the first day of training camp, Gaige had hung that moniker on him. Ironic since he was almost twenty-five, a good two years older than most of the other rookies. However, he supposed when someone had been in the league as long as Gaige, all the new guys seemed like kids.

"We're starting on the ground," Gaige instructed them in the huddle. "Sweep out left. Basic. Got it?"

Lining up as he had a thousand other times, Logan checked the defense. He knew he was fast. One of the fastest in the game. What set him apart was his anticipation. He had the uncanny ability to read the guy covering him. He knew when to fake left or when to fake right. Stutter step or flat out, in your face, catch me if you can.

His speed got him out of Denville, Oklahoma. His brains and determination got him to the NFL.

The sounds of the game were as familiar to Logan as the back of his own hand. The call from scrimmage. Each quarterback had his own unique cadence. Gaige was a master of mixing his up. Study him all you want. Good luck figuring it out. His teammates knew. A signal just before they broke the huddle.

Pay attention, you were golden. Slack off even once? Gaige could ream a guy out with the best of them. And he had no problem doing it in the middle of the game.

An entire YouTube channel had been devoted to Gaige and his rants. They were as legendary as the man himself. With a ball in his hand, he was cool as ice. The rest of the time, watch out.

No one would ever accuse Logan of lacking focus. Today was no exception. They were driving down the field. First and ten from the Arizona twenty-yard line. He already had three carries for at least thirty-five yards each. It was going to be a good day.

"Ready to take it in?" Gaige asked.

"Always."

"Then show them what you've got."

A quick snap later, Gaige handed the ball to Logan. The offensive line created a seam. Not a big one. Just big enough. Using the push of his powerful legs, Logan surged through. One more step. They wouldn't catch him. No one could.

Like everything connected with the game, Logan heard the snap of the bone with total clarity. The agony that surged through his body was so intense he almost passed out. In the next few minutes, he was going to wish he had.

"Get back." Logan heard Gaige through the haze of pain. "Goddamn it. Move the hell off."

The three-hundred-and-fifty-pound linebacker didn't get off by standing. He rolled. Crushing Logan's broken leg as he went. He would never know if the move had been deliberate. Now, it was the last thing on his mind. He only cared about two things. How bad was the injury and when would he be able to play again.

"Hold on, kid." Gaige took his hand. "They're bringing the stretcher."

The team doctor checked his eyes. Logan knew he was asked some questions. What they were and how he answered, he would never remember. By the time they carted him off the field, Logan knew the break was bad.

"Gaige." Logan reached for him.

"I'm here, kid."

"Is it over?"

"The game?" Gaige walked with him, his head bent toward Logan. "No. But I promise we're going to win the bastard."

They loaded him onto the open cart. They had him secured and the vehicle rolled away before Logan had his answer. He wasn't wondering about the game. It was his career.

To no one in particular, he whispered the question again.

"Is it over?"

AFTER THE RAIN—NOW AVAILABLE

An Excerpt from

Dreaming With A Broken Heart

(Hollywood Legends Book One)

THE ROOM WAS dark. Too dark for Garrett's liking. A little
stuffy, a slight antiseptic smell with an overlay of sex. That's what
you got from a cheap motel and furtive lovemaking. Odors and
memories you'd just as soon forget.

The sounds from behind the closed bathroom door indicated his
partner was trying to remove all traces of their recent activities. It
shouldn't hurt. This wasn't the first time, and damn his weak resolve, it
wouldn't be the last.

If he smoked, he would have something to do with his hands.
Watching his father struggle with lung cancer put the fear of God in
him and his brothers at an early age. All four of them had their vices;
smoking wasn't one of them.

Get up. Get dressed. For once, be the first to leave. Even if he could find the balls to walk out on her, he couldn't leave her alone at this time of night. In this part of town.

God, it was like a furnace in here. Despite having the AC wall unit on high, Garrett knew it must be hotter in here than outside. The sheet riding low on his hips was too much. Damn modesty. The room was too dark to see anything; if she didn't like seeing his naked body, she could turn away. Garrett whipped off the coarse cotton material at the same moment the bathroom door opened.

"You don't have to go," Garrett said to the shadowed figure.

"Yes, I do."

She always made sure the light was off. Her silhouette showed a tall woman, thin. Too thin. Even by L.A. standards. She was gaining weight — slowly. Garrett could attest to that. He knew it was a struggle. One she fought every day.

Garrett felt the anger drain from his body — his heart melt. Her demands were not capricious whims. They weren't her attempt to gain the upper hand. Her goal was not to manipulate. She had her reasons. They were real. Legitimate.

"It's still early."

Garrett kept his voice low and even. Shouting didn't help. She never fought back. Retreat. That was her coping mechanism. The last time he blew up it was two weeks before she would take his calls.

"I…" she cleared her voice. "His flight gets in at midnight."

"Don't be there."

"You know how he gets."

Garrett knew all right. She was devoted to a man who treated her like crap, forgot her existence ninety percent of the time, yet expected her to be there when he decided to come home. His fists clenched the mattress. It was the only thing preventing him from grabbing her, begging her to stay. *For once, pick me.*

"I don't know when I can see you again."

I don't know if I ever want to see you again. Garrett thought the words. He would never verbalize them. She was his drug of choice. Weeks passed. The need for her grew. Outwardly, his life looked smooth as glass. Inside, the itch grew.

Garrett became an expert at compartmentalizing. His work never suffered. His family never suspected. No one had the slightest clue about what was raging inside of him. *She* knew. Because she shared his unbreakable habit. Enablers. That's what they were. It was sick. Sometimes, like tonight, he hated himself. He wished he could hate her. Then, maybe, he could walk away.

"I'll be out of town for the next month."

Garrett wished he could see her face. Was she sorry he'd be gone? Relieved? Would she miss him half as much as he was going to miss her?

"Take care."

Garrett waited a second, letting the motel room door close behind her. Jumping up, rushing to the window, he pulled back the thin, dingy curtain. He never walked her to the taxi. Even the minutest chance of them being seen was too much.

The ritual of watching until she was safely inside the vehicle, seat belt on, doors locked, was something he never ignored. Nothing bad would happen to her when he was around. It was when he wasn't there that trouble found her. One more frustration. It wasn't his place to protect her. Knowing that drove him crazy.

Garrett grabbed his jeans from a nearby chair, pulling them on. Unlike her, he wouldn't clean up before he left. He would carry the smell of her with him — let it fill the interior of his car. Tomorrow he would pretend it was still there.

Damn it. Enough. He deserved more than this. They both did. One month. When he got back, one way or another, things were going to change.

DREAMING WITH A BROKEN HEART